# ASK FOR MERCY

JAMES BENMORE

# PROLOGUE

Shortly before he was murdered, Ray Tyler phoned the one person he needed to speak to in that wretched hour. The call went straight to voicemail.

'Christopher, mate,' he began, voice slurred. 'Chrissy? It's your dad. This still your number?'

The winter wind blew through the Deptford docks at unbroken speeds. Ray paused to collect his breath and continued.

'Listen, son,' he said, walking against the gale. 'It's a filthy night and I'm drunk. No surprises there, eh? I don't even know what time it is where you are. But I need to tell you—' he paused to cough. 'I know I've not been the best dad,' he went on. 'Understatement. But I understand... why you turned against me. I get that now.'

He shut his eyes, lifted his head and allowed the rain to wash his face. When he spoke again it was in a heavy, nasal voice that would be hard to hear over the furious weather.

'It was that afternoon in my office. When you was still my little boy. You heard me talking, right? Doing that deal with... the long needle.' He let go of the handrail on the river path and staggered off in search of somewhere more sheltered. 'Anyway,' he wheezed, 'I know you were listening.'

Ahead of him in the deluge a hooded figure approached at a steady trot from the direction of the road. Ray moved quickly, staying dry under a boat yard's awnings. He then cut through a children's playground and reached a high-walled alley that would lead him back toward the river. Having assured himself that he was not being followed, he rested against the wall.

'In spite of everything,' Ray told his child, 'I've always loved you, Chrissy. Believe that.'

There the call ended.

Ray was killed by being thrown against the wet steps that led down to the riverbank, his head impacting hard against slabs of stone. His attacker knew that this would look like an accident. The steps were treacherous and Ray stank of booze.

The killer crouched beside the body. Rain beat down around them both, washing the blood from Ray's head wound into the river, cleaning the scene already. Covering his mouth and nose, the killer made certain there was no life left in the man, then rolled his corpse into the freezing river.

Hours later, in Barcelona, the message was heard.

But Ray hadn't sent it to his son.

He'd sent it to his daughter, whose name was Mercy.

# PART I

*The Untrained Eye*

# 1

F*ebruary 14th 2020*

A CAB CARRYING Mercy Tyler drew up outside her father's old office in Southwark, a building with a huge peacock painted on the corner wall. The blues and greens of the bird, and the accompanying letters, had faded since the thirties. What had once been Peacock Fashions was now a Chinese takeaway, but the ghost of the sign remained. Mercy remembered it well from those few times when she'd visited her dad's office as a child. The image suited Mance & Tyler Investigations, she'd then thought. The distinct blue spots at the end of each tall feather reaching up to their top floor windows. Discreet little eyes, she thought, perfect for a detective agency.

'So, you've known this Bill guy since you were a little girl?' her Uber driver said. Mercy was in the back seat trying to collect herself before heading up to the office.

'Something like that.'

'Then why you so nervous?'

The driver had turned off the ignition and moved around to face her. He was handsome, although older than she'd imagined from the back of his head.

'You've got a good eye, Jamal.'

'People are always telling me that,' he grinned.

Throughout the journey this driver had been chatting to her about what she was up to today. Mercy hadn't minded; she'd been glad of the chance to go over things ahead of the impending appointment. She'd inherited one half of a detective agency, she told Jamal, and wanted to sort out some details with her dad's best friend, who owned the other half.

'I haven't spoken to Bill since Dad's funeral,' she replied. 'That was days after Christmas and I don't think I made much of an impression.'

'I'm sorry to hear about your dad,' offered Jamal. 'What killed him?'

'Drunken misadventure,' she said. Then she got out and glanced up to that top floor window. The figure of a large man looked down from the glass. 'Or so they tell me.'

Bill Mance drew back from the window once he was sure that it was indeed Mercy down there. He hadn't recognised her at first. She'd had dark blue hair at Ray's funeral but had now returned it to its natural black. She seemed to have been talking to the cab driver for a longish time before stepping out in a green leather jacket, jeans and boots. He straightened his tie, ready to do some forced smiling.

'Action stations,' he said to his secretary as she

pretended to busy herself on the computer, 'Mercedes has arrived.'

'*Mercedes*,' sniffed Barbara. 'Awful name for an awful person.'

'Be nice, Barb,' he said as he crossed over to the table where the kettle was, flicked it on and peered into the biscuit tin. It was empty apart from crumbs. 'This is Ray's heir,' he said as he opened a cupboard and found a packet of chocolate bourbons. 'Or rather his heiress. You partly work for the young madam that's about to walk in here.' He tore open the packaging and emptied the biscuits into the tin. 'So be polite.'

'I'll be *civil*,' she promised. 'Out of respect to Ray. But if you expect me to—'

The door buzzer interrupted her. Bill crossed over, picked up the receiver and let his late partner's child into the building.

THE OFFICES OF MANCE & Tyler Investigations occupied the top floor of the building, and as Mercy climbed the narrow staircase she was struck by the same musty odour she remembered from all those years ago. Perhaps it was the old carpet or maybe just a persistent mould. Either way, she couldn't believe that neither her dad nor Bill had attended to the bad smell in over two decades.

'Bill!' she beamed as he opened the door to greet her. 'Lovely to see you again. You never change.'

'Mercedes,' he welcomed her in. 'You're looking well too.'

'Call me Mercy,' she said, stepping into the office. 'Everyone does.'

The handshake felt too formal for someone she'd

known all her life. She almost considered kissing him on his cheek before realising that this might unsettle him.

'It must be years since you visited our humble agency,' Bill remarked, his northern Irish accent only mildly softened by his decades in England. 'As you can see, we've shifted things around since then.'

Almost everything about the office had changed since Mercy's childhood visits. She'd remembered it as being claustrophobic then; dominated by an old sagging settee for the clients, cork-boarded walls and an ashy stink. At the rear there'd been a small dark room for the development of photographs. She'd been forbidden from entering that room as a kid, so it had taken on a sinister aspect in her imagination. Now it had been knocked through and replaced with an open plan kitchenette. She was impressed by the alterations; everything was lighter, cleaner, more 21st century. She'd long associated this place with the fag end of the last millennium but the metal cabinets were gone, a stylish sofa had replaced the old lump and the computer the secretary was working on was brand new. The only thing that still reminded her of those dingier days was the secretary herself.

'Hello Mrs Gleave,' she said, as Bill shut the door behind her. 'Remember me?'

Barbara moved her eyes from the screen. 'I remember,' she sniffed. 'I should call you *Miss* Tyler, I suppose?'

'I'm still unmarried if that's what you mean,' Mercy smiled as Bill shot the secretary a hard look. 'But call me Mercy. I insist on it.'

'How's your mum?' Barbara asked.

'Good thanks, Mrs G,' Mercy replied and turned her back on her. She was more interested in inspecting the rest of the office anyway. 'I'll be seeing her later.'

'Send Julie our love then,' said Bill as he followed her towards the kitchenette. 'How's she doing?'

Mercy didn't answer. A small mini-fridge in the kitchenette had caught her eye. She moved closer and saw a familiar photograph that was stuck underneath a Union Jack magnet.

'That old fridge belonged to your dad once,' Bill confirmed.

'How could I forget,' she said and freed the photo from the magnet. 'Not every father had a fridge full of beers in his home study. Oh, I remember this being taken. It was that day at the golf club.'

The photo was of three men and two boys on a golf course and had been taken in the summer of 2000. The adults were her dad, Bill and another, shorter man who was stood between them, grinning like Mr Punch.

'Victor Neale,' Bill confirmed as she peered at the image closely. 'He was a major client in our early days.'

'Dad's old gangster mate,' Mercy nodded. 'The Met's Most Wanted. He paid for that whole day if I remember rightly.'

'That he did,' said Bill in a voice that, she felt, lacked enthusiasm. 'Vic was very generous to his friends.'

'Well, I imagine it's easy to be generous with stolen money.'

But what had drawn her eye to the photo was the image of her father. Ray Tyler – shorter than Bill but taller than Victor - smiling and suntanned with his hand resting warmly on the youngest boy's shoulder. He was wearing a golf shirt that he'd probably purchased for the occasion. She pointed at the boy's unsmiling face. *'Cheer up, Chrissy,'* she said, mimicking her dad. *'It might never happen.'*

There was a short pause in Barbara's typing. Mercy pointed to the other boy.

'This was Victor's son, right?' she asked. 'Remind me, why were there no girls allowed in this?'

'Vic wanted a boys' photo only,' Bill shrugged. 'Don't ask me why, he had a daughter of his own but some fellas are like that.'

'Your Lisa went ballistic when she found out she wasn't allowed in the shot,' smiled Mercy, replacing the photo under the fridge magnet. 'How is she?'

'Good thanks,' he nodded. 'Well, according to Facebook.'

There were two doors leading to separate inner offices, one of which used to belong to her father. Mercy asked who occupied it now.

'The new generation,' Bill replied in a fond tone. 'Two bright young operatives who've helped drag this agency into the digital age. There's Nina, who I think you met at the funeral, and young Robbie. They're both out working on a case so we can talk in peace.' He indicated the already open door behind him. 'Barb'll bring us in some tea and biscuits, won't you, love?'

'I'm busy, Bill,' Barbara protested from her desk.

'No you're not,' he mouthed as he went to shut the door between them.

# 2

The security at Berkeley Square House was tight if courteous, but Nina Markham, carrying a small bunch of flowers in one hand and a brown envelope in the other, blagged her way past it. Typically for her she was dressed in a smart but unobtrusive way, unlike her companion Robbie Ingleton. Robbie, with his bright orange hoodie and ungroomed beard, seemed conspicuous for an uptown setting like this. So she'd instructed him to wait for her on a red velvet sofa by the entrance. The young woman sitting behind the reception smiled at the flowers as Nina asked to see a Mr John Graycorn, who worked on the top floor.

'We're getting a lot of this today,' the receptionist said, indicating the extravagant collection of Valentine's bouquets lining the wall behind her, all of them more impressive than the drooping bunch Nina was holding. 'Leave it with us and we'll see that he gets them.'

'Can't do that,' Nina replied. 'His wife insists I hand him this myself. Either send me up or send him down. I don't care which.'

The receptionist's smile dropped but she phoned the hedge fund manager's office. Nina heard her say that his wife had sent flowers.

'He's coming down,' she told Nina in a frostier tone and then made a point of ignoring her.

While she waited, Nina took the time to survey this Mayfair building's high marble walls. She reflected on what a waste of time this was. She'd been feeling trapped in this job for a while now. What had seemed like a highly worthwhile assignment eighteen months ago now struck her as pointless.

When John Graycorn emerged from a gold-plated elevator, he seemed unimpressed by the sad flowers Nina was holding.

'Lydia sent *these*?' he asked. Graycorn was a tall man, at home in a tall room. He eyed the sorry excuse for a bouquet through thick-rimmed glasses, his expression suggesting that if you were going to make a romantic gesture towards him then it needed to be better than this. 'I only saw her a few hours ago,' he said, pushing his glasses back over floppy grey hair.

'I never said the flowers were for you,' Nina said, presenting him with the envelope. 'This is. Inside you'll find a solicitor's letter explaining that your wife wishes to begin divorce proceedings immediately. Also, there's telephone transcripts contained within which reveal that you are engaged in an affair with another woman. These were obtained within the parameters of the law and you're being served in front of this witness,' Nina indicated the horrified secretary. 'I work for M&T Investigations. You'll find our details among the documents.'

Graycorn glared, refusing the envelope. Resting it onto the reception desk, Nina reached for her phone.

'Another thing, your wife has a message.' She read from the screen. '*Thanks for the Bulgari necklace this morning which I'm keeping. See you in court.*' Nina then returned the phone back into her jean pocket. 'I'll see myself out.'

It still amused Nina that even the highest, most inaccessible people will come down from their ivory towers if they think you've got something nice for them. The flower trick was one of the many professional nuggets that Ray Tyler had taught her before his death.

Robbie was horizontal on the velvet sofa by the time she returned to the glass-fronted entrance, his concentration fixed on his phone. A security guard looked relieved when Nina came to take him away.

'I told you there was no point in us both coming,' Robbie said as she handed him the cheap flowers to dump somewhere. 'Bill just wanted me out of the way for the royal visit.'

Ignoring a passing purple supercar, Nina took out her phone and called the office while Robbie sloped off in search of a bin for the flowers.

'Hedge Fund's been served without incident,' Nina told Barbara, 'I delivered the client's message as written and we're heading home. Has the prodigal child left yet?'

By the time Robbie returned from dumping the flowers, Nina had news to relate.

'Barb says that Ray's kid has been speaking to Bill for over an hour now', she said as they both descended into the Green Park underground. 'I wonder what they're talking about.'

# 3

"*It was that afternoon,*" Ray's voice came crackling again through his daughter's phone "*...in my office. When you was still my little boy.*"

Mercy studied Bill as they both listened. He was sat across from her behind his large office desk, leaning forward and holding a pen over an as-yet unmarked pad. He tapped it as if ready to take notes, but his hand remained where it was. She'd wondered if he'd already heard about the existence of this voicemail message, perhaps from one of his old police contacts.

'*You heard me talking, right? Doing that deal with... the long needle.*'

Mercy paused the message. She looked at Bill, but he was a hard man to read.

'The Long Needle,' she repeated. 'That's what he says, right?'

'He does,' Bill agreed. 'And, yeah, it sounds like he's talking about a person.'

'And not literally a long needle,' Mercy nodded before

resuming with the message. 'Like my mother tried to suggest.'

Bill's office was large, tidy, and, aside from one potted plant, quite sterile. Mercy had begun by explaining that she believed her dad had been murdered. Even uttering those words aloud had felt like a confession. Perhaps it was this room; a place people came to voice their darkest suspicions to an investigator. Or maybe it was Bill himself who gave off a priestly air as he listened quietly to her theories.

Like the police and her mother before him, Bill had initially seemed sceptical when Mercy told him her murder theory. To be fair, the fact that her dad's voicemail had referred to an overheard meeting from over a decade before didn't prove much in itself. But now he was straining to hear every last wheeze of her dad's final message.

'Did you ever hear him talk about anyone called that before?' Mercy asked once the recording was over. 'Could it be a client?'

'I've never heard Ray, or anyone, use that name,' Bill told her as she placed the phone back into her jacket pocket. 'And I'd remember if I had.'

'Well, as I said,' she reached over to the tin of biscuits and took a chocolate bourbon as she spoke, 'I know who he's referring to.' She snapped the biscuit in half, 'Although I've never heard him referred to as the Long Needle before this call.'

Bill shook his head and leaned back in his seat.

'I have to admit,' he said, exhaling hard as he placed the unused pen down again, 'that was a tough listen. Poor Ray.'

'This message might not be enough for the police but it's enough for me,' Mercy continued after swallowing the biscuit. "And once we start uncovering more information about this Long Needle person, we should hopefully provoke them—'

'Hold that thought,' Bill interrupted her. '*We?*'

'You and I,' she replied, as if it was obvious. 'We're private investigators, aren't we?'

'I am,' he nodded. 'You're not.'

'I've inherited half of this agency,' she said, as if he was being dense. 'You've been paying me a wage for the past two months, so it's about time I started earning it. I plan to start officially on Monday.'

'Doing what?'

'Private investigating. I want to follow in Dad's footsteps.'

Bill studied her for some seconds, assessing her seriousness. Then he pulled his chair forward and placed his elbows on the desk, making an arch with his hands. When he spoke it was in a soft, frank manner, as if she was just another highly-strung client with whom he was discussing the infidelity of a spouse.

'Among other benefits,' he explained, 'inheriting half this agency entitles you to the share of the profits that would have otherwise gone to your dad. Our accountant advised I should present that to you as a wage because it's advantageous from a tax perspective. But nobody actually expects you to work here, Mercy. You're free to just take the money and let us get on with the running of things.'

'Dad always wanted a Tyler to continue working at the agency,' Mercy reminded him.

'I recall him saying something like that,' Bill gave a cautious nod, 'about how much he'd like it if little Chrissy became an investigator. But that was a long time ago.'

She wondered if he'd meant that to sound so callous. Bill had always struck her as the more diplomatic one in the M&T partnership, but she realised she didn't know him that well. A silence passed, one that he, at least, seemed prepared to hold.

'His will was explicit,' she then replied. 'Mum got his share of the house but I got the agency. And he'd made it recently too. The name Chrissy wasn't anywhere. So here I am, whether you like it or not.'

'I didn't say I was unhappy about it,' he backtracked. 'I'd welcome more hands on deck. But there are practicalities to consider. For instance, you'll need a license.'

'I can get one of those,' she shrugged. 'Besides, Dad told me that for the first five years in the job he operated without one.'

'That was a different time,' said Bill. 'And it caused us problems even then.'

'I studied law at university.'

'Did you finish the course?' he asked, knowing the answer.

'Listen, I've had a lot of different lessons in a variety of subjects,' she said, trying to appear unruffled. 'After all I've been through in recent years, I've a tougher skin than most.'

'Don't underestimate this job, Mercy. It's not as glamorous as it might appear in films.'

'You and my dad?' she smirked. 'Not glamorous? You astound me.'

'As for this idea that your dad was murdered,' Bill sighed and pushed back his chair, 'I'm sorry but I don't see it. I'm inclined to agree with the coroner's report.'

He stood and moved around the desk, perching himself on the edge of it.

'I don't mean to be patronising,' he said, failing at it. 'I'd love nothing more than to teach you our trade. But y'know, I've a business to run. Things have been tough since your dad died. Wages still need paying, rents, rates, lights and heating, various other debts. I still send money to Lisa every month, even though I never get a word of a thank you. So forgive me if I'm reluctant to drop my daily business and go haring after a killer I don't even believe in. And in the process,' he sucked through his teeth before continuing, 'possibly uncover some ugly truths about a man whose memory I hold dear. It would be unprofitable, unproductive and I don't even know if Ray himself would want us to. You can come across some distressing things while investigating a person's life and his daughter is the last person I'd encourage to do it. I suppose,' he shook his head, 'I'm one for letting sleeping dogs lie.'

Mercy placed her half-drunk mug of tea back onto the desk.

'You should put that on a business card,' she stared up at him. '*William Mance – Private Investigator. Letting sleeping dogs lie since 1989.*'

She stood and went to fetch her leather jacket from the stand behind her. She'd anticipated an obstructive attitude from him but was disappointed that he'd proven her right.

'Obviously I don't expect to be Sam Spade on my first day,' she spoke as if the matter was settled. 'And I won't be investigating Dad's murder during work hours. It'll be a side project until it gathers momentum. But I'll be starting here next week and I look forward to meeting the other… y'know… operatives, or whatever we call them. And it'll be a privilege to learn from your vast experience in this field, Bill.' She crossed over and made a point of kissing him on the cheek. 'See you Monday,' she smiled, exiting before he could voice further objections.

# 4

Gemma Bolton had just received a personal call from the boss himself. She'd only been working for Meantime gyms for a month and had met the notorious Victor Neale just once before, when the new state of the art entrances had been installed. On that occasion he'd been every bit as unpleasant as he'd been painted in the media. But today he'd managed to be much more polite as he impressed upon her the importance of not calling the police about what had happened during the spin class.

Gemma took one last look at the grainy black and white recording of the young man entering the gym at 9.25am before wiping it. She'd been watching the man at the time, live on her screen from behind the reception desk. And she'd known he'd be trouble from his cocky way of descending the stairs and by how he'd moved his neck from side to side, like a boxer on his way to the ring. However, when he'd eventually appeared before her in living colour she'd been struck by how well-groomed he was, like a reality star. Tall, with blonde, slicked back hair. Expensively dressed. The handsome impression was spoilt only by his sneer. There was a thick glass partition separating them and she saw him examining the sliding doors. She'd given him a pleasant wave, just as she'd been doing with other members who seemed confused by the recent changes. Then she'd moved out from behind her curving desk and approached the partition, ready to explain about the fingerprint ID. Suddenly, he'd punched the glass between them in anger.

'Open this fucking door!' he'd commanded, miming the doors opening as if unsure if she could hear him through the glass.

Gemma had paused before calmly explaining to him how the new system worked, paying him the respect she'd extend to another normally tempered visitor. There was no need to present a card anymore, she'd said, but she could get his fingerprint on the system now if he'd like. The young man had become even more apoplectic.

'This is *my* gym!' he'd shouted back through the glass. 'I ain't giving you my fingerprint.'

Gemma had then looked around for the management. But the only person she'd seen was Roz, a personal trainer, running towards her from the weight-lifting area. The loud volume of the workout music meant that nobody else had been alerted to the scene but the young man was by then shouting about how Gemma worked for him.

'This gym is owned by *Victor Neale*,' Gemma had replied, hoping that the name might carry some authority. 'I'm unsure who you are.'

'Fuck Victor Neale!' The young man had shouted, spittle landing on the glass partition in front of Gemma's face. 'That old bastard's trying to keep me out of my own business with this fingerprint shit. Where's Roz?'

'Let him in, Gem,' said Roz as she'd drew up beside her. 'That's Nick Neale.' Gemma had never liked Roz Stern much, but she'd felt grateful that somebody else was prepared to take charge. *'Lol's boy!'* Roz hissed before tapping her own finger on the sensor.

The doors parted and Nick Neale stepped into the gym like he'd been uncaged from captivity. Gemma backed away but he now appeared to be completely uninterested in her. Instead he went straight for Roz.

It looked like he was about to strike her but instead he grabbed her by the waist, pulled her roughly towards him and they kissed with an obscene passion. Gemma felt insulted watching them. She'd spent much of that morning wondering why she didn't have a valentine of her own, so was at a loss to see how these two abysmal people had managed to find each other.

'Where's Bruno?' the young man asked once he'd finally removed his tongue from hers.

'Taking spin,' Roz had replied with a wicked grin. 'Been in there for a good forty minutes. He'll be knackered.'

'Thanks babe.'

He released her from his embrace and set off along the 25-metre indoor track that led towards the studio. That morning's spin class was by then reaching its sweaty conclusion and Gemma saw Roz activate her camera phone as she followed behind Nick.

There was a longstanding joke amongst the older regulars of Deptford Meantime that they'd known classier gyms inside prison but hadn't been expected to pay a monthly direct debit for those. However, it was the cheapest membership in the vicinity and the only one that boasted Junior Bruno as a personal trainer. And that, as far as many of the spin class ladies were concerned, made it worth the fee. Junior was a minor celebrity boxer and failed DJ but he was a hugely popular presence in the gym. Whenever he took a class there was twice the usual turn out. On this particular morning he'd been working them hard and large patches of sweat spread out under every bike in that mirror-walled studio with its pounding soundtrack. Junior had been letting the session run on too long. There were groans of agony as he promised them "one more Rihanna song and you're free!" Nobody complained too much though. Some of the older ladies were under the impression that he was the illegitimate son of the former heavyweight champion Frank Bruno. Whenever they asked him about this he'd just wink and say *"You know what I mean, Harry?"* and impersonate Frank's famous laugh.

Counting the spinners in to the start of the song, Junior hadn't noticed Nick Neale enter the studio behind him until he'd strode right up to Junior's bike and punched him with full force in the back of the head. Junior had lurched over. Because he was such a heavy man, it was easy for Nick to kick his exercise bike after him until both it and Junior had crashed onto the floor. Nick crouched over the fallen pugilist and pummelled him hard as the entire spin class screamed in horror.

'Everyone out!' ordered Roz as she'd entered after Nick with her phone pointed straight at the unfolding violence. 'I'm filming this!'

'So I'm a plastic gangster, yeah?' Nick had roared at Bruno as he continued the savage pounding. 'That's what you've been telling people? You're lucky you don't end up like Ray Tyler.'

The spinners had begun running for the exit. Some made to help Junior Bruno, but Roz stopped them. She was dealing with it, she repeated, filming the whole scene. One woman produced her own phone to do likewise but Roz had shrieked at her to fuck off.

Through the studio window Gemma had just watched in horror, wondering what to do. She was relieved when both the general manager and the assistant manager finally appeared from the back office and asked her what the hell was going on.

'He says he's the boss's nephew,' Gemma had explained as they looked on. 'Should I call the police?'

'Don't you dare,' the general manager had told her before racing into the studio to break things up. 'Phone his uncle instead.'

*'I'M FILMING THIS! Fuck off, Elaine!'*

That was the bit that made both Nick and Roz laugh the most when they watched it back in their flat less than two hours later. Roz had briefly turned her camera away from the fight to catch Elaine the spinner's dumbstruck expression. It was, as far as they were concerned, comedy gold. Nick had told her to keep that bit in, but he was keen for her to cut the footage just before Junior Bruno took him by surprise.

'Coming up's where I want this to end.' He was blinking rapidly as he again watched her laptop screen, still rubbing the damp cloth against his battered cranium.

The camera had returned to the powerful image of him leaning over the former boxer and meting out a vicious punishment. The image was tight so the viewer would be unable to see the context of the rabbit punch that started everything or that Junior was just finishing up a long spin class that would place any fighter at a disadvantage. The only optics Nick wanted was of him beating up a Frank Bruno lookalike and one that worked for his uncle.

*'Tell Victor that I know what he did,'* Nick had been

snarling at his victim as he glanced up to the camera to check that she was capturing his best side. *'And he'll also end up like Ray Tyler when I—'*

'Cut!' Nick yelled beside her. Roz went to stop the image there, but left it too late. The reel kept running long enough to see Junior Bruno hoist himself up, grab Nick's ankle and punch his distracted attacker in the back of the leg. Nick had fallen hard onto the ground beside him.

'I said *cut!*' Nick grabbed the back of her neck as he often did when angry and on coke. 'I don't want all this in it, do I?'

Roz winced at the unmanly cry coming from her laptop where Nick was receiving a number of devastating counter blows to the head. She'd actually found the sight of Junior gaining dominance over her boyfriend to be quite a turn on but wasn't about to say so.

'S'alright, babe,' Roz pleaded as he continued to pinch her neck tight. 'I'll cut this so you'll look like the big man.'

'Which I am.'

He released her neck and leaned over the glass coffee table to clean off the last of the white powder. He'd told her he'd bought that stash of coke as a Valentine's present for her but, typically, he'd enjoyed the lion's share.

'I'm a born killer,' he declared as he got to his feet and began pacing about their large high-rise flat.

'Keep it shush!' she told him. 'They might hear us underneath.'

'I'm going to shoot my uncle Victor *dead.* And you keep it shush yourself.'

He was off on one of his coke rants now, the blinking becoming even more frantic.

'And what makes me sick to the dick is that no one believes I've got it in me.' He moved over to the window and looked out over their view of the Thames. 'Everyone knew my dad was deadly; he didn't have to film himself to get respect like I'm doing. But what can I do? I can't have people thinking Victor's the boss. Not after what happened on New Year's Eve.'

Beside her on the leather settee Nick's phone lit up with a new message.

'It was the truth as I've always known it,' Nick continued as she looked at it. `But I didn't *know it know it* until then. Victor had his own flesh and blood murdered!'

'Babe, who's Chrissy Tyler?'

Nick stopped pacing and turned to her. The bruise on his face was by now a fierce red. She dreaded the next time he'd look in the mirror.

'What about him?' he asked after a pause.

'Dan B just sent you a text. **Heard what happened to Chrissy Tyler?** Is he related to that dead private detective? The one who drowned.'

Nick said nothing for a few moments. Then he crossed over to his beanbag and dropped into it.

'He was Ray's son,' he explained. 'We went to school together. Dan used to bully him and I did too. And yeah, I've heard.'

Then Nick sank further into the beanbag and she couldn't get any further sense from him. Roz sighed, already regretting leaving her job at Meantime gyms. They were unlikely to provide her with a decent reference after today.

# 5

Gazing out through a scratchy train window at a landscape of soggy Victorian brickwork, Mercy found herself missing her life in Spain more than ever. She'd always struggled with London in the winter months. As she sped past more leafless trees further into suburbia, her thoughts ran again to that dismal day just after Christmas when she'd returned for her dad's funeral.

The last time she'd seen him alive was when she'd left for Barcelona five years ago. It had been a horrible parting of ways. He'd offered to drop her off at Gatwick Airport but they'd got into a vicious row on the ride there. Their fight had been about many things but, at its core, it was about the same thing it always was in those later years: his disapproval of how she was choosing to live. The snapping point had been when she'd mentioned her ambition to become a private investigator.

'*A person like you,*' he'd said with scorn, '*couldn't handle my job. That's a joke.*'

By the time she'd got out of his car she been made so upset by his dismissal that she wouldn't make eye contact and rejected his attempts to hug her farewell. Instead, not thanking him for the ride, she'd darted straight into the airport, not wanting him to see her cry.

To his credit, her dad had tried to make amends over the five years since then. Not just for that argument but for all the hurtful remarks he'd made. But she knew what he really thought of her, just as she knew he wished he could unsay it. During her time abroad they'd mainly communicated through her mother and had enjoyed no real relationship of their own. He'd sent her money whenever she had asked for it though, despite knowing what she'd spend it on. That made her feel guilty now. For all his flaws, she owed him much.

Ray had few remaining relatives but when they'd gathered for his funeral some acted as if Mercy was a stranger to them. She'd sensed their collective disapproval as they waited in the living room for the funeral cars to arrive, had caught disparaging whispers about her then dyed-blue hair, as well the tattoos visible under her sleeve. It felt unfair. She'd worn a dignified black dress, much like the one her mother had on, and her hair was mostly hidden beneath a hat. But she knew the reason they really hated her.

'If Ray is looking down now,' her mother had said as she and Mercy prepared cups of tea for everyone, 'he'd be cross that I haven't offered you all a stiffener. Would anyone prefer a beer or whiskey?'

'Cheers love,' replied Uncle Dennis, a greeting cards wholesaler who lived in Essex, 'I thought you'd never ask.'

Mercy was sent to the kitchen to fetch him a lager and, as she left, she'd heard her dotty Aunt Jean ask where Chrissy was.

'You'd think he'd come back for his own dad's funeral,' Jean had remarked as others tried to shut her up.

'Just because a dog thinks it's a camel,' Uncle Den was heard whispering with a mouthful of salty peanuts as she re-entered the room, 'doesn't mean it can cross the Gobi desert. Simple biology.' After handing him the glass of flat Budweiser, she'd then taken a large sip from the wine glass she'd brought for herself. She'd wished there was time to neck a whole bottle before the hearse arrived.

When it did Mercy, her mother Julie, and Uncle Den had ridden together in the first of the cortege cars. Den had ordered a floral wreath spelling out RAYMOND to be draped across the coffin but, on being told the cost, had shortened it to RAY. Julie had sat in the middle and conversed with her brother-in-law as he complained that passing pedestrians weren't removing their hats in respect.

Mercy had just stared out of her window feeling desperately sad. She'd always harboured a hope that one day she'd be reconciled with her dad but now that day would never come. She thought again about the terrible voicemail message she'd received and how defeated he'd sounded in his final moments. She'd contacted the UK police as soon as she'd heard that he was dead, played them his last message and told them what she understood, however little, about what he'd meant by the Long Needle.

But they weren't sure that his death was murder, so nothing as yet had followed.

The crowd at the crematorium was bigger than Mercy had expected. Uncharacteristic nerves had gripped her as she stepped out of the car with her family, grateful for the veil and hat that her mother had lent her. Some of Ray's friends had offered to carry the coffin, her mum had told her as she clung to her arm like a child.

'Just Bill, and some of the other usual suspects.'

Her father's coffin had slid out of the hearse and six

black-suited men stepped forward to shoulder it. At the front had been Bill, the tallest. Mercy also recognised some of her dad's other old cronies, including Tony Lamoreaux who'd first taken the final drags of his cigarette before dropping it onto the pavement. Beside him was 'Expanding' Alan McColl, a former policeman who now owned a spycraft shop. Collectively, those men had resembled out-of-shape, pink-faced, middle-aged Reservoir Dogs.

Then, with a jolt, she'd realised that Victor Neale was stepping forward among the men. She'd been a teenager when she'd last seen her father's notorious school friend, the man who'd been dubbed 'Britain's Public Enemy No 2' by the tabloids. Considering his high profile and reputation as a recluse, she'd not expected him to attend let alone act as a pallbearer. He was the shortest of the men and yet she could see that his presence put them on edge.

The Tyler family had followed the coffin into the chapel and Mercy had avoided the eyes of any onlookers. She and her mother had taken their seats on the front pew while the coffin was placed on two trestles. Beside it was a small table with football scarves draped over each side, one for England, the other Millwall. On the table was a photo taken roughly fifteen years earlier in some sunny locale. He was tanned, smiling and had sunglasses pushed up over his still brown hair. Ray of Sunshine.

The six bearers had then all taken the row directly behind her, Victor included. Mercy had felt even less easy to have a known murderer sitting behind her at a funeral.

Mercy had previously offered to read a poem at the service but her mother had dissuaded her. So, all she'd wished to do then was just sit and feel sad while others delivered his eulogies.

'For those of you who don't know me, my name's Bill

Mance,' her father's best friend had begun after positioning himself behind the podium. He'd placed on his reading glasses and was shuffling through some notes. 'Ray and I were private detectives together.' He paused for a small cough. 'It might be fair to say that I was the Watson to his Sherlock.'

Amid the polite laughter, her mother's hand had reached over and took hers. That day, for a change, they were bonded in grief.

'We're here to say farewell to a great man,' Bill had said. 'A better man than perhaps some of us ever gave him credit for. Someone with a strong sense of loyalty, who you could count on if you were in trouble. A man who would do anything for his family.' He consulted his notes again, his voice sounding a little stilted as he read from them. 'In these past ten days, since the shock of his death, I've come to know how poor old Watson must have felt after that fateful incident at the Reichenbach Falls. I've lost the best and wisest man I've ever known.'

This had all sounded like lip service. In particular, the assertion that Ray Tyler was known for his loyalty must have rung hollow for his widow who'd endured his infidelities over the years. The Holmes and Watson comparisons also struck Mercy as cheesy and she wasn't even sure if he'd pronounced Reichenbach correctly.

Bill had gone on to relate some second-hand stories about Ray's upbringing, failing to give them any colour. But the eulogy had picked up when Bill entered the story himself. He'd explained how, as a young policeman newly arrived in London, Ray had befriended him at a time when his Northern Irish accent counted against him.

'This was eighties England,' he'd explained. 'Unless you were Georgie Best, being a Belfast boy didn't exactly make you popular. Every time I ordered a drink in a pub they'd ask me where the bomb was. But Ray took me as he found me, when others wouldn't, and with him I had some of the best times of my young life.'

He'd told some well-worn stories then about their misadventures as two carefree bachelors in their twenties. Mercy had assumed they were not so much exaggerated as cleaned up for public consumption. It was Ray, Bill revealed, who'd persuaded him to quit the police and start up the agency.

'With the support of some generous benefactors,' he'd added, glancing at the pew behind Mercy, 'M&T Investigations was the second-best idea Ray ever had. Some of you may have even employed our services over the years. If so, don't worry, your secrets are still safe.'

He'd winked then, receiving another small laugh.

'I should fucking hope so,' someone had muttered from the rogues gallery behind her.

'But the best idea Ray ever had was, of course, marrying Julie.'

Her mother's head had lifted up in surprise, as if she hadn't expected to be mentioned during her own husband's funeral.

'I was with him when he first laid eyes on her,' Bill had continued, 'in a pub, you'll be unsurprised to learn. I had my back to the door and Ray suddenly leaned over and asked if I'd be best man at his wedding, as the most beautiful girl he'd ever seen had just walked in.'

Mercy's mother had gazed toward Bill as if bothered by what he might say next.

'I was his best man and, some years later, he was mine. I also had the great privilege of being asked to be godfather to his son, Christopher.'

Typical, Mercy thought, that he wouldn't want to mention her name at any point.

'Before I finish…' There was then a discernible shift in his tone toward something more serious. 'I want to stress the thing about him that I admired the most. His fierce sense of justice.'

He'd discarded his papers and had one hand rested on the podium, the other clenched. Mercy had sensed that this part of the speech might be aimed at someone in particular.

'If Ray felt that someone he cared about had been wronged,' he'd declared with a touch of fire and brimstone in his delivery, 'he wouldn't rest until he set it right. If he saw someone in need of justice, he'd help secure it, or at least settle the score. I've seen some bother in my time – we don't need to go into that - but I couldn't have asked for a stauncher ally than Ray Tyler. There was very little that would stand in his way once he was working your case. He'd pursue truth wherever it took him.' He'd paused as if distracted and Mercy had begun to see that his grief might match her own. 'He's an irreplaceable loss,' Bill had said, snapping out of it and returning to the row behind her as the funeral director resumed control of the service.

THE LANDLORD of the Pelton Arms was said to be so upset on hearing of her dad's death that he'd insisted the wake be held there after the service.

'Unsurprising,' her mother had remarked as the cortege travelled through the backstreets of Greenwich. 'Every publican in South London will be in mourning today.'

Tinsel was still hanging inside the pub and their tree was still up. As she'd entered Mercy had fought an urge to keep her veil on. But, not wishing to appear like a figure from Gothic melodrama, she'd removed it to make small talk with the few mourners who offered their commiserations. A divide had soon been created between her parents' family on one side of the bar and Ray's old mates on the other. That side was largely male, middle-aged and, with a couple of exceptions, white. Mercy had noticed a large man, the spitting image of the young Frank Bruno, who appeared to work for Victor as a chauffeur. Victor himself had ordered large whiskeys for all of the lads, including one extra that they left on the bar.

'For Raymondo,' Victor had toasted and they'd all chinked the extra glass before downing their own.

There was a discernible menace emanating from those men. Occasionally one of them crossed to her side of the bar to pay respects to either her mother or to Uncle Den. Few of them had acknowledged her. The old M&T secretary Barbara Gleave had been present too, deep in conspiratorial conversation with another woman. They'd both glanced over occasionally, clearly discussing her and saying nothing complimentary.

Bill had eventually arrived a while after everyone else. He'd been dealing with the funeral company that M&T had paid for and, typically, he didn't hesitate to cross the room toward her and offer his condolences. He was with a young black woman he'd introduced as Nina Markham and Mercy assumed that this must be his new girlfriend. But Nina was instead introduced as an agency employee and she told Mercy that she'd had huge respect for her dad. They were exchanging polite chitchat when Nina suddenly seemed distracted by who was at the far end of the pub.

'Isn't that...?'

'Victor Neale, yeah,' Mercy had answered. 'Short-arse gangster man.'

'Wow,' Nina had replied, transfixed by him while Mercy knocked back her drink. 'I mean, I knew that Ray had grown up with the Neale brothers, but I didn't think he'd be here. Who are those other guys?'

'A glittering array of criminal superstars,' Mercy had said and slammed her empty glass down onto the bar. 'Please excuse me, Nina, I'm going out for a cigarette.'

Mercy didn't smoke. Instead of heading to the pub garden, where she'd just seen Barbara go with her sickly-looking husband, she'd stepped out onto the front pavement and immediately put some distance between herself and her father's wake.

Her pace had increased and her breathing became hard, as if she'd been submerged underwater and had at last come up gasping. Sidestepping some discarded Christmas trees lying on the pavement, she'd kept going until she reached the Thames Path where finally, overlooking the river and under a grey sky, her emotions overcame her. She'd placed her hand on an iron railing; leant against it and cried the tears she'd been holding back all day.

She'd forgotten how isolated she could feel when surrounded by the people she grew up with and was shocked by how vulnerable that day had made her. But it was seeing Victor that had really set her off. She'd always harboured a profound sense that this man, whom she'd once been encouraged to call Uncle Vic, had damned her father somehow, that everything in their family would've been better without him. The Neale family, she'd often felt, were at the centre of everything that had gone wrong with Ray Tyler's life. It therefore followed that they must have had a hand in his death as well.

She'd buttoned her black coat against the wind and kept on walking. Eventually she reached an unoccupied bench that faced out onto the Thames, so she'd sat down and tried to ignore the spitting rain. A large patrol boat was heading upstream. She'd wondered if it could be the same vessel that had fished her father's dead body out of the water. He'd been found not that far from here, frozen to the bone. It was a bleak end for a man who earlier today had been described in such heroic terms by his partner.

*If Ray felt someone he cared about had been wronged,* Bill had asserted, *he wouldn't rest until he had set it right. He would pursue the truth wherever it took him.*

Was her dad really so righteous an investigator? Perhaps not. Bill seemed like someone who'd tell kind lies if the occasion demanded it. And so, to interrogate that thought further, she'd imagined a different funeral – her own with her father among the mourners.

If it had been she, Mercy, who'd been found dead in questionable circumstances – for example if her body had washed up on a Barcelona beach – how would Ray have conducted himself at her funeral? What would he have made of her sketchier friends had he met them? Her car thief ex-boyfriend, for example, or her druggy nightclub mates. Would he have been as suspicious of them as she was of Victor Neale and company? If so, she couldn't imagine that he would just leave the room in tears, as she'd just done, without investigating those suspicions. He undoubtedly would have begun asking questions, upturning rocks, and pursuing the truth wherever it might take him.

And if, in pursuit of that truth, he discovered that she'd been murdered, how would he act? He'd secure her justice somehow, just as Bill had said he would. That part of the eulogy she could believe.

'Excuse me?' a female voice had asked, snapping Mercy

out of her brooding. 'Sorry for disturbing, but are you Ray Tyler's daughter?'

It was a tall middle-aged woman wearing a thick grey coat with a black band around the right arm.

'My name's Helen Bracken and I was a friend of your dad. I wanted to offer my condolences. Mercy, isn't it?'

'Didn't see you at the funeral,' Mercy had said.

'I didn't want to intrude,' replied the woman. 'Not everyone there would've welcomed me.'

A new suspicion had pierced Mercy then. She took a closer look at this stranger who'd hidden in the shadows of a funeral. She was older than her mum and not especially attractive, but then her father had been a man of unexpected tastes. Mercy had always known he'd had other women and she'd wondered if any of them would have the gall to show up today.

'I knew him professionally,' Helen had explained as if having guessed at what Mercy was thinking. 'And I held him in high esteem, he was a very fine investigator. The people I'm avoiding are some of your father's friends. I'm a police detective. DCI Bracken.' She'd produced her police ID from out of her pocket. 'I've investigated the Neale family and their associates many times over the years. Part of me would love to go into that pub to rattle them all but it would be disrespectful to your family, so I've decided against it.'

'I wouldn't have given a shit,' Mercy had said and turned her head back toward the river.

'I'm here out of respect.'

'Followed me though, didn't you?'

'I saw you leave the pub and you looked to be in distress. I know how tough days like this can be. My mother died last year and it hit me hard. I thought I'd come and see if you were alright.'

'How thoughtful,' Mercy had replied in a flat voice. 'But, as you can see, I'm tickety-boo now. You can get back to whatever it was you were up to, skulking around a wake, spying on gangsters. Knock yourself out, I won't blow your cover.'

'Your dad told me you were like him,' Helen Bracken had said. 'He told me quite a bit about you actually.'

'Did he now.'

'He mentioned that you were interested in becoming an investigator yourself. He wanted you to join his agency one day. He was proud of you, I think.'

Mercy had side-eyed her. She couldn't imagine her dad saying anything of the kind.

'You wanted to be a police officer when you were younger, is that right? You know, that's not as impossible as you might think. There are a number of new initiatives to increase representation—'

'Just what are you trying to sell me, Helen?'

The woman had sat down next to her on the bench.

'Miss Tyler, I was wondering if we could talk about that statement you made to the police. The one containing the voicemail recording you received from him on the night of his death.'

Mercy turned to see her face.

'I heard the recording and read your official statement,' Bracken had continued. 'It interested me. Frankly, I was angry those details weren't sent to me earlier, before the coroner's report was in.'

'You believe me then?' Mercy had said, sitting up straighter. 'About Dad being murdered?'

'I can see why they ruled his death an accident,' she'd replied in a diplomatic way. 'There was a lot of alcohol in his bloodstream and the damage to his head and legs could easily have been caused by stumbling onto a rocky surface in that condition. But I'm hoping we might be able to talk about it more before you return to Barcelona.'

'I fly back tomorrow,' Mercy had told her. 'Let's talk now.'

'What about your father's wake?'

'Most of those people will be delighted if I don't go back. I'll text my mum to say I'm heading home.'

'Good,' Helen had nodded and got to her feet. 'Let's get somewhere warmer and I'll buy you some food. I'm interested to learn more about this Long Needle character.'

'You and me both, Helen.'

As DCI Bracken has led her back to her car, Mercy then remembered what her father had said to her during that drive to Gatwick Airport.

*'A person like you couldn't handle my job. You're not investigator material.'*

We'll see about that, Dad, she'd thought as she got into the policewoman's car.

# 6

Now, a girl sitting beside Mercy on the train was discussing her heart-shaped plans for the evening. It was only then that she remembered it was Valentine's Day. It made her wonder if Carmelo, the on/off boyfriend she'd left in Barcelona, would use the date as an excuse to suddenly switch it on again. Perhaps he'd suddenly appear before her in England, she imagined, as the train approached her station. Then she remembered that his extensive criminal record meant he was unlikely to be allowed outside of his own country.

But, as she was waiting for the train doors to open, she received a text from an unsaved number. It read **Happy Valentines thanks for the 5 stars. got plans tonite?**

She'd stepped onto the platform, was walking to the station exit and was about to put the phone away when a follow up appeared.

**This is Jamal from earlier btw. Uber driver. love to take u out?**

She smiled. Random blokes used to hit on her all the time in Spain but this was the first time it had happened in

England. From the back seat, her cab driver had seemed to be a good-looking guy and his chat had been entertaining. But she'd no intention of accepting his offer. She texted a response once she was the other side of the ticket barrier.

**Flattered. But can't unfortunately. Thanks anyway x**

She'd barely walked five steps before the phone buzzed again.

**Got boyfriend? cool. But if not I think you and me could have fun. FYI – Im a gentleman**

It was a short walk between the station and her family home, but Mercy wanted to get her head together before meeting her mum. She fired off one more text before turning her phone off.

**No doubt. But I've a complicated life so I'll do you a favour and refuse. Thanks again and I hope you have more luck with your next fare**

A pub on the corner of her old street was just opening up, somewhere she and her family used to go to a lot. She'd tried to get served in there once as an underage drinker but the landlord had recognised her and phoned her dad. She peered through the window. Surely nobody in there would recognise her now, she thought before carrying on down the street.

A little iron sign was still screwed onto the front gate of the Tyler residence with the words BEWARE OF THE ROTTWEILER emblazoned across it. The sign was a joke present given to Ray by one of the Neale brothers and referred to their nickname for him, Ray 'the Rottweiler' Tyler. Her mothers' allergies meant they'd never had a real pet.

Mercy looked up at the house, one in a long row of suburban architecture with its triangular, mock-Tudor design. Steam escaped from the top-floor bathroom and the tip of an electricity pylon that loomed behind it was visible from the front. There was a second path that curled around the side of the house and led down to the basement flat.

The front door opened and Julie was still wearing her pink dressing gown, smoking the last of an almost finished cigarette. Mercy noted that she was unwashed despite it being nearly afternoon.

'The merry widow,' Mercy smiled as she went to kiss her mother. 'Radiant as ever. On your own?'

'Of course,' Julie said after their embrace. Before closing the door after her, she stubbed out the cigarette on the outdoor brickwork. 'Been waiting for my girl.'

'I've been busy, busy, busy,' Mercy said as she swept through the house toward the kitchen. 'Got myself a new career.'

'So I hear,' her mother sighed as she followed her through.

A box marked "Christopher Things" was on the kitchen table ready for collection. Inside were some karate medals and belts, some true crime magazines and a rolled-up poster of Kylie Minogue. Also, a notepad with **Chrissy's Secret Diary** scrawled on the front.

'I've had Bill on the phone,' said Julie as she crossed over to the kettle and turned it on. 'He told me you'd been asking for your dad's old job.'

'I didn't ask,' Mercy replied as she placed her handbag on one of the kitchen stools and sat on another. 'I insisted, starting Monday. And I had no idea that you and Bill were so chatty.'

'We've always been friendly,' Julie told her as she fetched the teabags. 'He's been very supportive since your father died.'

'Has he indeed?' Mercy said as she flicked through the

diary. She was looking again for what she now called the Long Needle pages.

'He asked what I thought of you working at M&T, so I told him. It's a mistake.'

'Thanks for the support.'

'I'm sorry darling, but you're living in a dream if you think you're suited to it.'

'Dad wanted me in the business once,' Mercy replied.

'That was a long time ago, sweetheart. You should sell your half to Bill or someone else. Or take the money it'll bring in and get another job on top. But you're not the investigator type, you're too self-absorbed.'

'*Self-absorbed*,' Mercy lifted her eyes up from the diary. '*Living in a dream*. You've said those things to me before. According to you, I was delusional when I left for Spain. But, as you can see, I sit before you a changed woman.'

The kettle continued boiling. Julie brought over a tin of biscuits.

'Not for me, thanks,' Mercy said, her attention returned to the diary. 'I've had too many at the office.'

Her mother continued making the tea and, once a mug had been placed in front of Mercy, she took a seat opposite. A letter addressed to Chrissy had been sent to that address a week earlier and she read this as Julie watched her face. It was from Dylan, her former fiancé. Once Mercy had finished Dylan's letter, she placed it back in the box and took a sip of tea.

'I had a memory the other day,' Julie said then, 'from when I was pregnant with you. We were going to call you Elizabeth.'

'I didn't know that,' Mercy said. 'After Her Majesty?'

'Elizabeth Taylor actually,' Julie replied. 'Well, as far as I was concerned. But you know what a royalist your dad was.

We were going with Christopher if you were a boy but Elizabeth – Lizzie – if you'd been born a girl.'

'I was born a girl.'

'You know what I mean,' Julie rolled her eyes. 'If you'd been *assigned a female gender at birth* then. Fucking hell.'

'Been thinking about this Lizzie a lot, have you? She sounds less complicated than what you got.'

'Don't get defensive. I just thought you'd like to know what I would've called you. I mean I never would've come up with a name like Mercedes. It's a stripper name.'

'Mercedes was a close friend when I was in Spain,' Mercy explained. 'She was a sex worker and she was killed around the time I was transitioning.'

'And I just thought you named yourself after a car.'

'She was one of the sweetest women I've ever met. I took her name out of respect.'

'Well, it's nice to hear you've got respect for someone.'

'Now what's that supposed to mean?'

Mercy's back had become ramrod straight but a tap on the kitchen door interrupted them. A young man wearing a blue sweater and jeans had entered the house via the staircase that led up from the basement flat. He looked like he was already regretting intruding on the two women who were clearly poised for a fight.

'Hey Mrs Tyler,' the tenant said with a slight stammer. 'If this is a bad time I can come back later. I just wanted to know if I could borrow a Phillips screwdriver.'

'No problem, Craig,' said Julie. 'You remember my daughter.'

'Nice to see you again,' Mercy smiled. 'Bethan working today, I take it?'

'Yeah,' nodded Craig as Julie went to a low cupboard to find Ray's old toolbox. 'She's a nurse.'

'I remember,' said Mercy. 'Got any big Valentines plans?'

'Not really,' Craig said as he kept his eyes on her mother who was bent over and searching through various tools. 'Beth's always tired when she gets home.'

'Right.'

Julie crossed over, handed Craig a screwdriver and wished him a nice afternoon. She'd collected a packet of cigarettes from the cupboard while there too. Craig turned to Mercy and said goodbye.

'Quick thing, Craig,' Mercy said, before he could go. 'I'm curious. How many times have you screwed my mother exactly?'

'Woah!' he cried, staring at her in convincing amazement. 'Where did that come from?'

Julie had been pulling out the final cigarette from the packet. She stopped and glared at Mercy.

'Don't be a stupid cow,' she warned.

'Was today the first time or have there been other sessions?'

'You've got the wrong idea, my friend,' said Craig. 'I've never... we've never...'

'My suspicions were first aroused by the steam coming out of her bathroom window,' Mercy observed. 'I noticed it coming up the path. And yet clearly,' she waved her hand toward Julie, 'she hasn't washed today. What's that about? As the only other person in the building, you've been showering in her room. Also, she's smoking a lot which she always used to do after Dad had been at her.'

'The shower in our flat is broken' Craig spoke fast. 'Your mum was kind enough to let me use hers. Isn't that right, Julie?'

Julie said nothing. She just tapped the end of her unlit cigarette and stared at her daughter.

'Then that explains that,' Mercy nodded as she produced her phone and made to switch it back on. 'So if I send your Bethan a text – hard at work though she is in that hospital – she'll totally verify the whole broken shower story, will she?'

*'Don't do that!'* he stepped towards her.

'Go back downstairs, Craig,' Julie said.

'Please don't tell her,' he continued. 'It was a one-off. Never happened before, won't happen again. I swear.'

'Craig!' Julie hissed. 'Leave this to me!'

'Relax,' Mercy said and put the phone down. 'I'm not a grass. I don't even have her number. I was just trying to make a point to my mum who doesn't think I have what it takes to be a detective.'

'Please,' Craig continued. 'I love Bethan. It's just that we've both been working so hard lately—'

*'Craig!'* Julie shouted. 'Go to your room!'

With that, he darted out of the kitchen and scurried downstairs.

'Come on, Mum,' Mercy laughed. 'That was some serious Poirot shit you just witnessed.'

'Fine,' Julie said, grabbing a lighter. 'Be a private eye if you must, I'm past caring. Just do me a favour Mercedes, Mercy or whatever other stupid name you want to call yourself, take that box of old crap away and clear off.'

Julie walked out of the door and into the garden. She was still out there when her daughter eventually left the house.

# 7

A short time later, Mercy sat with a gin and tonic in that local pub with her heavy box of childhood things by her feet, trying to not cry.

'Cheer up, darling,' said a man in a Millwall shirt. He'd approached her table from the bar with a pint of bitter in his hand. 'It can't be as bad all that.'

'I'm fine,' she promised him. Because of his shirt she wondered if he were someone her dad might have known. 'Just having a crap day. Thanks though.'

'Lemme guess,' he persisted with a rueful smile. 'You got the Valentine's blues, same as me, right?'

'Nothing like that,' she said as she dried her eyes. 'But I'd rather be alone.'

Despite this, he pulled back a chair and sat at her table.

'Y'know, sometimes it's better to talk about these things. I'm Terry, by the way.'

'I don't care what your name is,' she snapped. 'Take your pint and piss off, Terry.'

'Alright love, no need to be a bitch,' he said, standing again. 'As you were.'

Terry stomped off, muttering that it must be her time of the month. She wondered if she should leave but Ella Fitzgerald's 'My Funny Valentine' was playing from the tinny speaker above her head and persuaded her to stay. So instead she went over to the bar and ordered another cheeky G&T then returned to her table and read the short letter from her ex again.

Years earlier, when they'd studied law together; Dylan had proposed marriage and she'd happily accepted him. They'd even enjoyed a big engagement party aboard a boat on the Thames which his rich parents had paid for. To be fair, she could've done an awful lot worse. Dylan had been handsome, kind, just about tall enough and, unlike her, had completed his degree and was now a practising lawyer. But he was also gay and wanted a husband, not a wife, so her announcement during the engagement party that she was a woman was very much the fly in their champagne.

In his letter, Dylan offered her his commiserations on her father's death, even though they'd never got on. He also congratulated her on her transition, mentioning that he'd seen a recent picture of her on social media in which she'd looked *really convincing*. He probably hadn't meant that to be insulting, she thought, as she placed the letter back in its envelope. Or perhaps he had.

She returned the envelope to the box of other relics and found herself longing for the company of the friends she'd made in Barcelona, the ones who had only ever known her as Mercy. She reached for her phone to order a cab back to her flat as more messages started appearing.

**With respect I get it,** the persistent Uber driver had replied. **it aint a thing for me if it aint a thing for you. just want to have a fun nite with someone beautiful**

She contemplated this message and wondered if the

cabbie was referring to her being trans or not. A follow up message appeared which seemed to stress the former.

**Imma open minded guy,** it read.

'Really?' she murmured, clicking on the third message.

**we could go to Brixton where I know cool places. meet at David Bowie at 7 take it from there? Let me know if into it**

She wondered how to phrase her rejection. Then she realised she might not want to. February the 14th was clearly a big day for pushy men chancing their arm, but Jamal was a much more attractive proposition than the hapless Terry. After all, she did want to get reacquainted with the London nightlife now she was back and it sounded preferable to another night in alone waiting for her mousetraps to spring. She could tell one of her friends where she was going and besides, she was confident she could handle herself if he turned out to be a creep.

**OK, you're on,** she replied. **Can we meet at 8 though? Also, what does David Bowie mean? A pub?**

Once that was sent, she ordered another cab and reached down for the box. Maybe this isn't such a miserable city after all, she thought, heaving it towards the door.

# 8

Around that same time Bill had called a staff meeting at the M&T outer office. As she watched him constantly checking his phone, Nina felt that there was something off about her usually self-contained boss. She was sitting on the clients' sofa while Barb was behind her desk and Robbie truculently swivelled on a chair he'd wheeled out from another room. With his back to the kitchenette, Bill then announced that Mercy Tyler would be joining the firm as a working partner, starting Monday. The meeting had been in session for just minutes before Barbara stood up.

'Beg pardon, Bill,' she said in a wobbling voice, 'but I can't remain silent any longer.'

This reference to her supposed hitherto silence struck Nina as funny considering Barbara had been making loud, disapproving huffs ever since Mercy was first mentioned.

'I've been working here for thirty years, nigh on,' Barbara continued. 'And I've seen you and Ray - God rest him - build this agency up from nothing. So, to hand

Raymond's hard-won legacy over to - whatever we're supposed to call it - is an insult to his memory.'

'We must honour Ray's wishes, Barb,' Bill replied with a patience Nina wouldn't have managed.

'No, it'll embarrass the firm,' Barbara persisted. Her chin was raised, daring Bill to call her bluff. 'If Chrissy's working here then I'll have to tender my resignation.'

'Sorry to lose you, Barb,' Bill replied with a swiftness that shocked Nina. She and Robbie exchanged glances. 'I'll expect your resignation letter on my desk sometime next week,' Bill continued, 'if you're serious.'

Barb sunk back down into her chair in defeat while he addressed his remaining employees.

'As for you two,' he told them, 'neither of you have any reason to fear losing your positions as a result of this new addition. Chrissy will be made to understand that his lack of experience means that he'll be introduced at a lower level. And it'll have no effect on any potential career advancement that you may have been anticipating.'

'You just called her *he*, boss,' Nina corrected him.

'Sorry, I wasn't thinking. And yes, her name's *Mercy*, not Chrissy.' It sounded like he was reminding himself.

'I left a decent job in an Apple Genius bar to work here,' Robbie reminded them. 'So she better not turn out to be my replacement. But, if she's below me, fine. I'll get her doing all the shit I don't want to do.'

'No you won't,' Bill told him in a raised voice. 'This is my godson - I mean goddaughter - and we'll treat her with respect.'

'Then what's her role?' Robbie asked, scratching his ginger beard and pretending not to be rattled by Bill's sudden flare. Bill's shoulders slumped. Nina couldn't get a read on how he truly felt about Mercy. He seemed tense just talking about her but was also acting like her arch defender. Nor could Nina quite decide how Mercy's sudden appearance impacted her own work goals. She was prepared to wait and see how the thing played out, but, for now, Mercy was an unknown quantity.

'That's not your problem,' Bill said, running his fingers through his hair. 'For now she'll share my office.'

Then his phone rang. Nina was close enough to recognise MEANTIME as the caller's ID and she knew instantly who that was. Victor Neale.

'Thanks for calling back, mate,' Bill said upon answering and indicated to his staff that this meeting was now over. 'I know you're a busy bloke.'

He headed into his office and shut the door behind him. Nina got up and pretended she was going to the kitchenette to make tea. But Bill was speaking too low to be heard through the door.

'One of his *special clients,* you reckon?' she asked Barbara. 'Victor, perhaps?'

'Wouldn't care to speculate,' the crestfallen woman sniffed. Robbie wheeled his chair back into his office as Nina stepped over to the photograph of that golfing day that had attracted Mercy's attention earlier.

'Did you know her at this age, Barb' she said, pointing at the child in the picture standing next to Ray.

'Yeah, I've known Chrissy since he was a baby,' Barb replied. 'He had bright blue eyes like his dad.'

'She still does,' Nina said.

# 9

'If it's a mystery you're after,' said Jamal as they walked through the curving avenues of Brixton, 'here's one for you.'

Mercy had almost talked herself out of coming on this date with a random stranger, but, after reminding herself that she could do karate, she'd decided a night out might be just the thing to lift her mood. When she finally arrived at the David Bowie mural across from the tube station, Jamal looked as though he was getting ready to leave. But his face had brightened on seeing her and she was glad she'd not misremembered what he looked like, considering she'd mainly seen his Uber profile and the back of his head. He was older than her; and wearing a blue denim jacket with very youthful trainers that he was just about cool enough to get away with.

'You'll need serious detective skills to solve it,' Jamal continued as they weaved their way through the market traders packing away their stalls. He was keen to tell her about, as he put it, the strangest thing that had ever happened to him in all his three weeks as a cabbie, but first he wanted to get settled inside the food market. She considered telling him private investigators rarely solve anything in the Sherlock Holmes sense. Her dad had always led her to believe that the job was more about spying on people and rooting through their bins.

After arriving at Pop Brixton, they sat on a table underneath some heaters in the middle of the market. A spicy Halal chicken for him and a Miso soup for her. Despite it being a cold February night, the place was buzzing with buttoned up Londoners. Mercy felt that she didn't fit in here, the city of her birth, as well as she had in Barcelona. The first time she'd ever gone out in public as a woman was when she strolled down La Rambla during her first month there, an easy action that she'd have found much harder had she still lived in London. The hot Spanish weather had encouraged her to wear less, exposing more of the extravagant body art she'd had done and she never seemed to mind if people identified her as trans or not. The London climate, by contrast, compelled her to dress in a more invisible way and, although this was partly to do with the weather, it was more than that. She felt an unwelcome pressure to pass here more keenly than she had in Spain where nobody had ever known her by the name Chrissy.

'So it's the early hours of the morning and I'm up near Richmond,' Jamal began after taking a swig of coffee. 'I get a call to one of those riverside theatres they've got there.'

They'd both ordered hot drinks instead of alcohol. She'd already had those two gins with lunch and was becoming conscious not to inherit her father's drinking habits.

'I pull up outside and there's no one about save for this young guy, early twenties. Good looking but a bit of a chinless wonder. The theatre is locked up and he's hanging down by the river before he sees me flashing him. He comes over, confirms his name is Simon and he wants to go to Shoreditch as it reads on my phone, only he says *Thimon* and *Thoreditch.* Seriously, it was one of the worst lisps I've ever heard. The guy was an actor and during the trip he told me that he'd just been cast in a lead role in his first Thakespeare play. *Love'th Labour'th Lotht.'*

Mercy had just taken a spoonful of soup and she smiled with her mouth closed. One of the few things she missed about Carmelo was that he wasn't forever trying to make her laugh like British men insist on doing.

'Simon said that he didn't get cast in many Thakespeare roles and I said, yeah I bet you don't. He kept on about how glad he was to get this part and that he was starting rehearsals on the following week. He'd been celebrating with some actor mates. At last we arrived in Shoreditch. Simon gets out, waves me goodbye, goes into his flat. Two minutes later I get a five-star rating from him plus a three quid tip. Nice guy, I think. Only thing is,' Jamal leaned closer across the table, *'he was never seen again.'*

'Spooky,' said Mercy who was finishing the soup that she'd not found filling enough. She was hoping this story of his wasn't going to go on forever, as she was keen to visit another stall and get a veggie burger. 'Police got in touch with you via his phone, did they?'

'Yep,' he nodded, 'days later. He'd failed to turn up for rehearsals. They'd broken into his flat and found his phone, keys, jacket, but no sign of young Simon. Also, weirdly, at some point that night someone broke into the theatre that I picked him up from. A bunch of costumes and props were stolen. I got shown some pictures that his parents had given the police and asked if I noticed anything odd about him during the ride. I mentioned the lisp but, supposedly, he had always had it. All the photos I saw showed him in rehearsals with the same set of actors. There was this same girl and boy who were in every image. They looked a close trio. There were pictures of the two boys trying to kiss the girl and of them wearing this knight's body armour and practising sword fighting. The girl claimed that she left Simon and the other boy drinking at that theatre after the show. There were just two of them there and they had the keys to lock up the place. The other boy told the police that he later left Simon alone while he took a night bus in the other direction. I received Simon's call over an hour later though, so what was he doing in the meantime? Stealing costumes? And, if so, why?'

Mercy finished the last of her tea. 'I've already solved it,' she told him.

'Go on.'

'You've made it all up. The police don't investigate missing people that quickly and it's unlikely they'd show you his photo with other people in them.'

He stuffed the last of the spicy chicken into his mouth. 'I knew I should have worked on my procedural stuff better,' he added after swallowing. 'It's from a screenplay I'm working on called *The Man with the Twisted Lisp*,' he said. She buttoned up her coat even tighter and suggested they move into the indoor area. 'Still, you haven't cracked it though,' he said. `All the clues are there.'

'I tell you what,' she said, glancing over to the burger stand, 'if I can work out what happened to this fictional Simon, you buy me a burger. If I'm wrong, I'll get you something.'

Once they'd relocated to a less crowded corner, Mercy went over the facts of his story again. She was glad that they'd found a darker spot.

'Simon was dead from the start,' she decided after mulling over the details. 'You never even met him.'

'Who did I meet then?'

'The other one. The boy who was in all the photographs you were shown. That's why you didn't realise they were asking you to identify the wrong actor in the pictures. They were both in all of them.'

'Okay.'

'Tristan killed Simon, stole his phone and ordered an Uber from it. Did an impression of his lisp so nobody would know that the real Simon was dead already. He was trying to divert attention away from the murder scene. Took his keys and jacket.'

'Alright but where's the motive?'

'Probably jealous of him for getting a bigger part. Or some other stupid actor shit. He killed him after the rest of the cast had left the two of them alone.'

'If that's true, where's his body?'

'Why else would you set the story by the river?'

'But bodies float. He'd need to weigh it down somehow.'

Mercy considered this before answering.

'The body armour from the rehearsal pictures,' she finally said. `He stole all the other costumes, so that particular loss wouldn't stand out. Simon is still in Richmond, at the bottom of the river dressed like a medieval knight.'

Jamal leaned back in defeat.

'You're in the right profession,' he sighed. 'What sort of burger you want?'

LATER, after they'd explored the market some more and she'd decided to risk another gin, Jamal brought up the texts he'd sent her earlier.

'So, remember that thing I said was no thing,' he half-whispered as they passed a snogging couple in the small garden at the rear of the market. 'I mean, it might be a thing. But it doesn't have to be. My family would go mental if they knew I asked someone like you out though.'

'Why did you then?'

'Because I hate being alone on Valentine's night,' he smiled. 'And besides, if two people make a connection then all that shouldn't matter, right?'

'Couldn't agree more,' she nodded, despite her irritation at how he was congratulating himself for dating *someone like her.*

'Also, you seemed sad,' he continued, 'and I thought a night out might cheer you up.'

'Well, it has,' she returned his smile.

'Something on your mind though,' he observed.

Pop Brixton had by this hour opened up some large wooden doors to reveal a dance floor, so aside from a few amorous couples, the crowd had headed over to where the music was blasting out. She and Jamal sat down on a discreet plywood bench on the opposite end of the market. They were underneath a line of soft hanging lights that set a seductive atmosphere and the music was far enough away for them to talk easily.

'I've got a little mystery of my own,' she said after taking another sip of gin. 'Only, unlike yours, mine is true. Maybe you can help me work it out.'

'Happy to try.'

'I told you that my dad died recently?'

'Yeah,' he nodded. 'He drowned, you said.'

'His body was found caught up underneath a rusty old landing stage near the Deptford docks in December. The coroners returned death by misadventure.'

'Man, I'm sorry.'

'They believe he stumbled into the river because his bloodstream was full of alcohol and he was too pissed not to drown. He hadn't been seen for days.'

'He fell in?'

'That's what everyone seems to think,' Mercy said. 'But I say he was murdered.'

Jamal was sitting close enough for her to feel his body stiffen. She guessed that he may have been planning on making some subtly amorous move now that things were getting more chilled but mention of a murdered parent was enough to dampen anyone's ardour.

'That's intense,' was all he said.

'Dad was a big drinker, true. And supposedly he'd gotten worse in recent years. But I'm not buying this idea that he just fell into the river like some knock-kneed old soak. Not Dad, he was better than that.'

She heard herself say that and knew how feeble it must have sounded to somebody else. But still, she believed it to be true.

'I've taken many walks since then, down by the river path where he fell in. And it's not so easy to just trip into the Thames by accident, I don't care how rat-arsed you are. No, I think that his murderer, or murderers, took advantage of his drunkenness. He was pushed over, cracking his head open and chucked into the ice-cold river. The strong current and hypothermia could finish off a sober, uninjured man so he had no chance. They didn't need to weigh him down with a suit of armour, they knew it wouldn't look like murder anyway.'

'Were there signs of a struggle?'

'Minor ones. But that's one of the difficult things about

my old man,' she sighed. 'There were always signs of a struggle.'

'A brawler, was he?'

'They used to call him Ray 'the Rottweiler' Tyler,' Mercy said. 'He loved a ruck. So the few bruises on his body might not have been connected to his death.'

'Fishy,' Jamal said although he didn't sound too convinced. Mercy had voiced such suspicions before and she realised that most people believed she was too grief-stricken to accept the fact that accidents happen, especially to hot-tempered drunks like Ray Tyler.

'That's not all,' she said after draining the last of her drink. 'I promised you a mystery and you'll get one. But first I need another of these,' she got up from the bench and walked the empty plastic cup over to a nearby bin. 'And it's my round so what yours?'

'Another coke,' he said, getting up also. There was a flicker of disappointment on his face as it became apparent that she was leading him away from the soft setting before any chance of romance could develop.

'You're a cheap date,' she said as they moved towards a crowded gin bar set within one of the more brightly coloured shipping containers. 'I like that.'

They settled with their drinks at a small table.

'When I was a kid, my dad used to take me to karate lessons. And after one class we were walking back to his car that was in an underground car park. As we drew closer we realised that the engine had been tampered with. Someone had cut through the hard rubber attached to the manifold with a sharp blade. Fuel was flowing all over the engine and if he'd turned it on it would've gone up like a fireball.'

'Holy shit.'

'Right,' she nodded. 'To this day the smell of petrol makes me want to puke.'

'Someone was trying to kill you both?' Jamal asked.

'More likely it was a threat because there's no way a person wouldn't smell that damage from a distance. Dad tried to assure me that it was just a fault with the motor, but, even at that age, I knew it wasn't.'

'Who did it?'

'Not sure,' she said. 'He went out of his way to hush it up and we didn't even tell Mum. But have you ever heard of the Neale brothers? Gangsters who were all over the papers back in the nineties.'

'Weren't they the guys who pulled off some big robbery at an airport?' he said.

'The Air Costelloe heist!' she said, glad that she wasn't going to have to go over the entire history of London's gangland with him. 'The older one, Lawrence, was a notorious armed robber from long before then.'

'*He* blew up in a car explosion,' Jamal exclaimed. 'Jesus, was your dad involved with those guys?'

'He was really good mates with them,' Mercy explained. 'As a kid, I met Lawrence a few times. He was a huge guy with fingers like cold sausages and he had a big broken nose. Everyone called him Lol. But it was Vic – the younger one – who Dad had gone to school with and they were very tight. It was Victor Neale who set up dad and his partner in the detective agency.'

'Wow,' Jamal said, sounding impressed. 'They were bad dudes, right? Didn't Victor...'

'... stab a policeman to death? Yeah. He escaped a prison sentence though because it was an undercover officer trespassing through his grounds in the middle of the night looking for Costelloe loot. Neale's lawyer was able to convince the court that Victor thought it was a home invader and that he'd acted in fear for his family. The weekend after the trial both the Neale brothers came round to our house to celebrate with their wives and families. They were making jokes about dead policemen. That was the day Dad let me have my first taste of champagne. Soon after that,' she went on, noticing that Jamal had stopped looking impressed, 'I overheard something I wasn't supposed to. I was at home one afternoon when I should've been at school. I'd expected the house to be empty as both my parents had day jobs, but Dad suddenly returned. I hid from him in his office which was downstairs by the back of the house.'

'Because he'd be mad at you for playing truant?'

'Sort of,' she shrugged. 'But the important thing is the man my father brought home with him to talk business. A man whose face I never saw but whose voice I heard clearly.'

'How come?'

'I was hiding behind some curtains.'

'Really?'

'And it was a beautiful sunny day,' she nodded. 'I was sure he was going to draw them back to reveal me hiding there, but he never did. That's how I knew they would be discussing something serious.'

The music in that bar was loud and there was a crush of people standing nearby. She leaned closer so she didn't have to broadcast the ugly truth to everyone there.

'They were conspiring to kill someone,' she said. 'From what I could make out, the visitor was some sort of hitman. My dad was hiring him to commit a murder, on behalf of some unnamed client.'

'My God. Are you sure?'

'One hundred per cent.'

'Who were they talking about killing?'

'I didn't hear a name.'

'Do you know who the hitman was?'

'Nope, never saw him. But if I heard his voice again, I'd recognise it. There was a creepy, cold edge to it. My dad clearly loathed him although the whole meeting couldn't have lasted longer than three minutes.'

'And they were definitely talking about murder? There's no way you could've been mistaken?'

'Dad had brought him back to his home to give him an envelope he'd hidden in the study. Inside that envelope, from what I could make out, were the details of the *target.* They used that word. Before he opened the envelope the man alluded to Victor Neale, made a point of saying he knew my dad was connected to criminals. Then Dad asked him how he'd do it. *"It won't look like what it is."* It was murder they were talking about, I'm certain. And get this; less than a week later, Lawrence Neale blew up in that car explosion you mentioned. He was dead before they reached the hospital.'

'Hang on. You're saying...' he squinted. 'Wasn't someone nicked for that?'

'A man named Bobby McAlonan was arrested soon afterwards. He'd already done time in his youth for identical attacks on rival businessmen and was known to hate Lol. And it *really* looked like he'd executed this explosion too. But I've always thought that the real killer had just borrowed McAlonan's *modus operandi.* Because what a great way to disguise a hit. Just make it look like someone else's handiwork.'

'Your mystery sounds more far-fetched than mine,' Jamal said, as she knocked back the last of her gin. 'And why would your dad do that to his mate?'

'Everyone thinks the Neale boys were tight,' she told him. 'But I grew up with them so I know; little brother *hated* big brother. You could feel that energy when they were in the same room. I believe Victor arranged the hit but, because the target was his brother, he couldn't use his regular guys. He needed the murder outsourced so he used my dad as the middleman.'

'Did you go to the police?'

'Of course not,' she replied. 'I was hardly going to dob my own dad in. I never mentioned it to anyone until after he died.'

The small bar was getting emptier. A man in a puffer jacket approached and told them to drink up before the whole place closed.

'Dad had a lot of gambling debts in those days,' she said as she collected her handbag from under the table and produced her phone. 'You want to hear his final words to me? On the night he died he mentioned the meeting with the hitman in a voicemail message.'

'I dunno,' Jamal said, with a scrunch of the nose. 'Sounds a bit personal.'

'Nah, it's cool,' she said, forcing it on him after finding the recording.

He listened to her Dad's voice with a finger pressed to his other ear and it was only then that she realised how inappropriate this was. She'd been getting steadily drunker all night while he'd remained sober and he seemed to pity her a little when he handed the phone back. Embarrassed, she put the phone away and wondered what had compelled her to share such an intimate thing. She was now regretting bringing any of this up.

'You've told the police now though?' he asked. The

music had stopped and the food vendors were all shutting up for the night.

'Sure,' she nodded. 'But you know how it goes.'

'You don't strike me as a liar,' Jamal said, answering a question she hadn't asked. 'Doesn't anyone believe you?'

'There's a police detective still investigating Victor Neale,' she replied. 'She seems like she *wants* to believe. But the case isn't open.'

'What about the rest of your family?' he asked, as they cut through the electric lit railway arches. 'Do they believe you?'

'My mum thinks I'm nuts,' said Mercy, using the moment to stop walking and turn to him. She'd chosen to do this underneath a darker spot between two orange lights. She hoped he was sharp enough to pick up on why. 'But that's nothing new.'

His cute smile told her he understood the reason she'd stopped walking.

'What about your brother?' he asked.

'I'm an only child,' she said and lightly tapped the front of his coat with her finger. He was slightly shorter than her but that still made him taller than Carmelo. Going in for a snog seemed guaranteed now and she felt good about the prospect.

'Who's Chrissy then?' he asked.

'Excuse me?'

'On the voicemail message your dad was talking to his son. He called him Chrissy.'

Her warm feeling sank away. Was he being obtuse? Did he genuinely not realise? She'd been giving him hints all night and had told him that the voicemail was for her, which was hardly ambiguous.

'That was my name when I was younger. Dad kept

calling me it even after I transitioned. You get that about me, right?'

Jamal stared at her for a couple of seconds and his face betrayed nothing. Then his head gave a very slight twitch and he took a step back.

'You're a man?' he cried, the words almost echoing off the railway arches. She felt her entire self sag. 'Are you serious? Is this another joke?'

'None of this is a joke, Jamal,' she said, taking a step back from him too. 'I'm transgender.'

'Why didn't you tell me?' he spluttered.

'I just did.'

'You think I'm an idiot or something?'

She felt suddenly cold and hugged herself while he grabbed his hair and turned away from her.

'I mean, you should mention something like that up front, shouldn't you?' he continued once he turned 360 degrees to face her again. 'It's only fair.'

'I thought you already knew,' she explained. 'Your texts suggested you knew. All that stuff being an open-minded guy. You even said that your friends would be mad if they knew you were dating *someone like me*. I mean, what was all that about if not me being trans?'

'I meant a non-Muslim!' he answered, and he looked upwards as if for help. 'I didn't mean a geezer!'

'Bloody hell,' Mercy groaned. 'You're the one having a laugh, Jamal, considering how strong you came on this morning. Don't pretend this is my fault.'

Mercy breathed out hard and began walking away from him, her disappointment replaced by a potent shot of anger.

'Thanks for the burger,' she called over her shoulder as she strode towards Electric Lane. 'I hope the next passenger you chat up is more suitable.'

'Hang on!' he called out and began following her. 'Don't leave like that. I didn't know, alright?' She quickened her pace. She needed to get the last tube home and was completely done with Valentine's Day at this point. Jamal ran up behind her. 'I'm sorry, OK. It was a shock and I handled that bad. I didn't mean to be an arsehole about it.'

'Well, you were.' Mercy let him catch up to her but kept her eyes facing forward. 'I'm not a *geezer*,' she told him. 'And I wasn't trying to trick you.'

'Yeah, alright,' he nodded, drawing up beside her. 'But thing is, I'm serious about my faith and that's what I was struggling with. And you know something? Maybe you would have picked up on that if you'd asked me anything about myself instead of just going on about your family all night. Some detective you'll be.'

'I'm not a detective,' she said as she stopped to face him. 'I'm a fucking private investigator!'

Don't start crying now, she told herself. There'd been too much sobbing recently.

'Listen, I've nothing against you... trans... people,' Jamal explained. 'And I think you're very cool to talk to. I'd like to be friends with someone like you.'

'What an honour for me.'

'Yeah,' he said appearing to miss the irony of her tone. 'But romantically...' he paused, struggling with how best to express himself. 'Well, that's a thing that *is* kind of a thing.'

'I'm going home,' she said, heading toward the bus stop. 'Thanks for a magical evening.'

## 10

It was past midnight as she trudged up the hill toward her home. Her bag was now heavy with a bottle of Rioja from an all-night off-license. She'd bought it to remind her of happier times in Spain and was now miserably listening again to her dad's voicemail message. She'd been doing this a lot lately.

*'In spite of everything, I've always loved you, Chrissy. Believe that.'*

Typical Dad, she thought as she reached the first crossing in the road. Even in his final moments he couldn't stop himself from dead-naming me.

The houses she passed were mostly building sites, with scaffolding and skips outside. Her neck was craning over onto her shoulder as she walked, her ear pressed close to the phone as she listened. She was so preoccupied with that dismal message that she wasn't focusing on the path ahead. So she didn't see the man with the knife until she almost slammed into him.

'Bag!' he commanded. 'Gissit.'

The blade was long, sharp and inches from her chest.

When she saw it, every nerve ending went into high alert. A cat yowled nearby and she jumped away from him in an impulse of panic.

His face was masked behind a thick red scarf and black hoodie and her fear on seeing him was primal. With his other hand, he lunged for the bag strap that was crossing her body.

Years of martial arts training kicked in. Her right hand grabbed his wrist in a blocking move just as the knife was cutting through her strap. Her left hand struck him in the stomach with serious force. She swoop-kicked his leg, he tumbled to his knees and the bag with the wine hit the pavement.

'Bitch!' he cursed from his kneeled position. His knife arm was surging toward her but she'd grabbed it and was holding it back as her heart beat hard. Fear coursed through her as her arms desperately struggled to hold the blade at bay.

Then his free fist punched her in the ribs and she collapsed, shocked by the pain.

'Don't move,' he said in a muffled voice, standing again. 'Or I'll cut you!'

Terrified, she screamed for help. As he reached down to grab her phone she scrambled away in fear, hoping he'd just take her possessions and leave.

Then she saw the wine bottle a few feet away, still intact. That knife forced every rational thought out of her head. In one swift move she grabbed it, swung it upwards and connected it hard with her assailant's head.

*'FUCK!'* he cried, dropping the knife and collapsing against the trunk of a tree. Mercy dived for the knife but he kicked her in the head as she got near. The pain was so

intense she thought an eye had popped out but she managed to fall over where the blade lay.

'Come closer,' she warned, grabbing it by the handle and coiled to spring if he tried another attack, 'I dare you.'

Just then a motorbike pulled up behind her. A black-clad helmeted rider pulled up to the mugger as he staggered away from the tree. A female voice shouted "*we done?*" through her helmet.

The attacker ran to the bike, climbed onto the back and they sped from the scene. Still breathing fast, Mercy watched, as they turned left into a road ahead. But she still clutched hold of the knife in case he returned. Her handbag was lying close by her; its leather strap cut.

Wincing, she rolled to her side and got up from her prone position. Her body felt sore from the fight. Then she spotted her purse, still inside the bag. She blinked and crawled towards her dropped items, her injuries cruelly revealing themselves with every movement. The wine bottle was beside the tree, still unbroken. Good, she needed a glass now more than ever.

Then she realised something strange. A single item had been stolen from her during the attack. Not the purse or even the bag itself, which wasn't cheap.

The mugger had only removed her mobile phone, the one with her father's voicemail on.

# PART II

*Secret Identities*

# 11

Mercy had been born in the same month that England had made it to the semi-finals of World Cup 90. She knew this because her dad would often refer to one of these events whenever the subject of the other was raised.

'Football fever was the reason I bought you that England shirt, Chrissy,' he'd told her twelve summers and three World Cups later. 'I thought it'd be a nice "Welcome to the Family" present for you.'

It was 2002 and they'd been sitting together in the back patio of their home. Their suburban garden was a decent suntrap despite several neighbouring houses and an electricity pylon overlooking it. Ray had been referring to a framed football shirt signed by England several players - men whose names he'd utter as if they were the very knights of Camelot. That shirt had been displayed on her bedroom wall ever since, despite her never having shown the slightest interest in it. Ray had opened another fizzing can of beer and threw the ring-pull onto the table between them as he spoke. He'd just returned, suntanned and triumphant, from ten days travelling around some Greek Islands where he'd been keeping track of a dodgy businessman in a big yacht for reasons left vague.

'Because someone paid me to follow him,' was the only answer he ever gave whenever young Mercy had asked why he'd been investigating certain cases. Then he'd swiftly change the subject back to penalty shootouts.

As usual on a Saturday, her mum was working at the hair salon, so she and Ray had been sat alone around the garden table. He'd given her another lager shandy and a *don't tell your mother* wink as they'd listened together to Talk-sport. She loved her parents equally but they were both easier to love when apart because then there were no rows. She'd recently insisted on being called Chrissy – not Chris or Christopher – and was daring to grow her hair longer despite his derisory comments.

Earlier that day he'd taken her to her first karate lesson. This had forged a rare bond between them. The thrill of throwing other kids about while wearing gender-neutral clothing had proven to be a wonderful release and Ray had seemed proud of her new skills. And it was in the afterglow of that, sat in that garden over that lager shandy, where she'd finally summoned the courage to tell him she didn't really like that football shirt on her bedroom wall and wanted it removed.

Ray took it surprisingly well. He even agreed to help her replace the frame with an image that she preferred. Kylie Minogue, in her white hooded jumpsuit.

'I don't blame you, son,' he winked at her as he helped hang the poster on the wall facing her bed. 'I had the blonde from ABBA on my wall when I was your age.'

During that period the Tyler family would socialise with the Mances almost every other Sunday. Bill's family had then consisted of his wife Moira, and Lisa, Moira's tomboyish daughter from a previous marriage. Lisa was a little older than Mercy but they'd gotten on well when young. They'd enjoyed roleplaying away from the adults, games in which the expected gender roles had been reversed by mutual unspoken consent. Lisa would pretend to be Han Solo while Mercy would be Princess Leia. It hadn't been a joke; just natural casting and they rarely acknowledged the switch as they played. But whenever an adult walked into the room, the roles would be flipped back in an instant.

'I'm Han,' Mercy would lie, knowing that their parents couldn't handle such harmless gender bending. '*She's* Leia.'

On one particular Sunday in 2003, the Mances had visited the Tyler home for a roast dinner. While the women had been preparing the meal, the men went to drink beers from Ray's little mini-fridge in his ground floor study. After a while Mercy's mum had sent her to tell them it was nearly ready and, on the way out of the kitchen, she'd pinched a crispy roast potato. She'd been chewing that as she'd moved through the already laid dining room, surprised that her dad hadn't already been summoned by the juicy smell of beef filling the house.

As she approached the study door, she overheard their conversation.

'Don't keep moaning about the Neale brothers, Bill,' she'd heard her dad say as she swallowed the potato and listened. 'Get over your issues with them, especially Victor.'

Bill had replied to that in a voice that was too quiet to overhear but her dad had interrupted it anyway.

'Yeah, Lol's a nasty cunt,' he said, much to her shock. It was the first time Mercy had ever heard him use that word. 'Me, you and half the villains in London agree on that. But his kid brother isn't so bad. Victor would be the first person I'd go to in a crisis. Apart from yourself obviously, mate.'

Mercy had often sensed that Bill was less comfortable with their criminal associates than her dad was, and she'd liked that about him. Her mum seemed to admire Bill too. In fact, she'd behave like a shameless flirt whenever he was near. Julie Tyler was an attractive woman who knew how to wear beautiful things, be they clothes, jewellery, or sexy smiles. She had a grace about her, Mercy had always thought, when she wasn't complaining of the constant headaches she held her husband responsible for.

'To think,' Julie had said as she touched Bill on the arm during that lunch, 'it could've been you and me if Raymond hadn't asked me out first. All our lives could've turned out differently if you'd been quicker off the mark, darling. Lucky thing for Ray and lucky for Moira, if you ask me.'

Mercy had made a throwing up face on hearing that, making Lisa snort out her coke in laughter. Ray just offered more wine to Moira who'd already sunk half a bottle. Bill had placed a hand over his own glass before Ray could refill it.

'You'd be welcome to his snoring, Julie,' Moira had hooted as she swirled her glass of Merlot. 'Not to mention the incessant grumbling I've to put up with. Bill's always tinkering for hours on end with his little gadgets when he isn't out spying at all hours. Mind you, Lisa's dad was much the same. Why I get stuck with these nocturnal types I cannot fathom.'

'Tell me about it,' Julie had said, glancing sideways at her husband who was now concentrating on his plate of roast beef. 'We should hire some investigators to look into these two, don't you reckon, Moira?'

'Look, people sometimes commit adultery at night,' Bill

had defended himself while patting his wife's hand, 'which means Ray and I have to work late unfortunately. I often wish these cheating couples would get their business over by 6pm, but what can we do?'

'S'right mate,' Ray had nodded, pouring himself the largest glass. 'Cheaters never spare a thought for the poor sods paid to follow them.'

'Like that married fella you were shadowing last Thursday, Ray,' Bill had then said, a false note entering his voice, 'who was carrying on with that young lass. He could've been more considerate.'

The words and tone had sounded oddly rehearsed. Mercy looked over at her mother and had seen her body language stiffen. When she spoke next, it had dropped the temperature of the room.

'Because what are mates for,' she'd looked at Bill with a less friendly expression, 'if not for providing false alibis?'

A sharp silence had followed then. The Tyler family were used to Ray's lies. He was generally better at it, so Bill's attempts to support a cover story had clattered like a dropped tin can.

'Well, I think it's disgraceful,' Moira had said after she'd swallowed a Yorkshire pudding. 'The way these girls carry on with other people's husbands. You wouldn't catch me having sex with a married man.'

'Including her own,' Bill had joked. Everyone laughed except for Julie. As Moira protested that she *hadn't meant it like that*, Bill leant over to kiss her.

The Mances' marriage had seemed functional enough, but Mercy thought it was unlikely that they'd ever loved each other. A decade later she'd not been surprised to learn that they'd divorced after Bill had been arrested for phone hacking. She'd always thought that he could do better than Moira anyway.

The real surprise was that her parents, clearly the more dysfunctional couple, had never split up. She could only imagine that it was because deep down they did actually love each other. In spite of all the pain that Ray caused with his countless deceptions, their marriage had somehow endured.

In the end, only his murder had parted them.

# 12

By the age of fourteen, Mercy had discovered what the term gender dysphoria meant and she knew that it applied to her. Inside she'd always felt she was female but now she had the terminology. According to the NHS website she might not be as adrift in this world as she'd previously feared, which was great because she'd grown tired of indulging in fairy-tale yearnings that her body would just transform overnight. The discovery she could do more than just wish for change was a sweet and miraculous relief.

However, while the world beyond the Tyler household was hinting that it might be prepared to accommodate her, inside those walls things were still 'Beware of the Rottweiler.' Her father was not a man she could imagine coming out as anything to, least of all as transgender. She'd often heard him speaking with unconcealed disgust about 'trannies.'

It was around then that the shoplifting started.

. . .

'WHOSE FUCKING EARRING IS THIS, RAY?' her mother's voice had rung out through the house. `Because I found it in our living room and it's not one of mine!'

It was the summer of 2004 and Julie's husband had just stepped through the front door after a day's work. Mercy had been sitting in her bedroom listening to Kylie Minogue's 'Fever' album for the hundredth time when she'd heard the ruckus. She leapt up from her bed, removed the silk scarf around her neck, and hid it inside her navy-blue pillow cover.

'Have you been shagging some tart on our settee?' she'd heard her mother crying from the hallway.

Feeling sick, Mercy had opened her bedroom door and crept along their dark landing toward the stairwell.

'It probably belongs to you, girl,' Ray said, defending himself. 'Or one of your mates.'

'You think me, or anyone I know, would be seen dead wearing this tacky shit?'

That had been a harsh blow. When Mercy had originally stolen both it and its earring twin from a branch of River Island, she'd thought they were quite classy. They were small glitter-lined gold hoops that she thought would go well with the outfit she'd been putting together. She'd slipped them into the pocket of her boy's school uniform, even though she hadn't had her ears pierced yet and simply glided out of the shop.

`It looks like it's fallen out of a Christmas cracker,' her Mum was heard saying.

The day before Mercy had left school early and returned while the house was still empty. She'd got out the pilfered accessories she'd been collecting. It was quite a haul - lipsticks, make-up sets, a cheap necklace swiped from a stall in the local market. Already at that age she'd started veering away from very girly stuff toward an alternative, grown up style. Her silk scarf had been a recent acquisition and she'd borrowed some killer heels from her mother's wardrobe. She'd already spent hours practising how to walk and dance in them and, by then, was no longer resembling Bambi on Ice. These were still some initial totters, but she'd eventually dared to go down to the living room to view herself in the large mirror there, with the earrings held up to her unpierced ears.

She'd been gazing at her reflection when her mother had suddenly returned from work. And, in the panic of scrambling back upstairs to her room, she'd not noticed that one of the earrings had dropped from her hand.

'Jools, I've had another crap day,' Ray was now grunting at the false accusation. 'I don't need all this.'

From the landing, Mercy could hear him shoving past her mother and knew he'd be heading towards his study, where he'd shut himself in to drink alone.

Horrendous guilt overcame Mercy as she heard her crying mother run up the stairs and then slam her bedroom door behind her. Her mum was in great pain, wrongly thinking that the gold hoop belonged to one of her husband's girlfriends. And she, Mercy, had been responsible for this poisonous misconception.

She dashed to the box above her wardrobe and removed everything that was obscuring her stolen stash. She'd pulled out her old briefcase with its combination lock, threw it on her bed and opened it to reveal her ill-gotten gains. Pushing aside her secret clothes and accessories she eventually found the matching earring.

She considered what to do with it.

Was she ready to go into her parent's bedroom and reveal that the earring was in fact hers? That would mean owning up to a lot more than just shoplifting. She placed the earring in her palm and thought about the consequences of confession. There had been many times where she'd been tempted to share her secret gender identity with her mother but Julie was a tricky woman at the best of times, and these were the worst. Ray was a transphobe - this was obvious - but she sensed that her mum could go either way. Julie was only in her late-thirties then and could hold progressive views when the fancy took her. Perhaps now was the time to trust her. Clenching the earring in her fist, Mercy moved into the landing.

'Mum?' she whispered as she tapped on the bedroom door. 'Can I come in?' It went quiet. Mercy repeated the question.

'Not now, Christopher,' Julie replied, sounding delicate and broken. 'It's not a good time.'

'Please Mum, I've got something to show you,' she persisted. 'It's important.'

Hesitantly, she entered the room where her mum was crying on the edge of her bed. She sat beside her and they hugged in a way that comforted them both.

'Sorry you had to hear all that, darling,' said Julie as her daughter pressed her face into the fluffy pink bathrobe she was wearing. 'It's not on.' Mercy pulled her face away from the robe. A mirrored wardrobe door was half open and she got a glimpse of mother and child together, hating how very boy she still looked. On the near bedside cabinet, the incriminating earring sat beside the alarm clock.

'He didn't do it,' she told her mum, `what you're accusing Dad of, I mean.' Julie held her closer and stroked her hair with her long fingernails like she used to when she was little. The feeling was like heaven.

'We love him, darling,' Julie whispered. 'But he is who he is.'

'No, it's true,' Mercy insisted. 'The earrings aren't his.' She opened her palm to reveal the matching one. 'They're mine.'

Julie peered down at the little glittered hoop. As she examined it, Mercy realised she'd been right. It *was* tacky shit.

'Did your dad put you up to this?' Julie asked, glancing over at the other earring on the cabinet.

'No!'

'Yours?' Julie made a frantic study of her child's ears for piercings. Tight panic passed over her face and, in that microsecond, Mercy had her difficult question answered. Julie wasn't ready.

'They're not *mine* obviously,' Mercy said, dismayed at how easily this lie had flowed forth. 'They're for a friend.'

'What friend?'

'You don't know her.'

'A *girl* friend?' Julie looked taken aback. 'I didn't think you knew any girls, Chrissy.'

'I met her on the bus.'

'What's her name?'

'Nadia.'

Julie pushed her blonde hair out of her face and wiped her eyes again. Her rapid facial expressions revealed a number of different thoughts happening at once. 'Is Nadia your girlfriend?'

'I'm in *love* with her, Mum,' Mercy declared about this girl whose name she'd just plucked from thin air. 'I bought her some earrings last Saturday - with granddad's gift vouchers - and I was going to give them to her. But she's going out with a boy from her sixth form. I'm gutted! I don't know how it eventually ended up in the living room but I was really upset.'

'I wish you'd told me, sweetheart,' Julie sighed. 'We should talk about these things.' She pulled Mercy close to her again for a long hug. 'I tell you something, honey,' she sighed into her child's unpierced ear. 'It's her loss. You're a handsome boy and one day you'll meet an even lovelier girl.'

'But it means you were wrong about Dad, doesn't it,' Mercy explained. 'He *is* being faithful.'

Julie exhaled, detached herself from the hug and reached over to grab the other earring from the cabinet. She placed it next to the one in her child's hand.

'If you say so, sweetheart,' she said and kissed her gently on the forehead. 'Why don't you give those to a girl who'll appreciate you more? Now go back to your own room, there's a good lad. Mummy's got a headache.'

# 13

They didn't see much of Ray in the following weeks, which was great because Mercy had started to prefer life without him around. Whenever her dad was at home he'd be in his study near the rear of the house where there was a sofa bed and a fridge. He'd leave before breakfast the next day and it was unclear where he was showering. Sometimes it smelt like he just wasn't. He rarely spoke to her now, other than to tell her to get a haircut.

Meanwhile, her mum spent a lot of time crying and talking to her friends on the phone. Mercy couldn't overhear everything but words like *Ray, bastard, shagging* and *slags* were said in quick succession.

One Thursday Mercy returned home later than normal due to an essential shoplifting spree that she was still buzzing from. She'd managed to lift the remaining items for the outfit that she'd been planning from a branch of Next. What's more, she'd been chased down the high street by a security guard who'd spotted her stuffing the expensive green jumpsuit into her bag and had pursued her for longer than store employees tended to. She'd found the experience strangely thrilling but had evaded arrest but now was itching to get home and work on the outfit in privacy. The right scissors were ready in her bedroom to cut the delicate garment down the neckline and up both legs.

But when she got home a white convertible Mercedes-Benz was parked in their pebbled driveway beside her mum's car. The number plate read VIC II. Despite not having seen the car before she knew whose it was.

Letting herself in, she ran upstairs with her stuffed bag trying not to be noticed. Her mum called up from the living room to come and greet their guest, but she was keen to hide the stolen jumpsuit first. As she passed the open door of her parents' bedroom, she saw that the wardrobe had been raided. A beautiful blue dress was lying on the unmade bed on a hanger.

'Christopher, look who's come to visit,' Julie was saying by the time she joined them in the front room. 'You remember Sarah.'

Sarah Neale stood up from the settee, extended her hand and smiled. It had been over a year since the Tyler family had visited Victor Neale's home in Kent and she'd first met the gangster's high-class wife. She looked as radiant as she had on that Sunday.

'How nice to see you, Chrissy,' Sarah said in her refined accent. 'You prefer to be called *Chrissy*, am I right?'

'Yeah, and well done for remembering,' she replied. 'Mum never does.'

Once again Mercy marvelled at how that vulgar spiv Victor Neale had managed to bag himself this poised specimen of a woman. She recalled her father having once told her that Sarah was, in some convoluted way, related to aristocracy, although that might have been just more of his bullshit. Her mother was certainly behaving as though Princess Diana had risen from the grave for a social visit. Their expensive tea set was out.

'Please to more tea,' said Sarah, placing a hand out to stop Julie from leaving the room. 'But only if there's some still in this pot. No need to go to the kitchen.'

Mercy noticed a tightness in Sarah's smile, as well as some skittish eye movements. She wondered why she was here. Folded beside her on the settee was Julie's favourite red summer dress. This explained the presence of the blue one in the bedroom above as the two women had swapped outfits in the past. Mercy longed to ask Sarah where she'd acquired her gorgeous skirt. She was already imagining stealing something similar at a future date.

'We're still waiting for Christopher... sorry Chrissy... to grow a bit taller,' Julie said as she poured out the last of the tea. 'Mother nature still has some work to do on you, eh boy?'

Nothing depressed Mercy more than being reminded that for her, puberty still hadn't relented in the damage it was doing to her, and that her days as a girlish boy were numbered. She didn't speak much after that, conscious of how much her voice must have deepened since the last time Sarah saw her.

Sarah's phone buzzed.

'Oh dear, it's Victor and he's hopping mad,' she said after picking it up. 'He's been in Antigua and has just learnt that the kids are on a school trip. He's saying I didn't tell him, which isn't true, but he's got a memory like an old sieve. I should head off.' She rose and air-kissed them both. 'Thanks for the dress, Julie darling. I knew I could count on you.'

Mercy stood beside her mother in the doorway waving

at their surprise visitor as she put the borrowed dress in the back of the convertible and placed on some designer sunglasses. Julie had been in full hostess mode until then but, as Sarah backed her car out of the gravel driveway, she hardened again.

'Did she come here just to borrow a dress, Mum?' Mercy asked.

'So she said.'

'You don't believe her?'

But, after the car drove off, Julie just went back inside the house, saying nothing.

# 14

The following day was, for a number of reasons, the defining episode of Mercy's young life.

It had begun as usual. She'd caught the bus before her mum left for work, but then got off again before reaching the gates of her school. She had no intention of enduring another day in that starchy all-boys place, getting bullied by arseholes like Nick Neale. Especially when, waiting in her bedroom, her special outfit was at last completed. Better yet, Ray hadn't been seen in over a week while Julie worked late on Fridays. Now was her time to dance as herself for once.

She'd spent the rest of that hot summer morning killing time in nearby woodland, reading a few chapters of a mystery novel and listening to birdsong. But, once she was certain that the house would be vacant, she returned discreetly, sliding over the lowest part of the fence in the back garden and then letting herself in through the kitchen with her backdoor key.

As soon as she was inside, the transformation began. Shedding her school uniform in a pile on her bedroom floor she took some disposable razors and a tub of shaving cream and went to the bathroom to prepare.

Mercy's original idea had been to fashion herself an outfit like the one Kylie had worn in the *Can't Get You Out of My Head* video. But she'd had a hard time finding a perfect white jumpsuit in any local shops. Anyway, she'd since decided the dark green one she'd stolen suited her more alternative style better. It had required some cuts down the neckline and up the legs, but it was a beautiful fit, which was a relief because she could hardly take it back. As she slipped her body into it for the first time, she felt wonderful. The sensation was liberating and for a second, she worried that she might pass out from it.

The long silk scarf she'd hidden inside her pillowcase made a perfect substitute for Kylie's hood but, until she saw the reflection of herself wearing it with the jumpsuit and a pair of her mother's high heels, she hadn't realised just how cool she would look. Kylie was the celebrity she flattered herself she most resembled, with her high cheekbones and short stature.

Luxuriating in the knowledge that the Tyler home was hers for the next few hours, she turned her CD player up loud so she could listen to her favourite album on repeat. Sitting on a small dressing table stool in front of her mother's vanity mirror she chanted along to the hook of her favourite song and opened her stash of stolen makeup. She made her selection from the eye-shadow palette, choosing a smoky colour to match the jumpsuit. Her cheekbones were, in her own estimation, her best feature and she hummed along to the music as she brushed gently at them. Then, once she'd attended to her eyelashes and the jumpsuit she'd briefly removed was back on, she applied some lipstick. The first few attempts resulted in graceless smears that she removed with some wipes before starting again. Eventually she got it right and the smile that flashed back was the truest she'd ever seen on herself. Bewitched by her own reflection, she leaned towards herself, distorting her face into something even more feminine, close enough to kiss. She sang along, mimicking Kylie's movements, her hand making the same delicate hush gesture that she'd been practising in her bedroom for weeks.

Her voice rose and she swiftly stepped backwards, spinning toward the full-length mirror behind her. The feeling of completion was electric and, just for a few moments she had to sit on the double bed to recover. Then, when another song began, she danced. Feeling fluid, alive and at ease with herself she watched her reflection as she continued through two more songs and then restarted the album. Aside from the silk hood that kept falling from her head, everything about the experience was sublime.

She returned to her own bedroom, her breathing heavy with excitement. It wasn't just the triumph of the outfit; it was more than that. While dancing she'd had a revelation.

She now knew that she could never accept what puberty was doing to her. Womanhood was her destiny, and, although she'd always felt female at her core, this was the first time it had seemed not like a curse but a blessing. Of course, she didn't really wish to be Kylie Minogue, or any pop star really, but she did wish to live as herself on her own terms. She'd planned that afternoon as a sort of farewell to this phase of her life. Now it revealed itself to be a celebration of everything that would follow.

A sudden impulse to dance around the house gripped her. She turned the music up high, placed the unruly scarf over her head again, and clumsily danced down the stairs, imagining that an appreciative audience was applauding her from the hallway. She was eager to view her reflection again in the wide living room mirror and was pleased with what she saw. Her hair looked cute poking out from under the hood and she was glad that she hadn't bowed to her parent's pressure to cut it short. She lifted her hands to her temple and broke again into the robotic moves that she felt she was absolutely nailing. She sang with uncontained glee.

Dancing out of that room, she took a new possession of the rest of her home. Then she headed into the kitchen to fetch an Evian to slake her thirst from the heat.

And that very second, while taking deep swigs from the plastic bottle and enjoying the cool of the open fridge, was when her happiness crashed to a halt.

An unfamiliar phone rang, and the sudden disturbance struck her like a whip. She dropped the bottle and it bounced across the kitchen floor, spilling water. On impulse, she ducked down to hide herself. It was the land-line phone that hung on the kitchen wall and it never usually rang! She'd misunderstood what it was at first and had been gripped by a primal urge to conceal herself.

Neighbouring houses looked into the windows of both the kitchen and the dining room. She had a paranoid certainty that whoever was calling had seen her bouncing about in this silly costume and was phoning to challenge her on it.

Shame had regained control. Staying low behind the counter she scuttled over to the water bottle to replace the lid before it could spill anymore.

The ringing continued for less than a minute but it felt like an age as she mopped the floor with a kitchen towel and placed the bottle back into the fridge. At no point did she consider answering. It was such a simple interruption, an unexpected phone call, but it had instantly killed all the joy that had been rising within her.

Then something far worse happened. From the front of the house she heard the sound of wheels crunching on gravel. As fast as a cat, she dashed into the hallway, staying low so she couldn't be seen through any front windows, and shot up the stairs with the borrowed high heels in her hands. She headed straight into her bedroom and turned off the song before whoever it was had time to get out of the car and hear it. Then she returned to the landing, treading lightly so she could peer around the top of the staircase to identify the driver through the windows.

'Shit shitting, *shit!*'

It was her father's car. She turned away from the staircase, completely out of sight; her back pressed against the landing wall. Why was he here? She'd barely seen him for weeks and now – *of all the moments* – he reappears. Thankfully, she was safely within reach of her bedroom where she could change so there'd be no evidence –

*SHIT!!!*

Her silk scarf! Where was her hood?

Her hands rose to her head but she knew without touching that it was gone. It must have fallen as she'd been dancing downstairs. Now it would just be lying there, waiting for her private detective father to discover like a smoking gun.

Maybe he'd just assume it belonged to his wife, fold it and leave it somewhere for her to collect later.

But what if he didn't?

For some reason, he wasn't getting out of the car. Perhaps he was making a call. There could still be time to race down and collect the scarf. As she weighed things up she heard another car approach and pull into the drive. *Who was this now?*

Barefooted, she moved down the staircase so she could get a better look at the new arrival. She couldn't see the new car but she heard her father turn his engine off and get out to meet the person. Oh God, maybe this one of the *other women* that Julie was forever accusing him of having?

The ignition of the unseen car turned off and she heard its door open. Her father addressed this unseen person aggressively.

'You've a bloody nerve,' she heard him say.

Swiftly, and almost on impulse, she made to retrieve the scarf. She dashed down, through the hall and into the living room, careful not to be seen by those outside. As she conducted a quick search of the settee that she'd been jumping on, she heard a quieter male voice beyond the curtained window. More ruinously, the scarf wasn't where she'd expected. She went back into the hall to return upstairs but it was already too late. Footsteps were approaching the door, the jangle of Ray's keys leaving her no option but to head through the house and escape through the back.

Then she saw it, through the open door of the dining room, her long silken scarf, ribboning beneath the legs of the wooden chairs. She had just enough time to dart in and grab it, but she could already hear the door opening. She realised that it was impossible for her to reach the kitchen door without her dad catching her in there, playing truant in a stolen jumpsuit. Her heart beat with painful urgency. If this other man were a client, then they'd be heading for his study and needed to go through this dining room to get there.

But the study itself had a patio door that led out into the

garden. Perhaps there was still time to leave through that and hide outside until the coast was clear.

Before the front door had even closed behind the men, she was inside Ray's dark room, which was mercifully unlocked, and crossed straight over to the thick scarlet curtains at the back. She pulled one curtain back and a shaft of daylight cut through the cluttered and musty space.

Even in her panic, the ashtray atmosphere of this once orderly room struck her. Empty beer cans on the desk, balls of paper and an old unwashed duvet on top of the sofa bed. It smelt, she thought, like a homeless man had been living there.

Worse still, there was no key in the back patio door. She yanked at the handle in desperation, but it wouldn't budge. There wasn't even time for her to search his desk as they'd be entering any second.

So, with no other moves left, she tucked into the narrow space between the back door and the curtains and then drew them over herself just before the door to the room opened behind her.

And that was when she heard the icy voice of the man she'd later refer to as the Long Needle.

# 15

'. . . A lovely home, Mr Tyler, I'll say that,' the voice was saying as it followed her dad into the study. 'Well, apart from this room. Had squatters?'

Mercy was pressing her body tight against the glass of the door like a pinned butterfly, careful that her movements wouldn't be detected through the floor-length curtains. The sun was on her back and sweat dripped from her body. The green jumpsuit, which had earlier felt so barely there, was now clammy and oppressive.

Surely her dad was about to draw back the curtains to let in some natural light. She almost let out a cry as she imagined his hands reaching out.

But, instead of opening the curtains, he pulled them closer together.

The room lit up from within. Ray had switched on the lights, even though it was daytime.

'Drink?' her father grunted, which told her that he was moving towards his mini-fridge at the other side of the room. There was a combination lock on that fridge that she'd always assumed was there to stop her drinking his booze. A cautionary note was stuck to the front under one of his Union Jack magnets warning her to not even try to crack it.

*'Daddy's beers! Keep out!'* she heard the other man say as he read the note aloud. 'An amusing insight into your home life there.'

'Stay out of my home life, alright?' her father's voice was a dry growl. 'This is bang out of order you even being here.'

'Steady,' warned the man. 'You've discovered more about me than I'm comfortable with. This is like for like. If you've a problem with that then you shouldn't have lifted my rock.'

'I could've handed you this anywhere.'

'But what would be my leverage then? I'm teetotal incidentally but thanks for offering.'

She heard something shunt and wondered if things had turned violent. Her dad hated a smartarse so she wouldn't have been that surprised if he'd punched the man.

'Here,' she heard him say instead.

'A cold one,' said the visitor.

Mercy remained as still as a statue and, with her pale skin and outfit of hanging silk, she may have resembled one. She didn't dare turn her head to see if anyone was watching her from outside but closed her eyes, wishing she could disappear.

'Have you looked inside?' asked the man.

'The seal ain't broken.'

'True, but a man of your talents doesn't need to break a seal to learn the contents of an envelope.'

The visitor's voice sounded educated and weirdly playful. She fought an urge to peek through the curtain at him.

'I'm the middleman,' Ray replied. 'I don't need to know

what's inside. My client assures me that all the information you need is contained within.'

'The mystery client,' the other man laughed.

'You'll see me afterwards for the rest of the payment but only once my client tells me he's satisfied with... what you've done. And don't come to my home again, understood?'

'I respect your precautions,' the man said. 'But, having researched you and your infamous friends, I can guess why I've been approached. Shall I show you who the target is?'

'No.'

'Deniability, eh?' She heard the tearing of paper. 'I prefer accountability. Take a look.'

Ray swore. There was a lengthy pause before the visitor spoke again.

'You recognise this person?' A silent beat. 'So do I,' said the Needle. 'So that's why the fee is so stupidly generous. But I like a challenge so consider it done.' Another pause. 'You look surprised, Mr Tyler. Are you? Or are you just very good at appearing to be surprised?'

Her father groaned.

'Well, if that's everything, I'll be on my weary way.' She heard the sound of a briefcase being opened and then clicked shut again. 'But before I do I need you to deliver a message back to your client. Tell him I'm protective about my identity.'

'Alright,' her father whispered.

'Tell him... and yourself... that nobody who betrays me lives. If I find out you're being indiscreet, there'll be consequences.'

'Hold up!' said her father. 'You get what we need, right? It can't look like what it is.'

'With me, it never does.'

'How will you do it?'

'I'll imagine doing absolutely nothing,' he replied, 'and hope that the person dies anyway.'

A sickness rose up in Mercy.

'And once I've imagined how they *might* die,' the man continued, 'that's how they do.'

Mercy remained petrified in her place, the breath squeezed out of her. She was no longer so much afraid of being exposed, as of the wicked business being conducted in her home.

'For instance,' he added, 'if someone strikes me as an alcoholic, then they'll probably just drink themselves to death. See you again, Tyler.'

She heard Ray follow the man out into the dining room, making assurances that there would be no problem with the money. He turned off the light as he went.

Once she was confident that the room beyond her thin space was empty, Mercy inched open the curtain and slipped through into a corner of the house that would now be forever contaminated. A conspiracy to murder underneath the same roof where she'd slept all her life. Now she knew a dreadful truth; her father traded in other people's death.

She crossed his disordered study to the open door, hoping that they were leaving the house. But their muffled conversation continued. Around her she noticed that the rotten room had altered during the time it had been screened from her. The door to the mini-fridge was open. Peering into it, she discovered what the shunting sound had been. She was surprised to see that the fridge door contained a false back, which had been removed, revealing a now empty secret compartment.

Standing again, she moved over to the desk. On it rested an opened A4 envelope that he must have kept in the concealed part of the fridge. It was deep pink and cold to her touch. She looked inside but found it empty. Whatever it had contained must have been moved and placed inside the briefcase she'd heard being unlocked.

The front door slammed and she heard footsteps returning to the study.

By the time her father re-entered the room she was again hidden behind the curtains but this time facing towards the garden. She scanned the windows of the neighbouring houses but saw nobody staring back, besides a wild urban fox. The fox was eyeing her from its place under the garden table.

Then, from behind her, at first quietly but rising to an awful pitch, she heard her father crying. It was as dreadful as anything else she'd heard that day. A low sob, that seemed to go on long enough for the sun to shift position. She rested her forehead and fingertips against the warm glass of the door as she endured the awful minutes.

At last he regained some self-control and his mobile rang. Ray swore and cleared his throat.

'Hello mate!' he answered in as breezy a voice as she'd ever heard from out of his mouth. 'Sorry about this, I'm still at the garage and they're fucking me royally over this carburettor. Shouldn't be much longer.' She was stunned by the ease with which he lied. 'Yeah, alright Bill, keep your hair on. I'm coming back now.'

She could hear him gathering things up, replacing the false back of the fridge door and locking it while he continued his conversation.

'I'll be there in half an hour,' he said as she heard him exit. 'Stop stressing.'

After some breathless minutes, she emerged again from the curtains and collapsed onto the sofa. Her hands touched her face and she felt how wet her cheeks had become. She wiped them using the silk scarf that she knew she'd destroy soon after.

Then, she pulled herself up and again inspected the room. The pink envelope had gone.

Upstairs, she surveyed herself in the mirror and burned with hatred at her reflection. She tore the jumpsuit off and dumped it in a bin bag.

# 16

'You've been upset lately, Chrissy.' Julie spoke in a soft tone as more of her child's long hair fell to the carpet. 'We all have.'

It was less than a week later and Mercy was sitting in front of that same mirror where she'd joyfully feminised her face while singing along to a pop song. Now her reflection was unsmiling.

'I'll admit,' Julie continued, standing behind her with her scissors, 'when the school phoned I may have gone too far.' Her mother was cutting her wet hair back to a more boyish length. 'But it was a wake-up call for us all. Your Dad and I have taken our eyes off the ball when it comes to you. We blame ourselves for all your recent delinquency. You deserve better from us, babe. That's what tonight is about; getting things back to where they were.'

Mercy's eyes pricked with tears as she regarded the miserable boy staring back at her from the mirror. Her mother misinterpreted her emotion.

'Things have been stressful for Dad at work, darling,' she whispered. 'Money troubles. But we've had a long chat, about you, about us, about our family, and well, we've made it up.'

This was already obvious. During the previous few nights she'd heard them making it up several times through too-thin walls.

'There,' said Julie once she'd finished removing all external traces of her child's femininity. 'Better.'

WHEN HE ARRIVED home that evening, Ray had also had a haircut. He beamed when he saw her coming down the staircase.

'Looking good, son. You're starting to look like me, you lucky devil.'

She attempted a smile as Ray came forward and forced a hearty bear hug on her. The gesture was warm but this was the first time she'd seen him since his secret meeting with a hired killer so it was hard to completely return his affection. She was awkward around him, unsure of who he was anymore, but he didn't appear to notice her shift in attitude.

'Karate lesson tomorrow,' he winked.

When Julie eventually joined them she looked amazing in Sarah Neale's blue summer dress.

'Before we go,' Ray said, 'I've something to say. An apology.' He lowered his head then in an expression of contrition and sighed before continuing. 'I've been a moody bastard lately. Don't try telling me otherwise.'

Mercy, who'd no intention of contradicting him, was already irritated by this performance.

'I've had a lot on my mind and I've been drinking too much, but that's no excuse. I shouldn't be taking it out on the two people I love most in this world. Which is you two,' he then added as if this needed clarifying.

'What's been upsetting you, Dad?' Mercy asked, curious to see how he'd answer. He was a liar; she knew this, but was keen to make a study of him as he lied. She looked for any tells in his voice or his body language, something she might look for in future interactions. 'Mum says money troubles.'

'It's true, son,' he nodded. 'The agency has been making losses and I suppose it got on top of me. But I've sorted it now. I've just done a deal with a new client who's brought an end to all our financial woes. And you know what that means?' he winked. 'I've got us an Aston Martin!'

He opened the front door of the house to reveal a gleaming vintage car. The sight of it made her want to vomit. Did he pay for this with murder money?

'No more driving around in a knackered old Honda for this family,' he declared. 'Let's get that curry.'

THEY DROVE to a Nepalese restaurant in Blackheath and, on entering, Ray ran into some former clients who happened to be there. He proudly introduced the couple to his family.

During the meal Ray joked with the staff and complimented the chef on an amazing lamb shank. He also made more glowing references to his child's haircut.

'This Nadia will change her tune when she next sees you,' Ray smiled as a phone started ringing from his jacket pocket. 'That was her name right, Jules?'

*'Ray!'* Julie snapped, while he reached for the jacket that was hung over his chair. 'I told you not to say anything.' She turned to her child. 'Sorry, love.'

'Barbara my dear!' said Ray, answering the phone. 'To what do I owe the pleasure?'

His smile dropped and he began immediately consoling his secretary.

'What do you mean?' Ray asked. '*Exploded?*'

Ray looked up then with a stricken expression. Julie asked him what the problem was but Ray just held up a hand, rose from his seat and took the rest of the call outside. Mercy and her mum were left sitting side-by-side watching him pace, his hands covering his eyes. He was ashen by the time he returned to the table.

'It's Lol,' he explained in a shaky whisper. 'Lawrence Neale.'

'What about him?'

'He's dead, babe. Barb reckons he's been blown up. Car explosion.'

Ray paid the bill soon afterward and the Tyler family left the restaurant, but not before Ray tottered over to where the couple he knew were still sitting.

'I've just heard some terrible news about a close friend,' she heard him make a point of telling them.

They went back to the car but instead of driving straight home Ray searched through radio stations. Sure enough, on a London news show they found a story of a fatal car explosion in Bermondsey.

*'We're receiving reports that Lawrence Neale, a notorious figure in London's gangland, was killed in the explosion. The incident bears the hallmarks of similar car attacks in recent months which also have links to organised crime.'*

'Scottish bastards!' Ray exclaimed and he banged the dashboard with his fist. 'This must be the work those McAlonan psychos!'

*'Mr Neale was the older brother of Victor Neale, the controversial businessman acquitted of killing a policeman in 2000. Both the Neale brothers are still under investigation in relation to the Air Costelloe heist.'*

'Jesus!' Julie said after switching off the radio. She was in the driver's seat because Ray had already drunk too much wine. 'Poor Maggie. Poor little Nick.'

'Vic'll make the McAlonan's pay,' Ray seethed. 'You watch.'

Mercy leaned forward to see her dad better.

'Maybe they didn't do it though,' she suggested. 'Perhaps someone just wanted to make it look like they killed him.'

Ray turned to her and, for a moment, she wondered if he realised she'd overheard his meeting.

'Bobby McAlonon is famous for blowing up cars,' he replied. 'It's his modus operandi. And who else would want Lol dead?'

Julie started the car and told Mercy to put her seatbelt on. The evening gently darkened as they drove home. Ray was quiet, staring out into the summer night.

'Poor Victor,' Julie broke the silence as they approached the Tyler home. 'He'll be devastated.'

'Yeah,' Ray agreed in a faraway voice. 'His own brother.'

# PART III

*The Spoils*

# 17

February 15th 2020

ONLY WHEN THE Thames is at low tide is Mercy able to visit the exact spot on the river's edge where her father's body was recovered.

Upper Watergate stairs, Deptford. Slimy steps with an installed iron rail that lead down to a small bank on the riverside. There, among the shingle, timber, and shards of clay, there's always an abandoned mobility scooter leaning against the foot of the brick wall. It has turned greener with her every visit but is too heavy to be washed away. Upstream, there's an old Victorian landing stage connected to a Grade II listed building hidden behind a high wall. Closer downstream, rising out of the river, is a three-legged structure once used for docking that reminds Mercy of gallows. Against this desolate landmark her father's body had snagged, preventing him from being carried too far from his place of death.

According to the post-mortem report, Ray had received a fatal injury to the head while tumbling down those steps. Traces of his blood were found on the stone at the top but, despite security cameras further up the alley, the moment went unrecorded.

The day after they'd met at Ray's wake, DCI Bracken had invited Mercy down to Lewisham police station and shown her what limited footage they had of him on that awful night. This included CCTV images of Ray stumbling along Dreadnought Walk as the storm battered the riverfront. He could be seen clutching onto the rail with one hand and talking into his phone with the other. Mercy knew that he must have been leaving that final, dismal message to her.

Seeing him stagger like that - unsteady and windswept, a depressed drunk – made her even sadder. It was a pathetic end for a man she'd always wanted to view as strong.

'Let me show you something else,' Bracken had said after they'd watched it through twice. 'The last footage we have of his car.'

Traffic cameras had captured Ray's Porsche 911 slipping into Greenwich via the southern approach to Blackwall Tunnel. This was about four hours prior to his voicemail recording. It was a distinctive model – a burgundy 1969 semi-convertible Targa – a conspicuous car for a private investigator to drive. Ray had purchased it from a vintage dealer just over five years ago and it was the same one he'd driven her to the airport in, the last time she'd seen him alive. It had been assumed that he must have parked it somewhere local and that it would materialise eventually, covered in parking tickets. Mercy had checked the DVLA to see if it had been towed away but, after many hours of online enquiries, there was no trace. She became fixated with locating it.

*Find the car - find the clues* she'd jotted down in her investigation notepad.

To that end, Mercy had photocopied a picture of the car and slapped it on lampposts all around the Greenwich area as if the Porsche were a lost cat. She'd included her phone number and hinted at a generous reward for its recovery that she couldn't really afford.

Since then, Mercy had made a habit of searching for the missing car while jogging along backstreets and through nearby housing estates. A set of spare keys had been hanging on a hook in their family home and she kept them about her person in case she came across it somewhere waiting to be reclaimed.

She was looking for it on the morning after her Valentine's date and, as she ran, she thought about the last night's mugging attempt. She'd reported it to the police immediately and had also sent DCI Bracken the details. But, as yet, she'd heard nothing back. But the incident reminded her of another piece of footage that Bracken had shared. A quick CCTV shot of an unaccounted-for figure that was also out on that stormy night in late December, a figure Mercy had come to refer to as The Jogger.

At the top of Watergate Street, a private art gallery with some outward facing security cameras had captured a blurred figure jogging past for less than a second. The image was not good quality so it was hard to tell if the person was tall or short, male or female. Whoever it was, they wore a black hood and shapeless clothes and had their head bent low towards a mobile phone. They flitted past the camera, heading quickly in Ray's direction.

Mercy wondered if this Jogger and her mugger were the

same person. Her attacker was definitely male, seemed young, and was a little shorter than herself. He'd gone to a lot of effort to hide his identity to steal just a phone, while leaving her purse and handbag untouched.

On her way home she jogged past a lamppost with one of her leaflets displayed on it. HAVE YOU SEEN THIS PORSCHE? Unfortunately, the contact details underneath were useless now as they belonged to the stolen phone.

# 18

In a no-star hotel on the other side of the river, a man who introduces himself as Jakob was keeping watch from a high window. He was looking down onto the sodium-lit street below, waiting for the south Londoners to arrive and chewing on a particular brand of bubble gum he'd enjoyed as a kid. His sister had sent him packets of the gum for Christmas, knowing he couldn't get the brand in England. The taste was like magic to him. Chewing, he was transported back to a time when he'd been more innocent.

Including Jakob, there were six men inside the honeymoon suite. Between them they were in possession of eighteen guns. His own was the small one concealed beneath his leather coat and his middle finger stroked its side as he waited. The light in the room was low and he was leaning against the wall by the window so most of his large self was hidden from external view. He heard the vehicle approaching before he saw it.

Leszek joined him by the window, summoned by the harsh sound of hardcore UK drill that was blasting out of a large black Range Rover. It was now trying to park between the two discreet cars in which their own collective had arrived. Les muttered that they'd never open the doors in such a tight space and, sure enough, the Range Rover abandoned the attempt and reversed out into the road again. The car had black 20-inch rims and tinted windows.

'Bruce Wayne,' Les sniffed and they laughed.

With the music still at full volume, the Range Rover eventually parked on the adjacent side of the road. Milos, from his seated position in the centre of the room, asked them if it was the idiot boy from the film.

He was referring to a video that he'd been shown hours earlier of a young blonde man beating up a spin-class instructor and talking to the camera as he did so. People who recorded their crimes were generally a rich vein of amusement for these men. But when Milos had been informed that the blonde man was possibly the same person they were scheduled to meet tonight, he became less amused.

Blaine, their south London connection, had assured them that the man he'd be introducing them to was a serious player, born into this life. His late father had been greatly respected and it was said that the son would soon be running things south of the river. He was the future, Blaine had promised, and confided that he'd already murdered a man.

*He's murdered that car,* Jakob thought, as the violent music was at last switched off.

Five people got out of the Range Rover. Jakob recognised Blaine as he opened the front passenger door and thought he appeared more agitated than usual. Then, from the driver's seat, a young man in a bright yellow tracksuit emerged onto the pavement holding a briefcase. His face was obscured from this angle by a white cap, but his movements were lively and he seemed to be shouting orders at the others. Another young man followed and then a much older guy who was wearing a leather jacket that looked older still. The last person to exit the vehicle was a woman wearing exactly the same outfit as the driver, except her bright colour was orange. Jakob noticed that she had something concealed underneath her tracksuit.

The cap-wearing driver lifted his face up to the hotel.

*Yes boss,* Jakob nodded to Milos, *it's the idiot boy.*

'Hide that money,' Nick Neale told Roz as they crossed the road towards the hotel. 'I don't want them thinking we're arseholes.'

Roz complained that it wasn't easy hiding large wads of cash underneath her top and she didn't see why she had to. The briefcase that Nick was carrying was empty because he'd had the last-minute idea to remove the contents and hide it about her person.

'If they make a grab,' he'd grinned after he'd wrapped it into a paper bundle and told her to stuff it inside her tracksuit, 'they'll go for the briefcase. This is clever.'

Blaine had repeatedly advised Nick that such a scheme was both pointless and potentially offensive to the men they were meeting. These were business people, he'd explained again, not bandits. But Nick liked his empty briefcase idea so it was happening.

As the five of them entered the hotel lobby, something happened which Roz found to be entirely predictable. Bob the Feet whistled for them to stop. When they all turned back to him, he asked if it would be a good idea for him to remain by the car.

'If something goes down,' he suggested, as if only

thinking of their safety, 'I'll be ready behind the wheel to make a fast getaway. I don't mind missing out.'

Bob the Feet was another bad idea that Nick couldn't be talked out of. He was 65, asthmatic, and whatever steel he may have once possessed had been left way back in the last century. But Bob had been a bank robber with Nick's dad in the eighties so her boyfriend was unable to see him straight. He'd been a key member of the Neale crew back in, as Bob described them, the glory days when Lol was in charge. Nowadays, Bob could be found drinking in the same Woolwich pub every day from 4pm onwards. Nick would drag Roz there so she could learn more about the legend of the Neale firm from Bob, whose fingernails, breath, and hair stank of old tobacco. As multiple pints of London Pride were bought for him, Bob would flatter Nick about how Lol's strength was born again in him.

'You should be the boss of the firm now,' Bob would wheeze as he stuffed his face with pub meals the younger man was paying for. 'You're the true heir, not Victor.'

Now, using the same leadership skills that had been attributed to him by a drunk in a pub, Nick laughed and gave Bob a friendly punch on the arm.

'You old warhorse,' he smiled. 'If it kicks off up there I'm going to want you up there with me, aren't I? You're the hardest geezer I know.'

Bob managed a smile but it looked like he was pissing himself. Roz wondered if this was the first time the retired bank robber had ever entered a dangerous situation without women's tights distorting his facial features.

The deserted lobby stank of cleaning liquids as they entered a cramped tin-walled elevator and took it to the fifth floor. Roz glanced over at Dan B, who was blinking heavily, no doubt in reaction to the too-many drugs he'd taken before leaving the flat. He was quietly rapping to himself. Roz had only recently discovered that Nick and Dan B had met at private school, which she found bewildering. Dan had once told her that he thought Middle Earth was a real place while Nick had once tried to spell the word cucumber with a Q.

Blaine led them through the corridors of the fifth floor. Behind almost every door she could hear sex. It was obvious that the hotel was mainly used as a brothel, but she hoped that the room that Blaine took them to was the one where nobody was getting fucked.

'Welcome,' said an unsmiling man with an Eastern European accent as he opened the door, 'to the honeymoon suite.'

Blaine fist-bumped him as he passed and then they walked into the large room beyond where the light was mostly provided by small lamps on the bedside cabinets. The dull click of the door being shut after them gave her a chill.

As soon as she saw the men she realised how out of his depth Nick was. These were nothing like the ones they'd seen on Instagram. They were serious, soberly dressed, and most of them were standing around the room with their hands hidden inside leather coats. The exception was a portly middle-aged man in a bland suit and he was in a chair facing them. Blaine introduced him as Milos but he appeared to speak little English. Another man translated for him.

'We've got your money,' Nick said and he raised his briefcase high as if about to perform a conjuring trick with it. 'Let's see the merchandise.'

On the bed were two large steel-cased boxes. They were already unlocked and one of the men peeled away from the flock wallpaper, crossed over and revealed their contents. Strapped inside were six Skorpion submachine guns, three in each box and with six ammo cases.

'Fucking Nora,' said Bob the Feet.

Nick moved closer, as one of the machine pistols was unstrapped. Roz was surprised by how compact they were but it made them no less threatening. Lethal little bastards, she thought, as Milos gave them some monotone patter in his language. She knew Nick would be sold on them; he only owned a couple of handguns and one of those used to be a starting pistol. These things were exactly the type of military-grade weaponry he'd been dreaming of. They looked alive in those cases, like they would spit venom.

'Czech army,' the translator told Nick as he pulled one out of the case. '1000 rounds per minute.' He then mentioned something about the bolting system that curled around the black barrel like an exoskeleton. He offered the gun for Nick to hold.

'Yes, yes, this is what I'm on about!' her boyfriend cheered as he took it by the pistol grip. She hoped the cartridge was empty, as she didn't quite trust him not to point it anywhere stupid. 'Where do we go now?' Nick said. 'To test them?'

The translator relayed the question. Milos responded in a weary tone.

'If you cannot tell the gun works from inspecting it,' the translator told them, 'then you shouldn't be buying from us.'

Everyone in the room shifted positions. Roz scanned the other men, knowing that they all had similar weapons concealed under their coats. They were terrifying to her, dead-eyed and menacing, and none more so than the huge man with the neck tattoos slouching by the window. He was chewing something with threatening slowness and studying them. This man, she sensed, would be the one to execute them if the order was given.

THE BUBBLE-GUM WAS delicious and Jakob would send a thank-you message to his sister as soon as this boring meeting was over. He knew the deal would not go down as soon as these amateurs entered the room. The boy holding the gun was as stupid as advertised and was accompanied by a tired old man, a scared woman and a boy who wouldn't stop blinking. Why was Blaine introducing them to these losers?

Although Jakob didn't speak much English he knew that Leszek had just mistranslated what Milos had said. The boss had not said that *you shouldn't be buying it from us* but instead *we shouldn't be selling it to you.* Milos had his own bosses and they wouldn't want him distributing their hard-won product to any fool who fancies himself as South London's answer to Scarface.

The excitable boy was asked what he intended to do with the guns. It was at this point the conversation really deteriorated. He started ranting about his uncle, a man called Victor, who he seemed to be in some sort of conflict with. There was something about an anonymous phone-call, his dead father and a long needle. It made no sense to Jakob but he knew a shit-storm when he heard one. He was unsurprised when Milos gave the smallest of indications to his men that the meeting was over before the boy had even stopped talking. Within seconds they took back the gun from him, strapped it back into the case and began leaving the room with Milos and the guns protected in the centre.

. . .

'Where are you lot off to?' Nick asked.

The men ignored him and shoved past Dan B who had been bobbing about in the passage to the door throughout the meeting. As soon as they left Nick turned on Blaine, demanding an explanation.

'They didn't rate you,' Blaine shrugged.

'Well, we'll fucking see about that,' Nick seethed. 'Come on, boys! Let's show these Czech twats who they're dealing with.'

Then he darted out into the corridor of the hotel, seemingly under the impression that his gang were hot on his heels. Roz looked to the other three men.

'I'm staying put,' said Bob the Feet.

Only she had the loyalty to step out into the hallway. The gun dealers were already out of view, but Nick was chasing after them making a tremendous row.

'Babe,' she shouted as she followed. 'Leave it!'

She could still hear him yelling abuse after he turned the corner. As she passed other hotel doors, one opened a fraction. Peering out of a dark room was an almost naked young girl. Roz was desperate to get clear of this skanky place. Ahead of her, Nick was heard confronting the men.

'You're either with me or against—'

Then he was silent. She turned the corner and saw him pressed hard against the opposite wall to the elevator. The gum-chewing man had Nick by the throat and was hissing in his ear.

'Leave him!' she cried but the man ignored her and continued squeezing Nick's purpling neck with his huge tattooed hand.

Aside from the strangler, the others were all cramped inside the lift. Just before the doors shut on them she heard the translator say 'don't see us again.'

Roz continued screaming and tried to pull the man away from Nick, but he just reached into his mouth. From it, he produced a wet glob of gum and stuck it hard onto the part of the wall just beside Nick's head. He released his hand then and Nick dropped to the carpet, choking. The man turned towards the shut doors of the elevator, cursed in his own language, and looked to Roz.

'Now I take stairs,' he complained as if it was her fault. Then he pushed past and left her alone with her wounded lover coughing uncontrollably on the floor.

Nick's three cronies finally appeared in the corridor behind her, all acting as if they'd rushed to get there. Bob the Feet was clutching the empty briefcase as if it still mattered.

The ride home was quiet. Blaine drove while Nick stared out at the walls of the Blackwall Tunnel. No music played and instead they all listened to the tunnel's low rumble and waited for Nick to break the silence.

'Why didn't they rate me?' Nick asked as they neared the light of the tunnel. 'My money's good.'

'It's not about that, is it?' said Blaine.

'What's it about then?'

'It's everything, mate,' Blaine said, pissed off. 'It's this car you rocked up in and the volume of the music. It's Bob and it's Dan and it's that you brought a girl with you. Nick mate, it's the stuff about your dad blowing up. They don't give a shit about all that. And, if they saw the spin class video, it was that as well.'

'They think I'm amateur?'

'They think,' Blaine said as the car emerged onto the south side of the city, 'that you're an arrest waiting to happen.'

# 19

Bill's phone woke him at six o'clock on Sunday morning and he instantly assumed bad news. He reached for it, as rain pattered against his window, afraid to look at the screen. For some reason he'd been dreaming that some dreadful fate had befallen Mercy and that it had all been his fault.

He sat up in bed and slowly turned the screen. The caller ID read MEANTIME.

Victor Neale.

Ever since Ray's funeral, Bill had been looking for excuses to contact their wealthiest client. He'd left several messages assuring Victor that M&T still welcomed his business even though they'd tragically lost the T. He'd received radio silence in return. So, when Mercy had played him Ray's final voicemail, Bill had used it as an excuse to reach out to Victor again. And this time it had worked. Predictably though, Victor had claimed he'd never heard of anyone called the Long Needle. But it was only later on that Bill realised he might have placed Mercy in danger by mentioning her interest in her dad's death. If Victor had felt threatened by her enquiry, might he send someone after her? Bill had been raised a protestant but the guilt that surged inside him at the thought was worthy of a Catholic.

'Victor?' he answered, after clearing his throat. 'Everything alright?'

'I need to see you, William. It's work.'

'Okay sure,' Bill rubbed his eyes with the other hand. 'When?'

'I'm sending Junior Bruno down to pick you up. He'll drive you to the Spoils and back.'

'Now?'

'He's on his way. Be ready for him.'

'There's no need. I can drive down first thing.'

'This is first thing. You're still interested in making money I take it.'

'Of course.'

'Then I'll see you shortly.'

'What's this about, Vic?'

'Work.'

He hung up.

By the time Bill was washed, dressed, and wearing his old Barbour coat, a silver Rolls Royce had pulled up outside.

'Mr Mance,' said Victor's man as Bill answered the door. He was wearing a well-tailored charcoal-grey suit, a neat chauffeur's cap and a broad smile. 'Good to see you again, sir. Mr Neale requests the pleasure of your company.'

'That's not how he put it,' Bill said as he gathered some things into a leather holdall and prepared to leave.

Junior Bruno opened the rear door of the Rolls Royce, providing Bill with a view of a large white bandage on the back of his head.

'That looks nasty,' Bill remarked as they drove through the lamp-lit streets of Denmark Hill. 'Boxing injury?'

‘I haven’t boxed for two years,’ the driver replied, his windscreen wipers on high. ‘I sometimes lead spin classes in one of Mr Neale’s gymnasiums.’

‘And you sustained that teaching spin?’

‘Sort of,’ the young man sighed. ‘I was punched in the back of the head during a session. By a surprise attacker,’ he added.

Bill felt Junior’s forced formality begin to ebb away.

‘Whatever rabbit-punching bastard did that to you, son,’ Bill said as he caught Junior’s eye in the rear-view mirror, ‘I hope you paid him back.’

‘Believe it, bruv,’ Junior replied, and Bill was glad that he’d finally dispensed with all the *sir* stuff. ‘He took a proper hiding from me. And I would’ve done worse if he wasn’t related to Mr Neale.’

‘Related how?’

‘It was Nick,’ Junior hissed the name. ‘The psycho nephew.’ Bill nodded. ‘I was coming to the end of a mammoth session when he punched me to the floor, shouting crazy shit. Once the element of surprise was over though, I battered him.’

‘Good for you. What had you done to piss him off?’

‘Fuck all. I barely know him. He went for me because I work for Victor and it was Victor’s place. He was ranting about how Ray Tyler had been killed and that Vic was next.’

Bill leaned forward.

‘He said what?’

Junior Bruno glanced up to the rear-view mirror again before returning his eyes to the road.

‘Nothing.’

‘Tell me.’

‘I dunno.’

‘Ray was my best friend, son,’ Bill demanded.

'I misspoke, sir. I apologise.'

'Not good enough, Bruno,' he insisted. 'What did the boy say exactly?'

'Mr Neale will tell you in good time,' Junior answered after some hesitation. 'It pertains to the business he wishes to discuss.'

THE JOURNEY CONTINUED in silence as the morning became drier. In the backseat Bill stared out the window as the car exited the M25 and entered the green Kent countryside. He leaned back into luxury seating and spent the rest of the 50-minute journey recalling the first time he'd ever been invited out this way.

Victor's fortieth birthday: it had been over two decades ago and the M&T foursome, as Ray liked to call them when they were with their wives, had travelled together in a mini-van cab. Also with them were Tony Lamoreaux, who'd gone to the same school as Ray and Vic, and his wife Jill. They'd all been in eveningwear and Moira had been taking swigs from a whisky flask during the drive. She'd told Bill he looked like Pierce Brosnan in his tuxedo, proving she was already a bit drunk.

Their other close friend, 'Expanding' Alan McColl, hadn't been invited. This was almost certainly because he was far too close to the police force for a party probably financed by the Air Costelloe heist.

It had been one of the biggest armed robberies in the history of UK crime. In 1998, £30 million worth of gold bullion and cash had been stolen from an airport warehouse in a raid that was both brazen and brilliant. Lawrence Neale had a long track record for armed robberies and so had been the police's immediate suspect. But this had been a much more ambitious heist than any of the jobs he'd been connected to until then. And Bill knew – because Ray knew – that it was actually the younger Neale who'd been the real brains behind it.

Victor had learnt about the bullion, bribed the right people, spied on others and mapped out the operation beat by beat. He'd arranged for the gold to be hidden, moved again and turned liquid before the police even had time to blink. Lol had been in charge of the actual robbery – which had involved him driving a giant metal spike through the warehouse doors like a battering ram - but Victor pulled the strings on logistics. Not one arrest had yet been made.

'You reckon there's any swag on the premises?' Tony had asked as they neared the Spoils.

'Well, if I were you,' Ray had replied after taking a swig from Moira's flask, 'I wouldn't get caught looking for it.'

The Spoils was a neoclassical mansion that Victor had been building for over ten years. A copper-domed palace, permanently encased in scaffolding. Victor had sunk fortunes into its construction and he'd claimed it was to be his ultimate legacy. Until recently it had been mostly uninhabitable after years of financial difficulties. But the construction had accelerated after Victor's recent windfall. At last, he was ready to show it off.

Victor had recently moved in with his new bride Sarah. They'd married in a small, rushed ceremony that had taken place on the same day as the big heist. The wedding had been Victor's alibi. Bill hadn't yet met her but had heard many things, both kind and unkind.

'You should see the ring he gave her,' Julie had told them on the ride over. 'It's fit for the finger of a princess.'

'It was probably stolen from one,' Ray had grinned.

The minivan had trundled up the Spoils' long rustic

drive and they saw that the external construction to the house was finally over. The scaffolding had gone and the entire front of the building was lit up for the occasion. As they'd approached, some black-suited men with walkie-talkies had stopped the vehicle and asked to see invitations. Underneath their jackets they'd appeared to be armed.

Other vehicles had been pulling up on the shingled driveway ahead and Bill had recognised affluent men he and Ray had met at various of Victor's club dinners over the years. He'd also spotted some of the old Neale crew floating about. It was a warm summer's evening and Bill had held his wife's hand while she tottered from the minivan. A young man in footman's livery had then informed them that Mr and Mrs Neale would receive them in the garden, which they could access by walking straight through the grand hall. The rest of the house, he'd informed them, was out of bounds.

The interior of the Spoils was a counterfeit Versailles, with giant mirrors and gold cornices. Rope barriers had prevented guests from sitting on any of the furniture. Huge, windowed doors opened out into the grounds where waiters were offering everyone flutes of champagne. That's where they had found their host, resplendent in a white dinner jacket and laughing like a man who'd stolen the sun. He'd greeted each one of the men with a warm hug and a Mafioso kiss. To the Victor the Spoils.

'William!' he'd cried when it was Bill's turn to be embraced. 'How are you, you old Paddy? And, more importantly, who's this vision of loveliness?'

Bill had introduced Moira and she'd complimented Victor on his magnificent home. A large white marquee stood behind Victor and from inside a swing band was heard playing Summer Wind.

'It'd be alright if it weren't for all the fucking ramblers,' Victor had told them as they surveyed his land, 'trespassing on my property. Still, they have their uses. Target practise!'

Eighteen months after making that comment, Victor had stabbed to death what he claimed to think was a trespasser. This trespasser had turned out to be a police surveillance officer named Shaun Kirby who'd been searching for stolen bullion. On his fortieth birthday however, everyone had roared with laughter.

'My husband is joking of course,' said a bright-eyed blonde woman in an elegant blue dress. She'd approached from behind, rested a hand on Victor's shoulder and smiled at his friends. 'After all, he's got enough enemies without upsetting the Ramblers' Association. Ray, Julie – how *are* you?'

Victor's radiant bride had met the Tylers many times before and greeted them warmly. Then she'd turned toward Bill and his wife.

'I could die of old age waiting for Victor to introduce us,' the new Mrs Neale had smiled, offering her hand, 'so I'll do it myself. You must be William and Moira.' In her cut-glass accent she'd pronounced her own name as *Sare*.

'Only Vic calls him William,' Julie had told her. 'The rest of us call him Big Bill.'

'Although only Moira here knows if he deserves the name,' joked Victor, punching Bill playfully on the arm. 'Or so we hope!'

Roars of laughter had followed and a sharp '*I better be!*' from his wife. Every head had turned toward him as if anticipating a witty comeback. But when he'd opened his mouth to reply, nothing had come out.

'He's called Big Bill,' Ray had explained, saving him, 'cos that's what we present you with after you've hired us.'

'Tell me about it,' Victor had tutted.

Ray had dominated the conversation after that - cracking jokes, telling stories about Victor as a schoolboy, flirting with his new wife. Bill always marvelled at his friend's easy manner and charm. Sarah had seemed captivated by him.

It was around then that Bill had heard a helicopter coming. He'd turned to see it coming from the far end of the land. Other guests had also turned their heads to the clear sky, but Victor was still in conversational flow. He hadn't registered it until it was hovering over his grounds with the low sun behind it.

'The fuck's this?' he then squinted, horror on his face.

*'MISTER NEALE!'* a voice had boomed through a loudspeaker. *'YOU'RE UNDER ARREST! PLACE YOUR HANDS IN THE AIR! WE'RE ARMED!'*

Shrieks of panic as both guests and caterers had headed into the safety of the main house. Tablecloths, dresses, and even the marquee had flapped from the rotor's wind. Nobody could hear what anyone was saying. Bill had noticed Bob 'the Feet' Walker dropping his champagne glass and heading off to hide in some bushes. From the marquee a Frank Sinatra impersonator had emerged holding his trilby up high to view the helicopter better. But Bill had already guessed what this was. He'd taken Moira's hand and told her not to worry. Sarah had touched her own husband's arm for similar reassurance but had received none.

Victor hadn't flinched. He'd just stepped away from his guests and had addressed the unmarked helicopter that was hanging in the air like a malevolent dragonfly.

'This is a private party!' he'd shouted up into the wind. 'You weren't invited!'

*'I REPEAT: YOU'RE UNDER ARREST. FOR BEING A SHORTARSE FORTY-YEAR-OLD GIT!'*

'It's only Lol,' Ray had then assured the rest of their group, 'fucking about.'

The collective relief had been palpable. Bill had noticed that Sarah, visibly shaken and abandoned by Victor, had raised her hands up to her forehead.

*'NOW A WORD FROM MY SUPERIOR OFFICER,'* the voice of Lawrence Neale had continued. Lol's beefy head was just about visible then. He was sitting behind the pilot with a headset on and had handed the speaker over to a passenger behind him.

*'HAPPY BIRTHDAY UNCLE VICTOR!'* a child's voice had rung out, summoning back the more cautious guests. *'SURPRISE!'*

When the helicopter landed Victor had made a great show of finding it all tremendous. He'd walked down towards his late arrivals, arms outstretched and laughing as the grass blew upwards. His open dinner jacket had flapped behind him like a sail as, inside the marquee, the swing band had struck up again with a vibrant rendition of Mack the Knife.

The first person to be let out of the helicopter had been little Nicky Neale, just nine years old. As soon as his feet had touched the grass, he'd run giggling up the field and into the arms of his uncle, his face overheating with excitement from the flight. Victor had picked him up and given him a big kiss as his parents were following him out of the helicopter. The older Neale brother, larger and more physically commanding than Victor, had strode towards him in his black evening suit laughing and pointing at the birthday boy. Victor had placed his nephew safely down and the two brothers had approached each other, both adopting a pugilist's stance. Sarah had greeted Maggie Neale to their home as their husbands danced around each other with their fists.

'Christopher would love a ride in that,' Ray had said.

The spectators had by then returned to their conversations and the caterers were back to work. But Bill had continued watching the Neale brothers at the end of the field. They were as different from each other as red and white wine. Victor had greeted his sister-in-law politely but when Lawrence had approached Sarah, he'd grabbed her by the waist, thrown her over his shoulder, and pretended to run off with her.

From a distance it had all looked like good fun. But Bill understood Victor well enough to know his sense of humour had limits, even if you were his older brother. No man wants to be upstaged in front of a new bride.

Inside the marquee the fake Sinatra had been reaching the end of his number as the Neale family, with young Nick in the middle, had strolled back up to the main house like the criminal royalty they were.

# 20

Now, over two decades later, Bill spotted the Spoils again through the first morning light. As the Rolls Royce turned off from an A-road, he saw it sitting atop a green hill and again encased in scaffolding.

'Are those gunshots?' Bill asked the driver, hearing soft popping noises coming from the far side of the grounds.

'Just some local pikeys,' nodded Junior Bruno. 'Sorry, *travelling people* I should say. Mr Neale pays them as security and they fire into the air as a warning to trespassers.'

'He can't get many of them after what happened to that poor copper?'

'Mr Neale enjoys his privacy,' replied Junior.

They came to some electric gates on the approach to the house. Bill watched as Junior tapped in the code and saw they were being surveyed via a discreet camera positioned nearby. Another new addition were the large mesh kennels closer to the house behind which at least two Rottweilers were prowling. Once the car had parked in the driveway, Junior turned to face his passenger.

'You must be hungry for breakfast, Mr Mance,' he said.

'Piper will make you a full fry-up while I go and locate Mr Neale.'

More gunshots rang out in the distance.

Bill had met this Piper person before. He was thickset, taciturn man, possibly Greek. Bill couldn't remember his real name, but it had many P's in it. He'd been a debt collector for the Neale firm once and was nicknamed Piper because there were severe consequences if you didn't pay him. Inside the mirrored entrance hall Piper greeted Bill with a curt nod of the head. Without acknowledging that they'd met before, he guided him silently through one marble-floored room to the next.

The walls of the Spoils had once been adorned with all sorts of conflicting art. Modern works had hung alongside classic oil paintings, the avant-garde and the traditional sharing the same awkward wall space. Bill didn't have much of an eye for art but then he suspected neither did Victor. It had been a magpie's aesthetic - old family portraits, but of someone else's family. Two thirds of a triptych, one half of a diptych. But now the walls were largely empty as if Victor himself had been the victim of a robbery.

'Where is everything?' Bill asked as they passed through another barely furnished room.

'Switzerland,' Piper answered and led him down some crooked steps.

The kitchen in this wing was not the main one. Piper was taking Bill to a tradesmen's parlour where a number of surly men were sat around a table eating fried breakfasts. There were some guns propped up in the corner. In a smaller room, just off this one, Bill saw a desk with CCTV monitors that covered different approaches to the property. Piper asked him what he wanted for breakfast.

'A bacon sandwich and a mug of coffee would be grand,'

he told him, turning to the men at the table. 'How's it going, fellas?'

No reply. One man stood up, gave him a quick pat down and inspected inside his leather holdall. Once the search was completed the rest of them got up, collected their weapons and left, leaving their unwashed plates on the table.

Bill ate his breakfast in silence. Piper washed the crockery in an earthenware sink then retreated into the small room with the monitors and shut the door after him, leaving Bill to make a closer study of his surroundings.

The parlour had a side door that, if the sound of furious barking was any indication, led out to the kennels. Despite it being winter, the radiators were cold to the touch. There were some windows that faced out onto the field beyond and Bill looked through to where, on a brighter day, a huge marquee had hosted Victor's party guests. He recalled the birthday boy and his new bride dancing to the hired swing band and how happy they seemed shimmying to *The Best is Yet to Come.* Bill had never seen Victor appear so at ease with himself before. And he'd never seen it again.

Another, darker memory surfaced then. Five year later in the M&T office, an after-hours meeting. Blinds drawn, lights low, staff lied to and sent home early. Victor sat in the client's chair, drinking more than one glass of neat Scotch and telling the two private investigators about his suspicions about his wife.

'I just want to know...' he'd said in a broken voice, 'that's all.'

The worst was yet to come.

Outside, the barking of the Rottweiler's became even more frantic and Bill heard their master telling them to shut it. Then the side door shoved open and in walked a man who bore little resemblance to the forty-year-old, light-footed, white-tuxedoed criminal genius of yesteryear. Here was a sour old codger in a dull fleece and muddy boots who slammed the door after himself and glared at Bill for an uncomfortable second.

'I like a dog,' he said in a colourless tone, 'who comes when I whistle.'

For someone who owned a chain of gymnasiums, Victor was in terrible shape. Bill offered to steady him as he bent to remove his boots but was met with an ungracious refusal. Once he'd liberated himself from the boots, Victor straightened and they shook hands.

'I'm glad you called,' Bill said after accepting the offer of more coffee. 'The agency still values your business even though we've lost our main man.'

'I know that,' Victor grunted and walked over to a coffee machine. 'You've left me several messages about it over the weeks.' He looked over his shoulder and winked. 'I was starting to think you fancied me.'

After some stilted small talk, Victor told Bill to accompany him to the games room and led him up some stairs. On the second floor they went through a concealed door in the cherry-wood panelling, one of many secret passages that Victor had built into the Spoils' architecture. Once through that, another two flights of stairs led upwards to a large room with a red baize snooker table in its centre. Tall windows opened on to a balcony that overlooked the length of the field, and Chesterfield sofas were dotted about. A woman was already in there, on her knees in front of a fireplace. The flames were rising when Victor told her to instruct all staff to vacate this end of the building for the next hour while he and Mr Mance spoke business.

Victor placed all the red snooker balls into the wooden

triangle. 'I'm going to knock some balls about as we talk if you don't mind. I find it calming.'

'No problem,' Bill replied. He placed his coffee cup on a nearby mantelpiece as Victor laid the table for his game of one. There was silence until Victor took his first shot.

'Don't know if I said so at the wake,' Victor said as he began prowling around the table, studying the layout, 'but that was a lovely speech you gave about Raymondo. Lovely eulogy. Made me wonder who'd give a speech like that for me when it's my turn.'

'They'll be a line of volunteers,' Bill remarked.

'I doubt it,' said Victor. 'Tell me, William, did you cry?'

'During the eulogy? No.'

'What about afterwards?'

'I don't think so. There was an awful lot to do on the day.' He walked back towards the opposite edge of the table to where Victor was hunched down and eyeing potential shots. 'But I did cry for Ray in the days after his death. It was a blow.'

'Takes a man to admit that,' Victor told him as he potted the pink ball. 'Some might think you were a poof for crying over another bloke, but not me. I know how close you were. Still,' he straightened up, 'I didn't shed any tears for him.'

Bill said nothing as he watched Victor reach for the square of blue chalk and attend to the cue-tip.

'Nothing against my dear friend of course,' he shrugged. 'I loved the man as you did. But I'm not someone who cries. I couldn't shed a tear when Mum died,' he said and looked at Bill to see his reaction. 'I ask you, what sort of man doesn't cry at his own mother's funeral?'

'Grief affects people in different ways.'

'You said it, son.' Victor's next shot that was too heavy-handed. Balls ricocheted everywhere but the pockets. *'Dick-heads!'* he shouted at them.

'What about when Sarah died?' Bill asked in an even voice after a few more shots. 'You must've wept then.'

'William, I've cried once in my adult life,' Victor said without taking his eyes off the table. 'And it wasn't on account of that treacherous cunt.'

Sarah Neale, a young mother of twins, had taken her own life at the age of 36. It had happened during a garden party she herself was hosting for her recently widowed sister-in-law Maggie. It was a summer's day and her young children were away with their nanny somewhere while Victor was out of the country on business. The garden party was for a small group of women. Maggie's friends, not Sarah's own. Among them were Julie Tyler, Bill's wife Moira, and M&T secretary Barbara Gleave.

They'd all given the same story - Sarah had been in a distracted mood ever since they'd arrived – *zoned out* according to Julie. Caterers served the ladies tea on the back lawn, but they hadn't seen Sarah for over an hour. They were becoming concerned even before they saw her step out onto her bedroom balcony, on the top floor of that mansion house. She was wearing a red summer dress that she'd borrowed from Julie Tyler less than a month earlier. Some of the girls called to her and encouraged her to come down and join them. It was only when she stepped up onto the balcony's ledge that her guests began to really panic. All of them ran towards the house, pleading for her to step safely down again. Sarah was said to be crying. Then she jumped, falling four floors and cracking her head open on the stone patio.

'I was sad for the kids, yeah,' Victor conceded after quietly potting the final red. 'Growing up without a mum, poor little mites. But, as a wife, Sarah was a disgrace and I'm better off rid.'

He complained about the manner of her death, how it had brought unwelcome attention onto the Spoils during a time when he was away and unable to manage things. He felt lucky though that he didn't have anything too hot on the premises while the police were sniffing about.

Bill watched in silence as Victor completed the game. The man revolted him. More than that, he was disgusted with himself for having to stand here and listen. Victor seemed to sense his disdain.

'You've gone quiet, William,' he said as the black ball dropped into the pocket closest to Bill. 'Have I shocked you?'

'I was wondering,' Bill said after a measured pause, 'what was the thing that *did* make you cry?'

Victor rolled the snooker cue onto the table and returned to his coffee that was resting on a round table between two red wingback chairs close to the fire. He indicated for Bill to sit with him now that it was in full flame.

'A dead dog,' he explained once they were sat opposite one another. 'You remember the tale?'

'Your daughter's Yorkshire terrier,' Bill said, his heart sagging. How many atrocious stories could surround one man? 'The one who got gored by a Rottweiler.'

'She loved that little rat,' Victor nodded. 'Forever brushing its hair and stroking it. I never should've let her play with it in the same room as my Tyson though. He got jealous I suppose, seeing Vix fussing over a smaller dog, and he fucking went for it. I was in the next room and the noise was horrific. Vix was in bits, as you can imagine. The terrier was still alive when I finally prised it out of Tyson's jaws.'

'Which dog made you cry?'

'Tyson. I had to put him down of course. Only reasonable action, considering. You can't let a dog get away with that, not with kiddies in the house. But I hated doing it, William. Got a gun, took him out the back and put a bullet in his head - bang. Fuck me, I'm welling up now just thinking of it.'

Bill sipped at his now cold coffee and looked over Victor's shoulder. There was a writing desk against the wall and something on it caught his eye.

'I wanted to spare him,' Victor sighed as he inspected his blue-chalked fingertips. 'But he brought it on himself.'

A long pause followed. Bill had a seasoned sense that they were about to arrive at business.

'It's about my nephew,' Victor finally said in an almost inconsequential voice, his eyes still fixed on his nails. 'Young Nicholas.'

Bill thought, *here we are.*

'He's a worry to me,' Victor continued. 'What have you heard?'

'Not much until this morning,' Bill replied. 'But your man Bruno told me about the spin class incident.'

'Unbelievable that! Attacking *my* employee in *my* business in full view of everyone. You've got to admire the bollocks on the boy,' said Victor with a faulty smile, 'if not his brains.'

'Apparently he was talking shit about Ray too,' Bill added. 'Claiming he was murdered. What was that about?'

Victor's small shark eyes flicked up towards Bill again. 'That's what I want you to find out,' he said, leaning forward, 'among other things. The boy needs monitoring.'

'Okay.'

'He's been talking shit about me, to anyone who'll listen about how *I* had something to do with my brother's death. Mouthy little shit.'

Bill went to ask a question but stopped himself. Victor answered it anyway.

'The suggestion is ludicrous in the extreme. But where's he getting it from?'

'I'll find out for you.'

'Nick's been telling people that he's going to avenge himself on me. Would you warrant it? And last night, according to a reliable source, he tried to buy guns from some Eastern Europeans to stage heists with; jobs he boasts will rival Costelloe. Military grade weapons, for fuck's sake. This dickhead's going to get nicked and, when he does, he'll be grassing to the gendarmes about me, tales that aren't even true! It needs nipping in the bud.'

'You want me to find out who's telling him lies about you,' Bill confirmed.

'You got it,' Victor clicked his blue-tipped fingers together. 'And if he's going to make a move against me, I want to know about it in advance.'

'If he's a genuine danger,' asked Bill with some caution, 'to you or to anyone...?'

'Don't insult me, William. The boy is family. I mean, if it was anyone else, they'd be removed already and you wouldn't be hearing about it. But this is Lol's only son we're talking about, not some Rottweiler.'

'What's the money?'

'Good boy,' Victor smiled, and got up from his chair. 'I knew you'd have your priorities straight.' He approached the writing desk and picked up one of the items that Bill had noticed. 'It's the usual arrangement,' explained Victor as he returned to the table and placed the fat envelope in front of him. 'You'll find half in there now and will get the rest – possibly more – when I'm satisfied with your findings.'

Bill looked at the envelope before picking it up.

'There's info in there concerning Nicholas and his mates. His girlfriend is an ex-employee of mine, would you believe? Rosalind. Worked in one of my gyms until last week.'

The envelope was a deep pink. Just like the one that Mercy had described to him in her account of the hitman meeting, the one that Ray had handed over on his mystery client's behalf.

'Count it,' Victor said.

'I trust you,' winked Bill and slipped the envelope into his holdall. 'Listen Vic, do you mind if I smoke?'

'Bit early for that.'

'I know but I've been gasping for a puff all morning,' he indicated the balcony window doors behind them. 'Could we continue this out there?'

'You can smoke by this fire,' Victor replied. 'I'll open the windows.'

'Trouble is,' Bill said, producing a black e-cigarette out of his holdall, 'I use one of these smelly things. Menthol Vape. It might be too much for indoors.'

Victor groaned but got up from his seat and headed over to the balcony. 'C'mon then.'

Outside the skies were a deep grey. Bill stood on the balcony that overlooked the grounds and realised that above him was another balcony, the one from which Sarah had fallen. He looked down to the stone patio below, onto which spits of rain were falling like sorrow. That was where her body must have landed, the same spot where Victor had greeted the guests at his fortieth birthday and had introduced them to his wife. How could such a new building already have ghosts?

'It goes without saying,' Victor told him as Bill assembled his e-cigarette with care, 'this is a one-man job. I don't want you sharing this with your employees.' Bill screwed the three parts of the already charged and personally customised device together. 'Don't involve that black girl that Ray liked,' continued Victor. 'His favourite.'

'Nina?' asked Bill. 'She's an exceptional operative.'

'So *he* kept saying,' Victor sneered. 'But I only want family on this. That's how I see you, William. Family.'

'I'm flattered.'

'And not a word to Barbara! I love the old girl but she's friends with Lol's widow and she's got a gob.'

'You don't need to tell me about discretion, Victor,' said Bill once the e-cigarette was ready. He then clicked the button enough times to activate it. 'I'm renowned for it.' He raised the e-cigarette to his chin as if ready to take a puff. 'I wanted to ask you about Mercy?'

'Who?'

'Ray's kid. We spoke on Friday about what she's saying about this hitman that Ray was talking to.'

'He's a fantasist, William,' Victor scowled. 'Thinks he's a woman, for fuck's sake.'

'Trust me, I've known what that kid is for decades,' Bill nodded after taking a small puff. 'But she's inherited her dad's sharpness. Plus, something about her story rings true. That's why I phoned you. I wanted your thoughts.'

'And you got 'em,' Victor said, surveying his grounds. Crows had gathered at the far end of the field but scattered after hearing another gunshot. Victor scanned the woods beyond as if expecting another policeman to emerge at any moment. 'Never heard of no Long Needle. End of.'

'Vic, I didn't say you did.'

Victor turned his head towards Bill again.

'If I wanted someone killed,' he hissed, 'I'd get someone I trust to do it. Or I'd do it my own fucking self. I wouldn't outsource a murder to a total stranger, would I? I'm not a cunt.'

'I know. I didn't mean to offend.'

'Why bring it up then?'

'Because I'm starting to believe her story.'

'*Her story,*' Victor scoffed.

'It seems unbelievable,' Bill admitted, after turning away from Victor so as not to blow any minty vapours into his face. 'But there's one detail that's lodged in my head. The colour of the envelope was pink, like the one you handed over to me just now.'

'And?'

'That stationary is from your club, the Never Setting Sun. Mercy couldn't possibly have known that.'

'What are you implying, William?'

'Nothing about you, mate. But if you didn't hire Ray to arrange that meeting, someone else from that club did. He knew all of those members through you, so it's not impossible.'

Victor blinked and shifted away. After another puff, Bill continued.

'Your brother died just a week after that meeting,' Bill said. 'Can you think of a Never Setter that might have had a reason to kill Lawrence?'

'Don't be obscene!' shouted Victor, loud enough to be heard at the far end of the field. 'Bobby McAlonan killed Lol! He died in prison for it.'

Bill felt suddenly afraid. He hadn't told anyone he was coming here. These grounds were large and armed men were everywhere. He'd wager that his wouldn't be the first body buried in them.

'Nick doesn't think that though, does he?' Bill persisted. 'Someone is telling him otherwise. Listen, I'm not just bringing this up to antagonise you. But could there be a link between what Mercy's overheard and Nick's recent behaviour? If Nick thought Ray was involved in killing his dad, then he might wrongly assume it was at your request.'

Victor puffed up his cheeks. 'And to think,' he said after exhaling, 'we all thought that Ray was the brains.'

'Let me help you sort this,' Bill told him. 'What are you not telling me?' Victor coughed and Bill apologised for the smoke.

'Alright,' Victor relented. 'Give me a moment.'

'To clarify,' Bill added, 'Mercy doesn't get the relevance of the pink envelope. She's just a kid who eavesdropped on a conversation she didn't understand. She's not a problem so let's leave her out of this.'

'I don't give a shit about that weirdo,' Victor said, straightening up. 'But okay, I admit, it wasn't true what I said before...'

'Go on,' Bill said.

# 21

Monday morning and Barbara saw her bus at last emerge onto the Elephant & Castle roundabout. It was still dark and, as the Number 63 approached, its interior lights revealed to her that a seat would have to be fought for. Every morning was a battle, she thought, as she huddled under a rain-battered bus shelter.

A morose weekend had come and gone since she'd threatened to quit M&T. On Saturday afternoon, while her poorly husband Bernie had been watching an old western, Barbara had written her official letter of resignation at the kitchen table and placed it inside her handbag. It was still in there now, ready to be presented if Bill still wanted it. She bustled her way through the standing commuters to the back of the bus, where she planned to glare at a young person until they found the grace to offer her a seat.

But the truth was she couldn't afford to lose her secretarial work at M&T Investigations and nor did she wish to. She'd come to respect both Bill and Ray over the years, just as she had the Neale brothers. They were old school, like her, and had provided her with much-needed financial aid during the long years of her mother's decline, often in the form of ready cash. For all his mistakes Bill was a decent bloke, so perhaps she owed him more loyalty now that Ray was dead and his shit-stirring kid had reappeared.

Barbara positioned herself close to where a young man wearing bright red earphones was sitting, hoping to catch his eye. But this ungallant generation of men couldn't compare to either Bill or Ray, both of whom would have been off their arses for an older lady in seconds. Earphone boy continued to ignore her as the bus travelled towards Southwark. Accidentally on purpose, she poked him with her wet umbrella but even that didn't give him the hint. Christ, this country had turned to crap.

A small digital screen by the bus staircase alternated live shots of the commuters from various angles. Barbara's own slumped image frowned back at her from under an anorak hood. She looked away, cursing this modern obsession with filming everything. Earphone boy jumped out of his seat once they reached St George the Martyr and, as she was about to take his place, a West Indian lady of her own age tried to occupy it.

'Don't take the piss, love,' Barbara warned before shoving in ahead. 'This is taken.' The two women eyeballed each other for the rest of the journey.

After stepping off the bus, Barbara headed straight into the nearest newsagent for a paper and a packet of Silk Cut. Since Bernie's heart murmur she no longer liked to smoke around him, so she was gasping by the time she got to work. Thankfully, there was still time for a quick fag before heading up to the office. It was lighter by then and the rain had almost abated. Under a covered loading alley across the road from M&T she could stand and enjoy the first blissful puff of the day. She unwrapped the packet and placed a cigarette into her mouth.

Then she noticed something odd.

From where she was standing she could see the agency windows. And, although the blinds were all down, she could tell that the lights were on. Someone was in there already.

She placed the unlit cigarette back into its packet and reached for her phone. Aside from her, there were only two other people who had keys to the office and knew the alarm code. She called Bill and he answered within seconds.

'Bill. You at work?'

'Stuck in a gridlock,' he said. 'I'll be another hour. What's the problem?'

'Someone's in our office,' she spoke with urgency. 'I'm stood across the road and the lights are on! Did you pop in over the weekend?'

'No, I did not,' he answered.

'Nina then?'

'She's just texted to say she won't be in until midday.'

'Then we've an intruder,' Barbara whispered. 'And I ain't going up there to confront him. Should I...' her voice lowered to a whisper, '*call the police?*'

'Don't you dare,' he told her. 'I'll deal with it when I get there. You just get your phone out and film whoever comes in or out of that building.'

Barbara was ready to do just this; glad that her vigilance had proven invaluable. Then one of the window blinds was suddenly pulled up.

'Hold up, Bill,' she said. 'I can see her. It's a woman.'

'Don't tell me,' he sighed. 'I think I know.'

The other blind was also drawn up and the tall figure

was clearer now. She was pressing her face closer to the glass, peering out onto the street below.

*'It's Christopher!'* Barbara spat as she stepped back into the alleyway, ignoring the lorry that was trying to reverse into it.

'She's called Mercy, Barb,' Bill said. 'I won't tell you again.'

'Mercy then,' Barbara conceded as the intruder's face turned to where she was. 'Whatever you want to call the shameless bitch, she's up there now waving down at me.'

MERCY KNEW that Barbara was a secretary and not one of M&T's skilled investigators, which was just as well as she didn't seem to have much in the way of surveillance expertise. She was the most conspicuous person on the street below, shifting around up a path between a bookie's and a newsagent's and yammering into her phone. A large refuse van was trying to reverse down the alley, but Barbara seemed oblivious to it until one of the bin-men leaned out of his window to shout at her. Barbara was doubtless telling Bill about Mercy's early appearance in their inner sanctum.

Mercy hadn't wished to surprise anyone with her presence, which is why she'd pulled up the blinds. But she had wanted them, and Bill especially, to be impressed by her talent for entering a locked office without raising the alarm. Most of all she wanted some time alone to search for clues into her dad's death. And to that end, she'd had a productive morning.

Moving away from the window, she returned to the photocopier. She'd been copying whatever paperwork she could find in the filing cabinets pertaining to M&T's dealings with the Neale family. She'd picked their locks, using a long needle of her own, and had collected anything mentioning Victor, his dead brother or anyone else in their rotten family. There was far less documentation than she'd expected though, considering that the Neales had been clients since the pre-internet age.

On paper Victor Neale was a legitimate businessman who owned a successful chain of gymnasiums. Like her dad, he was a working class Greenwich kid who'd risen in the world. As schoolboys they'd forged a tight friendship that had lasted well into adulthood. Mercy understood that this friendship had been an unbalanced one, lacking in the real affection found in Ray's later bond with Bill. But as her dad used to say, 'I'd rather be Vic's mate than his enemy.'

Lawrence Neale, meanwhile, had been your classic celebrity gangster. Every old tabloid photo of him showed a large, brylcreemed man who was respected by the public, probably all out of proportion to his true wealth and power. Officially he'd only owned two minor nightclubs and a dog track, but it was in armed robbery he'd made his real money. Victor may have been the more successful brother, both in legitimate business and otherwise, but Lol was the one that true crime books had been written about. His explosive death had captured the public imagination and in 2008 a former footballer had played him in a straight-to-DVD biopic.

Victor's profile was less sentimentalised. The tabloid-reading public hated him because he'd killed a police officer named Shaun Kirby and had somehow gotten away with it. He was also aggressively litigious and had only appeared as a character in the film about his brother once, in an early scene played by a child.

The only invoices she'd found with Victor's name on were for 'commercial investigations' and covered a range of dates up to two years ago. No figure was mentioned; just the letters TBA and addressed to the Spoils.

Decades ago, the Tylers had visited Victor's extravagant home. She'd found the Spoils itself – much like Victor – to be ugly and ostentatious. And she had little in common with Victor's spoilt children. She'd been transfixed by his wife Sarah, however, whose feminine beauty was so perfect it had made her want to cry. Years later, when her mother had described that horrific day when Sarah had fallen from a fourth-floor balcony in front of several party guests, Mercy had asked if Victor might have been responsible. Don't be ridiculous, Julie had replied. He'd been out of the country.

'What the bloody hell,' exclaimed a voice behind her as she returned the original documents to the file, 'are *you* playing at?'

Mercy turned to see Barbara coming through the door. The secretary's little body was shaking in anger and in her hand was a rolled-up newspaper that she was brandishing like a club.

'Morning Mrs G,' Mercy said, offering a welcoming smile. 'I got in early to make a good impression on my first day. And look,' she pointed at the kitchenette where a baker's bag was resting on the worktop, 'I've bought pastries. There's an almond croissant in there, which you can have first dibs on if you like. Your reward for being the first in after me.'

'Stuff your croissants,' Barbara replied with a scrunched-up face. 'What's happened to that fridge?'

The door to the small mini-fridge was open, it's interior hanging loose and there was a flat screwdriver lying beside it.

'Yeah, sorry about that,' Mercy bit her lip. 'I recognised that fridge from my dad's home study. So I prised the door open to have a look inside. Awkwardly though, I can't get it back on again.'

'Why d'you do that?'

'I was looking for a secret compartment,' Mercy explained. 'My dad used to keep things hidden in it and I was curious to see if he still did. Turns out I was right.'

Barbara stared at her like she was insane. Mercy walked over to her green leather jacket on the desk and reached into the pocket.

'I found a secret phone, would you believe?' she said, pulling out a small burner that she had connected to a portable charger. 'My dad was such a character, wasn't he?'

'You don't have a key,' Barbara said. 'How'd you get in here?'

'Oh, that's simple,' Mercy explained. 'I broke in.'

'You what?'

'I crept here under the cover of darkness, picked the locks, shut down the alarm. Child's play.' She placed a carton of milk back into the fridge and tried again to shut the door. 'I used to date a burglar when I was in Spain and he taught me some tricks.' She flicked on the kettle and produced some plates from out of the cupboard. 'Not the sort of thing you can put on a CV though,' she laughed.

'You're lucky we don't call the police on you,' Barbara said, shutting the door behind her. 'I've told Bill and he's fuming.'

'He'll be cool once I've explained things,' Mercy said, laying out each of the pastries on a plate. 'And there's nothing illegal about breaking into a business you co-own. At least I don't think there is. I never actually finished my law degree. Here,' she placed one of the plates at Barbara's desk and picked up her jacket, 'have a *pain au chocolat* and don't worry so much.'

'What've you been making copies of?' Barbara asked once she'd hung her anorak on the rack and placed her umbrella in the stand.

'Well spotted, Mrs Gleave. I've been collecting anything I can find relating to the agency's dealings with Victor Neale and other dubious clients. You know, the high-paying ones that stink of shit.'

Barbara eyed her with suspicion as she reclaimed her ground beside her swivel chair.

'What's your interest in Mr Neale?'

'He's an interesting man,' Mercy replied as she reached for the teabag tin. 'For one thing, he murdered a copper.'

'Police incompetence was to blame. It was proven in court.'

'You've always been close to the Neale family, right?' said Mercy. 'I saw you chatting with Victor at Dad's wake. What sort of work has he been getting this agency doing over the years?'

'I'm not at liberty to say,' Barbara raised her chin. 'M&T treat our clients' business with the strictest confidence, Mr Neale included.'

Mercy sighed.

'Oh, Barbara, – may I call you Barbara? – oh, Barbara. *I'm* the T in M&T now. There's no point keeping secrets from me, darling woman. I'm partly your boss, in case you haven't comprehended that, so you *are* at liberty to say.' She crossed over to the other side of the desk so she could stare Barbara down and placed her fingernails on the edge of it. 'I'll be a good boss, I hope. One who surprises her employees with croissants occasionally. But still very much a boss.'

'You're Ray's daughter,' Barbara winced after some hesitation. 'I accept that.'

'Good, because that's not going to change.'

'By which I mean,' Barbara continued, seemingly unsure of what she did mean, 'I accept that you're my joint employer. But Bill's the other one. And I'd be uncomfortable talking such matters without him present, if you don't mind.'

Mercy let the awkward pause hang there for a bit as the kettle finished boiling behind them.

'Fair enough,' she smiled, letting the matter drop for now. 'I hope I haven't made things uncomfortable. We'll talk later. Now what do you prefer, coffee or tea?'

'I should make it for you, I suppose.'

'I won't hear of it,' Mercy waved the suggestion away. 'It's my pleasure. You're a milky tea girl, am I right?'

A young man with a laptop bag and wearing a cycle helmet entered, his attention connected to the phone in his other hand. He looked startled on seeing Mercy standing there, not to mention Barbara with a face like a terminal patient and a chocolate pastry in front of her.

'I thought you'd resigned,' he said to the secretary.

'You must be Robbie Ingleton,' Mercy smiled, stepping forward as he removed his earphones. 'I'm Mercy, Ray's daughter.'

'Right,' said Robbie, shaking her hand. 'I've heard about you.'

'All of it flattering I'm sure,' she said. 'Now, the kettle's just boiled and I've bought us some treats in the hope of ingratiating myself. Barbara's already snagged the one *pain au chocolat* but she's been politely saving it until we're all here. But there's an almond croissant still available if you want one.'

'Yeah, that'd be sick.'

'It *will* be sick. Also, could you help me fix the fridge door?' she asked him, heading back to the kitchenette. 'It needs one more shove.'

# 22

Dirty clouds were concealing the sky as Bill parked in a garage underneath some railway arches. Before leaving the warm car and negotiating his way around the puddles of Southwark, he saw that he'd missed a text from Matt Wren, a man he'd hoped to never hear from again. Wren was a high-functioning irritant and Bill held him partly responsible for his 18-month stay at Her Majesty's pleasure.

**Got a text from Tyler asking if I knew where his car was. No idea but glad he's reaching out again. You boys back in the game?**

This was followed by the fingers-crossed emoji. Bill wondered if he was winding him up, because, unless he'd come into possession of a Ouija board, he hadn't heard from Ray.

**Ray's dead,** he texted back. **And I'm still not interested. Don't engage with me again.**

A train rumbled overhead as he collected his leather holdall and locked the garage door. Then he headed towards the agency.

Bill had been dismayed to learn from Barbara that Mercy was at work already. He'd been hoping that she would've reconsidered joining the firm by now as she was a factor he didn't know how to deal with. And he had no intention of involving her in Victor's case.

He felt guilty thinking bad thoughts about her though. After all, he'd known her all her life and had always cared about her, under any name or gender. She'd been his godson once, and now she was his goddaughter. For him, that was all there was to it. But he wished her father had seen it like that. Ray may have been a sharp detective, but he had often been blind to what was happening under his own nose. Bill had been disappointed in his old mate's reaction when Mercy had announced she was transgender. He liked to think that he'd have been more accepting in the same circumstance, if he'd been blessed with a child.

Entering the office, he found his flustered secretary alone behind her desk. Laughter came through the door of the smaller room where Robbie worked, enough to tell him that this wasn't going to be an ordinary Monday.

'She broke in,' Barbara whispered, as if scared that Mercy might overhear. 'Like a burglar. Picked the locks and shut down the alarm. She's been making copies of invoices made out to Victor, and has been asking questions. But you know me, Bill, I kept *schtum!*'

'What would I do without you, Barb?' he said, putting his umbrella in the rack and removing his coat. 'But we've nothing to hide so don't get worked up about it.'

'Also, she's been interfering with the fridge. Look!'

Bill crossed over to the kitchenette and opened the mini-fridge that he'd originally bought as a gift for Ray and Julie when they'd moved into their first house. The inside of the door had been tampered with.

'Ray had a secret compartment in there,' Barbara informed him. 'He'd been hiding a phone inside.'

Bill was astounded. He inspected the damage Mercy had done to the old fridge and realised it was true, there was a space created inside of the door to hide things in. Fucking Ray, he thought. How many other compartments did he have hidden around the place?

'Where's this phone now?' he asked.

'Chris... Mercy's got it on her.'

He moved over to the door behind which he could hear his usually taciturn data expert conversing with enthusiasm. He tapped on the glass screen before opening it to find Robbie showing Mercy how to break the security code on a standard laptop.

'She's just called the Doctor,' he was telling her as they searched through the laptop's history. '*Doctor Who* is the name of the show.'

'Is that right?' Mercy murmured and then swivelled her chair around to Bill. 'Morning chief!' she beamed. 'And it's a good job you are the chief or you'd be in trouble. What time d'you call this?'

'We can't all be up with the larks, can we?' he smiled at her after nodding hello at Robbie. 'From what I hear you gave Barbara a bit of a fright this morning.'

'Ha, sorry about that,' she said in the same cavalier tone that her dad had used whenever he'd been up to mischief. Oddly, Mercy reminded him much more of Ray nowadays than she ever had as Christopher. 'Did Barb tell you that I picked the locks and disabled the alarm too?'

'Yeah, although I'm guessing that you just had Ray's spare keys. I know he kept them at home with your mum.'

'The alarm code has changed but that didn't matter,' Mercy confirmed. 'Got it on my second try.'

'Solid detective work,' he congratulated her. 'You're in the right trade after all.'

The six-digit alarm code had been his stepdaughter's birth date, information Mercy could have easily got from Lisa's social media accounts. Her first try, he assumed, would've been her own birthday, which she must have known was the code back when M&T first opened for business. He wondered how she felt about the code having been changed.

'Mercy brought us pastries,' Robbie said, looking up from the laptop. 'But I've had two.' He then returned his attention back to the flickering images on the screen.

'That's okay, I'm supposed to be on a diet,' Bill said coming closer so he could see how the data retrieval was progressing. 'I see Robbie's been showing you the digital ropes,' he said to Mercy as a series of extremely startling images flashed up. 'That laptop needs to be back with the client by five at the latest. Before her husband gets back from abroad. Find anything yet?'

'Porn,' Robbie said, after slurping his tea. 'Plenty of it. But nothing as horrible as his missus is worried about. Nothing dark web.'

'That'll be a relief to her,' Bill said and patted him on the shoulder. 'Remember, if you find anything illegal, we're duty bound to report it to the police.'

He wondered if that sounded forced. He was keen to show Mercy that M&T was a straight-edged business nowadays, operating within the boundaries of the law. Frankly though, he couldn't remember the last time they'd reported something to the police that clashed with a paying client's interest. Keen to move away from ethical grey areas he suggested that Mercy join him in his office so Robbie could get on with his search undisturbed.

'We'll carry on with our discussion about who should be the next Doctor Who later, Robbie,' she said before leaving. 'Happy hunting.'

'She's called the Doctor!' Robbie corrected her as the door was shutting.

But they'd already left. He reached for another croissant and carried on looking through the graphic images on his screen.

# 23

Mercy felt the energy shift once she and Bill were alone in his office. She'd sensed the same tension during her visit last week, a studied lightness Bill adopted in front of others that he struggled to maintain when it was just the two of them. Not that he was hostile. If anything, he became more courteous as they began the awkward negotiations about what her role in their agency might be. But she could tell she made him uncomfortable by how much he hid behind formality. She sat across from him in the same chair as she had on Friday, one usually meant for clients, and they drank hot tea. The positioning felt antagonistic.

Bill began by talking her through the current clients and describing a typical working day in the agency, as much as any day was ever typical. He explained that, while most of the bigger agencies were specialising in lucrative corporate investigations, most of the jobs that came to M&T these days involved matrimonial stuff, tracing missing persons, running background checks, and the odd bit of vehicle tracking. He made a number of practised jokes as he ran through the spiel and she wondered what she might read into his stiltedness. Perhaps he wasn't relaxed around trans people. While regrettable, that was more his problem than hers. But perhaps there was more to it, she wondered. What might he be hiding?

'So we never do commercial investigations?'

'I never said never.' It was obvious that he knew she'd been looking at the Neale invoices. 'For instance, Victor has employed us in the past to investigate what happens in his various gyms when he's not there. Untrustworthy management, that sort of thing. Commercial investigation can be a very catch-all term.'

'Does Victor hire M&T a lot?'

'Less so nowadays,' Bill shrugged. 'Besides, your dad tended to deal with his business more than I did. They were old school mates and had a special understanding. Although Vic was very supportive of me during my time away. Speaking of which, can I ask you a question?'

'Sure.'

'Have you been sending out texts from your Dad's phone?'

Mercy sat up straighter, feeling like a guilty schoolgirl in a headmaster's office.

'His phone was never found,' she answered. 'It's probably lying at the bottom of the Thames.'

'I'm talking about the one you found this morning inside the fridge.'

'Oh yeah,' Mercy grinned and opened her palms in a bang-to-rights gesture. 'That!'

'It's funny,' he smiled back. 'I bought your dad that fridge and I didn't know he had a secret compartment in it. How did you?'

Last time they were in this office she'd told him about

the afternoon she'd spent as a teenager eavesdropping on her father and the hitman. She'd relayed what she remembered of their conversation and had even mentioned the pink envelope. But she'd deliberately omitted the part where her dad had produced it from inside the fridge's compartment. Having noticed that the same fridge had somehow ended up in the M&T kitchen, she wanted to be the first to open it.

'There are nine mystery numbers stored into the phone,' Mercy explained. 'All of the contacts are saved in initials. CB, NI, MW, SJ, etc.'

'MW stands for Matt Wren,' Bill told her. 'He contacted me about forty minutes ago and told me Ray had sent him a text asking where his car was.'

'Yeah, I sent that message. Technically, that car belongs to mum and me, so it wasn't a lie. And I was curious to see who'd respond. Who's Matt Wren?'

'He's a tabloid journalist,' Bill answered with a pained expression, 'who writes for the London Crier. It was Wren who hired me to do all that work. You know, the hacking.'

Mercy felt a pang of regret at having rattled this cage. She knew Bill's tabloid shame had cost him a lot.

'He used to pay for the jobs that landed me in prison. The royal phones, the celebrity stuff, and, worst of all, that missing girl. I'm not proud of that phase in my life – I was in a bad place – but I've sworn never to work with the press again. Lesson learnt. Ray and I made a decision to discard Wren's details years ago, but it seems he'd kept the number.'

'I'm sorry all that happened, Bill. Dad said the tabloids made you a scapegoat.'

'That was good of him,' Bill nodded. 'But I'm a grown man and I take responsibility for my own actions. They called me Bin Man Bill then because I'd literally go through people's rubbish looking for personal details. And the reason tabloids pay so much for investigators to do their dirty work is the deniability so I knew what I was getting into. But at the enquiry,' he spoke in a bitter voice, 'those bastards really did a Saint Peter on me. As if no tabloid editor would ever suggest bugging a phone or a hotel room. As if I was just some maniac operating of my own volition and they'd only expected me to make discreet enquiries into the lives of the rich and famous. In the end, I took the hit and got 18 months for my trespasses. In fairness, that was deserved. But they wouldn't even pay my legal fees. And now here Wren is, asking if I want to go back into business with him. I honestly wouldn't piss on him if he was on fire.'

'Why does he still want you to work for him?'

'Because I was the best,' Bill replied, with a reluctant measure of pride. 'At the dark arts, as they call it. Well, until I got nicked.'

She sensed the open wound left by that shabby period in his life. Bill had lost more than 18 months. Moira had divorced him while he was in prison and his relationship with his stepdaughter had also deteriorated.

'Am I right in thinking that Victor paid your legal fees?'

'At Ray's request no doubt,' Bill confirmed. 'Yeah, he was a good friend to me.'

'Victor?'

'No, your dad. Victor's just a friend of a friend. Listen, I've been meaning to say something...'

There was a tap on Bill's door and he seemed glad of the interruption. It was, she noted, the second time he'd moved the conversation away from Victor. Behind her, Nina Markham entered to report on her morning's surveillance. Mercy rose to greet her.

'I'm afraid I wasn't at my best when we met at the funeral,' she said, offering Nina her hand. 'I hope to make a better impression now.'

'Good to have a Tyler back in the firm,' Nina said as they shook. Her smile felt forced though. Perhaps she thought her job was no longer safe with Mercy here. Or maybe she just disliked smiling.

'Barb's been telling me about your dawn raid on the filing cabinet,' Nina said after handing over her camera to Bill so he could upload her new stuff onto his computer. 'Bit keen. I didn't realise we had anything going with Victor Neale at the moment, Bill.'

'We don't,' he said, as he looked through the images of a client's wife dropping her kids off at a school. 'Mercy was just showing an interest in her new job. These are fantastic, Nina. Were you spotted?'

'Am I ever?' Nina answered. She crossed over to Bill's side to talk him through the pictures.

'Your dad used to call Nina here the Invisible Girl,' Bill told Mercy as she joined them at the screen.

The photos showed a pretty woman in her thirties speaking with an older man under the sheltered awnings of a school that seemed to be for disabled children. Despite the rain, the picture quality was excellent. The man had a downs syndrome daughter of around seven who, in one image, was refusing to leave her father. The client's wife was comforting this girl and persuading her to hold hands with her child.

Then there were shots of her sharing a coffee with the man inside a Costa. They were holding their own hands under the table.

'Nina gets close enough to touch,' Bill declared, 'but they never clock her. Astonishing work.'

The final picture in the sequence showed the client's

wife by a tall fence up a sodden lane, kissing the man as the rain held romantically off. Nina had somehow positioned herself above them and the shot captured everything the client needed to know.

'They parted company soon after, so I left it there. But if the client wants audio as well, it'd obviously be worth the extra money.'

'He may not,' Bill said, closing the file. 'Depends if he's thinking divorce or not. Some men just want to know. I'll call him now to arrange a meeting. Why don't you two get some lunch out of petty cash? You've done well, Nina.'

Before following Nina out of the room, Mercy asked him a question.

'What did you want to say before she came in?'

'Oh, don't worry,' he looked up as he placed his hand on the landline phone. 'We'll leave that for now.'

'No, go on,' Mercy insisted.

'We had a burglary,' he answered at last, 'about four years ago. It wasn't serious but I wanted to explain why we changed the alarm code from your birthday.'

'Okay.'

'Just in case you thought... I don't know what.'

'That I'd been disowned!' Mercy laughed before leaving his office. 'The thought hadn't occurred.'

# 24

'So how long have you been spying on married women for a living?'

Mercy had meant the icebreaker to sound funnier than it was, but Nina didn't seem offended. They were underneath the pavilion shelter of a café not far from the office and had ordered some shawarmas and a Diet Coke each. Until this morning Mercy hadn't really considered how useful Nina might be in making sense of her father's death, but that had now changed. She'd just witnessed a demonstration of some exceptional spying skills, so here was a woman who surely knew many useful things.

'Two years, just under,' Nina replied as she took a swig of Coke and surveyed a passing teenager who was carrying a guitar case. She was a born watcher, Mercy could tell that. A middle-aged man with a grey ponytail, a younger guy wearing white paint-splattered overalls, a couple quarrelling in Arabic – Nina's quick eyes took them all in. But she rarely made eye contact with Mercy.

'Feels like longer,' Nina added.

'That bad?'

'Nah, it's cool. I like the work and I'm good at it. But the load is heavy. Especially since… well, you know.'

'Sure,' Mercy said. 'Well, I'm here to help with the workload now. M&T were lucky to find you. Who did you meet first, M or T?'

'Your dad,' answered Nina. 'We were introduced through a friend of my ex who drank in the Lord Clyde. Ray had heard that I'd left the police force with some surveillance experience and was keen for work. As luck would have it, he and Bill were looking for a new operative, so it worked out well.'

'I didn't know you were in the police.'

'Only for a short time,' Nina explained. 'I dropped out to have Kyle and never went back.'

'I didn't know you were a mother!'

'Yeah, he's four,' Nina nodded and pulled out her phone to show Mercy her screensaver of her and a little child. 'Mummy's little soldier.'

'Adorable,' Mercy smiled.

'Ta. Mum and Dad look after him when I'm working long hours. I'm a single mother.' Mercy returned the phone 'That's why it was such a lifeline when Ray convinced Bill to take me on. I owe your dad a lot. He was a good bloke.'

'So they say.'

Their lunch arrived. Mercy leaned forward to smell the spices on her vegetarian shawarma.

'When I was a kid,' she said picking up a fork, 'I loved having a private eye parent. So will Kyle.'

'Hope so,' said Nina after taking her first bite.

'I used to have these daft fantasies about Dad and Bill. I'd imagine they were the stars of some buddy-buddy TV show about two detectives who'd tear around the city in cars, solving crimes.'

'Like Starsky & Hutch?'

'Sort of,' she said. 'I had Dad down as the tough one. The wise-cracker, the brawler. While Bill was strong but silent. Dad barked but Bill bit.'

'Tough guys,' Nina smiled.

'Yeah,' nodded Mercy. 'But good guys.'

A silence fell and Mercy regretted bringing up so childish a thought. She sipped her drink and wondered what questions she should be asking.

'Why are you sniffing around Victor Neale?' Nina asked first. 'What's with all the printouts this morning?'

'I'm investigating him,' Mercy replied. 'In relation to Dad's murder.'

Nina chewed on her shawarma for some quiet seconds.

'Are you now?' she said after swallowing.

'Him and some others.'

'Why d'you think your dad was murdered?' Nina asked. 'And why would Neale be involved?'

'Victor Neale is a notorious criminal,' Mercy replied between bites, 'even if he's never been brought to book. And M&T have had a lot of concealed business with him over the years. Maybe he had Dad killed because he knew too much about a crime he'd helped to arrange. Or maybe someone else killed Dad because of his dealings with Neale.'

'What have you discovered so far?' Nina asked. 'About all this secret business that's supposedly been going on?'

'Not much,' Mercy admitted. 'Have you ever worked one of Victor's cases?'

'Never,' she told her. 'That was Ray's territory.'

'Before he died Dad referred to someone called the Long Needle. Any idea who that is?'

'Sorry,' Nina shook her head. 'Can't help you there.'

Mercy considered if Nina might be lying but she was a tricky person to read.

'You don't strike me as someone who always takes things at face value,' she said. 'Did you never question Dad's death?'

'The thing is,' Nina answered after wiping sauce from her lips with a tissue, 'your dad was a heavy drinker. You knew that, yeah? He used to hide bottles of whiskey around the office. We used to find them in cabinets, down the toilet cistern. His breath often stank of booze during the day. He was a functioning alcoholic, until his final weeks when he wasn't so functioning. So, if I'm honest, I do believe it was drunken misadventure.'

Her words hit hard, although Mercy didn't doubt that they were true. She'd found an almost empty whiskey miniature in the fridge compartment along with the phone. But it was still hurtful to hear her father's disease described in such a stark way.

'That all fits in with my theory,' she persisted anyway. 'If you were trying to kill him then his alcoholism would make a booze-related accident easy to fake; you can blame any disaster on a drunk. People would just think either an accident or suicide.'

'Some people did think suicide,' Nina told her, and Mercy wondered if she'd meant it to sound so harsh.

'And those people would be wrong.'

Another awkward moment followed. A homeless man approached their table and asked for change. Mercy gave him some coins as Nina carried on eating. She couldn't shake the insidious idea that Ray was possibly suicidal in his final hours and it ruined the food she'd been enjoying. Had he sounded like he was about to destroy himself in his final message? Mercy had to admit that she hadn't interrogated that dark possibility enough. She herself had once contemplated suicide years back when she'd been an unhappy young person with a wrongly assigned birth gender. But she'd battled those demons and won. The thought that, unlike her, her dad may have lost his own fight with depression caused her sorrow.

'Is that why you want to become a PI?' Nina asked after finishing her meal. 'To look into these suspicions?'

'Mainly,' Mercy nodded. 'Although I do need gainful employment, so there's that too. But I'm taking the career seriously. I've had some business cards printed up.'

Mercy reached into her handbag and produced a small box full of freshly printed cards. She handed one over for Nina to see.

**MERCEDES TYLER - PRIVATE INVESTIGATOR**

Underneath these words she'd already handwritten something in dark blue ink. *Ask for Mercy.*

'Nice peacock feather,' Nina said, referring to the little plume illustration that adorned the left-hand side of the white rectangle. It was designed to look like one of those on the M&T exterior wall. 'Y'know, that sign's been up there since the forties. It's got nothing to do with the agency.'

'True, but it's a cool icon.' Mercy pointed to the inner sleeve of her leather jacket. 'I've got a tattoo of a peacock feather here actually. Blue and green are my colours.' Nina went to hand the card back. 'Keep it,' Mercy waved it away. 'I've got loads.'

After putting the card away, Nina brought the conversation back to Victor Neale. Mercy found it interesting that, unlike Bill or Barbara, this one didn't mind talking about their controversial client.

'I've only met him once,' she told Mercy, 'at your dad's wake. Bill introduced me to him in the pub garden.'

'What was your impression of him?'

'Cunt.'

Mercy had just swigged the last of her Coke, but she snorted fizz out of her nose. They both laughed.

'Succinct,' Mercy complimented her. 'And fair.'

'He was boasting about how his brother's funeral had triple the amount of mourners as your dad. As if funeral numbers were competitive! Some guys will make a status symbol out of anything. And his cronies were all laughing at his every comment, like he was Oscar Wilde or someone.'

'Who was sniggering during Bill's eulogy?'

'Tony Lamoreaux and a few others. Oh, and the guy who owns the spyware shop where we get most of our gear. Alan McColl, former copper. He was thrown off the force years ago but I don't know why.'

'He was on the take,' Mercy told her.

'I hate to say it but some of these dicks were making jokes about you.'

'I can imagine the sort of thing.'

'Bill stood up for you though. He told the boys they were out of order for making fun of Ray's kid at Ray's funeral, which they were. Victor agreed.'

'How does Bill behave around Victor?'

'He sucks up to him, like he does with any big client.'

After they'd paid, Mercy reflected that she'd just revealed much more to Nina than she'd learnt in return. As a first-day detective, Mercy felt that she'd just been outplayed by a professional.

They walked back to the office in relative silence, their route taking them past the site where Marshalsea Prison once stood. Mercy paused to read a sign attached to a remnant of the old prison wall that told how Charles Dickens' father had been imprisoned there for debt. Her own difficult dad had once told her about this local claim to literary fame and how many of the streets around here were named after Dickens characters.

'Bill took a phone call from Victor last week,' Nina said in a confidential tone as they then passed by some children playing in Little Dorrit Park, 'during a staff meeting. I'm not sure, but it sounded like he was phoning Bill back. I couldn't hear what they said.'

'Well, that sheds a different light on Bill's claim that he's not an active client,' Mercy said, irked to discover that he'd lied to her.

'I'll say this,' Nina added, 'I'm not one for murder conspiracies. The world's too chaotic for that. But I'm no fan of Victor and I liked your dad, so if you can prove to me that something is up, I'll be your ally.'

'Cheers Nina, that's appreciated.'

They crossed the street towards the Chinese takeaway on the corner of Nadgett Street. From the high window of the office, just above the peacock feather, Barbara could be seen keeping her own beady eye out.

'Until then,' Nina said as they reached the side door of the building, 'let's get back to work. We've got married women to spy on.'

# 25

That afternoon Nina was sent out on another surveillance job. Mercy had asked to tag along but Bill had shaken his head.

'There's no telling where the mark will lead her,' he'd explained. 'Your inexperience might give Nina away,'

While conceding that this might be true, she suspected that there was another reason that Bill thought she'd be conspicuous. She was transgender and trans people drew attention to themselves, or so he probably thought. She wanted to tell him that since transitioning she'd become adept at moving invisibly through a crowd, not least because her safety often depended on it. But, for now, she just agreed to learn how to be an indoor detective.

To be fair, her dad had always warned her that poking around in other people's affairs was all good fun until the paperwork began. Mercy had always assumed he was exaggerating but the rest of her first day proved him right. The business was so incredibly mundane that she suspected they must be playing a prank on the new girl. But it was Barbara who fielded the lion's share of the bureaucracy.

'Fair fucks to her,' Robbie whispered in the smaller office later, 'she can type like the wind. But Barb makes plenty of mistakes. Your dad tried to fire her last year before Bill overruled it.'

'Fire her?' asked Mercy. 'Why?'

'Something about a phone conversation he overheard,' he answered while making hardcopy printouts of some disturbing images he'd found in the laptop's search history. 'I arrived one morning, normal time, and it was only the two of them here. Your dad was angrier than I'd ever seen him. He'd got a cardboard box from somewhere and was telling Barb to fill it with her stuff and clear off. Bill came in soon after me and she was in floods by then, saying how sorry she was. Ray was all, *tough shit, Barb.* Bill ended up dragging him out of the office until he calmed down.'

'Was he drunk?'

'Probably,' Robbie admitted. He pointed to a small folding bed stood against the wall. 'Ray used to sleep in here sometimes when he couldn't drive home. As far as I know, Barb came in early that morning and was gossiping on the phone. She didn't realise that Ray was in here listening. I dunno what she said but it must've been *bad.*'

'How was Dad with her after that?'

'Not sure,' Robbie shrugged, zipping the laptop into a bag. 'He died a few days later.'

When it came to running discreet but enhanced background checks, Robbie was their man. He talked Mercy through the elaborate and just-about legal means by which an investigator would typically verify identities, conduct financial searches, or check for criminal histories that a subject might be concealing.

It was possibly the dullest few hours of her life.

Of course she was impressed – even mildly horrified –

by how easily Robbie could negotiate online loopholes and drag up personal information. But she was also questioning what her own role at M&T might prove to be. They already had a respected boss, a surveillance expert, a computer genius and someone to type the letters, so what was she for? She knew that she'd exerted an unearned privilege in forcing herself into a job that wasn't even vacant, but she hadn't expected to feel quite so fraudulent this fast.

Six o'clock came but Robbie had left early so he could bike the laptop and its attached report back to the client before her husband returned home. Nina had contacted Bill to say she'd follow her mark throughout the evening and he'd agreed to pay her usual overtime fee. Before leaving herself, Barbara told Mercy that Bill had asked to see her.

She knocked on his office door before entering. Bill looked up from his laptop as if he'd momentarily forgotten who she was. The day had darkened by then and there was little natural light in that room. He was wearing half-cut spectacles and had been tapping his chin with a ballpoint pen. In the light of the computer screen, and with his short hair sticking up as if he'd been ruffling it, he looked older than he had that morning. What could be preoccupying him?

'Could be cocaine,' Bill said, referring to the large sums that the subject of her first background check seemed to be spending at regular intervals. 'These sorts of unaccounted for withdrawals sometimes lead to hard drugs. Good work, Mercy. A productive first day.'

'Thanks,' she said, pulling back the client chair before sitting. 'Was that all you wanted to see me about?'

'Not just that. I wanted to chat about your little discovery this morning.'

'Dad's secret compartment,' she nodded.

'More specifically,' he said, tapping the desk lamp to a brighter setting, 'Dad's secret phone and its mystery numbers. I'd like to take a look at them.'

She considered what the most diplomatic answer she could give might be. 'I'm sorry Bill,' she said, settling on polite-but-frank, 'I'm not ready to share those details.'

'Excuse me?'

'I'm prepared to pay for a new fridge if it won't shut properly,' she held his gaze. 'But I found the phone. It belonged to Dad and now it belongs to me. That includes any information it may contain.'

'I only want to see if I recognise any of the numbers,' he replied. 'Your man, the Long Needle – his details could be on there.'

'I thought you weren't interested in helping me find the Long Needle.'

'I didn't say *not interested*.'

'When we sat in this office on Friday, you made it plain that you wouldn't help me investigate my dad's death. Let *sleeping dogs lie*, remember? Fine. It's my investigation now.'

'Now hold on—'

'Information is transactional,' she told him. 'If you want these numbers, you need to provide me with something I don't know.'

'I might be able to tell who they belong to,' he answered with a restrained huff, 'I can trace them for you.'

'Robbie can teach me how to do that. He's already started.'

'Why won't you trust me with them?'

'Why won't you trust *me?*' she replied.

She almost asked him then why he'd lied about speaking to Victor Neale on Friday. Instead, she let her question hang there for him to work out. Bill removed his glasses and leaned back.

'Suit yourself,' he sighed. 'I was only trying to help.'

'I'll give you the number of the phone itself,' she said, after a pause. 'You can contact me on it. My own was stolen on Friday night.'

'Stolen how?'

'It was taken by force halfway up Lewisham Hill by a man with a knife.'

He sat up straight again.

'You're joking?'

'It was around midnight.' She shook her head. 'I was coming home from a night out when he jumped out at me from behind a dark corner. He had a hood on and a thick scarf obscuring most of his face. It was too dark to see the colour of his eyes. I almost had a heart attack when I saw the size of the knife.'

'My God,' he said. 'That's appalling. Are you okay?'

'He punched me hard in the ribs,' she nodded. 'It's still a little painful when I sit down. But got the knife off him and hit him over the head with a wine bottle. Hopefully I've left a bump.'

'You overpowered him?' Bill looked sceptical.

She nodded.

'Was he a big guy?'

'I'd say he was about a foot shorter than you. I used karate on him.' She enjoyed the look of astonishment on Bill's face. 'A girl on a motorbike pulled up, he jumped on the back and off they vanished.'

'A girl?' His face screwed up.

'Black helmet, medium height. She asked him "*we done?*" before they took off with my phone but nothing else. My purse, my credit cards, my jewellery. Didn't even take the handbag. They just wanted my standard little mobile. That's suspicious, right? Why make a point of stealing that?'

Bill had begun grinding his teeth. Aside from the police, he was the only person she'd told about the phone message.

'You were targeted,' he said. It wasn't a question.

'I know. I think it was an attempt by someone to get Dad's phone message off me. A waste of time, I have back-ups.'

'Jesus, Christoph - *sorry—'* he winced at his mistake, '... Mercy. If that's true, it may have been my fault.'

The confession took her by surprise. She'd expected that getting him to admit it would've been harder.

'Why's that, Bill?'

He lifted his large hands up and rubbed his face in a vigorous motion. Then he exhaled and stared at her.

'After you left my office on Friday I spoke to Victor,' he said in a lower tone. 'I wanted to know if he knew someone called the Long Needle. I told him what you overheard in your dad's study and about your voicemail message. I'm so sorry.'

'What did he say?'

'He denied all knowledge.'

'Why didn't you tell me before?'

'I didn't want to worry you. But I had no idea masked men would start jumping at you from the shadows. It was stupid, I'm an idiot.'

'You think that he sent them to steal the voicemail message?'

'Perhaps. But this is why I was trying to dissuade you from stirring things up. Investigation can be dangerous. You must be careful if you're going up against people like Victor.'

'No, it's a good thing. I want dad's killer to come for me. I'm glad it's getting around that I'm a problem.'

He stared at her like she was mad. 'You want to get killed?'

'Visibility remains my best tactic,' she explained. 'Asking unwelcome questions, poking around, being a nuisance. Waiting for the right person to strike. I'll be ready.'

'Unacceptable,' Bill snapped. 'And if your father knew you were endangering yourself like this, he'd be furious with me for allowing it.' She was taken aback by how agitated her story had made him. 'From now on,' he continued, 'I'll drive to you to work and back. You can't keep walking up and down that road if there are attackers lurking, regardless of their motives.'

'Bill, you live miles away,' she said.

He shut down the computer and began collecting his things from the desk, indicating that he was ready to leave.

'It's no bother,' he said as he placed his glasses into their case. 'I should've offered earlier but I didn't realise you lived in such a rough area. It won't happen again.'

'Lewisham's fine,' she answered. 'It has a huge police station.'

'There's a reason for that.'

She was glad to accept a daily lift though. It gave her a chance to question him further.

'And on the way,' he said as they were walking down that musty staircase, 'we can talk more about your dad's phone. If it's information you want in return, I may have some.'

THE INTERIOR of Bill's car was more impressive than its exterior. This made it the opposite of anything her father ever drove. Ray was always a sucker for something that looked more beautiful on the outside and her earliest memories involved watching him wash down a blue second-hand Jag with a sponge and big bowl of soapy suds. The car would glint brilliantly in the summer sun, but she recalled broken glove compartments, sticky upholstery and scattered tape cassettes, none of which were in the correct container. He would have slept in those cars too, when he'd been out all night.

Bill tended to drive more what Mercy would expect a private eye to. Sensible, under-the radar vehicles that you wouldn't notice if you saw one in your rear-view mirror several times in the same day. His current Nissan had dull cutlery colours and plastic hubcaps, but the insides were immaculate without a trace of dirt or disorder. It was a family car for a man who no longer had a family.

'I take it you and Barb had a confrontation this morning,' Bill said as he pulled onto the main road. 'I could tell from her face.'

'Yeah,' Mercy said, with a pang of guilt. 'I was asking what she knew about the Neale family and I may have been too rough.'

'She loves the House of Neale with the same fervour that some people love the House of Windsor,' Bill smirked. 'You won't get any dirt out of her.'

'I feel bad, I behaved in a very entitled way. It's not cool to pick on an older woman, but she's always been such a bitch to me. It felt good to push back. I don't know how you've been putting up with her so long.'

'Look Mercy,' he said, his tone becoming firmer. London was still wet from the day's intermittent rain and the traffic was slow. 'I know Barb might seem like an old misery, but she's been with us since the Stone Age. And her husband Bernie is very ill, he may not last the year out. This little job is all she's got and she's unlikely to get another one that pays the same.'

'I wasn't suggesting you *fire* her,' Mercy said, chastened. Barbara's antagonistic attitude could be challenging but she also knew that she, Mercy, was the one who'd leave if their personalities couldn't be reconciled. 'Barb's part of the furniture. I get that. But it's not just me who finds her difficult. Didn't Dad try and sack her?'

'Robbie told you that, did he?'

'I couldn't possibly betray my source.'

'I'm impressed,' he smiled. 'I can barely get two words out of him if it isn't about *Game of Thrones*.'

'He didn't say what the argument was about,' Mercy explained. 'I was hoping you'd be more forthcoming.'

Bill let out a heavy sigh as he indicated right at an upcoming roundabout. 'She'd been talking to Maggie Neale,' he said at last. 'Lol's widow. Remember her?'

'Nick's mum,' Mercy nodded, 'they used to call her the Cleaning Lady because she laundered all the dirty money.'

'Maggie spends much of her year in Nevada now, but she and Barbara are close. Maggie's a night bird; Barb is a lark, so they speak on the phone early our time. They were gossiping that morning and Barb didn't realise that Ray was in the other room. Barbara was slagging off all the wives. Bitchy comments. Supposedly she'd been running down my ex-wife and also your Mum. I won't repeat what exactly.'

'Dad was defending my mother's honour?' Mercy asked, not meaning to sound sceptical.

'Something like that,' nodded Bill. 'Ray was a righteous fellow when defending his family. You're like him in that way.'

'Am I?'

'Sure, all these lengths you're going to investigate his death. You're a good daughter to him. I wonder if my Lisa would try to hunt down my killer, if she thought I had one.'

'I certainly would,' Mercy told him. 'You're my family too.'

'That's a nice thing to say,' he glanced towards her. They continued down the Old Kent Road and he turned the radio on. They listened to one of his Motown playlists and began chatting about their favourite tracks. She even managed to coax him into singing along to Sitting on the Dock of the Bay with her. They laughed at his self-consciousness and soon, as musical conversations tend to, things turned nostalgic.

'I was literally sitting on the dock of a bay when I first heard this,' he told her. 'Belfast Harbour, where they built the Titanic. My dad worked there and took me with him when I should've been at school. Those lads had the radio on all day and we'd sing along. I should've become a docker, it would've been a simpler life than this one. My old man was furious when I eventually told him I was crossing the channel to become a copper. He couldn't comprehend it.'

She asked him if he regretted coming to London.

'For a time,' he said, 'until I met your dad.'

Bobby Womack was still halfway across 110$^{th}$ Street as their car rolled up Lewisham Hill. Bill turned down the music and slowed. He asked her to point out the spot where she'd been attacked on Friday. She talked him through where her assailant had sprung out from and in which direction the bike then headed.

'Where's the knife now?' Bill asked.

'I gave it to the police.'

'Pity,' he said, before continuing the journey. 'I could've told you more.'

Night had fallen by the time they pulled up outside her home. He killed the engine and pointed to the glove compartment.

'Take a look,' he said. 'See if you recognise anything.'

As the compartment lit up from within she noticed a small pair of binoculars and a folded up packet of Golden Virginia tobacco.

'Under those,' he said, and she pulled out a neat bundle of car insurance documents. Among them she found something that made her gasp. A deep pink envelope.

*'Is that your card?'* Bill said in the style of a conjurer as he turned on the interior light. She pulled the envelope out.

'This is it!' she exclaimed, touching something that she'd last seen fifteen years earlier in her father's office. It had the same wax seal. 'This envelope contained the details of the hit.'

'It's not the same one,' he told her. 'But that brand belongs to the Never Setting Sun. They're a gentlemen's club.'

'You and Dad went to a charity dinner there once,' she remembered. 'It's where he bought my football shirt.'

'Victor's top boy at the club,' Bill confirmed. 'He's been a member for decades and this is their exclusive stationery. The theme is the British Empire and, traditionally, pink represents how that was coloured on a map of the world. In the dining hall there's a portrait of the Queen and there were endless toasts being made to her throughout the night. Your dad was very taken by it all but, being Irish, I was less enthralled.'

'This envelope proves a link between whoever hired Dad and the Never Setters,' she said with excitement. 'Where'd you get it?'

Bill reached into the backseat for his leather holdall. From that he produced an e-cigarette.

'Listen to this.'

# 26

'If *I wanted someone killed,'* Victor's rant could be heard through the speaker, *'I'd get someone I trust to do it. Or I'd do it my own fucking self. I wouldn't outsource a murder to a total stranger, would I?'*

Mercy leaned closer to the dashboard so she could hear more clearly. The sound was crackly and the recording occasionally cut out whenever Bill had taken a puff of his e-cigarette.

*'I don't give a shit about that weirdo,'* she caught Victor saying about her. *'But okay, I admit, it wasn't true what I said before.'*

*'Go on.'*

Mercy looked at Bill, sat beside her in the driver's seat. He was stroking a finger under his stubbly chin. His customised e-cigarette was plugged into the charger and the balcony conversation sounded tinny coming out of his car radio.

*'I have heard of the Long Needle before.'*

*'Who is he?'*

*'That's what I'm paying you to find out. Whoever he is, he's got it in for me.'*

*'How so?'*

*'Nicholas received a phone call,'* Victor's voice went on, *'on New Year's Eve. Anonymous.'*

*'New Year's Eve just gone?'*

*''Course. A voice said to him, "I killed your daddy."'*

*'Were those his exact words?'*

*'That was the gist. I'm told he had an American accent. He goes on to say that he was hired by Raymond to murder Nick's dad* – my Lol! - *and then asks the boy to guess who hired him to do it. And that's when the bright spark jumps to the conclusion that I must have had my own brother killed. The impertinent little prick.'*

*'Did the caller name you?'*

*'He did. "Your uncle had your dad killed," he says. Nicholas explodes. Starts demanding to know who the caller is,* "I'll kill ya, I'll kill ya" – *all this.'*

*'But why would someone say that to him, Vic?'*

*'I'm a man with many enemies,'* Victor replied as if proud. *'But I need to find out what's going on before my nephew does something that'll disgrace the family name. Now finish that poofy fag and let's go back in. It's brass monkeys out here.'*

Bill turned off the listening device from his radio.

'Sorry about not sticking up for you when he misgendered you,' he said. 'I don't see you that way.'

Mercy didn't respond to that but picked up the e-cigarette for inspection.

'I thought you'd given up this filthy habit,' she remarked, weighing it in her hand.

'I don't normally record private conversations,' he responded in a defensive tone. 'But this is Victor. Next time I'll learn even more.'

Mercy unscrewed the device and looked inside at the tiny recorder hidden below the battery. She had to admit, it was smart. When people go outside for a smoke they're often less discreet in their conversation than they are indoors with the non-smokers. She wondered if he'd bugged many other people this way. Vaping was too recent a phenomenon for this to be a relic of his pre-arrest heyday.

'I'd love something like that,' she said, handing it back to him. 'A lipstick container perhaps.'

'I'll go one better than that,' he nodded. 'I'm going to need help in monitoring his nephew and I'm developing a plan that involves you. Are you comfortable with the idea of wearing a wire?'

Mercy listened to his plan and agreed to it. But she knew he was only involving her to gain access to her dad's phone numbers.

He then told her what Junior Bruno had said on the drive over; that Nick had boasted about killing her dad as he assaulted him during the spin class.

'If I can get footage of that spin incident,' she said with excitement, 'or even an eyewitness account, then we could perhaps use it to convince the police to reopen his case.'

'Nick is telling everyone about this Long Needle call,' Bill explained. 'Including an old bank robber called Bob 'the Feet' Walker. Bob tells Victor whatever he can in exchange for cash and a pat on the head. Before I left, Vic handed me Nick's mobile numbers, which he expects me to bug. I promise you, Mercy,' he continued, 'if we discover any hard evidence that Ray was murdered - and that Victor had something to do with it - then we go straight to the police. Fuck him. Justice for your dad is paramount.'

'Do you think Victor was behind the hit?'

'Absolutely,' Bill said. 'If he wanted his brother dead he

*would* outsource. In those days Victor's men and Lol's men were the same men. Ray was hired to arrange an assassination without mentioning Victor's name.'

'That's a strong motive for arranging for Dad's murder then,' she said. 'Maybe Victor decided he could no longer be trusted with the secret.'

'Or perhaps the hitman killed him,' Bill suggested tapping the steering wheel with his fingers. 'There's a chance that your Long Needle had a grievance. He kills Ray, makes it look like an accident, then tries to manipulate Nick into taking out Victor for him. It's worth considering.'

They both went quiet, thinking their separate thoughts. The Nissan had been parked outside her home for over an hour with the headlights off. It was pitch black outside.

'So, we a team?' she asked.

'It seems so. Now you get a good night's sleep.' He nodded towards her building. 'I'll pick you up first thing. Until then, just stay safe, can't you?'

As she was climbing out of the car, he took her by the arm.

'Nice try, Nancy Drew,' he said, grabbing the pink envelope back with his other hand. 'This stays with me until you've shared those numbers.'

She watched as his car three-point turned away, wondering if she trusted him more or less after today.

# PART IV

*Other Women*

# 27

F*ebruary 20$^{th}$ 2020*

A MAN who resembled Hitchcock was gliding through the streets of Soho as if cameoing in his own movie. He was wearing a tailored suit and also bright orange trainers, making him easy to track through a crowd. Hitch appeared to know where he was going, and it seemed as though he'd walked this route many times in other stolen hours.

Nina had been instructed by Bill to start teaching their new recruit how to perform a two-person tail. The previous day she'd taken Mercy out on an even easier job and had been tasked with reporting back on her progress. It seemed that training up Bill's godchild was now the most crucial challenge facing the agency. It was only Thursday, and Nina was much more curious about the sudden urgency to fast-track Mercy than about wherever the Hitchcock lookalike might be leading them.

Hitch took them to Vegas, a video game arcade in the heart of Soho with a colourful display of hearts, clubs, spades, and diamonds on the front. The two investigators sat and watched him from inside a Starbucks across the street.

'He's the oldest guy in there by about twenty years,' Mercy had observed as she sipped her tea. 'Too much pocket money, that's his problem.'

'And to think,' Nina said as she examined the photos she'd already taken of their client's husband, 'she was worried he was spending her cash on prostitutes.'

Against Nina's advice, Mercy entered the arcade to get a closer look, as Hitch played a zombie shooting game near the back. Their subject was about a foot shorter than her and she'd positioned herself at a nearby machine. Mercy, with her supermodel height, seemed to be too striking a figure not to get clocked by their mark. But fortunately, Hitch was too transfixed with his post-apocalyptic survival adventure to notice her. Soon Mercy exited Vegas and crossed back to Nina. The only intelligence she seemed to have learned from this risky approach was that Hitch sweated profusely as he played but, whenever he won, his jowly face would explode in joy.

'It's a lost youth thing,' Mercy suggested after she'd bought them both another drink. 'He's getting a nostalgia fix in there. I guess that's why most middle-aged people still come to Soho when they don't have to; to remind themselves of a more carefree time.'

Nina found Mercy's attempts at amateur psychology wearisome. It was an investigator's job to uncover hard facts about a person, discover where they went, who they saw and for how long. Observation and exactness were the tenets of the trade. Speculations about what subconscious motives their subjects might have was a professional irrelevance she had little time for.

Mercy's phone buzzed. To Nina's irritation, it was Bill. Typically, if she were performing a two-person tail with Robbie, the boss would contact her but now it seemed that the new girl was the direct line. She studied Mercy's face as they spoke. Something was up.

'Must dash,' Mercy told her after the call. 'Bill needs me.'

'Right now?' Nina asked as Mercy collected her handbag with its replacement strap. 'Is this for the new case? The one he's being secretive about?'

'Not sure,' Mercy shrugged. 'But I'll leave you to it. Sorry.'

'All due respect,' Nina said to her, 'if that's urgent then maybe I should help him. I'm a bit more qualified after all. You stay and watch on the Master of Suspense over there,' she indicated the gaudy exterior of the arcade.

'Speaking of which, he's on the move.'

Nina turned to see that Hitch had left the arcade and was heading up Brewer Street at a brisk pace.

'You better hustle,' Mercy smiled as she zipped up her jacket. 'See you tomorrow.'

'A CLASSIC EXAMPLE OF UNEARNED PRIVILEGE,' Nina's ex sympathised. 'Pure nepotism.'

'She's an obstacle, that's for sure,' Nina said, her voice low enough for their son not to hear.

It was eight thirty the next day and they were stood in the tight hallway of his home. Kyle's father worked weekends, so this was his day to look after him. She was trying to make a speedy exit so she could get to work before Mercy got there. She wanted a chance to speak to Bill alone.

'How long have you been in that shitty place now?' Ian continued. 'Two years? What a waste of time.'

'Cheers for that.'

'I'm saying it's a waste of *you*,' Ian qualified. 'There's been no progression for ages. And now that Tyler's dead, I don't understand what's to be gained.'

Ian had made the initial introduction to Ray, when they'd still been married. Even now they were divorced, he understood how devastating Ray's death had been for her in a way that few others did.

'I get what this is about,' Ian lowered his voice so as not to be heard by four-year-old Kyle watching cartoons in the living room. 'It's about your brother. But, well, Tyler's gone, and he was who mattered, right?'

'The *agency* matters,' she told him. 'At the end of last year I was making strides. But I was Ray's girl. I don't have that same relationship with Bill and now, with Mercy here…'

'There's nothing of value at M&T anymore,' Ian told her.

'Look, I don't need all this,' Nina said as she made for the door. 'Just try not to give him so much sugar this time, yeah? You're not the one who has to get him to sleep at night.'

She was agitated during the drive to Southwark but, as her car neared the office, she attempted to pull herself together. She practised how to phrase her complaint; that Bill had been overlooking her career-wise and that it wasn't fair for Mercy to be the one working the bigger cases when she'd been there longer. Ray had begun to trust her with sensitive clients, she'd point out, and it felt as though she'd taken a step back since his death.

However, when she eventually entered the M&T office neither Bill nor Mercy were there. Barbara was typing something and there was a small vase with pansies on her already cluttered desk.

'*Mercedes* is still trying to worm her way into my affections,' Barbara remarked by way of explanation as she pushed her computer's mouse around its matt. 'She thinks that if she buys me muffins and flowers, I'll start gossiping like we're old pals. Fat chance.'

Nina removed her coat and looked at the time. It wasn't even a quarter past nine. Through an open door she could see Robbie wearing earphones and toiling over a new laptop.

'Has Bill been in yet?'

'He's working from home,' Barbara replied without much energy. 'Again.'

Disappointed, Nina moved to the kitchenette and noticed that the old photograph of Ray, Victor and company had been removed. Only the Union Jack magnet remained on the fridge door, which was now held shut with masking tape. She opened it and pulled out a bottle of water.

'She hasn't inherited Ray's work ethic,' Barbara huffed, her eyes fixed on the screen. 'Madam told me that she was off to the gym. Let's hope she stays there.'

'She's supposed to be working with Bill, right?' Nina asked, pouring herself a glass of water, 'on some new case. What's that about, you reckon?'

'Couldn't tell you,' Barbara answered in a tone that suggested that she wouldn't if she could. Nina crossed over and sat on the leather settee reserved for clients.

'It must be for one of their *special* clients,' she said, during a pause in Barbara's typing. 'Those mystery benefactors you're always alluding to.' Barbara said nothing but began typing again. 'Do you think he'd ever involve her in that sort of business? I mean, could Mercy end up dealing with someone like – oh, I don't know – Victor Neale? Because I can't see—'

'Don't *you* start!' Barbara demanded, stopping abruptly. 'I've had enough from *her* this morning, pestering me with questions. I don't need the third degree from you.'

'Alright Barb,' Nina sat up straighter. 'I didn't realise I was getting on your nerves.'

'I don't care to be cross-examined,' the secretary continued. 'I've enough on my plate, with all these forms piling up. I don't need people keeping on about matters that, as far as I'm concerned, are long buried.'

'Jesus, I'm sorry. I was only making conversation.'

Barbara slumped and, to her amazement, Nina realised that she was about to cry. There was a box of tissues on the desk that weren't normally there.

'It's not you,' Barbara said and reached for one of the tissues. 'It's *Mercy*. She was grilling me about that phone call her dad overheard. The one that almost cost me my job. I suppose *you* told her about that.'

'I'm no gossip,' Nina said, guessing that Robbie would have been the source on Barbara's infamous bitching session. 'Did she have a go at you about it?'

'No, it's all sweetness and light with that one, which gets on my tits even more. What d'you call it when someone smiles and pretends to be your mate as they stick in the knife?'

'Passive-aggressive.'

'That's it,' Barbara sniffed into a tissue. 'Well, I prefer aggressive-aggressive. Give me a stand-up row any day. But what can I do? She's a Tyler, her names on the door.'

'It can't have been that bad,' Nina said in a *there there* voice. She got up from the settee as Barbara wiped her eyes with the tissue. Nina went over and rubbed her back in a consoling fashion.

'She wanted details about the suicide at the Spoils,' Barbara said, her throat starting to convulse. 'She knows I was one of the witnesses and was asking for every morbid detail!'

'Sarah Neale, you mean?'

Until now, Nina had never heard Barbara speak of that horrific incident when Victor's wife had thrown herself off of the top floor balcony in front of almost a dozen witnesses, including Barbara. She gently prodded for more.

'We were there to celebrate Maggie Neale's birthday, of all the jokes,' Barbara elaborated, her hands flying in between tissue dabs. 'She was turning fifty. It was this little summer party held in the grounds – all women. There was bunting, for fuck's sake. It'd been less than a month since Maggie's husband had exploded in that car bomb and they hadn't even arrested the McAlonan boy yet. The idea was to cheer her up.'

'Was Sarah close to Lol's wife then?' Nina asked.

'Not remotely. The Neale wives hated each other. There was bad blood between them because of all the rumours.'

'What rumours?'

'Well, if you don't know I'm not telling you,' Barbara said. The drawbridge had been pulled up again.

'Come on, Barb,' Nina persisted. 'Tell me what you told Mercy. I know my name isn't on the door, but...'

'I told her that Ray had been cross with me for slagging off his wife,' Barbara spoke rapidly. 'But she wanted to know what had upset him specifically. So I told her. I'd been complaining about Julie because of how she handled things after the suicide. I felt it was disrespectful to the dead.'

'How so?'

'We were all in shock,' Barbara's head bowed as she spoke. 'But as soon as the ambulance was called Julie started bossing us about. Spinning lies before Sarah had even been declared dead.'

'You mean she was asking you to lie to the ambulance crew? To the police?'

'Don't be daft,' Barbara shrugged. 'It was obvious to them what had happened.'

'What was she concealing then?' asked Nina, moving around to face her. 'What did Ray find out from that phone call that he didn't already know?'

Barbara's swivel chair shifted inches away.

'Just the state of Sarah that morning. How drugged up she was. Now,' she turned her chair again to face Nina, 'that's as much as I told Mercy and it's as much as I'm telling you. So why don't you stop pretending to be my friend and get back to work.'

Nina stared back for a few hard seconds. Then she moved away from the desk and went into Robbie's office where he still had his earphones on, seemingly oblivious to all else. She collected the small file on her current case, gathered the camera equipment and stepped back into the outer office where the typing was again reaching incredible speeds.

'Barb, neither of us is a Mance or a Tyler,' she said after placing her coat back on. 'This isn't your agency any more than it's mine. Maybe remember that and don't treat me like I'm your problem.'

Barbara's smile suggested little worker solidarity. 'Oh, I know how I fit in, love,' she said with a trace of threat. 'And just because I'm not one of you investigators doesn't mean I'm blind to what goes on.'

'Meaning what?'

'Just that I find it rather rich,' Barbara explained, 'you complaining about the new girl and the boss forming a little gang of two. Next thing, they'll be meeting up for after work drinks in The Blue-eyed Maid, finding themselves a dark corner and whispering while they think no one's watching.'

Nina was stunned to realise what Barbara was implying. She then realised that Barbara probably knew the regulars in The Blue-eyed Maid.

'Our Ray was always carrying on with other women,' Barbara informed her. 'It'd be enough to make you pity his poor wife, if she wasn't such a slag herself.'

'You've got it wrong, Barb,' Nina pointed a finger but kept her voice low. She definitely didn't want Robbie hearing this. 'My relationship with Ray was only ever professional.'

'Let me play Emily Maitlis for once,' Barbara interrupted, lacing her fingers together. 'It's only fair, considering that I've spent the morning under interrogation.'

'I don't need to explain myself—'

'Where were you on the night that Ray died?'

'I beg your pardon?'

'You heard. When they fished him out of that river he'd been AWOL for days. So had you.'

'My little boy was sick,' Nina replied, her voice sounding as close to a hiss as the human throat could. 'He had the measles and a high temperature and I wasn't about to leave him alone before Christmas. Ask Bill; he read the doctor's note. I don't know where Ray was before he took the plunge but he wasn't with me.'

'Well, if I knew Ray, he was with someone and it wasn't his wife,' Barbara taunted. She produced a tin of powdered travel sweets that she reserved for special moments from her desk drawer. 'There was always another woman involved in his lost weekends.'

'I don't care who his final fuck was,' Nina insisted. 'Because Ray and I weren't sleeping together.'

The secretary unscrewed the tin of rhubarb and custard flavoured sweets.

'You can see a lot from the top deck of a bus,' she said, after taking a sniff of them. 'Ray getting out of your car up a side road in the morning. You arriving to work fifteen minutes later, trying to make it look like you'd come in separately.'

'Some nights he stayed on my sofa bed. Nothing in it, but we were keen not to set tongues wagging. Might as well not have bothered.'

'Then there was that phone call *I* overheard,' continued Barbara, as she carefully selected one of the sweets. 'Bill was out on a case and Ray was drunk again, on the phone to you, saying *I need you Neen, I need you now.*' Barbara's impression of their inebriated boss was horribly accurate.

'I was his employee,' Nina tried not blink as she defended herself. 'What's so remarkable about that?'

'Nothing,' said Barbara, raising the chosen sweet up to her lips. 'Except he was found dead days later and it sounded like you *were* going to meet him.' She popped the sweet into her mouth and began to suck. 'Which surprises me,' she added with her mouth full, 'considering how ill your little boy supposedly was.'

'Go fuck yourself,' Nina said, before slamming the door behind her, loud enough for Robbie to hear through his headphones.

Barbara sucked harder on her sweet and felt a rare surge of happiness. It turned out she could do passive-aggressive after all.

# 28

About four miles away, behind a different desk, Gemma Bolton's bored eyes drifted toward the same live feed on which she'd first seen Nick Neale enter the gym two weeks earlier. She'd spent the morning squirting cleaning products onto the many cross trainers and wiping the sweat off them, and was dismayed to realise that it wasn't even ten o'clock yet.

On the screen in front of her she saw a tall, black-haired woman from behind coming down the staircase from the street above. As with Nick, she could immediately tell that this would be no ordinary visitor even from a fleeting image. The woman was wearing a leather jacket, jeans, and boots but had no sports bag. She was moving with a purpose, as if she too had come looking for a confrontation. However, the young woman made a much better impression when she appeared down in the gym itself. She smiled at Gemma through the glass as she realised that the entrance required a fingerprint ID. Gemma rushed out from behind the reception desk and allowed her access to Deptford Meantime.

'Cheers Gemma,' said the woman. 'You're a star.'

For one slow moment Gemma forgot that she was wearing a nametag on her Meantime brand shirt.

'What am I like?' she laughed and then invited the woman, who'd come to talk about potential membership, to the reception area to explain about their exciting new discounts. She handed her all the relevant leaflets and, as she began babbling about their opening hours and range of classes, she found herself struck by how beautiful this woman was. She had extraordinary ice-blue eyes and the style of some cool rock chick you might meet if you blagged your way into the VIP section of a festival. In other words, Gemma thought, she's exactly my type.

'Call me Mercy,' said the woman when asked for her name, and went on to explain that she'd just moved back to the area and had heard good things about their spin classes. 'Am I right in saying Junior Bruno still works here?'

'Sometimes,' Gemma told her. 'But he's taken some time off right now. He's a friend of mine though,' Gemma lied. 'It's a friendly place!'

'Just what I need,' smiled Mercy. 'Are you going to give me the grand tour or what?'

Gemma was wearing a fitness tracker on her wrist. Later that day it informed her that her heart rate had increased a discernible degree during her encounter with Mercy. She proceeded to show her around but, on this occasion, she found herself becoming acutely aware of what a horrible place the gym was. Sweat, both new and old, had invaded the air and Gemma was annoyed at herself for having gotten used to it. As she led her past the out-of-service rowing machines she worried that it all appeared too shabby. She continued trying to impress Mercy though and spoke about the planned renovations that she didn't really believe would happen.

'Where are the spin classes held?' Mercy interrupted her.

'Right here,' Gemma replied and took her into the empty studio.

The first thing Mercy remarked upon when they entered was all the violent black marks in the centre of the floor. The exercise bike that Junior Bruno had been riding had fallen with him during the Nick Neale attack and had badly scarred the rubber flooring as it had been dragged around during the conflict.

'What's happened here?' Mercy asked as she inspected the damage.

'There was an incident recently' Gemma bit her lip. 'An upset, we're calling it. But the floor won't be like that when you next come, if you do.'

'Hang on,' Mercy said, her smile widening. 'The mate of mine who recommended this place, the one who told me about Junior Bruno working here, she told me about some punch up that happened. Something to do with Lawrence Neale's son, she said. Are these marks from that?'

'Well,' Gemma said with a little smirk, 'I'm not at liberty to say.'

'Why not?'

'Management wouldn't care for it.'

'Go on, Gem,' Mercy appealed to her, 'I love a bit of drama.'

Gemma glanced over to the mirrored walls as if considering whether she should betray the confidence of the gym, but she already knew that she would for this hot girl. The reflection of them standing next to each other was nice and she wondered if they looked like a plausible couple. Yes, she eventually decided, they very much did.

'It happened on Valentine's day,' she began in a conspiratorial whisper, and continued to relay the whole shocking incident as she remembered it, including how a former employee of the gym had helped Nick Neale ambush Junior.

'I watched the whole thing through the window.'

'So you didn't hear what was being said?'

'Not a word,' Gemma replied. 'I was too terrified to go in.'

'Sure, sure, it sounds distressing. I see there's a camera up there though,' Mercy pointed at the small CCTV in the ceiling corner. 'Did that catch anything?'

'Um, I don't think they were switched on. It's a very safe gym most of the time,' Gemma assured her. 'It's the only time anything like that's happened since I've been working here.'

'Sure, but what about camera phones?'

'People tend not to bring their phones to a class,' Gemma said, although she was growing a bit suspicious about why Mercy was asking. 'Someone did film it all though,' she added. 'Roz Stern, the girlfriend I told you about. She had a camera running throughout the whole fight.'

'Why was she filming it?'

'Because she's as cracked as her boyfriend.'

Soon after that Mercy went to leave despite Gemma's attempts to keep her chatting. She seemed keen to take some cards about the various trainers who worked there which was encouraging. Gemma handed Mercy more leaflets, each one detailing a different reason why Meantime was the only worthwhile gym in London.

'Deptford's the best branch though,' Gemma smiled as she tapped the sensor with her card to open the glass doors again. 'It's the one with Yours Truly in it!' She immediately regretted saying that.

'You've been very helpful, Gemma,' Mercy smiled back, 'if I do join a gym, it'll definitely be this one. Maybe see you again.'

'I'd like that.'

Once the partition was closed between them Gemma thought how nice it would be to see Mercy regularly. She returned to her place behind the reception desk and glanced at the live feed of the staircase that Mercy was still walking up. She watched as Mercy reached the top of the stairs where a small litterbin was placed nearby.

Then she saw her dump the leaflets straight into it and knew she'd never see her again.

# 29

Even pretending that she might join a gym owned by the odious Victor Neale had been a stretch on Mercy's limited acting ability. However, her visit to this branch of his business empire had proven fruitful. Emerging back onto the street, she breathed in the wintry air and inspected the one item that she'd spared from the bin; a card advertising the services of Rosalind Stern: Personal Trainer.

She'd seen police mug shots with more charm than was displayed on that sharp-cheeked, unsmiling PT profile. Rosalind's dirty blonde hair was pulled back so tightly on her reddened forehead that it looked like part of some pain endurance exercise. According to the card she took classes in Muay Thai, Brazilian jiu jitsu and mixed martial arts. Mercy wondered how she'd do in an even contest against Rosalind, should the situation ever arise.

She slipped the card into her wallet, keen to get to Bill's house to share her findings with him. According to Gemma, this Rosalind person had visual evidence on her phone of the incident during which Nick had reportedly boasted of killing her father. Mercy was already planning ways to get hold of the video as she headed in the direction of a bus stop.

Now that she was at street level again she noticed she'd received a text while underground from an unidentified number. She tapped the screen to reveal it. When the message appeared, she had to slow down in order to take it in.

**Porsche is in a driveway off Rafferty Road SE10. The property owner would appreciate its removal, thank you.**

Mercy paused outside a shut-down second-hand vinyl shop. Leaning against the locked door she tried to figure out who'd sent this to her. It had not come from any of the saved contacts in her dad's phone. This text was from an unfamiliar number and when she tried to call it back, she found it blocked.

Excitement coursed through her. Surely this was a response to her Send All question about the missing car. And if whoever this was knew its whereabouts, then they'd know a lot more besides. Unfortunately, Ray's second mobile was not a smart phone so she couldn't trace the mystery number or find the address on Google maps. Continuing onwards, she called someone who might help.

'Robbie, I need a favour and fast,' she told him as he answered. 'I've had an anonymous text sent to my phone and I want to find the caller. It's for a case,' she added not wanting to divulge further details.

'Send it over,' he said between yawns. Robbie had already helped her trace three of the contacts on her dad's phone and she'd been able to rule out all of them from being the hitman. She'd briefly suspected Matt Wren, Bill's old tabloid nemesis. But she'd ruled him out after listening to him on a true crime podcast, as his Liverpool accent sounded nothing like the killer she'd heard speaking in her family home. That left five mystery contacts still unaccounted for.

'If I get any info,' Robbie asked after receiving it, 'am I sending it to you or Bill?'

'Me,' she insisted. 'Bill's got enough on his plate. Cheers.'

At the bus stop she considered if she should go straight to Rafferty Road now and collect the Porsche. That way, she could examine it and its location for clues before anyone else got to it. But, if she did that, she'd have to tell Bill what she was doing and she was reluctant to share her discovery just yet. For now, she'd head, as per his instructions, to his address in Denmark Hill. He was working Victor's case from home, away from the other M&T staff.

When she alighted from the bus at Surrey Quays she noticed she'd had another voicemail. This one had come from an unaccounted number on her father's phone, saved under the contact **OG**. She stood on the train platform, listened to the message, and recognised the sober female voice.

'Hello Mercy, DCI Helen Bracken here,' said the policewoman. 'I hope this is the right number to reach you on. I've only just learnt that you were recently attacked and had your phone stolen which possibly explains why you haven't been returning my calls.'

Mercy frowned. She'd been trying to contact Bracken on a regular basis ever since their brief chat in Lewisham police station but hadn't received much response. So to hear Bracken now tell it like she'd been the one trying to reach out was unconvincing. Her phone had only been stolen a week ago.

'I hope you're recovering well. I know how traumatic these experiences can be,' the DCI said with a note of practised sympathy. 'I'd like to meet you later today if that's possible. For an update into what you've learnt about your father's death. You can reach me on this number.'

Mercy stepped onto a train. She was unsure how she felt about police interest in her investigation now. Her initial plan had been to cast enough suspicion on her dad's death for the police to reopen the case and that, she'd thought, would be enough. But now she bridled at the thought of handing her hard-earned leads over to the police when they'd made no progress themselves. She was starting to think she could find his killer independently.

Still, there was more to be gained from engaging with Bracken than from ignoring her, so she put aside such truculence and called her back. She answered on the second ring.

'Helen, my dear,' began Mercy brightly. 'I'm glad you've called. I've missed our little chats.'

'Yes, I've been meaning to touch base with you for a while now, Mercy. I'm curious to know what you might have for me.'

'Have for *you?*' Mercy replied with an undisguised edge. 'I was hoping it might be the other way round. Any clue as to who killed my dad yet?'

Sat across from Mercy a middle-aged lady reading a book about Jesus glanced in her direction.

'I think you know that his death wasn't returned as murder,' Bracken replied. 'But when we last spoke you expressed a willingness to keep me informed about anything you might discover that could shed light on his demise.'

'What are you expecting me to have found, I wonder?'

'I mentioned I was interested in learning more about your late father's dealings with certain clients,' Bracken's tone remained firm. 'And you were prepared to tell me if you discovered anything. Has that changed?'

'Actually I have discovered one interesting lead,' Mercy whispered. 'You're still a contact in Dad's phone. But rather than having you listed as Helen or DCI Bracken he has this number registered as OG. What does that stand for? Original Gangsta?'

'Old Granny probably,' Bracken laughed.

'Seems secretive to me.'

'Well, your father was a secretive man. Perhaps we could meet up in person to discuss this more fully?'

Mercy's gaze was fixed upon an advert above the window for headache tablets. 'To be honest, I'm busy at the moment,' she said. 'And I'm not really sure what's in it for me.'

'Meaning?'

'I'm still looking into things regarding to my dad. Every day I'm discovering more about him. But to be frank, I'd prefer it if you'd report to me with some news.'

'You sound agitated. Is this a bad time?'

'The exchange of information in this relationship strikes me as unequal,' Mercy elaborated as the train continued onwards. 'I feel *you're* holding things back. If this isn't an official investigation then I'm under no obligation to share with you my findings.'

'So you *have* made some findings?' Bracken said.

A new text came through. Robbie.

**Got zip on that number. Burner phone. Soz mate**

'Oh, I'm making all sorts of inroads,' Mercy said, returning the ear to her phone. 'I'm about to bust this case wide open.'

'I wish you'd be more specific,' Bracken persisted. 'I could also be available tomorrow or on the weekend.'

'You're cracking up, Helen,' Mercy apologised as the train approached her stop. 'I'm about to go under a tunnel. Speak later.'

She hung up on the policewoman.

# 30

As a child Mercy had visited the Mance family home many times. Back then Chez Mance was over-spilling with books, vinyl records, pets and unruly pot plants. Lisa was growing her own vegetables in the garden and they had a beautiful French bulldog which they'd named, in a witty reference to Bill's profession, Sam Spayed.

But that had been during his family man days. Now he lived in a neat single person's apartment on the second floor of a new-build. He'd been forced to sell his former home following his release from prison and subsequent divorce. There was no dog anymore, no garden, just basic furnishings and no plants. He'd sold his vintage Motown collection on eBay years ago. The only relic she recognised from that time was a small oval picture of the Virgin Mary. Here it was again, positioned above the kitchen door, and it surprised Mercy. She'd always attributed the icon to Bill's wife who wore a cross around her neck and was more openly religious than her husband.

'Are you expecting anyone else?' she asked Bill in his

narrow kitchen as he was producing some teabags from the cupboard. She'd moved over to the far window that was still dirty from yesterday's rain. It overlooked the street below and she was convinced she'd recognised a car as she'd walked up from the station.

'You're the only person I'm trusting with this job,' he replied, fetching milk from the fridge. 'Why?'

'It's nothing,' she shrugged and turned from the window. 'Following people around with Nina must be making me paranoid.'

An estate agent would've described Bill's kitchen as compact. Whenever one of them moved they had to squeeze past the other.

'How did you take to the tail?' he asked, pouring out her tea. 'On Wednesday Nina told me you were almost a natural.'

'Almost?'

'She claims you did a fantastic job of keeping track of the marks, staying close when you needed to, giving them distance as wisdom demanded. She was impressed,' he said as he handed her the mug. 'Or at least as impressed as our Nina ever gets.'

'What were the criticisms then?' Mercy said, blowing on the brew.

'She said some onlookers clocked you.'

'Clocked me?'

'Noticed you following the mark,' he clarified. 'It wasn't a big deal but she says you drew attention at certain points. You were behaving like an actor in a film pretending to tail someone. And anyone watching you watching the mark would've seen that.'

Embarrassment prickled as she remembered her first professional attempt at a one-person tail. Nina had given her the simple task of following a woman on her way to work on the Jubilee Line. Mercy had stepped into a separate carriage of the train and watched her through the intervening windows until she got off. At the time, Mercy had considered this to be subtle stuff, but Nina had been further down, monitoring her performance. In her report, she'd described how some passengers had noticed her giving off, according to Nina, *stalker vibes* as she tracked her mark.

'It's a rookie error and we've all done it,' Bill consoled her. 'You'll get better with practice. Speaking of which,' he indicated to follow him into a different room, 'let's discuss how best to monitor young master Neale.'

Bill's tall body had been obscuring the fridge door until then and it was only as he moved away that Mercy noticed something familiar. There were a number of postcards and photographs stuck to the front and one of these, on first glance, looked like the photo stuck to the mini-fridge at the office showing her father, Victor and Bill on a golfing day. Once Bill had moved through to the hallway Mercy was able to examine it properly. Although it captured another beautiful sunny day with a similar line up, it was of a different occasion.

'When was this taken?' she called over to Bill, wondering why she'd linked the two images in her mind.

'When was what taken?'

'This photo with my mum and dad in,' Mercy pointed at the ensemble. 'You all look fantastic.'

There were five figures in the picture and they were all dressed smartly for summer, with a white marquee behind them. Her parents looked young and happy but were positioned at opposite ends of the quintet. She could hear her father's dirty laugh just by looking at him and his arm was around another woman. Bill was in the middle looking as awkward as he often did at social gatherings.

'Victor's fortieth birthday,' Bill informed her from the doorway. 'It was a memorable evening. His brother arrived at the Spoils by helicopter.'

'Yeah, Dad told me about that. And this is Sarah of course,' she noted, recognising the stunning woman in the blue dress who her dad was making laugh. 'He seems to have taken a shine to her.'

'Your old man loved to flirt,' Bill agreed.

But the really interesting thing about the photograph was who wasn't in it. There had originally been six people, but somebody had been snipped out. A white jacket sleeve was visible on the far right next to where her mother was, his arm linked in hers. She was certain that the edited party had to be the birthday boy.

'Why isn't Victor in this?' Mercy asked.

'He was taking the photo I think.'

Mercy turned to see if he was serious because it was obvious that Victor had been removed. Bill was stood in the doorway underneath his plastic icon of the Virgin Mary and said nothing. Bill clearly hated M&T's criminal benefactor, he'd not bothered to conceal it over the past few days, but to have a photo in your home of *Victor's birthday* only with the man himself removed seemed weird. There was her dad with his arm around Sarah's waist, while Victor's visible arm was entwined with Julie's. And Bill was in the centre of it all next to his ex-wife Moira. What was this photo for?

'Shall we crack on?' Bill said, beckoning her through. 'Clock's ticking.'

The curtains in Bill's living room were pulled shut despite it being midday. He switched on the lights to reveal a sizeable whiteboard covering the far wall but didn't elaborate on how it had ended up there. Overuse had turned the board a scratchy grey but it could still display photographs, maps, and financial records. While Mercy had been learning the tail from Nina, Bill had begun a preliminary surveillance of Nick and his associates as they went about their day. The resulting photographs were now stuck to the top half of the board with small silver magnets. Mercy approached the images to see if she'd recognise her old school bully in adult form and, as she saw him, a long-held repulsion stirred within. Even after years of therapy, you never forget your first tormentor.

The clearest photo of Nick showed him at a petrol station filling up a black Range Rover that, with its tinted windows and black hubcaps, might as well have had DRUG DEALER as a number plate. He was wearing a purple Puffa jacket, matching beanie, and some wraparound shades even though there'd been no sun for months.

Part of the original reason she'd asked her dad for karate lessons was so she could defend herself against Nick's attacks. From an early age she'd endured his taunting but, as they'd grown older, the threat became more physical. On one afternoon, Nick had cornered her alone in the changing rooms while the rest of the class were out on the pitch. They were both half-dressed and he was whipping her with his towel. She tried to run but he grabbed her by the wrist and pressed her hard against the lockers. The experience was sickening and it was unclear what he wanted as he held her against her will. '*Why are you such a girl, Christopher?*' he'd sneer, as if it were her fault that he wanted to touch her so much. When the other boys came clattering in, football shirts muddy from the game, Nick released her in a guilty second and stomped out before anyone else could spot the erection through his shorts.

She'd never told her parents about Nick's behaviour. Her dad was too involved with the Neale gang, and she feared if he lost his temper with Lol's son, there'd be nasty consequences.

Deliverance had come in the form of a crime. Nick had broken into the school tuck shop when he should've been in an exam and stolen over £200 in coins and a box of Lion bars. But, whereas the Neale brothers had been made rich by their robberies, all Nick had ultimately earned was a swift expulsion. She remembered him standing in the middle of the quad on his last day, shouting that he was going to come back and "kill the grass" who'd informed the headmaster that the stolen Lion bars could be found in his locker. She wondered if he'd even suspected that the informant had been her.

'That's Dan Beesley,' she told Bill, pointing at a photo of another young man in a baggy tracksuit who was shuffling toddler-like behind Nick. Bill's long lens had captured Dan with his head bent over so his face was hard to make out underneath a gold-lined cap. But Mercy recognised him from his servile body language towards his friend. 'He also got expelled. In his case for keying the word *Paedo* onto a teacher's car bonnet. I think he spelt it wrong.'

'This one,' said Bill, pointing at a third photo of an older, lank-haired man licking a tobacco skin on the forecourt, 'is called Bob Walker. Bob the Feet, they call him; a former armed robber and an old crony of Nick's dad. He's been inside countless times and now appears to be working as Nick's gopher. He drives the Range Rover when the lads are too high. As I've previously mentioned, he's also the person telling Victor about the anonymous calls.'

The only other person in Bill's photos was a scowling

young woman with whom Nick was seen quarrelling outside his home.

'Rosalind Stern,' Mercy revealed and showed him the personal trainer card she'd obtained an hour earlier. 'And get this,' she added as Bill placed the card underneath the photo he'd taken, 'according to my source at the gym, she was filming the fight between Nick and Junior. If that's true, there could be hard evidence of Nick talking about my dad's murder.'

'Good to know,' Bill nodded.

On a round coffee table in the centre of the room was an old phone scanner, a bowl full of bugging devices, and a dog-eared handbook on how to locate individual mobiles via mast.

'I haven't hacked a phone since 2011,' he told her, as she flicked through the book about obsolete tech. 'Back in my day, we'd access a voicemail if we had the phone's PIN, which was usually on a factory setting. A bit of blagging to the relevant phone companies and we were in like sin.' He seemed impressed by his former audacity. 'Nowadays the security on smart phones is radically tighter. But I've been in touch with some colleagues who've kept up with things and I should have Nick's phone bugged by this time tomorrow.'

He stepped back to survey his whiteboard. The only other photo showed an older woman wearing a garish pink fascinator on her head. The hat suggested she was at a wedding even if her snarl would've blended in better under an C18th gallows.

'Nick's mum Maggie,' Bill said as he drew an arrow between this picture and her son. 'Or as she's still known in underworld quarters, The Cleaning Lady. She lives in Vegas now and is the answer to the question of where he gets his money. He's spending like an oil baron but doesn't seem to have a job, legal or otherwise.'

'She's funnelling funds to him?'

'Has to be,' Bill spoke with a harsh edge, 'I've followed drug dealers before, and the successful ones tend to be more industrious than this lazy shit.'

'He bugs you, doesn't he?'

'Nick's a loser who's forever being told he's a winner by other losers,' Bill nodded. 'He wants to be thought of as a gangster, but, unlike real gangsters, he's never needed the money. Maggie subsidises him through snaky channels so it's all posturing without the work ethic. He's benefitting from the graft, brains, and balls of his elders. No wonder Victor resents him.'

A silence followed. She wondered if he'd ever held similar opinions about her inheriting the agency. While in Barcelona she'd accepted subsidies from her dad although they weren't speaking. Bill would've known that and she hated to think that, in his eyes, she and Nick were part of the same ungrateful generation.

'Of course Victor already knows where the money's coming from,' Bill remarked after finishing his tea. 'He just wants to find out what stupid thing his nephew intends to do next. Most importantly, he wants to know the identity of this mystery caller who's been winding Nick up.' He turned to face her. 'Are you sure you want to do this, Mercy? If you want to back out, I'll understand.'

'Courage,' she answered, putting her jacket back on, 'is in my factory setting.'

'In that case,' he smiled, 'let's go shopping.'

Bill went to use the bathroom while she took their empty mugs back to the kitchen. There she approached the photo of Victor's fortieth birthday again. It had initially reminded her of the golf day photo in the M&T office but now she realised the two summery images were otherwise quite different.

An electric thought suddenly occurred. She realised what had initially caught her attention and it wasn't the photo itself. Mercy stared at the fridge and tried to make sense of her quick epiphany.

But, from the hallway, Bill was calling for her to hurry along.

# 31

From above a red unnumbered door, a discreet camera was pointing straight at Bill and Mercy. After pressing the doorbell, Bill gave the camera a subtle salute.

'You have to phone ahead with Alan,' he said as they waited to be allowed in. 'He keeps odd hours.'

3rd Eye Electronics, the once thriving retail empire of disgraced policeman Alan McColl, now had only one branch left. It was situated, with unplanned irony, above a branch of Specsavers. From the high street an A-board displaying the 3rd Eye logo was the only thing helping prospective customer identify the entrance and it gave instructions to look for the narrow door squeezed between the opticians and a computer repair shop.

The door buzzed open. A corridor with sickly yellow walls led them towards a staircase that seemed to get thinner as you climbed. Only one unshaded bulb dangling from the ceiling provided any light. Mercy counted two more cameras pointing at them before they came to another door with yet another bell.

'I'm loving the Orwellian aesthetic,' she said, as they waited for the door to be opened, 'but it can't encourage passing trade. Is he trying to go bust?'

'Most of Alan's business is online now,' Bill told her. 'I don't think he likes customer-facing transactions much.'

'I'm not surprised, considering most of his customers are probably peeping toms.'

A pretty young woman that Mercy immediately recognised as Kittichai McColl opened the door. Alan had married the sweet Thai girl during a holiday in Pattaya after knowing her for less than a fortnight. She'd been in her late teens then, just a few years older than herself, and Mercy remembered feeling uncomfortable about it. The idea of marrying any of her dad's friends – and especially Alan! – was gross and she'd assumed that Kittichai must've been sold into marriage or something. But here she still was, fifteen years later, smiling with delight and giving Bill a big hug. She hadn't aged much. Her black hair was pulled back into a ponytail and she was wearing a small blue polo shirt with the 3rd Eye logo on the breast pocket. Her hug seemed to take Bill by surprise, but then he often became flustered when people behaved affectionately toward him.

'Hello Kitty,' he said. 'Lovely to see you again. This is Mercy.'

'Nice to meet you,' she said without a flicker of recognition.

'We've met before,' Mercy corrected her with a smile. 'Loads of times.'

'This is Ray's kid,' Bill explained. 'His daughter.'

Kittichai allowed them to cross the threshold into the shop, her forehead creasing in confusion. 'Ray?' she asked, closing the door after them. 'He didn't have a daughter?'

'He did but didn't know it,' Mercy explained, keen to see

her expression change as the penny dropped. 'At the time he thought he had a son.'

Surprise – big and bright – burst onto Kittichai's face.

'Wow!' she laughed and threw her arms out in congratulation. 'You became a girl!'

'It's good to see you too,' Mercy laughed back, accepting the hug.

'You look *amazing,*' said Kitty, pulling back to take a better look. 'What name again?'

'Mercy.'

'Like pray for mercy?'

'That's it,' she nodded. 'Short for Mercedes.'

'Cool name.'

'Thanks,' Mercy replied. 'I've been waiting for someone to say that.'

During this exchange Bill drifted further into the showroom to examine the products displayed behind glass cases. State-of-the-art drones, nanny cams, GPS vehicle tracking systems, hidden camera detectors and other gadgets were locked in, as if they were priceless jewels. The top half of a mannequin stood in the corner of the room wearing a blast proof vest and night vision goggles.

'Is your old man back there, Kitty?' Bill asked, nodding towards an open door at the far end of the store. 'Hiding away like some seedy Wizard of Oz?'

'I don't mind *seedy,*' a rough voice called out from the backroom, 'but a bit less of the *old,* if you please.'

Although hitherto concealed, Alan had clearly been monitoring their arrival. He now emerged through the far door wearing a blue polo shirt that matched his wife's, except his was XXL. Mercy had last seen him at her dad's funeral where he failed to offer her his condolences despite having known her since birth. He was still a heavy man, although less pink in the face nowadays. His cheeks sagged like a cartoon dog and what little hair he had was grey and stubbly. He was wearing an extraordinary pair of glasses that made his eyes appear grotesquely huge. He removed the thick-lenses and strode towards Bill.

'A rare visit from the main man!' Alan laughed as they patted each other on the back. 'We're honoured. You usually send whatshername down, so this must be a special occasion.'

'Her name's Nina,' Bill nodded. 'And I fancied getting out of the office for a change. Good excuse to visit an old mate.'

'Someone's after a discount,' Alan rolled his eyes and laughed. When he turned toward Mercy his smile became less natural.

'I see you've joined the family firm at last, Chrissy,' he said as his body leaned forward so they could shake hands. 'Your dad would be chuffed.'

'She's called Mercy now!' Kitty corrected him.

'Righty ho,' nodded Alan, as if only now being made aware of this development. 'Well, that's fine by me. As it happens, we've got some lady-boys in the family, haven't we Kitty? On her side obviously.'

'That explains why you're so comfortable with us,' Mercy said, noticing that he hadn't yet once looked her in the eye. Alan appeared to miss the sarcasm.

'Tell me you're getting back into the bugging game, Billy Boy,' he turned back to Bill with a hungry grin. 'You were always the master eavesdropper.'

'I never left,' Bill replied, as he studied some night vision binoculars. A sign on the shelf warned **TOUCH IF YOU MUST. PAY IF YOU BUST.**

'You know what I mean,' Alan persisted. 'I'm not talking

about these play-it-safe operations you give to the minions. I'm talking proper spy craft – custom made gadgets, creative solutions, camera-in-the-bowtie work. You were like 007 back in the day.'

'In which Bond film,' Bill said in a weary tone as he held the binoculars up to his eye, 'was he sent to prison?'

'Oh *that,*' Alan's right arm waved away the months Bill had spent at Her Majesty's Pleasure. 'A long forgotten red card, unfairly presented to a superb player during an otherwise stellar career.' He turned back to Mercy, nodding his head towards Bill. 'Has this one told you about the Bag of Nails pub?' he asked. 'Oh, that was blinding.'

'That was a different age, Alan,' Bill said, returning the binoculars firmly to their place. 'We don't need to bore the ladies with that last century stuff.'

'The Bag of Nails is just round the back of Buckingham Palace,' Alan proceeded regardless. 'It's a tourist pub and generally busy of an evening. Anyway, there was this group of palace staffers who'd frequent it every Friday, for an after-work pint and a grumble about their lot. In particular, a couple of footmen and some press office girls – just a bunch of workmates unwinding after a long week. But Bugger Bill over there learns about them and they pique his interest. He makes it his business to get into the pub on a late afternoon, buys himself a pint and a paper and sits at their favourite spot, saving it. He waits until they all come in and then gets up and leaves, certain that they'll sit in his vacated place. Only he's left a few little toys behind, ain't that right, Bilbo?'

Bill was pretending to inspect some telescopes that were propped up by the windows. At Alan's prompting he looked over to Mercy with a sheepish expression.

'I'd placed a few listening devices underneath the table,

that's all,' he elaborated. 'He's making it sound cleverer than it was.'

'With chewing gum!' Alan wheezed with uncontainable delight. 'There were three or four bugs stuck under there, picking up every word. He returned hours later to collect them. And blimey, could they gossip! You played me some, remember Bill?'

'Yep.'

'It started off tame, just moaning about the visiting Highgrove staff. But, after a couple of rounds, it'd get even less discreet. Stuff about where the young princes would be that weekend and where they could be papped. Priceless information for the tabloids! This was all just after Diana's death, so it was hot stuff.'

'Alright Alan, don't rub it in.'

'It was harmless fun and you did very well out of it, son,' Alan wagged a naughty-naughty finger at him. 'So did I, for that matter. You'll enjoy this next bit, love.'

His wife looked up from an open laptop in front of her, startled by the sudden attention her husband was paying her.

'Every year at Royal Ascot you can place a bet on what colour the Queen's hat's going to be. Not huge odds but it's a closely guarded secret and only a handful of courtiers know in advance. Oh, and just one other nosey bugger. For over five years the Bin Man over there called it correctly every fucking time. He'd tell his mates in advance and we all had a successful flutter on the day. Ray used to call him the Magic 8 Ball.'

'How did you know the colour?' Kitty asked. 'Chewing gum under the table?'

'I'm afraid not,' Bill told her, returning to their side of the room. 'By then I was illegally listening to the mobile phones of the ladies in waiting. It's one of the reasons I was sent to prison.'

'Oh,' said Kitty.

'Well, for that,' he continued, with unconcealed irritation, 'and for hacking the voicemail of a missing teenager who was later found murdered. The courts took a much dimmer view of my antics than your husband seems to. So, Alan,' he clapped his hands together, 'shall we back out of Memory Lane or what?'

Alan mumbled something about having touched a nerve there. Then he shrugged and asked what Bill was in the market for.

'Police standard undercover tech,' Bill said. 'A mike feed, discreetly hidden underneath clothing or perhaps even within it. For high quality live audio.'

Alan raised his eyebrows, glanced over towards Mercy who was stood next to the blast proof dummy.

'And there was me thinking you'd become a pipe and slippers man, Bill,' he said after a beat. 'This sounds a bit fucking sexy. You working for Victor again?'

'I have numerous clients,' Bill replied.

'Send him my regards if you see him,' Alan sniffed. 'It's been years. Water under the bridge as far as I'm concerned. He still owes us money for the kit we set up at the Spoils, but he's a hard man to chase, if you know what I mean.'

'It'll need to be discreet,' continued Bill, 'or it could be dangerous for the wearer. I don't want the shit you sell to amateurs.' He indicated the glass case in front of him. 'I've a smartphone that'll pick up more than these devices can.'

'A live feed, eh?' considered Alan. 'I can accommodate. You'll be the listener, I take it.' Bill nodded. 'Annnnd that means...?' he swivelled on the ball of his foot towards Mercy.

'She'll be the wearer,' Bill confirmed 'yeah.'

Alan chewed this over for a second before nodding in approval.

'Mance & Tyler are back!' he exclaimed. 'But now it's the next generation. Nice one.' He approached Mercy and eyed her jacket. He studied its zipped front and popper fastenings as if the woman inside it was just another dummy in his shop.

'Will she be wearing this?' he asked Bill.

'She will,' Mercy answered for herself. Alan raised his eyes to meet hers. 'We're hoping you'll wire it so that Bill can still hear what I'm saying even if I remove it but keep it close.'

'Risky,' said Alan. 'It's not how the police generally do it.'

'We're not the police,' Bill answered, crossing over to them. 'And Mercy's had minimal surveillance training, so we don't want anything that'll let her down.'

'You insult me,' Alan said, 'I'm not a cowboy.' Then he reached out and touched the collar of Mercy's jacket. 'Leather is perfect,' he told them. 'Thick enough to hide our handiwork in but you can still hear a pin drop through it. Unless the device rubs against the fibre in which case it won't work. Take it off and hand it to Kitty.' Mercy removed the jacket. 'Show her the lining.'

He turned to his wife and they began talking in Thai. Kittichai pulled the green jacket across the counter and examined the inside stitching. It had been purchased from a market stall in Barcelona and, although not expensive, Mercy was very attached to it. It had always fitted her shape well so the idea of the McColl's opening it up and stuffing it with listening devices wasn't appealing. She watched Kitty's swift, work-hardened hands knead the inside of the jacket, as if searching to see if it was already bugged.

'Okay if I change these?' Kittichai asked, indicating the

silver buttons near the collar. 'I have better ones for disguising a feed. They'll all match,' she assured her. 'It'll pick everything up and still look good.'

'I'm sure it'll look killer,' Mercy nodded. 'How long is it going to take?'

'Depends on how much your boss here wants to spend on you,' Alan answered. 'If it's just for recording, then no time. You could stick it in your pocket and walk out now. That'll set you back £150. But if you want strong quality, expertly hidden live feed,' he sucked through his teeth like a luck-pushing plumber, 'well, that's another matter. And your agency hasn't always been the quickest on the draw when it comes to invoices.'

'It was only ever Ray who tried to knock you,' Bill responded. 'I always paid promptly for my orders, and for many of his too.'

'*Bill pays the bills,*' Alan sniggered and turned to Mercy. 'That's what your dad used to say whenever I chased him. He died owing me a grand. God bless the old reprobate.'

Mercy didn't smile back.

'Let me take a proper look at what equipment you're planning to use,' Bill said, indicating that they go through to Alan's backroom. 'I need a new GPS tracker too. We can haggle afterwards.'

'You know, I don't let just anyone into my inner sanctum,' the spyware expert said, 'but as you are one of my oldest – and I do mean *oldest* – friends, I'll allow it. The girls won't mind staying out here for a natter while we talk business.'

As soon as they left the room, Mercy began to untighten. Like many of her dad's old cronies, Alan set her on edge. She marvelled at how Kitty had managed to stay married to him for so long. She'd by then folded up the jacket and placed it on the counter in front of her.

'Sorry to hear about your father,' Kitty said, gazing at her with tranquil eyes. 'He was a *nice* man.'

'Was he?' Mercy asked, remembering some of the unkind jokes her dad had made when Kitty had first arrived in England.

'We never spoke much,' she admitted and seemed to struggle to think of a positive thing to say. 'But he was always laughing.'

'Yeah, the old man loved a giggle,' Mercy muttered. By then she'd circled the glass case in the centre of the showroom. Displayed inside was a collection of innocuous objects that were designed to hide listening devices in. A baked bean can, a computer mouse, a cigarette lighter, plus a hardback copy of *The Perfect Spy* by John LeCarre. She kept browsing around the shop but felt that she could learn more information from Kitty than she could from any intelligence-gathering gadget in the place.

'It must've been difficult,' Mercy said idly while pretending to be impressed by the telescopes. She peered through an eyepiece to see what special meal deals were on offer at a McDonalds across the road. 'When you first arrived in England, I mean. Not really knowing anyone.'

'I knew Alan.'

'Sure,' Mercy nodded, although she wasn't certain that their three-week romance counted. 'But were his friends kind to you?' She turned away from the telescope and back toward Kitty who was still behind the counter. 'I have memories of that time and you were ignored a little I think.'

'Some people were nice,' she smiled. 'I spent time with the other wives, in their houses drinking and gossiping. Your mother was sometimes nice. And Bill's wife. Maggie Neale was... not so nice. But they spoke to each other, not to me much. My spoken English was not then good. But I would sit and listen as they gossiped about whoever was not there. I learnt better English from that.'

'Who did they gossip about?' Mercy asked.

'My favourite,' Kitty didn't even hesitate. 'Sarah.'

'Sarah Neale?'

'Poor woman,' Kitty sighed. 'Even before she fell, everyone talked about her *all the time.'*

'What did they say?'

'Some hated her,' Kitty expanded. 'Some loved her. *I* loved her most. She was the nicest.'

'Did my mother like her?'

'Not always,' Kitty admitted. 'She said Sarah had her nose in the air too much. But she liked how she dressed.'

'What was the gossip about?'

'Sarah took drugs.'

Mercy already knew that Victor's late wife had spent time in rehab so that wasn't new information.

'Did she have affairs?' Mercy asked, 'with any of the husbands?'

'Not with Alan!'

'No, obviously not with him,' she said, with perhaps too much certainty. 'But I've heard rumours about Sarah over the years.'

She paused, curious how Kittichai might respond to that. After lowering her eyes for a second, Kitty whispered.

'I heard rumours too.'

'Yeah?'

*'Lol,'* Kitty said. 'I mean, Lawrence.'

'Really?' Mercy asked. 'Sarah was fucking her husband's older brother. That's hard to believe.'

'I don't believe it!' Kitty insisted. 'But Alan told me it was true.'

'And how would Alan know a thing like that?'

Kitty indicated all the spyware surrounding them.

'He knows many things he's not supposed to. When Lol's car exploded, he made a joke that Sarah would be most upset. I told him he had the wrong name. Maggie was Lol's wife, not Sarah. He laughed and told me that Sarah slept with Lol. They were *lovers!*'

'Did he have any evidence?'

Kitty glanced towards the door through which her husband had walked. She shrugged.

Mercy was now standing across the counter from Kittichai, her treasured green jacket lying folded in the space between them. She reached over and touched her hands.

'I wish we'd been better friends in those days, Kitty,' she said. 'There you were, spending all that time with older women when we were much closer in age. We could've been like sisters.'

'You were a boy then,' Kitty reminded her.

'I was pretending to be one,' Mercy replied.

'Boys don't play at being Kylie Minogue,' smiled Kittichai with a cheeky wink.

The significance of that remark didn't impact immediately. When it did, Mercy withdrew her hands as if having experienced an electric shock.

'What did you say?'

*'Chrissy Tyler likes to dress as Kylie and dance around.'* Kitty placed a hand over her mouth and giggled. 'That was the gossip about *you*. I didn't believe it then but now... seeing you... maybe it was true.'

'Yes, I did do that,' Mercy eventually nodded. 'I dressed up as Kylie once.'

'Fun!' Kitty's hands gave another swift little applause. 'I love her too.'

'But *only* once.'

'I hope,' said Kitty, her smile vanishing, 'I haven't upset you.'

'Not at all,' Mercy assured her. She tried to process what this meant though. As far as she was concerned nobody had ever seen her on that one afternoon she'd spent impersonating a pop princess, the very same hour she'd overheard her dad talking to the Long Needle.

'Did Alan tell you about my Kylie costume?'

'I *have* upset you!' Kitty said, shaking her head.

'You haven't,' Mercy insisted. 'I'm just confused. Did my dad tell you about it?'

Another shake and one that was easier to believe. Mercy didn't know at what point Ray had learnt that she'd been listening in on him, but he was hardly the type to brag about his son's cross-dressing hobby.

'Sarah told me,' Kitty then revealed.

*'Really?'* Mercy asked in an even more incredulous tone. 'When?'

'It was *our* gossip, just the two of us,' Kitty answered fast. 'She was the only person who ever spoke of it. I just remembered because I see you're a girl now. I got excited thinking, *oh, Sarah said this many years ago. She was right.* I wish she was still alive to see she was right!' Kitty paused to catch a breath. 'She was nice.'

'Sorry if I'm being weird,' Mercy said, trying to adopt a friendlier approach. She wondered if the men in the other room could hear this conversation via a hidden bug. 'But this is really interesting to me. I'd be fascinated to know how the subject even came up.'

'We were at her big house in the country.'

'The Spoils?'

'Yes, and it was late in the evening. We were sitting together on a beautiful sofa, drinking wine.'

'I didn't know that you and she were close.'

'I used to work there sometimes,' Kitty explained. 'I helped with catering jobs.' She then glanced to the backroom and lowered her voice. 'My husband and her husband were friends,' she continued. 'But it was not a good friendship. Alan got angry when ignored or treated bad. Victor would not let him join a club he belonged to. But my husband *really* wanted to be friends again, so he asked if they had jobs for me. Immigrants worked at the Spoils a lot then and most couldn't speak good English. Many couldn't get jobs because we didn't have proper papers. Victor paid us in cash to help out.'

Mercy nodded, knowing that it was probably all stolen money that Victor knew wouldn't be traced.

'But I didn't see the husband much anyway,' Kitty continued. 'He was *always* away. He would phone Sarah with orders and she would pay us. But she treated me different to the rest, like a friend. I once stayed overnight when there was a party happening the next day and that was when she told me about you!'

From out in the backroom, they heard Alan laughing at something.

'I remember our conversation well,' Kitty went on in a quieter voice, 'because she was so happy. Sarah had not been happy for a long time but that night she was acting like a teenager. We were eating sweets from out of a bowl when she asked me about lady boys from my country.' Kitty rolled her eyes. 'I told her my cousin was one and we call them *Kathoey*. For some reason, English people always want to know about kathoey. But Alan's friends are interested in the operations they have, how can you tell if you meet a kathoey, do they trick men into sex, those things. But Sarah asked if Thailand was kind to kathoey and if the word lady boy was considered an insult. People rarely had asked *these* questions. Then she asked what I thought about *you*. Could I tell if you were transsexual or not? I said no. Then,' Kitty pointed to Mercy, 'she asked if I would be surprised to learn you *were* transsexual. That you dressed up as Kylie Minogue and danced to her music around the house while everyone was out.' She raised her hand up to her mouth. 'Sorry to say we laughed about it.'

'I forgive you,' Mercy said, turning the possible meanings of this over in her head. Sarah Neale was such a peripheral person in her life and the last person she'd ever expected to know she was transgender. *So who told her?* Suspicions unfurled.

'Who else was in the house with you when she said this?'

'Nobody! We'd been preparing for all the guests to come for the summer party the next day. It was the birthday of Maggie, her sister by marriage.'

'Hold the phone!' Mercy said in stunned realisation. 'You're talking about the garden party that she threw for Lol's widow? That was the day after this conversation?' Kitty nodded. 'But that's *the* day, right? When she... y'know?'

Kitty answered in her smallest whisper yet.

'...fell from the balcony.'

'Nobody told me that *you* were there, Kitty.'

'I was serving drinks and helping with food.'

'Did you see her do it?'

'I dropped a tray of champagne glasses when she landed.'

'But you just said she was happy the night before? Drinking wine, laughing, gossiping.'

'She seemed very happy.'

'Then how did she go from that to killing herself the next day?' Mercy asked, 'in full view of witnesses?'

'I don't know.' Kitty's eyes had become wet.

Feeling bad for pressuring her, Mercy moved around to her side of the counter and went to hug her. Kittichai allowed it.

'I didn't mean to upset you. It must be a terrible memory.'

'It was,' she cried.

The low murmur of Bill and Alan's conversation could still be heard from the other room. Mercy fumbled through the leather jacket she'd removed and found a pocket-sized pack of tissues.

'Wipe your eyes,' she whispered, handing them over.

Mercy thought about the little she knew of Sarah Neale. The last time she'd seen her was the afternoon she'd made a surprise visit to borrow a summer dress from her mum, the same dress she'd been wearing as she threw herself from the top balcony weeks later. Since then, her suicide had rarely been spoken of in the Tyler home.

'What a traumatic thing to witness,' Mercy sighed. 'I can't imagine. Mum never speaks about it.'

Kittichai pulled away then with surprising forcefulness.

*'Your mother,'* she hissed the words, '*never* wanted *anyone* to speak about it. She stopped us all from saying what we saw.'

'Excuse me?'

'Her and *the cleaning lady*,' Kitty seethed.

'Do you mean Maggie Neale?' Mercy asked. 'Or an actual cleaning lady?'

'They bullied the rest of us,' Kitty said, with a fast-rising anger. 'Told us not to tell what we saw.'

'What *did* you see?' Mercy asked, surprised by the shift in temper. They could both hear Alan and Bill getting louder as they headed back to the showroom. Kittichai regained composure and suddenly changed the subject.

'Alan likes hot chocolate,' she said and gathered up the leather jacket. 'I'll fetch some for him. What about Bill?'

'Um, not sure,' Mercy replied as she took the jacket back. 'Black coffee, I think.'

'Let's go before they get back,' she said and darted towards the door, beckoning Mercy to follow.

As they queued for hot drinks in the McDonalds across the road, Kittichai ignored Mercy's questions. It wasn't until they'd been served that she suggested they sit in some chairs by the window. She seemed quite paranoid, which was perhaps a symptom of her trade. Mercy glanced up at the windows of the spyware shop, wondering if the men were watching through telescopes.

'I told the police everything I saw,' Kitty resumed. 'But my English was not yet good. I was truthful even though I might get in trouble because my work visa had not come through. The police used her death as a chance to search the house for illegal things. All the staff were frightened. One boy even ran away before the police arrived.'

'A caterer, you mean?'

'He was frightened about having no visa. He was from Morocco, I think. There was a girl there also who I never saw again. But I don't remember much about her.'

'Did the police catch up with this Moroccan boy, or the girl?'

'Don't know,' Kittichai said. 'I didn't tell the police about him because I'd promised.'

'Okay,' Mercy said, making a mental note to investigate these missing caterers further. 'But, aside from that, you were honest with the police even though my mum asked you to lie?'

'It was our husbands she wanted us to lie to.'

'You've lost me. Lie to them about what?'

'Your mum didn't want people knowing what had been going on,' Kitty said after some hesitation. 'And I never told my husband because he would sell Sarah's secret to the newspapers.'

'I still don't understand.'

'Victor had been gone for *too long!*' Kitty spoke fast. She dropped her hands down to her waist, indicating a round belly. 'But when Sarah jumped from that balcony,' she explained, *'she was pregnant.'*

# 32

Nina's confidence as a surveillance expert had taken a dent that morning. That Barbara, of all the ridiculous people, had clocked her clandestine relationship with Ray had caused her to seriously reassess how good her covert abilities were. More importantly, she feared; did Bill also know what had been going on?

Almost immediately after her row with Barbara, Nina had dumped her workload onto Robbie and set off in her car toward Bill's home, hoping to speak to him. She had arrived just in time to see Mercy emerging from the train station in her green leather jacket, also heading toward Bill's flat.

Nina pulled back and watched as they remained in there for half an hour. Around one o'clock, they emerged from the flat and drove off together in his Nissan. From the route he was taking, she could soon tell they were headed to Third Eye Electronics for some spyware. Certain that she would be noticed if she followed in her familiar car, she decided to instead use the time to return home and borrow a less familiar one.

It was only two weeks after Nina had joined M&T that Ray Tyler had made his first clumsy pass at her. He'd been drunk, of course, and the two of them had been in The Blue-eyed Maid pub in Southwark. Earlier that day she'd helped him close a big case – a missing persons thing that had led them to a homeless shelter in Oxford. She and Ray had learnt of the subject's whereabouts, travelled there together in his vintage Porsche, located the missing man, and sent a photo of him to his parents, along with the address of the shelter. Their payment had hit the agency account by the time they were back in London. To celebrate their success, Mance, Tyler, and Markham had all gone to the Maid where, as usual on a Thursday, karaoke night was in full swing.

Bill left soon after the first round though, just as Ray was getting up to sing a rendition of *I Heard it Through the Grapevine*.

'Marvin Gaye was murdered by his father,' he'd said to Nina as his swaggering partner took to the stage, 'and now Ray's going to murder his best song. You two have fun.'

Ray's voice had indeed been a keyless travesty. But what he lacked in talent he made up for it in booming enthusiasm and the rowdy pub had gone wild for him. He must've been a hot guy in his youth, she'd thought, as he belted out some high notes, and he seemed to think he still was. After more drinks, Nina had been persuaded to sing Diana Ross' *Chain Reaction* with Ray on Bee Gee backing vocals. For all its tackiness, it had been the most fun night out she'd had in a while and she'd stayed late, knowing that the best way to ingratiate yourself with a man like Ray was to get drunk with him.

However, when they returned to their table as last orders were being called, his hand reached out for her knee. Moving away, she told him that she was going through a divorce and wasn't looking to complicate things. Smiling, he'd just pulled it away, shrugged and got another round in.

Despite this awkward start, an easy intimacy had developed between them. But it wasn't until about two weeks before his death – when Ray had overheard something that had sent him into an alcoholic spiral – that he came to really depend on her.

And from then on, she'd had him right where she wanted him.

## 33

The last time that Mercy had worn any traditional male clothing was five years earlier, on the day she'd left for Spain. And even then she'd had on light make-up, earrings, and a blouse underneath her old denim jacket. The jacket though, as well as her jeans and shoes, were fairly blokey. She was wearing them partly because it was early in her transition and couldn't yet afford an entirely new wardrobe. But, also, her father was driving her to the airport and he was so uneasy with her female identity that she'd wanted to compromise for his sake. However, on the way to Gatwick he'd behaved like such a prick that afterwards she'd wished she'd worn a pink floral dress just to spite him.

During the drive she'd casually mentioned that, despite her decision to fully transition abroad, she still harboured ambitions to follow in his professional footsteps. Ray hadn't hidden his contempt.

'You can't work surveillance dressed like *that*, Chrissy,' he'd mocked. 'People tend to notice when a pantomime dame is following them around.'

Looking back, she wished she'd remained calmer. She should have just replied that an old fart driving around in a vintage sports car wasn't exactly inconspicuous either. But his words had carried such a sting that she was crying about them in the departure lounge an hour later. As soon as she'd arrived in Barcelona, she'd bought the first female jacket she'd ever loved from a market stall - the one she'd just left with Kittichai McColl.

'Alan promised we'll get your jacket back tomorrow,' Bill assured her, taking his first vape of the day. 'The gear he's placing inside will catch a dropped pin.'

Six Nations bunting flapped above them and the sky was as grey as the slabs beneath their feet. It was later in the afternoon, they were in a pub garden having just eaten and Bill was now puffing on the same e-cigarette he'd used to record Victor at the Spoils. The garden was mostly empty so the two investigators could speak freely about the case, although Bill had been doing most of the talking.

'You've gone quiet,' he observed, after exhaling more sweet smoke. 'Is it the coat?'

Bill had offered Mercy the use of his black Barbour as soon as they'd left Third Eye, as she'd been cold without her jacket on. It was the first time she'd been enveloped inside a man's clothing since that drive to Gatwick and it felt like a forgotten weight had been placed back onto her shoulders. She was glad that she no longer had to wear such things, but as she'd been listening to him explain a plan he had to trap the Long Needle, his lingering body warmth felt nice. Bill was showing her much more respect than she'd ever received from her dad. It also occurred to her that it had been a long time since she'd been held in a man's arms.

'The coat's alright,' she murmured, placing her fork down beside the unfinished vegetarian lasagne. 'But there's been something on my mind concerning Dad. I wonder if now is a good time to bring it up.'

'Go on.'

She pushed her plate to the side and considered how to phrase her question.

'I want to ask,' she said, resolving to just come out with it, 'about his extra-marital affairs.'

'His what now?' Bill squinted.

'Who was he fucking, both back in the day and more recently?'

Bill took another drag on his e-cigarette. They weren't the only people in that pub garden but everyone else seemed engrossed in their own intrigues.

'You're assuming I'd know.'

'I very much am,' she replied, making a study of his response. 'Good old Bill, his best mate. I'm not assuming you'll answer honestly though. But I'm hoping you might.'

'I never approved of the way he ran around on your mum, Mercy,' he said, following another pause.

'I can believe that.'

'Don't think it was a laugh between us, or anything. But yeah, it was no secret that Ray saw other women.'

'Did he discuss his affairs with you?'

'Not often,' he said, 'but not never.'

'Who were they?'

'I couldn't tell you.'

'Couldn't or won't?'

Bill straightened. She could hear the antagonism creeping into her own voice but was unwilling to adjust it. The idea that he might hold out on her out of some lingering loyalty to a dead philanderer was as aggravating to her as suits and ties had once been. She'd been developing an idea that her father's tomcat behaviour could somehow be linked to his death and her conversation with Kittichai had pushed this idea even further to the forefront.

'Ray had secrets,' Bill replied. 'And while I did know that he was involved with various women, he wasn't boasting about it to me. I was family.'

Mercy wasn't ready to accept that. Certainly, she could imagine her dad wanting to conceal his weakness for adultery from a man he respected. But if she'd learnt anything about Bill in the past week, it was that he didn't miss much, so she wasn't buying that he was oblivious to his partner's recreational activities. He probably knew more about Ray's women than Ray had.

'You covered for him though,' Mercy persisted, recalling Bill's attempts to support her dad's alibies.

'He occasionally asked me to lie for him, yeah,' Bill shrugged a *mea culpa*. 'But he understood that I hated doing it. And I rarely knew the details of what he was up to, I only knew what he'd told your mum and what I was expected to stick to.' His eyes dropped in what looked like shame.

'How was he meeting these women?'

'Sometimes,' Bill said, placing his e-cigarette away, 'they were clients. Married women who'd hired us to prove that their husbands were cheating on them. In a situation like that, they often know the truth and all they want is hard evidence showing hubby in the act. If the wife was attractive, Ray would sometimes go round to their home with a file full of incriminating evidence. Her husband having sex with another woman, or sometimes a man. That's a hard thing to see, even if they suspected it beforehand. So, the wife would become emotional. Vulnerable. And your old man...' Bill searched for the right words, 'well, he was a devil when he wanted to be.'

'You said that right,' she sniffed. Throughout her own

messy love life Mercy has encountered many bullshitting players, so it was dispiriting to learn that her dad had been the king of them.

The clouds above were getting fuller. The publican took away their plates and asked if they wanted another drink. Bill answered with a fast no.

'I'm not sure how long these affairs went on for,' he continued, 'or if you can even really call them affairs. But I can dig up some details for you.'

'What about Sarah?' Mercy asked, just as he was getting ready to head back to the car park.

He lowered back down again. 'What about her?'

'What was Dad's relationship with her like?'

'She was his best friend's wife.'

'I thought you were his best friend.'

'All right then, Sarah was his *oldest* friend's wife. Why are you asking?'

'Because by your account,' Mercy replied 'he didn't mind sleeping with other men's wives.'

Bill gave an incredulous laugh.

'Your dad was a handsome rogue,' he admitted, 'but she was well out of his league. Plus, you can't underestimate how shit-scared people were of Victor in those days. Nobody, outside of a maniac, was trying to fuck that guy's wife.'

'Then how come Sarah had been pregnant when she died?' Mercy asked. 'Despite her husband having been out of the country for so long?' Bill tried to look surprised, but didn't have much of a poker face. He knew what she was talking about. She was even willing to bet that Sarah's gravid state was the controversial detail that her dad had overheard during Barbara's phone discussion with Maggie Neale.

'*That's* what had upset him,' she added after voicing the suspicion, 'not the insults about my mum.'

'Yeah,' Bill admitted, as if wondering how she would have learnt this. 'You're right.'

It had started raining. Mercy downed the ice at the bottom of her glass and handed him his keys from the coat pocket. They didn't speak as they walked to the car and he got in the driver's seat. Quietly, Mercy put her seatbelt on as he placed a hand on the steering wheel. But, instead of starting the car, he turned to her.

'I knew that Sarah was with child when she died,' he confessed. 'My Moira was at the garden party and wasn't great at keeping secrets. But I never told Ray because it was just another horrible detail to an already horrible incident. And I knew that he liked her.' The rain outside wasn't stopping and Bill turned the windscreen wipers on at a slow setting. 'But when he learnt the truth from Barb at the end of last year,' he sighed, 'he went into meltdown.'

'Why was it a secret?'

'Because you're right, the baby probably wasn't Vic's. Which left a bit of an unanswered question among the wives.'

'You just told me that nobody, outside of a maniac, would try to sleep with Sarah. So, who was the maniac?'

'I should warn you,' he sighed, 'that our agency doesn't reflect well in this story. There are some shady things here that could come back to haunt us, from a legal standpoint I mean.'

'Okay.'

'And I've done as much time inside as I want to.'

'I'm not recording this.'

'Sure,' he nodded. 'But I want you to understand why

I've been reluctant to speak about this episode. Your dad and I don't come out of it covered in glory.'

She waited for him to continue.

'Months before Sarah died, Victor hired us to spy on her. A 24-hour round-the-clock surveillance to go on for as long as it needed to. Big money, absolute secrecy. The only people he'd trust were myself, Ray and Alan, who back then worked for us on a freelance basis. Vic gathered us together late at night in the office and said that he was going abroad to take care of his offshore interests. But he was concerned about leaving Sarah. She'd been a junkie when he'd met her and had a history of depression. He'd helped rehabilitate her during their marriage but was worried she'd revert to her old habits.' He switched the windscreen wipers to a faster setting as the rain beat down. 'The three of us worked shifts. Alan, who she knew the least, monitored her in the mornings as she did the school runs, etc. I kept watch in the afternoon while your dad did the night shift. She socialised a lot in those early weeks, cocktails with the girls, pop concerts. Nothing scandalous. No drugs or other men. Nannies were hired to watch over the kids so she could enjoy life without Vic around. It seemed a boring assignment at first.'

'Ray didn't report any gentleman callers during the evenings,' he said after a pause. 'But one night she went to a party at Lol and Maggie's house. Ray had managed to blag an invite for himself and your mum so he could monitor her up close. He watched as Lol cornered Sarah and offered her a line of coke. Soon after, she vanished into the bathroom with him and came out high as a kite.'

'Didn't Dad try and stop it?' Mercy asked. 'He knew she had issues with addiction.'

'Investigators aren't paid to intervene,' he replied. 'We're like David Attenborough. We watch and report. But we all hoped it would be a one-off thing and that would be that. Unfortunately, though, Lol became obsessed with his sister-in-law and started visiting her home. Soon he had her hooked on heroin. Victor hit the roof when we told him. But the worst was yet to come.'

By then, the rain had become strong and steady. Bill's eyes remained fixed on the puddles forming in the empty car park.

'Therapy was part of her weekly routine,' he explained. 'She went to see this woman every Thursday afternoon and never missed an appointment. On my own initiative I booked an hour with that therapist on the same day during Alan's shift. And I left one of my devices inside her room.'

'How?'

'I paid some kids to set her car alarm off,' he explained 'and, while the therapist was attending to that, I hid the bug. Of course, that meant I had to book a second appointment for later in the week, and arrange another distraction so I could get the bug out again. Those were the only two hours of therapy I've had in my life.'

'What was discussed?'

'Just stuff about my marriage and how I wasn't happy in it.'

'No, what came out in Sarah's session,' Mercy clarified, 'that you'd illegally recorded.'

'Self-harming,' he replied. 'She had a history of it and had started cutting herself again.'

'Jesus.'

'Yeah, it was brutal to listen to.' She saw him sag at the memory. 'And it was all Lol's fault. She kept the details vague, but it was obvious he was using her drugged state to force sex on her. She said it wasn't rape but I didn't believe it and neither I think did the therapist.'

Mercy sat in furious silence. To think that neither Bill nor her father had stepped in to prevent this abuse made her want to vomit.

'I sent the tapes to Victor hoping *he'd* intervene. But he kept paying us to maintain the surveillance. I know,' Bill said, one hand still gripping onto the steering wheel, 'I should've gone to the police. But well... I didn't.'

'How soon after this did Lawrence Neale die in that car explosion?'

'About a month.'

'And when you heard that he'd been killed,' she asked, 'did you honestly think it was the work of the McAlonan gang? Or, considering what you knew, did you suspect it was Victor's revenge?'

'I always wondered if Victor was responsible for his brother's murder. And when you told me about the hitman I became sure of it.' He reached for the ignition key to start the car. 'But, quite honestly, it didn't matter to me who'd killed Lol. I was just glad that *someone* had.'

# 34

Nina had been sitting in a state of sharp-edged tension for over an hour now, behind the wheel of a borrowed blue Smart car. The day had grown dark and she'd parked in an obscure spot out of sight from Mercy's flat, away from any streetlamps. The engine was running and the back windscreen wiper was working hard against the pelting rain. Her headlights were turned off.

She'd just got off the phone from her ex-husband, Ian, who had been asking her what time he could expect her to collect Kyle, as well as return his car. She'd been explaining that she needed more time when, in the rear-view mirror, she'd seen Bill's car drive into the far end of the street. After hastily hanging up on Ian, she'd pulled the cap on her head down and lowered further into the seat.

She again inspected the mirror that she'd angled towards Mercy's home. The passenger door of Bills' car opened, turning the interior light on. Nina made a note of the time as Mercy stepped out onto the wet pavement wearing what looked like Bill's coat.

Avoiding puddles, Mercy reached her front door and

waved back at Bill as he three-point turned and drove away. Nina bit her fingernail as she considered what to do next.

She'd come to this address to log their time of return and then follow Bill at a safe distance in an unfamiliar car. She was hoping to learn more about this secret investigation of theirs but also felt a strong impulse to get back to her son before his bedtime. Spending more time with Kyle had been her only New Year's resolution and, so far, she'd stuck to it. She raised her phone up to her ear, ready to phone Ian back and tell him she was coming home.

But before she had a chance, Mercy's front door opened again. Out she came, still wearing Bill's winter coat, holding an umbrella and a small torch.

Again Nina slunk down, but Mercy turned the other direction, following the same route that Bill's car had just taken and walking with purpose. Where could she be going in weather as filthy as this? Nina lowered her phone as Mercy reached the end of the street. Then, after allowing her to walk far enough, she slowly followed in the car.

Pulling up at the nearest corner, and taking care not to be seen, Nina saw that Mercy had crossed the road and was waiting under the shelter of a bus stop on the edge of Blackheath. Her umbrella closed, her attention was now directed fully at her phone. Wind blew in wild gusts across the heath, but Mercy had tied up her long hair. Nina remained in her car, wondering if it was worthwhile tailing Ray's daughter to wherever she was going. Perhaps she was just out on a date or something? But she couldn't shake the idea that this journey was somehow important.

A bus crawled up the hill. Nina watched from the shadows as Mercy put her phone away and positioned herself on the lower deck of the bus. Thanks to a travel app that told her the route, she could allow the bus some distance before she'd lose sight of it, so it was just a case of staying close enough to see where her quarry would get off.

She hadn't needed to track it for long. Mercy disembarked at the end of a long residential street called Rafferty Road. Nina discreetly parked up and watched as Mercy raised her umbrella against the light rain and set off down the road. Once she'd walked on far enough, Nina stepped onto the pavement and followed. Mercy must be visiting someone, she assumed, and so perhaps she could just make a note of the house number for now and then return home to her child. Ahead on the dark street Mercy turned on her torch, making the task of following her easier. Once again, Nina was struck by how hopelessly visible Mercy could be for someone who fancied themselves an investigator.

It soon became apparent that she was not looking for a particular house but rather at *all* the houses. She was flashing her torch at every address, often crossing the road back and forth and crouching down to aim her torchlight low through iron gates. This end of the road boasted a number of affluent homes and Nina hung back, pausing behind trees and between lampposts. But Mercy was too busy to turn around anyway, peering over front garden fences and venturing up driveways. As she travelled further, the houses became smaller and the driveways less far apart, speeding up her search until she vanished round the back of a block of flats. Nina remained in a discreet spot behind a timber-filled skip until she could get eyes on her again.

Mercy eventually emerged from behind the flats and continued on in the same direction. She explored the parking spaces of council flats and old people's homes. At the corner of a mini roundabout there was a white art deco house with a tall unwelcoming gate. The lights weren't on and Nina, who'd by then crept up the steps of a nearby estate to survey her progress from further away, watched as Mercy shone her torch through the iron rails. She couldn't see exactly what Mercy could, but she registered a sudden spasm of excitement in her body language. *Bingo!*

Mercy rattled the gate, finding it unlocked. She pushed it open and entered the driveway, moving out of Nina's sightline.

Not understanding what was happening, Nina risked getting closer. Once she was back on the street, she strode across the mini roundabout to the far side and glanced toward the open gate of the white house. Inside the driveway she got her closest look at Mercy tonight. She was opening the door of an old burgundy Porsche that, with a jolt, Nina immediately recognised.

It was Ray's missing car. The same one she'd driven to Oxford and back in eighteen months earlier. It had been a bright, summer's day then and a section of its roof had been removed. What she mainly remembered about the journey was how much they'd both been laughing. But it looked pitiful now, like a lost, broken toy.

Then, a teenage boy on a bicycle narrowly avoided crashing into Nina. He apologised, despite the near-collision being absolutely her fault. Concerned that this had blown her cover, Nina turned back toward Mercy, but she was still flashing her torch around inside her dad's car in sharp, searching movements. Nina decided to withdraw.

Back at the car she reached for her second phone which she'd hidden under her seat. On it was a contact she had saved as **GREENWATER.**

'Mercy Tyler is becoming a problem,' she told the voice on the other end once it was answered. 'I may need you to get rid of her.'

# 35

'Anyone home?' Mercy called into the large house. 'I'm about to remove this car. *Don't try and stop me*!'

Blinds blanked out most of the windows in the art deco place and no lights appeared to be on. To shout through the letterbox, she'd had to remove some local leafleting which was half-soggy from weather exposure, telling her that not even squatters were living here. The white house looked like it had passed a few rainy seasons since it's last paint job and the front lawn needed weeding. To get round the back would involve venturing through a dark, narrow passageway that only a bad actress in a horror movie might attempt. The rain had abated by now, but the wet muddy ground was still slippery.

After receiving no answer, Mercy stepped back to further examine this mystery house outside which her father's pride and joy had been found. It wasn't a place that revealed much about itself. There was nothing about its façade that hinted at what sort of people might reside there. This, in itself, interested her. You can usually tell if children live in a place, even from the exterior. Or perhaps if a business is run from there. But this poker face of a building suggested neither. There were two refuse bins around the side, both empty.

*If I were to imagine where the Long Needle might live*, she thought as she shone her torchlight into the guttering, *I'd imagine a house as blank as this.* Could this be his home? Had her dad visited the assassin on the same night he'd died?

She shoved the small garage door to see if it would yield as easily as the front gate. It was locked. She estimated that this driveway was large enough to accommodate around four vehicles but her dad's Porsche was parked right by the gate, barring others from entering. Mercy hadn't even needed her torch to read the number plate from the street; the recognition had been instantaneous. She'd stopped in her tracks on seeing the car and pushed the gate open for the family reunion. The Porsche had been backed so tightly against the gate that she'd needed to squeeze through a thin space to gain entrance. Once in, she stroked the cold metal of the car. It was the exact one that he'd driven her to the airport in when she'd last seen him. The paintwork had faded since then but it was definitely the same 1969 semi-convertible Targa. It had been in almost perfect condition when he'd bought it seven years ago from a vintage car dealer. To find it here now, abandoned, unloved and in a state of serious disrepair, was another testament to her dad's own decline. Her fingers slid gently along the freezing bonnet.

She reached into her coat pocket for the key ring with the matching Porsche insignia. The police had returned it to the family after the coroner's verdict and, when she slid it into the lock, the door opened like a granted wish. No interior light came on but she couldn't recall if any were supposed to. She shone her torch inside and saw that a steering lock was in place but her ex-boyfriend Carmelo had taught her how to pick them. In less than a minute she had released that and placed it on the passenger seat. Then she sat behind the steering wheel, placed the key in the ignition and turned.

Nothing.

She tried again, her foot pressing the accelerator all the way down and her fingers pulling at the choke but the battery was dead. She cursed, shining her light across the dashboard and around the indicators. Her dad, or whoever else had driven it here, had left the fog-lights on. Thanks a bunch.

She made a quick study for clues. The mileage count was very high and the passenger seat was pulled in tight, as if for a child. But nothing else struck her as suspicious. No ID's of any secret acquaintances lying dropped on the floor. No alien objects that would lead her to the next puzzle piece.

Somewhere on the street, she heard a voice apologising to another person. Getting out of the car, she saw a young cyclist splash through a puddle outside the gate and turn into the neighbouring driveway. There were some trees between the two houses so she wasn't sure if he'd seen her. She slammed the car door, wanting to draw attention to herself.

'Sorry to be a nuisance,' she called over in the least threatening tone she could manage. 'I'm having some car trouble. Might you have any jump leads I could borrow?'

She saw him dismounting from the bike and peer over

the fence at her. His house was a pretty, gabled home with a well-tended garden and it formed an unlikely contrast with the lifeless white property she was standing in front of.

The young man stepped closer to the fence between the trees. He pulled his hood down and the light from a nearby lamppost revealed him to be a shaggy-haired boy of about nineteen. He seemed initially surprised to see her but then gave an open, trusting smile.

'Jump leads, yeah sure,' he nodded, as if keen to show that he understood the concept of them. 'We've got some. Definitely.' Then he paused and extended his already long neck out even further toward the Porsche. 'Are you taking that away?'

'Yep,' Mercy replied. 'It belongs to my dad and I've come to remove it. But the people who own this house don't appear to be in.'

'I'm not surprised,' said the boy. 'They live in Canada. Don't you know them?'

'Not at all,' she explained. 'I was told I'd find his car here but I don't know much beyond that. I'd like to leave them a note actually, if you have their details.'

The boy stepped out of his own driveway and moved around to the other side of the gates. He looked back at the path he'd just ridden down.

'Is it just you?' he asked.

'That's right,' she answered. 'I have documentation that proves this car belongs to my family if you want to see it.'

'Sorry,' he said, in a confused way. 'I assumed this car belonged to the house. It's been here *weeks.*'

'How many weeks exactly?'

'Weeks and weeks,' he said.

'Since Christmas?'

'I guess,' he replied as he pushed the gate open enough to squeeze through. 'I was staying with my dad around then so I'm not sure. But it was *definitely* here at New Year's Eve. We wanted to use these spaces for some party guests but it was in the way. No offence to your dad but he left it in a pretty inconvenient spot.'

'Well, he was a pretty inconvenient man,' she sighed, as he joined her at the car. 'He died about week before Christmas and the family has been wondering where he left this thing.'

'Oh shit,' said the boy, pulling himself up. 'Sorry to hear that.'

'That's alright,' she said. 'It wasn't your fault.' Then she narrowed her eyes. '*Unless it was.*'

'Excuse me?'

'Kidding,' she smiled. 'Seriously, I'm grateful to you for shedding some light on this. And I'm sorry if it's made things difficult but once I've driven it away you'll have the whole driveway to use. Are the Canadian owners cool with you using this as free off-road parking?'

'Never met them,' said the boy.

'Then how do you know they're Canadian?'

'Mum spoke to them once. One of them has, like, this Russian accent though, she said. They're only ever here for a few months in the summer and seem rich. That's why I thought this was theirs. They look like the types to be into vintage cars.'

'Can you describe them?'

'Why?'

'No reason,' she shrugged, 'just curious who my dad was visiting on the night of his death. I feel I owe them an apology.'

'They're a couple of older guys,' he told her, 'like fifty or something. They have a sort of academic look, like they could be university professors. I think they're a couple. To be honest, mum used to joke that they might be spies.'

'Why's that?'

'They just seemed a bit shifty.'

'But nobody lives here during the winter? That seems a shame. Don't they rent it out?'

'Not that I've seen,' the boy said, puffing out his cheeks with air. 'This place is dead.' He seemed to be getting bored of her questions, so she brought the subject back to the jumpstart.

'So if you don't mind, I've already released the handbrake and we just have to give it a little push to allow your car in here. The engine's in the boot on this one so we don't need to turn it.'

'Cool,' the boy nodded again, admiring the Porsche. 'Your dad had good taste.'

Once they'd rolled it further into the driveway the boy, whose name she learnt was Jason, bounded off to get the keys to his mum's Hyundai. Mercy followed him up to his front door in the hope of asking his mother some questions about the pair of possibly Russian-Canadian spies who owned that strange house. But when the woman opened the door, she didn't seem very friendly. Unlike her son, she was short, unsmiling, and seemed irritated as Jason explained what they needed.

'I'm very appreciative,' Mercy called up to her. 'My mum and I have been searching for this car for weeks.'

Jason's mother handed him the keys and said that his dinner would soon be ready. Then she shut the door, claiming she didn't want to let the heat out. Her more gracious son drove the car into the other driveway and they set about recharging the Porsche's battery.

'Why did you ask if I was alone?' Mercy asked once the two engines were connected and the Hyundai was ticking over.

'I thought you were with someone,' Jason said as he sat in his mum's car, revving it. 'When I cycled in, I almost hit a woman stood just there,' he thumbed over to the mini roundabout. 'She was looking over.'

Mercy turned to look in that direction. Was someone still watching her?

'That might be my friend Brenda,' Mercy said, wanting to know more. 'I told her to meet me here, but she gets easily lost. What did she look like?'

'About your age,' Jason replied, 'bit older. Is Brenda black?'

'She sure is.'

'That may have been her then.'

Mercy stepped toward the pavement and scanned the road for this person. She couldn't see anyone. But she'd spotted a familiar car outside Bill's flat earlier so had an idea who it might be.

'It might be worth trying it now,' said Jason, who was doubtless getting hungry for dinner. Mercy returned to the Porsche, sat behind the wheel and, with one turn of the key, the engine inside the boot roared back into life. On came the fog lights.

'Jason, you're a star!' she cried out. 'Thanks so much.'

Soon afterwards, she was waving him goodbye and driving it home. The handling was stiff but to get it out on the road felt like a well-earned triumph. The last time she'd been in this particular vehicle, her dad had insulted her on the way to Gatwick airport, pouring scorn on her ambitions to become a private investigator.

But now here she was, recovering a lost car that even the police couldn't find. The radio was set at a high volume and an Elvis Costello had come blasting out of the tinny speakers, mid-chorus, as she'd turned on the engine. She tapped her fingers on the steering wheel and sang along to a song about detectives.

# 36

Julie's Hair & Beauty salon was, contrary to local opinion, not owned by Mercy's mother, but instead by an entrepreneur named Juliette Jaquest. That Julie had been a celebrity hairdresser in the late nineties and now lived in semi-retirement on the Kent coast. Julie Tyler had been running the place as manageress for over two decades but every Saturday afternoon *the real Julie* would phone up to ask about business. Sometimes the stylists would dare to refer to Mercy's mother as *Fake Julie*, but never within her earshot. That said, most of Fake Julie's customers assumed that it was her name above the door, a misapprehension she'd encourage by answering the phone with *'Julie's Hair & Beauty. Julie speaking.'* It was more of a mislead than a lie, but it was interesting to note that she never answered the phone like that on a Saturday afternoon.

Mercy had often visited her mum's workplace as a child. Rather than finding it boring, she'd been entranced by that intoxicating world of blow-dries, hairspray and happy female chatter. She'd proven a helpful addition to the salon too, sweeping up hair and making cups of tea. Years later, when Julie's own mother had learnt of her grandchild's transition, she'd condemned those early visits as being the *start of the trouble.*

Julie was feeling at ease with her world on that particular Saturday morning. Yesterday's rain had cleansed the air and she was chatting to her assistant Tania by the window, holding a mug of tea and waiting for the first bookings of the day to arrive. It was then that she saw a vintage burgundy sports car approaching, one so familiar that she almost dropped her tea in shock.

*'Raymond!'* she exclaimed as the Porsche swung into a vacant space in one swift and decisive turn. Tania, who'd been arranging hair products on a nearby shelf, turned to see what had startled her.

'Isn't that's your husband's car?' Tania asked, with a bottle of Moroccan Oil Treatment in her hand. 'I thought it was missing?'

'It was,' Julie exhaled.

The door to the Porsche opened and out stepped Mercy wearing a man's coat. She was gesturing toward the car like she'd won it on a game show.

'That Chrissy?' Tania asked. Julie placed down the tea she'd been enjoying until then on a counter and stepped toward the door.

'Yeah, but that's not her name anymore,' she said before greeting her daughter outside.

MERCY GAVE her mother a warm hug, keen to prove that, despite the nasty scene that had unfolded the last time they'd spoken, she was a bygones-be-bygones sort of girl.

Julie kissed her on the cheek, told her it was lovely to see her and called her by the correct name.

As a mother, Julie hadn't really done much wrong. She'd been supportive of Mercy's decision to transition in another country, sent funds when asked for, worked hard on the pronouns. During Ray's funeral, she'd defended her against transphobic comments made by other relatives. So aside from their recent spat, and especially when compared to her husband, Julie had behaved in a way that was hard to rebuke her for. But there had always been some light behind her eyes that had once shone for the child she'd called Chrissy. Mercy noticed its absence every time they spoke now.

Her mother looked dumbstruck by the reappearance of the Porsche, which made Mercy glad. Like her dad, Julie had doubted that Mercy had what it took to be an investigator, so she'd of course been the first person she'd wanted to present the recovered car to. Besides, the Porsche rightfully belonged to Ray's widow anyway. No doubt she'd want to sell it on the vintage car market at the first opportunity, so driving it to her like this was simultaneously an *I told you so* and a peace offering in one smooth action.

'Where did they find it?' Julie asked, as she peered into the open door of the last vehicle her husband had ever owned.

'Where did *I* find it, you mean,' Mercy corrected her, while waving to Tania through the window. 'It was in an empty driveway not that far from here. Rafferty Road. Do we know anyone who lives there?'

Julie shook her head and continued inspecting the interior, sniffing the leather as if she suspected it of not being real. 'Did the DVLA tell you where it was?'

'No, I found it on my own. I'm not sure if I've mentioned this before but I'm a private investigator now.'

'Did Bill help?'

'Would it make more sense for you if he had?'

'I'm just asking, darling,' Julie said as she bobbed her head out from the car again. 'Don't get defensive. And to be fair, you are wearing his coat.'

'You've a suspiciously good eye for your late husband's best friend's clothing,' Mercy said. 'He lent it to me. My jackets in for alterations. Listen, have you got a couple of quid?' she pointed at a traffic warden approaching from the other end of the high street. 'I'm going to be here awhile.'

Julie continued staring at the car. Eventually she snapped out of it, gave her daughter some coins for a permit and asked if she wanted to come inside for a cuppa.

'Actually,' Mercy said once the permit was displayed inside the windscreen, 'I came here to get a haircut and a blow-dry, if you're not too inundated.'

'You want *me* to do your hair?'

'Well, I was hoping for the Real Julie,' Mercy smiled as she locked the car door, 'but you'll do in a pinch. I'm going clubbing later and I need to look sharp.'

Inside the warm salon, Mercy made small talk with the excitable Tania, who had much to say about Ru Paul's Drag Race and told Mercy that she envied her husky voice. Julie suggested Tania put the kettle on and then directed her daughter towards one of the sinks and placed a smock around her neck.

Mother and daughter had enjoyed few civil interactions since Mercy's return to London. And she knew she couldn't leave here without some difficult questions answered first. But, as Julie's fingers lathered her scalp with shampoo in a calming way, she hoped that this didn't have to turn into an argument as well.

'We'll need to store the Porsche inside your garage if that's okay,' she said over the sound of the hose, 'because it'll just collect parking tickets outside my place.' Her hair was being held in a ponytail as Julie's fingers ran through it. 'I've already searched it for clues but I'd rather you didn't sell it straightaway. The police might want to examine it once I've proven to them that Dad was murdered.'

'That's not convenient, darling,' Julie replied, her hands pulling unusually hard as she drained the hair of water. 'I've got a new tenant moving in soon who wants to keep his car there. If I can't put it straight on the market I'd sooner you kept at it yours. Have a word with the council about getting a permit.'

'New tenants? What happened to Craig and Bethan?'

'After your performance last week,' her mother said, 'they split up and moved without warning. From the sound of the rows they were having down there, he must've confessed to something. She stormed out, never to be seen again. Then *he* had the nerve to act as though it was *my* fault,' she added, with a trace of a wicked smile.

'Blokes.'

'What are they like? I tell you what, he won't be getting his deposit back.'

They both laughed at her naughtiness. Ever since she was little, Mercy had known that the best way to get this woman to thaw out was to have a giggle with her.

'What are *you* like?' Mercy beamed up. Julie was only in her early fifties, still a beautiful woman and being in her presence always had a raw effect. Throughout her life, people were forever telling her she looked like her dad. But here was the parent she'd always longed to resemble. 'Craig was half your age, mum,' she said. 'I'd be scandalised if I wasn't impressed. What with Dad and his escapades and you carrying on with toy boys, it's a wonder that I turned out so well adjusted.'

'We weren't always like that,' Julie assured her as she rinsed conditioner out of her hair. 'When your father and I started out we were the very model of the perfect couple. Like Paul Newman and Joanne Woodward, people used to say. Well,' she qualified, 'Ray used to say it. Flattering himself.'

'I've seen your wedding pictures,' Mercy said as her mother detangled her hair. 'There's no denying, you were a gorgeous couple.'

'That must explain why we produced such a gorgeous kid,' Julie smiled, squeezing Mercy's shoulder in an affectionate gesture. 'Now let's see if we can't give you gorgeous hair to match.'

She moved her round to face the mirror.

'Try not to give me a short back and sides this time,' Mercy said. Her mother assured her that she'd be getting sexy, voluminous hair like all her other customers. Mercy closed her eyes, radiating in how glorious it was to have this woman, who'd been responsible for so many of her harsh boyish haircuts when young, finally deliver the feminine treatment she'd always wanted from her.

'How's Big Bill?' Julie asked as she snipped. Reflected in the mirror, his Barbour jacket was hanging from a coat stand behind them. 'Coping without Ray?'

'He's been very supportive,' Mercy told her. 'Teaching me the tricks of the trade.'

'He always was a lovely bloke.'

'Unlike Barb,' Mercy agreed, 'who's been less welcoming, to put it mildly.'

'The biggest mystery to come out of that place,' scoffed Julie, 'is how they've been putting up with her for so long.'

'It isn't for her winning personality. What do you make of Nina Markham?'

'I only met her the once,' Julie considered as wet triangles of hair fell onto the smock around Mercy. 'She seemed moody. Mind you, we were at your dad's funeral, so fair enough.'

'Did Dad trust her?'

'*Trust* her?' Julie asked. Her scissors paused and their eyes locked in the mirror. 'What d'you mean?'

'Nothing,' Mercy shrugged. 'Just trying to get a sense of how he rated my new colleagues.'

The snipping resumed.

OK, Mercy thought, time to stop pussyfooting and go in for the kill.

'Guess who I ran into yesterday,' she said, in her sweetest manner. 'Kittichai.'

'Kitty who?' Julie asked.

'Kitty McColl,' Mercy explained. 'You remember her. Alan's Thai wife.'

'Blimey,' Julie raised her eyebrows. 'Are those two still together? I wouldn't have put money on it.'

'Yeah, she works at his shop now. Her English has improved and we had a long chat about the good old days. Nice girl.'

'Imagine being married to Expanding Alan,' Julie whistled. 'She deserves a medal.'

'Kitty remembers you fondly too,' Mercy said. 'She was telling me about that awful afternoon at the Spoils.'

'What afternoon was that?'

'The garden party when Sarah Neale killed herself,'

Mercy said, studying her mother's reflection as she said it. 'You can't have forgotten.'

Julie winced. She looked at Mercy through the mirror.

'I don't know what she's been saying,' Julie told her, pointing with her scissors, 'but she wasn't even at that party. It was for Maggie Neale's birthday and she'd hardly invite a copper's wife, even if he'd retired. The only people invited were me, Mags, Jill, Moira and Barb.'

'Kitty wasn't a guest,' Mercy replied. 'She was there as a caterer. Perhaps you don't remember because she was quietly pouring the drinks and is a person of colour.'

'It was over a decade ago,' Julie defended herself. 'I can't be expected to remember every little detail. It was very traumatic.'

'I can imagine,' Mercy sympathised, 'a young woman throwing herself from a high balcony like that straight onto the ground in front of you all. And wearing *your* red dress! Must've been extremely distressing.'

'It was like something from a horror film,' Julie confirmed, while glancing over at the rest of the salon. The other stylists were busy chatting to their clients. 'One of the worst things I've ever witnessed.'

'You've never talked about it much.'

'Can you blame me?'

'I guess not,' Mercy said and left a respectful pause before continuing. 'Poor Sarah. Did she say anything before she jumped? Any last words?'

'No. She just stepped up onto the ledge of the balcony and then plummeted.'

'Could she have been pushed?'

'Who by?'

'That's what I'm asking.'

'There wasn't anyone up there with her.'

'You sure?'

'Sarah wasn't all there, mentally,' Julie explained, her focus having already returned to Mercy's hair. 'She'd been a drug addict earlier in her life. Party girl gone wrong. And that stuff never really leaves the blood. Victor helped get her clean. Whatever else might be said of him, he did good there. She was a troubled soul and he'd sorted her out; got her into expensive rehab clinics, helped her kick all her filthy habits. But, as he spent more time abroad, nobody was around to protect her from toxic influences. Sad waste of a beautiful woman.'

'Did she seem high,' Mercy asked, 'when she welcomed you into her home that day?'

'If memory serves, someone else let us in. It was all immigrants working there around that time, none of them spoke much English, but they showed us out the back and kept our champagne glasses full. We didn't see much of Sarah until she was on the balcony ready to jump. But yeah, the hospital said she had a wide variety of drugs coursing through her when she died. Which explains *everything.*'

'Kitty says she was impressed with how well you handled things. She reckons you and Maggie really took charge.'

'We had the presence of mind to call an ambulance, if that's what she means.'

'I'm not sure it is,' Mercy said, nearing her point. 'Sarah died on the way to the hospital, right? Did any of the guests travel with her?'

'Only Moira Mance had the stomach for that. The rest of us stayed in the house until her death was confirmed. Maggie kept drinking her birthday champagne, which was a bit off, but nobody had the guts to say anything. Then, one by one, we all dispersed back to our own lives.'

'Including the staff?'

'I suppose.'

'If you had to guess,' Mercy asked, as her mother picked up a flat iron hair straightener, 'how many weeks pregnant was she when she died?'

The straightener was marble-coloured, making it appear heavier than it probably was. Julie clutched it like she was considering giving Mercy a sharp clout.

'Your little Thai friend told you that, did she?' Julie asked, their eyes meeting again in the mirror.

'Not just her,' Mercy nodded, 'Barbara was overheard talking about the baby bump too. And Bill admitted he was told the same thing – that Sarah took her own life and also that of her unborn child.'

There followed a weighty pause before Julie answered.

'She'd have been in early in her second trimester, I'd say. I mean, she wasn't showing on that day she visited our house to borrow my dress and that was only weeks earlier. None of the others knew about the pregnancy before the party either.'

'But why didn't you want anyone knowing about it?' Mercy persisted. 'Apparently once her body had been removed you and Maggie started bullying all the other women into not mentioning it.'

'Kitty's exaggerating,' Julie said as she pulled the straightener down, twisting her daughter's hair as she did so. 'Do you think we could keep a baby secret from the paramedics? Do me a favour. Now keep your head still while I work on these waves.'

'According to Kittichai,' Mercy remained as still as she could, 'it wasn't the authorities you were trying to conceal the fact from; it was from your own husbands. She told me that you didn't want any of the men to know about the belly.'

'I think I preferred pretty Kitty,' her mother said in a light voice, her attention still fixed upon Mercy's hair, 'when she couldn't speak English.'

'I've been racking my brains as to why you'd form a conspiracy of silence around that. Because Victor obviously would've been told that she'd lost a baby, so it wasn't for his benefit.' Julie kept on working the hair straightener. 'However, if my Neale timeline is accurate, he would've been living in Antigua for most of the previous year while she'd remained in England. I suppose that makes her bump a bit controversial.'

'If you're going out tonight you'll need your eyes done,' Julie remarked. 'Your lashes need work and the brows are a state.'

'A smooth change of subject.'

'What sort of mum would I be if I let you leave here without looking your optimum? I tell you what, once we're done with your hair, why don't I give you the full Julie treatment?'

'I can't afford the full Julie treatment,' Mercy admitted. 'To be honest, I can't really afford this.'

'You're in Julie's Hair & Beauty,' her mother winked. 'And I'm Julie. Don't worry about the money.'

Despite the transparent attempt at distraction, Mercy was delighted. She'd come here hoping for as feminising a makeover as possible, so wasn't going to refuse.

'You'll need to shut your eyes though,' Julie added in a sweet tone, 'and maybe your mouth as well. All I ask is for you to lie back and open your ears. I promise to tell you every bit of gossip I know about Sarah's mystery bump – and gossip is *all* it is. When we're finished – and you're looking more like my daughter than ever – that will be that. Deal?'

'Deal,' said Mercy. Then she shut her eyes and allowed Julie to finish twisting her hair into subtle waves.

'SARAH FIELDS-FOX WAS your classic double-barrelled, upper class It girl,' her mother began once they'd moved to a discreet waxing room in the back of the salon. 'Tatler famous. I'd seen her in magazines socialising with minor royals and the children of rock stars. The magazines had described her as an aristocratic wild child and that was before she'd started dating a gangster several classes below her.'

Mercy was leaning back on another chair, her eyes firmly closed as her mother softened her follicles with damp cotton wool. There was no radio playing in this private room, just her mother's voice and a faint scent from the reed diffusers.

'Basically, she was the sort of woman who people enjoy making up stories about,' Julie continued, 'regardless of whether there was substance to them. She and I got on well,' she claimed with a hint of a boast, 'we used to swap clothes because we had similar figures. To this day, I have this beautiful blue dress she wore to his fortieth birthday hanging in my closet. Obviously I haven't worn it since but it feels wrong to give it away. Victor was besotted with her at that party. But, well, Vic was still Vic. He could be controlling.'

Mercy thought *controlling* was a bit of an understatement considering he'd paid M&T to run constant surveillance on her while out of the country.

'The real problem though,' Julie explained, 'the *bigger* problem, was his brother Lawrence.'

Something got sucked out of the air as Julie uttered that name. Her eyes still closed, Mercy could sense her mother bracing herself, reluctant to cross this line in the narrative.

'Lol was difficult. He had a bad reputation around women.'

Another pause.

'So yeah, back in the day, that was a thing we talked about, we wives. *Don't get left alone with Lawrence Neale,* we'd say. It didn't matter that we were married to his mates, in fact that probably turned the dirty fucker on. He was always touching us up and there were stories of him... well, forcing himself on girls in his clubs. When we were all teenagers, Jill Lamoreaux's sister Debbie claimed he pulled her into a gentlemen's toilet and raped her. I'm sorry to say that nobody, including Jill, believed her at the time, which on hindsight is a bit shaming. Keep your face still, Mercy, or I'll mess the shape up.

'He cornered me once,' Julie continued, 'during a party at their house. Maggie was heavy with her Nick at the time and I was less obviously pregnant with you. We were having a nice barbecue and Lol was turning the meat while Ray, Victor, and the boys were all kicking a ball at the end of their garden. I asked Maggie which loo I could use and Lol answered for her.

'"*Use the upstairs bog, girl,*" he called over. "*The flush is fucked down here.*"

'So up I went, relishing the chance to explore their big house and found the lavatory. Afterwards, when I unlocked it, there he was, occupying the doorway like a leering gorilla, blocking my exit. My whole body went into high alert.

'"*Wiped your whiskers?*" he grinned. His arm was placed

on the door so I couldn't shut it again. Outside I could hear your dad cheering because he'd just scored another goal. *"He's a lucky boy, your Raymond."*

'I tried to push past but he wouldn't let me. I told him to stop fucking about or I'd call his wife. He fucking laughed. Said, *"Maggie hears what she wants to,"* whatever that meant. I told him I was serious and almost managed to slip past, but he grabbed my hand to stop me leaving. Then he tried to force me into the bathroom. I was terrified. He was a *massive* bloke.'

Mercy had to open her eyes. Above her, Julie had gone pale. looked down at her daughter and gave her a thin smile.

'Jesus, darling,' she said, before reaching out with her fingers to motion her daughter's eyelids shut again. 'I haven't thought about this in years. I went into full panic mode and was about to scream when I was rescued by Barbara of all people.' Mercy raised her eyebrows. 'She only had her job at the agency because she was tight with the Neale boys, so she was at the barbecue too. She must've noticed that Lol had crept off after me and had come to investigate.

'*"See to the sausages, Lol,"* she said to him. *"Before they burn."*

'Lol released me, pushed past Barb and went back downstairs. He left me trembling. I reached out to thank Barbara but she just told me to dry my eyes and followed after Lol. Never mentioned it again.'

Mercy sat up on the bench and went to hold her mother. Julie responded, and they remained like that for a minute. The sick memory of Lol's only son accosting her in the school changing room slithered through her again. Two generations of Tyler women attacked by the same rotten family.

'That's horrible, Mum,' she whispered into her ear. 'Did you ever tell Dad?'

'Rottweiler Ray? With his explosive temper?' Julie reached for a nearby box of tissues to dab her eyes. 'No way. He would've done something about it and then where would we be? Lol was the most dangerous man in Britain. It would've been a death sentence for your dad. Lie down again so I can do the other brow. You're asymmetrical.

'I wasn't the only one with such a story,' she eventually continued. 'Jill told me he grabbed her in a hotel lift once and ripped her blouse. She believed her sister a bit more after that.'

'This is monstrous,' Mercy cried from her prone position. 'How was this not reported? He was a famous gangster. The police would've taken you seriously, the media even more so.'

'I thought we agreed you'd keep your mouth shut and your ears open,' Julie replied, plucking out a stubborn lash so hard that it stung. 'We were all terrified of Lol but it was a different time. Also, there was a lot of money being funnelled to the agency from the Neale direction. Criminals can be very generous with their friends, partly because they can't do much else with stolen loot. So yeah, blind eyes were turned. Lower your eyebrows, love; you're making this difficult. Anyway, it came to a stop when his younger brother married Sarah. I didn't realise at the time, but the pig turned his attention to her. Amazingly, they started an affair.'

'A *consensual* affair?' asked Mercy. 'I don't believe that for a minute.'

'One night, Maggie received a midnight phone call from her brother-in-law who was still in Antigua. He was in tears. Imagine that, Victor Neale crying. He told her that she needed to keep a tighter rein on her husband. He'd intercepted a message written from Sarah to Lol, saying that she loved him.'

'Mum, why didn't you tell me this earlier? This totally fits in with my theory about—'

Julie placed a finger over her daughter's lips.

'Quiet darling, Mummy hasn't finished. Shut your eyes. So, a short time later,' she went on, 'Lol was murdered in a car bomb. So that was the end of that.'

Mercy recalled that night in the Nepalese restaurant when her father had told them about the explosion. *Poor Maggie,* Julie had said about his wife. *Poor Nick,* about his son. Never poor Lol.

'Most of us were thrilled,' Julie said. 'But his wife and son were devastated, so we rallied around for their sake. From abroad, Victor insisted that we use the Spoils to celebrate Maggie's birthday a fortnight later, you know, cheer her up. That's why we were having that dreadful garden party. I mean, we all thought Lol was the father when we saw the bump. And maybe that was why she'd done it. Perhaps her druggy brain just couldn't live with bringing his kid into the world. We kept the secret for Maggie's sake, not Sarah. She'd been humiliated enough by Lol's antics. Why make that worse? The newspapers would've had a field day, so we insisted that nobody say anything about the pregnancy. No good would come of broadcasting it. Now then,' she said, pulling away from Mercy's face. 'I think that's everything. Open your eyes.'

Mercy looked up at her mother. Was she imagining it, or did Julie seem unburdened now? Lighter.

She sat up to see how her mum had made her look.

Delighted by the result, Mercy thanked Julie who also seemed proud by how beautiful she'd made her daughter. Considering the unpleasant events they'd been discussing, the hour they'd spent together had felt therapeutic. They were celebrating with a hug when Tania knocked on the door to tell Julie that she had a customer waiting and that Mercy's parking permit was about to expire.

As THEY WALKED BACK through the busy salon Julie asked Mercy who she was going clubbing with.

'Just an old school friend,' she answered.

'Well, you look stunning,' Julie smiled, before they embraced again 'if I do say so myself.'

Julie watched her late husband's car drive away through the window, before letting out another audible sigh and going back to work.

# 37

Leaving her mother, Mercy drove straight back to Rafferty Road and parked the Porsche once again within the open-gated driveway of that mysterious art-deco house. However, by now, she no longer cared who owned it. She had since realised that her dad must have left it there because he knew it provided free off-road parking. And he must have known that for the same reason she did.

Because a neighbour had told him.

A basic background check had revealed that the taciturn woman who lived in the pretty house next door was called Claudia Beech. She was a divorcee with a long career in glossy magazines and a habit of hiring private investigators. Her more forthcoming son had mentioned he'd been staying with his dad when the car had been left there, which explained its presence. Dad had been visiting Claudia.

Jason's bike was missing from its chain as Mercy rang the bell. She was glad he was out; it would be easier to interrogate this woman alone. Some impatient moments followed, and she pressed the doorbell again.

Through the window she saw Claudia coming down the

stairs. She had curly blonde hair and was somewhat short; at least, much shorter than her mother. Claudia reached the bottom of the stairs and recognised who was at the door. She froze. Mercy tapped on the window regardless.

'Ms Beech?' she called through to the startled homeowner. 'Claudia? My name's Mercy Tyler, I'm Ray Tyler's daughter. I believe you knew him. Your son was very helpful last night in allowing me to remove his car, which I'm sure was becoming a nuisance. It *was* you who sent me the anonymous text, I take it?'

The woman remained where she was. She looked terrified.

'Thank you for that,' Mercy continued. 'It's a huge relief for my mother and me. We could really use the resale money. But I have some questions about how it got here in the first place, if that's not inconvenient.'

Claudia took tentative steps towards the door. Then she paused again.

'I checked our database this morning,' Mercy persisted, 'and discovered that you were one of my dad's clients in 2017. I know that you knew him. Seriously Claudia, I'm not here to give you shit or anything. I don't care if you were having an affair or whatever. I simply want to ask about—'

Claudia moved. She strode up to the door and Mercy heard a shuffling behind it. Then it opened, a brass chain acting as a barrier between them.

'Get off my property!' she hissed. 'Or I'm calling the police.'

'Why would you do that?' Mercy asked, cocking her head. 'I only want a chat.'

'You've got the car. Good. Now just leave my son and I alone! I'm not in any way involved and nor do I wish to be.'

'Involved in what?'

Claudia produced a phone from her pocket. 'I'm calling them,' she threatened.

'Do it,' Mercy replied. 'I've been meaning to tell the police about my dad's car being found anyway. I'm not doing anything illegal.'

'You are *not* who you say you are!'

'I think you'll find I am.'

'Ray Tyler didn't have a daughter,' Claudia informed her. 'He had a son who lives in Barcelona. You're an imposter.'

'Okay, I see what's happened here,' Mercy rolled her eyes and reached for her wallet. 'He was telling you about me. I transitioned in Spain. Here, take a look.'

She held up a Spanish driving license with her name on and then reached into her handbag. From there she produced the photograph of the golfing day that she'd removed from the office fridge. She indicated the child who Ray had his arm around.

'That's me,' she told her. Claudia compared them and looked up again.

'*You're* Chrissy?'

'I prefer to be called Mercy now.'

The IDs were handed back, but Claudia remained on edge. She was an attractive enough woman, Mercy supposed, if diminutive. But she had nothing on Julie in the beauty department, so what was the appeal to her father? Perhaps it was simply that she was a bit more middleclass than he was used to. In Mercy's own experience, cockney boys are often a sucker for a posh voice.

'If you're really his child,' Claudia challenged her in an accent that hit every consonant her mother would miss, 'then answer me this. When Chrissy was born, Ray bought him a shirt. What was it?'

'A Three Lions shirt signed by several England players,' Mercy answered, shaking her head in weary disbelief. 'Let me get this straight. He never mentioned that I was transgender, but he found the time to boast about *a football shirt?* That fucking guy.'

Claudia removed the chain from the door.

'Sorry for the third degree,' she peered up in a sheepish way. 'I thought you were dangerous.'

'Well, as you can see, I'm perfectly benign.'

'Your text about the car freaked me out,' she explained. 'Pretending to be Ray when I knew he'd was dead. I thought...'

'Thought what?'

'I thought perhaps you were working for Ray's enemies,' she answered with a slight raise of the chin. 'And, oh I don't know, that you were using his phone and meant trouble. Look, I just wanted the bloody thing out of the way. Seeing my dead lover's car every morning wasn't exactly great for my mental health.'

'Enemies?' asked Mercy. 'I'd love for you to elaborate on that.'

'I wouldn't know who they were,' the woman answered, quick, nervous, unconvincing. 'I assume he had them.'

'Listen Claudia, I think my dad was murdered.'

The woman widened her eyes, but Mercy wasn't buying the surprise. She'd made similar declarations to others in recent weeks, but this was the first time she'd sensed that someone agreed.

'The police have footage of him driving that very car into this vicinity about four hours before he died,' she continued. 'So let's cut the crap. You were one of the last people to see him alive and you're obviously scared about getting *involved,* as you put it. So, I'm assuming that you do know who his enemies are. If you'd prefer, I could return later and ask Jason.'

'Don't you *dare* involve my son,' she snapped. 'He doesn't know anything about this.'

'Fine. Let's talk now then.'

Claudia bit her lip, took a step back and gestured for Mercy to cross the threshold.

'I'm putting the kettle on,' she told her. 'You can join me if you take your boots off.'

Claudia's living room was light, colourful, and had an extremely soft sofa that Mercy sank into. There were little rips near the bottom of it though and, in the corner, there was a cat's scratching post. If the cat itself was in the room, it was hiding, but Mercy had expected a feline presence. The coronary report had mentioned little animal scratches on her fathers' hands and so at least one of his attackers had now been uncovered. Mercy examined the place while Claudia was in the kitchen brewing her a cup of tea. There were moody black and white photographs on the walls and some abstract art. The coffee table books were all about fashion or architecture. It was curious to think that this was where her rough-edged dad had spent his final evening.

'Ray and I were an on-and-off thing,' Claudia eventually explained as she sat on an opposite chair, holding her own cup and saucer. 'We met when I was divorcing Jason's father. I hired him to gather hard evidence of his infidelity and, I have to say, I was pleased with the service. If it weren't for him, I'd never have got full custody of my son.' She took a sip of the tea. 'Not to mention this house.'

'It's beautiful,' Mercy said, blowing on her own tea. 'Did Dad visit you often after your divorce, or just when Jason was away?'

Claudia's jaw shifted a little before answering.

'I knew he was married – I won't pretend I didn't. But he told me that he and your mother were only together for your sake.'

'Ha!'

'Well whatever,' Claudia said, after sipping at her tea. 'That's what he said.'

There was a well-stocked wine rack near the fireplace and while Claudia had been making the tea Mercy had established that many of the bottles were empty. Here might be the real reason why her alcoholic father and Claudia had enjoyed each other's company so much. Drinkers love other drinkers.

'Occasionally he'd phone me up and ask if I was still single. And always on that number you contacted me on. He'd take me out to dinner; we'd drink some wine and laugh about our respective jobs. He wasn't the sort of man I could imagine introducing my friends to, but we had fun. He told a good story.'

'What sort of story?'

'Oh, stuff about the agency, his friends, the colourful characters he'd met throughout his life. The celebrity scandals he knew about, the criminals with whom he'd grown up. I never knew whether to believe any of it but it was entertaining at the time.'

'When did it stop being entertaining?'

'How do you mean?'

'When did he stop referring to "colourful characters" and start talking about enemies?'

Claudia's right hand had become a little unsteady as she held her teacup. She was withholding something.

'He must've told you he was friends with Victor Neale, right?' Mercy prodded. 'The guy behind the Air Costelloe heist.'

Claudia placed her teacup onto the table. Her eyes were scared.

'It's not a world that has anything to do with mine,' she said after a pause. 'Perhaps you should leave.'

Mercy placed her own half-drunk cup beside Claudia's. She reached into her pocket for the recorder she kept her father's message on.

'Let me play you something before I go,' she said. 'Dad sent it to me hours before his body was found in the river. Please, Claudia, if you ever cared about him at all, I'd like you to tell me if anything jumps out.'

She pressed play.

*'Christopher mate. Chrissy? It's your dad. Is this still your number?'*

On hearing Ray's voice, Claudia immediately leaned backwards into her chair as if spooked.

*'It's a filthy night and I'm drunk.'*

'He was probably drunk on your wine,' Mercy said. Claudia's eyes darted towards her as Ray was assuring Christopher that he'd always loved him.

'Your dad was pissed when he got here,' Claudia informed her with a measure of spite. 'He *drove* drunk quite a lot.'

*'It was that afternoon in my office,'* his voice continued, *'when you was still just my little boy.'*

She watched her dad's girlfriend as he talked about the Long Needle. Claudia didn't react to that but continued looking at the phone as if it was a third person in the room. Mercy's own response on hearing the message again for the umpteenth time was complicated. She'd begun to find his whimpering words pathetic, especially considering he'd been cheating on her mother with this woman a short time before his death. She longed to rebuke him for the complicated mess he'd left her to solve. *He* was his own killer, she wanted to tell him, and that she'd deserved better from a father.

*'In spite of everything, I've always loved—'*

Mercy turned it off before he finished.

'God, he sounds broken.' Claudia said in a sorrowful voice. 'Oh Ray.'

'Hearing it takes a toll on me too,' Mercy said as she placed the recorder away again.

Claudia dropped her head into her hands, her long curly hair concealing her face. She emitted a little *woo* sound and then rose up again, eyes glistening.

'Does anything stand out?' Mercy asked, keen to return her own attention back to the investigation and away from clouding emotions. 'Did he mention any of that when here?'

Claudia turned her head towards her magazines, lifted an elbow up and placed her hand over her mouth. A moon grey cat at last appeared from behind the sofa. It slinked towards its owner, sensing distress. Then, almost imperceptibly, Claudia gave a tiny nod.

'On that final night,' she said, after reaching out to stroke the cat, 'he wasn't his usual happy self. Possibly I saw a different side of him than you and your mother were used to, but, when he was with me, he played the clown. Smiling, joking, making saucy comments.'

'A cheeky chappy,' Mercy said, with an edge. She remembered that side of his personality too, but hadn't seen much of it since she'd come out as trans. It irked that he'd still been performing it for others.

'One of the things that endeared him to me was how upbeat he could be. It was cheering, especially after my divorce. But I hadn't seen him in over a month and I'd rather moved on. Started dating other people. Then, out of the blue, he called me up one morning. He told me he'd love to see me that night, meet at our restaurant, come home afterwards, early night. I told him that it wasn't appropriate, that I had a new boyfriend. Which wasn't strictly true, I'd had about three Tinder dates with a chap and they hadn't gone well. And Ray, pushy bastard, got me to admit to it. So I said, fine, sure, suit yourself, lets meet later. In all honesty, I was keen for a good fuck.'

Her eyes lifted from the cat but she didn't apologise, which Mercy appreciated.

'He was late to the restaurant,' Claudia continued. 'I waited almost an hour which was humiliating as I'm a regular there. No call or anything. I was about to leave when the Porsche screeched up outside and in he bounded, as if being pursued by the Hounds of Hell. I told him he was too late, I was going home, but he insisted on driving me, which wasn't exactly appealing considering the smell of booze on his breath. But it saved me an Uber,' she shrugged.

'On the drive home he told me he wouldn't be staying the night,' she continued, her voice rising a note, 'which wasn't unusual. Normally, he went home afterwards which suited me fine. But I reminded him that Jason was away with his father so he could stay if he wanted to. That's when he told me he had a business meeting later near the Cutty Sark in Greenwich. "*Tonight?*" I asked, "in *this* weather? At what time?" Midnight, he replied. He was brokering a deal between two people and he needed to introduce them. Well, I assumed that this was just a wild excuse to vanish after he'd had his fun with me. "You can piss off now," I told him, "if you're going to be like that."

'But he pleaded with me to let him stay. Some undisclosed business-related reasons meant he needed somewhere to "lay low." From who Ray, I asked? I admit, I was sceptical. I just thought it was some bullshit he was coming out with to secure sex after having upset me. But he told me there was a dangerous woman he was trying to duck and he couldn't sleep in the office.'

'Did he say the dangerous woman's name?'

'Yes actually,' Claudia told her. 'He'd said she was called Greenwater.'

'Just Greenwater?' asked Mercy. 'Not Mrs or Miss?' Claudia shook her head. 'Did he ever mention the Long Needle to you?'

'No, I've never heard him say that until you played me that voicemail. All he said was, "Greenwater's after me." I asked, who is this Greenwater? He mumbled, "you don't know her."'

Interesting, thought Mercy, making a note to look through the client database for that name later on.

'That's why I was scared to see you sniffing around his car last night, asking your questions. I thought you were this Greenwater woman he was stressing about.'

'His use of a female pronoun suggests he wasn't talking about me,' Mercy said, more to herself. 'So then what happened? Why did he leave his car?'

'He was here for a few hours, we drank too much and ordered a takeaway,' Claudia explained, as the cat padded away from her. 'But he was awful. Pacing around, checking his phone, rubbing his face like he was trying to force his own nose off. Swearing to himself. He kept going to the toilet and was in there for ages. I thought maybe it was a cocaine thing but all I could hear was sobbing. It was horrendous.

'Eventually I said, "seriously Ray, what's going on? Why is this Greenwater woman after you? What've you done now?" But I couldn't get any sense out of him. His phone was off and when I asked why he said his battery was dead.'

The cat had begun scratching the sofa beside Mercy's legs. She reached down to stroke her. Ray's second phone with Claudia's number on it had been found inside the office mini-fridge, which explained why he hadn't phoned ahead to say he was going to be late. But the battery to his main smart phone had been working when he'd left her that final message hours later. So why pretend it was dead? Was he trying to make sure nobody could track his movements?

'He drank and drank and wasn't much use to me beyond a certain point,' said Claudia. 'Sex was obviously off the agenda. So as midnight approached I asked him to leave, quite forcefully. It had begun raining again and he was reluctant to go. "*I won't survive the night!*" he suddenly said. "*Someone out there wants to kill me.*" I told him that someone was thinking about killing him in here and I insisted he go. He called me by a misogynistic slur, which I won't repeat, and stormed out. I watched from the door as he wobbled over to the car that he'd left in the neighbour's drive. The rain was battering down and I shouted over that he shouldn't be driving anywhere in his condition. But he was calling a cab.'

'I thought his phone battery was dead.'

'He must've turned it on again,' Claudia shrugged. 'He waited inside his Porsche for almost an hour, fog lights on, until a cab pulled up. I watched from the window as he got out of his old car, without turning off the lights.'

'Are you certain it was a cab?' Mercy asked.

'I didn't see the driver, but I was just relieved he was going. I expected him to return when he'd sobered up,' she sighed, 'but, as history records, he never did.'

'When did you realise he wasn't coming back?' Mercy asked, her head down and focusing on the young cat. She was fighting not to become upset by this wretched description of her father. She didn't want Claudia using that as an excuse to clam up. 'How did you find out he was dead?'

'Days past and I kept expecting to hear from him. An apology, an explanation; something. I'm a bit ashamed to admit that I was sort of hoping he'd show up on my doorstep with an expensive gift and a sunnier attitude. But Christmas passed and Jason was due to come home from his father's place and that bloody car was just *sitting* there in next door's driveway. Rather than go through the indignity of him ignoring me on either of his phones, I called his office and asked to speak to him, acting as if I were still an important client. And that miserable secretary told me they'd buried him the previous day.' She lifted her face to the ceiling. 'I was devastated, sure,' she spoke with a crack in her voice. 'But... more than that...'

'You were scared,' Mercy helped her, 'because he'd told you he was going to die that night and then did.'

'I asked for some details about what had happened,' Claudia said after a cautious nod, 'and was told he'd had an accident down by the Deptford docks days before Christmas. I knew it must be the same night because of the car.' She looked down at the cat who'd grown bored and was leaving them to their conversation.

'Why didn't you tell the police this?' Mercy asked. 'How come I was the only one saying the word "murder" to them?'

Claudia's eyes met Mercy's own. It was difficult to tell if they were wet from grief or fear.

'I mentioned that he was a storyteller,' she said, after briefly wiping her eyes. 'Well, on hindsight, one of the more fanciful tales sticks in the mind. He told me once, over a very drunken dinner probably six months ago, that he knew a contract killer. That if I wanted someone *whacked* – his word – then he had the number of a man. He was trying to impress me, as pathetic as it sounds. Even more pathetically, I was impressed.'

Mercy straightened. It seemed too good to be true, but here at last was a thread that might lead to a needle.

'I said, what makes you think I don't have hitmen in my own contact list, Ray. "Maybe you do, darling," he answered, cocky shit that he was, "but not like this guy. This is the guy you call when you don't want it to look like a hit." I encouraged him I suppose. Asked him what he meant by that and he just said that he knew a young man who was as deadly as a shadow. Shadows aren't deadly, I said, and he replied, "*his is!*" which made me giggle. We were both quite sloshed.'

'A young man?' Mercy said. She was struck by an impulse to record all this but was concerned it might silence Claudia. 'How young?'

'Young enough for Ray to have been surprised when they first met,' she said. 'He told me that when he'd originally contacted him he'd expected an older, gruff-voiced man, gun in a violin case, that sort of thing. But actually the hitman was just a kid. He was shocked by his youth.'

'Like a teenager?'

'I don't know about that. But Ray said baby-faced, if that helps. Baby-faced killer.'

Mercy considered what age that might make the hitman.

Back then, someone in his late twenties would've been a kid to Ray.

'Your dad didn't say what his ethnicity was, probably because he didn't know, but he was mixed race. Apparently that was part of his success, being able to pass as either African, Arab, Spanish, Italian, sometimes Indian. There were many crowds he could disappear into. And he was well spoken. "*Plummier than you*", Ray had enjoyed telling me.'

'How did he first come by this baby-faced killer?'

'Didn't say,' shrugged Claudia. 'He mainly spoke about his methods, which were chilling. Supposedly, once the contract had been accepted, he set about researching his targets. He'd unearth whatever weaknesses you might have and use them against you. If you drove a motorbike fast, you'd have a motorbike accident. If you were a druggy, you'd have an overdose. Weak heart, he'd weaken it further. The manner of your death wouldn't seem suspicious if it was how everyone expected you to go.'

Mercy scanned again her long held theory.

*If you were a gangster with rivals known to blow up cars...* but then stopped and considered her newer theory.

*If you were a former drug addict with a history of self-harming, then a suicide would look very real.*

'Ray was an alcoholic,' Claudia said with admirable bluntness, 'and he died an alcoholic's death. If he hadn't told me that someone was trying to kill him that night, I wouldn't have been suspicious. As I say, that one story stuck. He never told me a name.'

'Did he tell you anything else?'

'I remember him saying that he rarely met Baby-face in the same location twice. Sometimes he went to Camden, Kings Cross, Little Venice, Limehouse. He moved all over London and beyond.'

Mercy felt sick to imagine her dad bragging about *doing business* with a creature like that. The idea that he'd continued his relationship with the Long Needle for years after that first meeting was a blow she hadn't expected, and she'd expected blows. How many murders had Ray brokered? Whatever remaining sympathy she felt for him was ebbing fast.

'I'm diabetic,' Claudia told her. 'So I suppose if the baby-faced killer targeted me that's what he'd use. He'd gain entry into my home, which you managed easily enough, and make it look like an insulin mishap. My son would presumably find my body.'

'If he wanted to kill me,' Mercy said, recalling the glinting knife in the dark, 'he'd make it look like a transphobic attack. Or a mugging gone wrong.'

*There'd been two of them,* she remembered, *a man and a woman.*

'Well, this has been a delight,' Claudia said with a tight smile as she stood. 'A shame we had to meet under such circumstances, but I think it's time for you to fuck off now.'

Mercy tried to think of one more question as Claudia walked her to the front door and she placed her boots back on.

'If I find out who killed him,' she said as the door was opened, 'whether it's this baby-faced man, the Greenwater woman or someone else – do you want me to come back and tell you?'

Claudia's face showed exhaustion. Then, this woman with whom her father had spent his last night alive, shook her head.

'No thanks,' she said, shutting the door after her.

On the previous evening Mercy had felt proud to be an investigator as she'd driven her dad's car away from Rafferty

Road. Today she felt the opposite. She'd been making advances in her case, sure. But, to get there, she'd pressured two women into sharing painful secrets about themselves – three, she rebuked herself, including Kittichai – and had learnt that her dad had been profiting from a contract killer for over a decade.

This time, as she drove away, she kept the radio switched off.

# PART V

*The Never Setting Sun*

# 38

Nick could remember visiting this pub before in a previous dream. It was called the Hell on Earth and it had a warm, welcoming glow. As before, it was packed to the walls with dead villains.

He was moving through the countless saloons of that golden-lit maze, passing all the old faces that his dad had told him about. Jack Spot with his black cheek mole propping up the bar, Billy Hill dealing cards at a table, the twins keeping their counsel in a dark corner. Nick glided past them. Ahead in the smoke he could hear his father's boisterous laughter.

He pushed through brass swing doors into another bar. The only people he found in there were some once-great train robbers playing darts. He kept searching through the different chambers, climbing staircases, calling out his dad's name. Behind the bar, a phone was ringing.

Nick came to a charred-black room on the top floor with part of its roof missing. Stinking of ash, Lawrence Neale was sitting in a red leather chair while Roz – Nick's girlfriend, wearing only a black thong – gave him a lap dance.

'Cracking bird, son,' his father leered.

The phone finally succeeded in waking him. He turned to find Roz lying beside him in a drug-induced sleep that even a fire alarm wouldn't wake her from. He looked at the phone. Unknown caller.

'Who this?' he demanded on answering. There was a pause on the line before a deep American voice spoke. He recognised it as the same voice that had called him on New Year's Eve.

*'But that I am forbid to tell the secrets of my prison house,'* the voice wheezed. *'I could a tale unfold of which the slightest word—'*

'You again?'

*'—would harrow upon thy soul—'*

'You got some front, mate!'

*'—freeze thy young blood—'*

'It's three in the fucking morning,' Nick told him, rubbing the sleep from his eyes and sitting on the edge of the bed. 'We're trying to sleep here.'

*'So art thou to revenge,'* the voice warned, *'when thou shalt hear.'*

'Stop fucking about,' Nick glanced over his shoulder to the slumbering Roz, her long blonde hair a dreamy mess. 'Tell me who you are.'

*'I am thy father's spirit, doomed for a certain term—'*

'You cheeky cunt!' Nick roared. 'If you really killed my dad then at least have the stones to come down and face me. Don't call in the middle of the night talking bollocks.'

*'What's the matter, Nicky? Don't you like Shakespeare? It's the Long Needle, by the way.'*

In a state of rising apoplexy, Nick strode out of the bedroom. 'This has gone beyond now,' he seethed. 'I'm gonna rip your head off and *shit down your neck-hole*!'

Just then he hit his foot on a discarded dumbbell. Crying out, he collapsed onto the sofa, clutching his foot with the other hand. '*You* made me do that!' he told the caller.

The curtains were open and moonlight illuminated the room. The voice on the line cleared its throat.

*'You and Hamlet have much in common,'* it explained. *'You've both been informed that your uncle killed your dad, but you dither so. There's a lot of big talk from you both but the serpent that stung thy father's life still wears his crown.'*

Nick rubbed his foot. The window overlooked the river and the outline of an industrial sugar factory could be seen on the north bank of the Thames. Getting up, he limped over to the glass door, pulled it back and stepped out onto the balcony.

'I've been prepping,' he whispered while scanning the path below to see if anyone was watching. 'But I need proof of what you're telling me before I can make my big move.'

*'Evidence is for pussies. Think your dad made his name by coming up with reasons* not *do whatever he liked? He was a man of action.'*

'*I'm* a man of action,' Nick insisted. 'But he's not an easy guy to get. If he was here now, it'd be done already. Bare hands. But he lives in this big mansion in the country and never comes out. What can I do?'

*'I'd like to meet you tomorrow night. I have a gift I'd like to give you by way of an apology for blowing up your dad. Where is good?'*

'Jack Spot's,' Nick answered without hesitation. 'I'll be mob-handed from 7.'

*'Mark me,'* the voice said before hanging up.

# 39

Under a wet sky, Mercy walked alone through the flower garden in Greenwich Park. It was hours after she'd spoken with Claudia but the day was still light. There weren't many other people around, just some passing joggers and pram-pushers. Once confident that nobody was following her, she continued speaking aloud.

'Fact:' she said, 'in the summer of 2004 my dad met with a contract killer inside our family home. Another fact: in a voicemail sent to me just before his death, Dad made explicit reference to this meeting. He then called the visitor the Long Needle.'

An elderly man was sitting on a park bench ahead of her, feeding pigeons. Hands in her jacket pockets, she moved away from the path and crossed the large lawn, passing between flowerbeds.

'Next fact: Lawrence Neale died in a car explosion less than a week after that meeting. Rival gangster Bobby McAlonan was tried and convicted for that crime but he always denied it. But yesterday, *you* told me that Victor had a solid motive for wanting his own brother dead.' Her chin was resting in the black scarf around her neck as she spoke to Bill. 'An anonymous caller has recently been harassing Lol's son,' she continued, dropping her voice even further to better test the recording, 'calling himself the Long Needle and revealing that he was the person who arranged for Lol's car to explode. This caller also stated that my dad acted as broker for the hit on Victor's behalf. I've no clue what his motive for admitting that might be but it fits perfectly with what I previously thought; which was that Victor had his own brother killed.'

Mercy opened a low steel gate to let a jogger pass through. She then continued into the main park and was quiet for a bit. Ahead of her at the top of the hill was a cloaked figure in a three-corner hat, his back to her. The statue overlooked the rest of the park, the curving river and much of architectural London, old and new.

'I've developed a new theory though,' she whispered, approaching a water fountain that a man was drinking from, his terrier lapping at the spillage beneath. There were some cars parked nearby including her dad's Porsche and Bill's Nissan. She gave the dog a gentle stroke before the owner led it away.

'Want to hear it?' she asked.

The fog lights on Bill's car flashed.

'I don't think that Dad had opened the sealed envelope before the meeting. Like me, he just assumed that the victim would be Lawrence Neale. He knew that Lol was a sexual predator who'd hooked Sarah onto drugs, so he may have even approved of the hit. *I* could've lived with it.' She was whispering now, and not just for the sound test. 'So he hadn't seen the actual contents of the pink envelope until the Long Needle insisted on it. So, what if he suddenly learnt that it wasn't

Lawrence's death warrant he'd handed over? What if Victor had instead arranged a hit on someone else? Namely, the innocent mother of Victor's own children. That might explain why Dad wept once the meeting was over. Fancy a hot drink?'

She crossed over to a coffee stall, cross with herself for speculating her dad might have felt guilty about his actions. This was not a fact. It *was* a fact that he did business with killers. Everything else about him, including the reason for his tears, was theory.

'I'm not making excuses for him,' she assured Bill as she walked two hot cups back towards his car. 'But when Dad eventually learnt that Sarah had been pregnant when she'd died, he went nuts. Could that revelation have triggered some action on his part? Something that got him killed?'

Bill had lowered the driver's window as she approached. 'Cheers for this,' he said, taking the coffee. 'And it sounds brilliant.'

'My theory?' she asked.

'No, the recording sounds brilliant,' he indicated the speaker through which he'd been listening. 'Your theory sounds implausible. Get in and I'll explain why.'

Once she was settled in the passenger seat, he played back everything she'd said while strolling through the park. As much as she hated hearing her own voice, she agreed that the recording was crisp. She'd begun her walk by telling him what she'd learnt from Claudia.

'What you're suggesting,' Bill said, fiddling with his new hacking gear once they'd listened to it all through, 'is that this Long Needle fella convinced a pregnant woman to step from a fourth floor balcony under her own volition? As well as her unborn child, she had two other kids. So how did he persuade her? Hypnotism?'

'He pointed a gun at her,' Mercy suggested 'while she was high on drugs.'

'I don't know...'

'It's known in the hitman trade as a Russian Suicide,' she told him. 'An assassin leads their target at gunpoint to a high place, like a cliff edge. *Jump or I shoot.* According to this podcast I listened to, most people take their chances with option A, assuming it will be less painful or that they would be more likely to survive. So, the hit looks like suicide. Now you imagine that same choice, but with the gun trained on a pregnant belly. And Sarah unable to think straight. I reckon she'd jump.'

Bill placed a finger in his mouth and bit at the nail.

'Kittichai told me that two caterers had gone missing soon after the fall and have never been accounted for. Could this be the Needle and a female accomplice? A man and a woman stole my phone, don't forget.'

'Maybe this Greenwater woman your dad was worried about?'

'Actually, I think Greenwater is someone else.' She produced her dad's secret phone. 'One of the contacts I found on this is marked OG. Last week I discovered that it belonged to a policewoman named Helen Bracken. She approached me after Dad's funeral where she claimed she was an old friend of his. Ever heard of her?'

'No.'

'I think the G in OG stands for Greenwater. Could he have been a paid informer?'

'That certainly would be a turn up,' Bill said, raising his eyebrows. 'Because your dad hated a grass. He used to say *snitches get stitches.*'

'Well, he received more than a few stitches. Maybe he

was about to snitch on Victor, or the Long Needle. Someone got to him first.'

Mercy considered telling Bill about Nina. But she wasn't completely certain that she'd been followed by her last night and so, for now, she decided to keep that suspicion quiet.

'Well done on tracking that down,' Bill said, thumbing at the Porsche beside them. 'Slick detective work.'

'I blush.'

'I've not been idle myself,' he said, attaching another lead to his hardware and searched through his files on a computer tablet. 'Here's what I caught fishing in the early hours.' After dropping her home on the previous night, Bill had driven to Woolwich and positioned his car close to Nick's apartment block. Using the new state-of-the-art equipment he'd bought from Alan, he'd managed to lock in on Nick's number. 'And just as I was dozing off,' he told her, 'there was a pull on my hook.'

*'It's three in the fucking morning,'* she heard Nick's voice coming out of Bill's speakers. *'We're trying to sleep here.'*

Then an American voice replied, *'so art thou to revenge when thou shalt hear.'*

They listened as the caller then introduced himself.

*'It's the Long Needle, by the way.'*

'Got him,' Bill smiled.

Nick then threatened to tear off the caller's head and shit down his neck hole. It then sounded like he'd tripped over, making both Mercy and Bill laugh.

The caller told Nick that he had a gift for him. Then he asked where they might meet.

*'Jack Spot's,'* Nick replied. Bill had already discovered where that was. A grimy little nightclub in Woolwich that

was once owned by Nick's dad. *'I'll be there mob-handed from 7.'*

'The American accent sounds fake to me,' Bill said, once the audio was complete. 'Like when Benedict Cumberbatch tries to play a superhero. Do you recognise the quotes he's coming out with?'

'We did Hamlet at sixth form,' Mercy nodded. 'But Nick had been expelled by then, so I doubt he got the reference.'

'You know, this could be enough for Victor. He wants hard evidence that his nephew is planning to harm him and, well, there it is. Job done. We could get paid full fee on this alone. But if there's a chance that this hitman will make an approach tonight then we need to be watching. Are you ready?'

'Willing and able.'

'Good. I'll be monitoring you closely, but you must walk away at the first sign of danger.' He handed her another phone. 'If *I* see trouble, I'll ring that as a signal for you to get out of there. But, if I call your other phone then it's not a red alert situation.'

She took it and got out of the car. As she opened the door to her dad's Porsche, he called over through his open window.

'By the way,' Bill grinned, before driving away. 'Love the hair!'

# 40

'Know this, babe' Roz said as she and Nick were preparing for their night out, 'you were a lot easier to live with before this Long Needle started winding you up.'

Nick had been dousing himself with the aftershave she'd got him for Christmas. His shirt was unbuttoned and he'd been checking himself in the mirror, striking bad boy poses.

'Because I was in ignorance then,' he snarled, turning on her. 'I was walking about like some kind of arsehole, thinking my dad's killer was dead and I had nothing to avenge. So yeah, I probably was easier to live with!'

'Alright babe, keep your voice down.'

'Sorry if you can't handle me now,' he said, not sounding very contrite. 'But this is family honour!'

'I'm not saying you aren't well within your rights—'

'Whoever this geezer is, he's opened my eyes to the obvious. He's made me see Uncle Victor for what I already knew he was, only now I *know it-know it*.'

She stepped towards him, made a gentle shushing

sound, and buttoned his shirt. Around his neck he was wearing a gold chain that had once belonged to his dad.

'What's his game though?' she asked. 'If he planted the car bomb, why's he telling you? And why does he *keep* phoning?'

It had been only minutes into the New Year when Nick had received the first of those mystery phone calls. They'd been in Spot's nightclub with his usual entourage and they'd just finished singing Auld Lang Syne. Nick had assumed the call was from his mum in Vegas wanting to wish him a Happy New Year. But, on answering, Roz saw his joyful, coked-up face turn sour. He'd lifted his free hand up to his ear to block out the club noise and asked the caller to repeat that. That's when the line went dead, leaving a highly agitated boyfriend for her to deal with amid the artificial smoke of the club.

They'd left soon afterwards. Nick had pushed his way into the street and almost got into a needless fight with the bouncers, one of whom had earlier sold them the coke. Once clear of the place, she managed to calm him down. He told her that an American voice had just wished him a Happy New Year and boasted that he'd killed his dad.

'He said my uncle *paid* him to do it,' Nick had cried. 'Said to *thank Victor for the money!*'

Nick had immediately wanted to get a gun, travel to the Spoils, and shoot his uncle dead. Roz had talked him out of it.

'It's bollocks, babe,' she'd reasoned. 'There's no way that's real.'

Two weeks later, he received another call. This time he'd placed it on speaker so she could hear too. An American accent saying hi, it's me. Shut up and listen.

*'Your uncle fucked me,'* the menacing voice had said. *'So*

*did Rottweiler Ray. They put me up to whack your dad and they broke my big rule. I've already drowned Tyler in the river like the rat he was. Question is, who's doing Uncle Vic? You or me?'* The more recent phone calls had added a strange name. '*Tell Victor that the Long Needle sends his regards.*'

Each time this happened, Nick went crazier.

'Fuck the bloke,' she reasoned now. 'I mean, why not just let him kill your uncle? Let *him* take the risk.'

The intercom buzzed, interrupting them. The usual crew were all downstairs. Nick told them he'd be down in a minute, grabbed the Range Rover keys and told her to hurry the fuck up.

## 41

Bill was parked in a secluded spot close to Nick's apartment building. Through tiny binoculars he watched Nick emerge onto the cold street where he tossed some keys to Bob `the Feet' Walker. Bob shuffled off to the rear of the building. Nick remained on the pavement, play-fighting with three other men as Roz appeared through the door behind him. Bill recognised Dan Beesley and the other guy they called Blaine. The third was a heavy-set man wearing an army camouflage jacket and a woollen hat. Bill could hear his bellowing laughter from across the street.

The black Range Rover with its tinted windows rolled out from a concealed garage. The driver's window lowered so he could see Bob flicking his cigarette once he'd pulled up beside them. Nick sat in the passenger seat while the big man squeezed in the back with Roz and the boys.

Bill allowed the Neale-Mobile a head start before following. He could afford to hang back. Earlier that day he'd managed to place a tracking device underneath the Range Rover. As he pulled away, Mercy's voice came back through the mike feed.

*'My make-up's on, my hair looks fine, and I'm ready for my big night,'* he heard her say. *'I'll be at Spot's before he is.'*

Hearing her voice come through unsettled him. Something was telling him that it was a mistake to involve her, that it would be his fault if she got hurt. Mercy had only been training for a week and even though Nick's crew seemed idiotic, they were volatile people. He considered cutting her involvement immediately, cancelling the job before it was too late. But Mercy had inherited Ray's bravery. Whenever Bill had tried to discourage him from a perilous action it had always proven futile. If he'd wanted to extract her, he should've done it sooner.

He wished Ray could have seen her now, he reflected drawing up to some traffic lights. Taking to their trade with such enthusiasm. How could he not be proud? Bill was, and she wasn't even his daughter.

Approaching the club, Bill saw Nick and company get out of the vehicle and head toward the main doors, skipping the already long queue of clubbers. Mercy was there among them, in her green leather jacket. The Range Rover drove off after letting the passengers out. Bill couldn't afford to get too close, as Nick would recognise him on sight. Mercy, however, was the secret weapon.

He found a place to park and raised the volume on the mike. He could hear Mercy's breath as she queued and then her quick exchange with the doormen. Then things got noisy. For an old Motown guy like Bill, the atrocious din of this nightclub was a challenge even through a feed. Over the thumping base, he became concerned that they wouldn't be able to record anything worth using and he wished that Nick had suggested somewhere quieter to meet the hitman.

*'G&T,'* he heard Mercy order at the bar. *'A double.'*

That was another thing she'd inherited from Ray, he thought. He liked to drink on the job too.

## 42

That first sip of gin had an immediate calming effect, the familiar taste assuring her, as it always did, that everything was going to be cool. Mercy propped herself on a stool and surveyed Spot's. From what she'd seen so far it was a below-standard high street club and reminded her of some the old dives she'd frequented during her unhappy teenage years. She'd hated those nights, partly because she'd hated herself, but also because such rammed-to-capacity sweat-palaces were objectively awful. She hadn't really enjoyed clubbing at all until she arrived in Barcelona. Carmelo had a lot of flaws as a boyfriend but, fair play to the old crook, he knew the best venues and coolest people. It was on the Spanish scene that she'd met most of her real friends, trans or otherwise. These included the beautiful Mercedes after whom she'd later named herself, as well as a tattoo artist named Gina with whom she and Carmelo had enjoyed a threesome within hours of meeting and who'd designed much of the body art she'd since had done. She remembered every night out during that time as having been utter euphoria, although that could've been the drugs.

Here in Spot's however, the vibe was less appealing to someone who flourished in an alternative culture. The men were men, the women were women, and it seemed important to everyone that they were viewed as such, in both behaviour and appearance. The fashions were boringly conservative. Her leather jacket felt too heavy in this hot environment and she would've removed it had that not defeated the purpose of the evening.

She explored the dance area below, keen to see if anybody there matched up with what she knew about the Long Needle. Her dad had described the assassin as a mixed-race baby face. But everyone present seemed too young to be the man she'd heard talking fourteen years earlier. Mercy felt like she was one of the oldest people in the place and she was only 29.

She returned to the upper bar. A curious feature of this otherwise generic nightspot was all the large portraits of hard-looking men that adorned the walls. She recognised the Kray twins and assumed the rest were all famous gangsters too. Then she saw a portrait that made her jolt. There was a reserved section elevated one tier from the rest of the club, allowing whoever occupied it to look down over the dance floor. On the wall, above a velvet settee, was a picture of the man who'd once attempted to sexually assault her mother. The image of Lawrence Neale – bank robber, rapist and car bomb victim – was positioned so it overlooked the whole club. Surely then the spacious round booth itself was reserved for his son and heir. Mercy drifted by the booth and saw two bottles of champagne waiting in a silver bucket. The words NEALE RESERVATION warned anyone else from crossing the rope cordon.

So this was what her childhood bully liked to do with his free time, she thought. Sit underneath a portrait of his more famous dad, waiting to be recognised by teenagers in a shit nightclub in Woolwich.

# 43

Nick nodded at the doormen but, much to his annoyance, it wasn't the usual staff. The bruiser controlling things placed out a hand and asked him his name.

'Neale,' said Nick, making it sound like a command.

'Neal who?'

'Neale is my second name.'

'You on the list?'

'I don't need to be.'

Roz drew up beside him, gesturing that she'd sort this out.

'We're regulars,' she explained to the big man. 'We spend a shit tonne in here and *we* decide who's on the list. Where's Janine?'

'Holiday.'

'Benny knows about us.'

'Don't know any Benny.'

'We've reserved a booth,' she tried again, 'it's underneath a picture of his dad.'

The towering doorman surveyed Nick and then glanced

towards a shorter woman who'd appeared behind him with a clipboard. She nodded.

'Not much of a likeness,' the bouncer said, but stood aside.

'I get my looks from my mum,' Nick told him as he produced a £10 note and handed it to him. 'And my cash from my dad. Remember me next time.'

Inside they pushed past another queue for the cloakroom and Nick heard a young voice whispering behind him.

'That's Nick Neale,' the impressed teenager said. Nick smiled as he handed over his coat. 'Victor Neale's nephew,' the voice continued. He stopped smiling, turned and shot the boy a vicious *shut the fuck up* look.

The club was heaving as he entered. Four of his rowdiest mates greeted him at the bar, all with vodka shots for the new arrivals. Nick downed one, slammed the glass down and, in a sudden burst of affection, assured his friends that they were all daft cunts. This provoked a huge laugh, although none of them would've dared to return the compliment. They then all forced their way towards their roped-off section. Nick took his regular place in the centre of the low-backed, horseshoe shaped furniture, positioning himself underneath the portrait of his late father. Roz slid in next to him.

From there he had a decent view of most of the upper level. If anyone wanted to approach him, they'd have to get past his crew first. Collectively, Blaine, Dogger, the Asfaw brothers, Dan B, and Paul the Sweets were enough to keep any mouthy chancers away and he needed that protection. When you grow up Neale, he'd often told his crew, people are always challenging you to fights. Your job, he'd wink, is to protect them from *me*.

So he sat in his booth, flanked by his most trusted and

well-paid friends, and scanned the crowd for someone who might be this Long Needle prick. He doubted that anyone fool enough to boast about killing his dad would approach him in this environment, but you never knew with psychopaths. He placed his phone on the table facing up in case he received another call and told Roz to pour some champagne.

'There's a hostess who does that,' she sulked and indicated the three blokes who were now blocking her way out of the booth. 'Besides, I'm stuck.'

Dan B did the honours, but his actions were so jerky that the flutes overflowed with bubbles as he poured. The lads all called him a clumsy twat and Roz said he should've waited for service. Once the champagne had settled, Nick took a sip and wished that he'd left Roz at home. None of the others had brought their girlfriends and she was being fucking needy. The champagne slipped down his throat, but what he really needed was another line of coke to take the edge off.

They were soon onto the second bottle and had already ordered a third, a cocktail for Roz, and another round of shots. Dogger made some leering remarks about the hostess and the rest of the lads started assessing which girls in the club they'd like to pull. Billy Asfaw was on the dance floor grinding against a random girl. Blaine and the other Asfaw approached a group nearby and asked if they'd like to join them behind the rope. Roz squeezed closer to Nick, as if to remind him who he was with, but he wasn't even interested in these young girls in matching white dresses he was being introduced to. They were fine for boys like Blaine, who was still dating teenagers a good decade after being one.

However, sitting unattended near the edge of the bar was a woman he *did* want to meet. She was alone, sipping at a drink through a paper straw and wearing a green leather jacket. He thought he recognised her and wondered if she'd been on television.

What's more, he was certain she'd been eye-fucking him ever since he'd entered the place.

# 44

What an absolute wanker he still is, Mercy thought as she sipped from another G&T. Observing Nick with his perma-sneer and unearned swagger made her want to drink even more. His clothes were surprisingly preppy; beige trousers, smart collar and a black V-neck jumper. His trainers were bright red though, the bubble soles of which reminded her of a human blister, which is how she saw him. When he'd strutted through the club doors, a bunch of raucous men had greeted him with boysy embraces and profane banter. She made a rapid study of them, the group Nick entered with and anyone else in the club who might be registering his arrival.

Across the other side of this bar she'd already spotted someone interesting; a man in a blue untucked shirt who was nursing a bottle of Bud Zero. He'd stood out because, aside from herself, he was the only loner in there and the non-alcoholic drink struck her as suspicious. While Nick was downing shots at the bar, the man had made a finger-to-ear phone call, his eyes never leaving Nick.

'Black guy in a blue shirt,' she whispered, loud enough to be heard by Bill through the mike feed, 'watching Nick as closely as I am. He's a bit too old for the crowd and is on his own. Maybe our guy?'

She took a surreptitious photo of him with the phone Bill had lent her. The suspect continued speaking on his own call and she considered moving closer to eavesdrop. Would she recognise his voice from fourteen years before? He looked to be in his late thirties, old enough to be the Long Needle at a push, but she didn't want to draw attention to herself. She was still trying to master invisibility.

'He's flashing daggers at Nick,' she observed, as she sent Bill the photo.

'First sign of madness,' the barman told her. 'Talking to yourself.' He indicated her almost empty glass. 'Another?'

Soon Nick and company situated themselves in their reserved area and proceeded to argue like clowns. She recognised Dan Beesley among the group. He appeared even twitchier than he'd been at school as he messed up the simple task of pouring champagne. From the photos on Bill's whiteboard, she also identified Blaine, the boy who'd set up the meeting with the arms dealers.

Aside from Nick, there was only one other person of real interest sat around that booth and, like Mary Magdalene in *The Last Supper*, she'd positioned herself to the right of her man. Roz Stern looked hotter than the Earth's core tonight. She was wearing a killer black cocktail dress and her hair, which had been pulled back into a severe ponytail in her gym profile, was now styled with Viking-style braids making her look like a sexy warrior-woman. She'd obviously made a huge effort and, if her body language was anything to go by, it was all for the benefit of the unappreciative daddy's boy sat beside her. Her hand was resting on Nick's bicep and she seemed insulted by the giggling presence of the girls Blaine was inviting into their reserved area. Roz got up from the booth, stormed away and, for one thrilling moment, it looked like she was leaving the club. Instead, she veered towards the ladies' room with a deadly expression on her face. Mercy's eyes flicked back to Nick who looked unconcerned and had summoned Dan over to whisper something.

Mercy was tempted to follow Roz into the ladies'. Perhaps she'd be crying in there and this might provide her an opportunity to console, befriend and charm, and that way learn more about the mysterious calls. She could perhaps even manipulate Roz into sharing the spin class footage with her. Might be worth a try, she thought, although it would mean losing eyes on Nick if the Long Needle made his approach.

She glanced over to the man in the blue shirt, in time to see him exiting through the tall doors of the club. The music was too loud for her to speak into her jacket, so she reached for her phone and texted **blue shirt exiting - follow him?** to Bill. She paused to see if he'd respond with another thumbs up emoji. Nothing came. His communication had become minimal since she'd entered. But she'd done her due diligence and now she was ready to pursue Roz. However, looking up, she found her path blocked by a tall, grinning idiot stood directly in front of her.

'Looking for your boyfriend?' asked Dan Beesley, his expression as moronic as it had been when he'd tried to sell weed to her during double maths. 'Maybe you found him!'

She cursed herself for having absolutely no game when it came to surveillance. Surely this meant they'd noticed her watching.

'Pretty girl like you shouldn't be drinking alone,' he shouted over the noise of the club. 'Not when we've got quality champagne over there.' He pointed over at Nick who was leaning back, one arm resting over the top of the seat that Roz had just vacated. Staring straight at her. 'Know who that is?'

'That's Nick Neale,' she answered, staring back. The strobing lights of the club lent Nick an even more sinister air as he ignored whatever the large man on his right was saying in his ear. 'And the guy in the picture behind him,' Mercy continued, 'is his dad. They're gangsters or something.'

Dan raised his eyebrows, impressed. Then he wagged a finger.

'You shouldn't believe everything you read in the papers, my darling,' he laughed through bad teeth. 'He's a businessman!' He began bobbing from side to side to the music.

'I know Nick actually,' she relayed in a confidential manner. 'From way back.'

'That right?' he said, dancing on the balls of his feet and looking over her shoulder at someone else. 'P'raps that's why you caught his eye. He wants to say hello, you up for it?'

'Sure,' she smiled. 'I'll have a drink with an old mate.'

She followed as he weaved his way back through the crowded club towards the Neale party. Nick seemed wholly uninterested in everything going on around him; his eyes were just locked onto hers.

'Who's your friend, Daniel?' he asked in a languid tone as they drew near. Dan seemed confused.

'This is who you told me to fetch, right?' he asked, like he was unsure if he'd collected the right girl. Nick shot him a shitty look.

'Has she got a name?'

'Didn't ask,' Dan blinked and then turned to her. 'What is it?'

'Mercy,' she answered with a modest smile.

'I like it,' Nick nodded. 'Like the French way of saying thank you.'

'Is her surname *Beaucoup*?' grinned the big man, pronouncing the p.

'No, it's Tyler.'

'I was joking, love.'

'Have some Veuve Clicquot, Mercy,' Nick said. He turned toward Blaine who'd been concentrating on the girls in white. 'Be a gentleman and pour her some fizz before they guzzle the lot.'

Blaine rose and handed Mercy a flute glass. Nick asked if she'd care to sit, indicating to Dogger that he should squeeze his hefty self out from behind the booth so she could take his place. Nobody now formed a barrier between her and Nick, which suited her fine. Before taking her seat, she removed her leather jacket and folded it so that the mike feed was placed to best advantage and laid it on the table between them. If the quality of the wire was as good as Alan boasted, then Bill should be able to catch and record everything.

'You've already met,' Dan then said to Nick, sliding in after her. 'You go way back, she says.'

Mercy sensed Nick studying her profile as she took her first sip of the champagne. She placed the glass on the table, beside Roz's half-empty one.

'I've met you both before,' she told the men either side of her. It occurred to her if this were to turn bad she'd be trapped between them with little room to get out. 'Many times.' She quickly reminded herself that Bill was listening; she was on public display, the law of the land was on her side, and that she knew martial arts.

'I thought you looked familiar' Nick said, leaning forward. 'Where'd we meet?'

'Guess.'

'Space!' said Nick, clicking his fingers.

'Correct,' she beamed back. 'It was aboard the Starship Enterprise.'

'That ain't what I meant and you know it,' he laughed. 'Space the Superclub in Ibiza. Around 2014. You was with that big group Carl Cox introduced us to.'

'Sounds fun but that was someone else.'

'You used to buy ketamine from us back in the day,' Dan suggested. Mercy shook her head.

'You're going to kick yourselves when I tell you.'

'Go on then.'

'See, Mercy *is* my real name,' she explained in as breezy a way as she could manage. 'But at school you knew me as—'

'Who's this bitch and why's she in my seat?'

Roz was standing across the table from them, hands on hips and with murder in her eyes. Some of Nick's mates had come back, thirsty from the dance floor and seemed entertained by what was threatening to unfold.

'This is Mercy,' Nick informed his girlfriend in a *whatcha-gonna-do-about-it* tone. He was projecting his voice to be heard over the loud, pulsing sounds of the club. 'We're old mates and we're having a catch-up.'

'I've never heard you mention that name before,' Roz replied, matching his volume. 'And she better not be drinking *my* champagne.'

'This is yours,' Mercy moved the correct glass towards Roz. 'Sorry to barge in, but we're having a school reunion.'

'You're full of shit,' Roz sneered. 'Tell her why, babe.'

Nick turned toward Mercy, his expression stonier. She wondered if he'd already made the connection.

'Our school was boys only,' he said. 'Aside from dinner ladies, there wasn't a girl in the place.'

'There was me,' she replied, holding his gaze.

'Who are you?' he asked, but quieter, making it harder for the others to hear. Mercy breathed in before spitting out her old and hated name.

'You knew me as Christopher,' she said.

'Chrissy?' asked Dan, straining to hear from her other side. 'You were friends with that little poof?'

'Christopher Tyler was my dead name,' she elaborated, keeping her eyes on Nick. 'I'm Ray Tyler's kid.'

'His sister?' Dan blinked.

'No!' she persisted, ready to perform a blocking move against either of them should she need to. 'I'm an only child.'

Nick's left arm, which had been resting on the seat behind her, pulled slowly away.

'People thought I was a boy then,' she continued so there could be no ambiguity, 'but I was a girl.'

The music continued beating away as nobody said anything. She wondered what Bill might be making of this as he listened. Roz broke their silence; her machine gun laughter cutting through them like it was the St Valentine's Day Massacre.

'Oh, that's classic, babe,' she raised her hands up to heaven. 'I leave you alone for two minutes and you pull a geezer.'

She appealed to all of Nick's mates to join her in mockery. His gang were more muted in their response. The big man scrunched his round face up as if trying to suppress laughter but, like all of them, he seemed to want to gauge how Nick would take it first. Blaine and the snow princesses had all turned to Mercy to inspect her and Dan blinked like he still hadn't understood. But it was only Nick that mattered. She'd come here to speak with him and didn't want to get ejected this soon.

'You think I didn't know who this was the moment I set eyes on him?' he eventually scolded Roz, as if she'd just interrupted some grand plan of his. 'I've known this boy since we were kids and all the boob jobs and make-up in the world can't disguise him.'

'It's not a disguise,' Mercy corrected him. 'It's my life. Otherwise, I wouldn't have just literally told you who I was.'

'I can *see* who you are, Mrs Doubtfire, with my fucking own eyeballs,' he grinned. 'You look like your dad!'

'And sound like Barry White,' added the big bloke.

Nick's crew erupted into oafish hooting, freed up now that the derision was aimed at her. Nick slapped the table with his hands and mimicked her voice. Even the snow princesses were giggling.

Mercy wished death upon them all. Her every sense recalled the verbal and physical abuse she'd suffered when younger and her inner child was screaming at her to flee the club. Somehow though, her outer adult held fast.

'I already heard you were tranny,' Nick informed her. 'That's why I wasn't fooled!'

'Again, I wasn't trying to fool—'

'You always were a girly little boy.'

She burned at the ignorance of these people. It never failed to cut her to the marrow to have a company of losers like this treat her as if *she* was the biggest joke in the room. Forcing her anger down, she told herself to use the rage for when she needed to stick in a metaphorical knife. Or perhaps a literal one.

'Maybe that's why you couldn't stop touching me,' she asserted.

Nick told her to shut up. The others hadn't heard that remark over the volume of music and he probably didn't want her to repeat it.

'What you doing here though?' asked Roz, who'd stopped laughing around the time that the others had started. 'Are you a stalker?'

'A pertinent fucking point, babe,' Nick agreed. 'Did you come here to see me?'

'What do *you* think?' Mercy replied. 'One doesn't come to Woolwich for Woolwich. Ever since I've been back in Britain, I've been asking people where you can be found. And they all gave the same answer: this dump.'

'What for?' he cried. 'I ain't interested in you.'

'I came to speak on a personal matter.'

'Drugs,' Dan nodded with confidence.

'I hardly need you for that, Dan,' she told him. 'I just want a conversation.'

'If you've come to show off your new tits and this face-lift you've got yourself,' Nick finger-circled the air, 'you needn't have bothered. I've got a real woman over there.'

Roz seemed suddenly flattered. She pulled up a seat opposite and stared straight at Mercy with the smug smile of a chosen queen.

'Here's a question for you,' Nick said with an arrogant jut of the chin.

Before it had even left his lips, Mercy could feel a brutal, transphobic taunt coming.

# 45

Fury overwhelmed Bill as he listened to the vulgar question that Lol's shithead son was daring to ask his goddaughter. He was stood at the back of the largely unmoving queue for the club, enduring Nick's vulgar interrogation and the laughter of his moron mates second-hand through earphones. It had started raining again and he'd rushed to the club as soon as he heard Mercy announce her identity. This was happening too fast and he was convinced events were about to spiral.

*'That's hardly your business, is it, Nick?'* he heard Mercy answer through the feed. '*I don't care where you keep yours.*'

She was handling Nick's insults better than he would've managed. He knew that if he was in there now, he'd punch the insolent boy. He'd already tried to queue-jump by telling the bouncers that he was here to collect his daughter who he suspected of underage drinking inside but, if anything, that just made them more obstructive. He was a man in his early sixties trying to get into a club full of, as far as he was concerned, children. He felt like an awkward dad at the fringes of a school disco.

*'Don't stay out too late'* a booming voice was saying. Bill guessed it belonged to the big man in the camouflage jacket. *'Else your beard will grow back!'*

His fists clenched as he heard Nick's cackle. The queue was at last starting to move and Bill considered approaching the bouncers again and offering them fifty quid to let him in. That would be the right figure; any less wouldn't work and more would suggest that he could be trouble. Then he noticed that the blue-untucked-shirt man had returned. Bill hadn't recognised him when sent Mercy's blurry photo and had dismissed him as unimportant. But now he was lurking by the corner further up the street. He appeared to be waiting for someone.

*'Aren't you curious as to why I'm here?'* he heard Mercy ask Nick as Blue Shirt waved at an approaching car. It pulled up and Bill watched the man as he leaned in to speak to whoever was in the passenger seat. Headlights shone in Bill's direction.

*'You want pimping out?'* Nick's voice sniggered.

Three huge men got out of the car and greeted Blue Shirt. It seemed clear to Bill that these were who he must have called from inside the club.

*'I came to ask you questions,'* he heard Mercy tell Nick as Blue Shirt led his friends up to the door of the club, not bothering to queue. The bouncer waved all four of them in. It was then, with a sudden alarm, that Bill recognised one of them.

'Christ!' he exclaimed. The man who'd been sitting in the passenger seat of that car was about to become a major problem for Mercy.

*'My first question is,'* he heard her voice saying as he tapped out an emergency warning text, *'did you kill my dad?'*

# 46

'The reason I ask,' she explained to her audience of plastic gangsters, 'is that apparently Nick, you've been telling people that you're his murderer.'

The laughter stopped, which made asking the question immediately worthwhile. Nick shrugged like he had no idea what she was talking about.

'I'm informed that you violently assaulted a man during a recent spin class,' she said, hoping her voice would be loud enough for the recording. Her green jacket was still on the table, but it was closer to Nick than her. 'And during this assault you declared, in front of several witnesses, that you'd killed my dad for some unspecified reason. Not only that, but *she*,' Mercy pointed at Roz, 'captured it on camera.'

Nick's head whipped towards his girlfriend.

'It was *your* idea to film that, babe,' Roz defended herself. 'Don't give me that look.'

'I haven't seen the footage myself,' Mercy admitted, 'but I know people who have. They say that you're quite insistent that you killed my dad with your bare hands.'

'Your dad was a loser,' he shot back. 'A drunken waste man.'

'Be that as it may,' she shrugged. 'Do you stand by your claim?'

'No I do not,' he declared. 'I was having a laugh.'

'What a relief,' she said, reaching for her champagne glass again. In her jean pocket she felt her phone buzz. Bill had said he'd only contact her in an emergency, but she couldn't check it yet. 'I'd hate to think of that sweet little boy I knew growing up to be my dad's killer.' Nick leaned closer like he wanted to sting her.

'He had it coming though.'

'His death was recorded as accidental,' she said after taking a strengthening sip of alcohol. 'Do you know different?'

'His sins caught up with him.'

'Which sins were these?'

'The sins of *your* father,' he growled and then indicated the portrait on the wall behind them, 'against *mine*.'

'Could you be more specific?'

'No, he fucking couldn't,' interrupted Roz. She reached over the table and touched her boyfriend's arm. 'Nick, I love you, but you need to shut the fuck up, yeah?'

Lying on the table in front of Nick was his mobile. It had a silver skull-and-crossbones sticker on it and every so often Mercy noticed Nick checking to see if he'd missed a call. This presumably was the phone to which the Long Needle calls had been made. It hadn't rung once since she'd been present, but across the table Dogger was receiving his own surprise call. He had a finger in one ear and was shouting 'YOU WHAT?' down the line.

'Question time is over,' Roz pointed at her with extreme

aggression, 'and so is our hospitality. Down your drink and fuck off.'

'Fucking off soon,' Mercy assured her, 'but first I have to tell you something important.'

'FUCK'S SAKE, BOB,' Dogger was shouting into his phone. 'GET TO THE POINT, MATE!'

'We have an identical problem,' Mercy explained to Nick, who seemed distracted by the outburst. The big man was now on his feet and was pacing around the reserved area as he shouted. Nick checked his own phone again to see if he'd missed a call but there was nothing. 'I want to know who murdered my dad,' she continued, 'and so, I think, do you. To that end, we could share information.'

'IS IT STOLEN OR NOT?' Dogger bellowed.

'What's the situation over there?' Nick called over.

'It's Bob the Feet,' Dogger said, lowering the phone from his ear. 'He's at the Ferryman.'

'And?'

'Someone's interfered with the Range Rover. He doesn't want to say what over the phone, but he's talking like he's seen a ghost.'

Nick got up from the booth, forcing Blaine and his girls to make way, and took the phone from Dogger. All eyes were on him, and Mercy, briefly forgotten, checked the message Bill had sent her.

**Junior bruno in club with blue shirt man and 2 more. Prob coming for Nick! Watch out!!**

She lifted her head and surveyed what little she could see of the rest of the club from her seated position. Nick's mates were crowding around him to discover what had gone wrong with the Range Rover and were obscuring the main dance floor. She stood to get a better look. Roz eyed her as she edged out from behind the table, taking her handbag but leaving the jacket.

'Going to the loo?' Roz asked. 'Use the right one.'

Ignoring her, Mercy scanned the nightclub looking for any sign of Junior Bruno who she'd only ever seen once at her father's funeral. The dance floor was bathed in a flashing green light, making a visual study hard, but Bruno looked like a famous heavyweight boxer so he shouldn't be too difficult to spot in a crowd.

'What d'you mean you won't turn the key?' Nick was asking Bob the Feet over the phone. 'What d'you think is going to happen?'

He turned back towards their booth, and, for a moment, Mercy thought he was looking at her. Then she realised he was staring beyond her toward the picture of his father on the wall, a man who'd died in a car explosion.

'Oh,' he said.

That was when Mercy clocked Junior Bruno and his friends, including the blue-shirted man. They were cleaving their way through a packed dance floor searching for someone. Blue Shirt looked over in their direction, saw Nick on the phone with his back to the rest of the club and patted Junior on the shoulder. Then Victor Neale's chauffeur, bodyguard, and occasional gym instructor immediately began cannonballing towards Nick. The last time these two men had encountered each other Nick had rabbit-punched Junior during a spin class with zero warning. It seemed like a return attack was about to happen within a matter of seconds.

'Don't be a pussy, Bob,' Nick was saying into the phone as his surprise aggressor neared their area with a frightening rapidity. 'Start the engine and see—'

'Look out Nick!' Mercy shouted over the deafening music.

Nick's entire crew spun around in time to see Junior climbing the steps to the raised section, followed by three equally fearsome companions. Junior took a hard swing at the back of Nick's head, but Mercy's warning had arrived before it struck. Nick turned and blocked the punch, but this didn't prevent Junior from crashing straight into him with tremendous force. They both barrelled through the reserved section and landed straight onto the table inside the booth with a mighty crash, toppling an ice bucket containing two more champagne magnums, scattering beer bottles onto the floor and causing Dan B, the only person still at the table, to scream out in shock.

Roz had managed to dodge out of their path of destruction. But she began freaking out even more as Bruno pressed her boyfriend's skinnier body down onto the table and punched him repeatedly in the face. Mercy gasped when she saw the blood.

'*You asked for this, bruv!*' Bruno roared as he meted out Nick's brutal punishment. '*Have it!*'

'Leave him alone!' Roz shrieked. She jumped onto Bruno's back to pull him away. But he was far too strong, so she cried out for help from the rest of Nick's gang. Mercy looked to Dan, who remained frozen, but she then saw Blaine rush to Nick's aid. The rest of the crew had all turned on Junior's boys and a full on rumble had erupted.

Mercy tried to back away from the violence. However, violence followed her in the form of the blue-shirted man and Dogger who were locked in combat and staggering towards the wall she was standing against. She darted out of their way and, realising that all other paths were blocked, turned back towards the booth where Nick was still receiving a savage beating underneath the disapproving face of his father. Roz grabbed an empty champagne bottle and whacked it over Bruno's head. It didn't shatter but he cried out and turned to shove both her and Blaine away. Nick tried to retaliate. But he still couldn't get up and so remained lying on the table as the assault continued, with Mercy's green leather jacket pressed tight under his back.

# 47

Bill hadn't been listening for some minutes. He'd finally reached the front of the queue, removed his earphones, and negotiated with the doorman to be let in. He pushed through to find a place packed with teenage clubbers and music and lights that were an assault on his ageing senses. He forced a path through the crowded bar, heading towards what he assumed was the main area of the club. As he did so, he was shoved out of the way by a man in a puffer jacket and a walkie-talkie in his hand. Bill saw other men, clearly club security, all rushing toward the same direction. Further in, he was able to see what the fuss was. On an elevated platform a huge fistfight had broken out that reminded Bill of a scene from an old western. Even through blinding lights he knew that this had to be the Junior Bruno/Nick Neale rematch in full bloom.

'Security!' he cried out in an effort to get to the dance floor quicker. 'Let me through!'

Drawing nearer, he gained a better view of the action. Junior was being pulled away from a rabid and bloody Nick. Mercy was helping to separate them as the security guards reached the area and tackled the warring parties. Amid the carnage, the big shaven-headed man grabbed Mercy and threw her against a far wall.

'I'm police!' Bill shouted at the oblivious dancers still blocking his way. 'Clear a fucking path!'

# 48

'You!' Dogger bellowed at Mercy. He'd already grabbed her arms and was banging her against the wall. 'You told these fuckers where we are!'

Mercy had been so preoccupied by the surrounding violence that she hadn't seen this brute's grab-and-pull coming. And she was glad that her old karate instructor wasn't around to see how easily she'd been overpowered and struggled to free herself. She attempted to sweep his legs away, but they were like tree trunks rooted to the spot. Over Dogger's shoulder, she watched the security guards pounce not just on Junior Bruno but also Blaine, Blue Shirt Man, and several others.

'Cool it,' she warned him, 'or you're next.'

With mounting dismay, she realised he was reaching back into his throat. She could tell what was coming.

Mercy had been spat at twice before. Both times it had been in Barcelona courtesy of complete strangers during her early transition years when she wasn't passing as well as she did now. But it had been a while since someone had communicated their disgust for her lifestyle via the universal language of saliva. She scrunched her face up tight as he made a honking sound and then she felt her cheeks get covered in gross spit. Her soul sank, the degradation stinging hard.

She wanted to curse him, but her larynx was too clogged up with rage to form the sound. He opened his mouth, either to insult her or to spit again, she'd never know. Because that was when Bill appeared and elbowed him hard in the side of the head.

'Get off her!' he shouted as his arm collided with Dogger, his Northern Irish accent thicker than ever. 'You're a disgrace!'

Dogger howled and staggered away, clutching his head. Released, Mercy allowed her body to flop against the wall and she wiped the gob off her face with the palm of her hands. She looked at Bill and saw her own rage reflected.

Around them, the struggle between Junior's boys, Nicks crew, and the club security continued. Mercy noticed Roz pressing reddened tissues against Nick's upturned nose. Chaos reigned.

'You alright?' Bill asked her. But before she could respond Dogger was back in the game and he charged at Bill like a battering ram. On impact, Bill fell down the steps he'd just climbed and he landed badly on his back. By then a second wave of security had arrived and they descended on Dogger. Mercy dashed over to Bill. His face was contorted in agony and he couldn't get up again.

'Where's the jacket?' he asked through clenched teeth. 'Don't say you've lost it. It's expensive Mercy, and arguably illegal.'

She raced back to the table inside the booth, underneath which Dan B had heroically slid. She examined the jacket, feeling for any damage to the hidden microphone inside the lining. It was probably useless now, she reasoned as she placed it back on and collected the handbag she'd dropped during the fight. Then she noticed something else that had been left unattended on the table.

A mobile phone with a skull-and-crossbones sticker on it.

She looked about for its owner. The reserved area had thinned out as most people had either been dragged off or scarpered. Then she saw Nick. He'd reached the opposite end of the dance floor and Roz was guiding him towards the exit, with a towel that had been produced from somewhere pressed against his nose.

Mercy slipped the abandoned phone into her jacket pocket. Then she returned to Bill who had grabbed a railing to pull himself up.

'I've done my back in,' he winced as she helped him get steady. While they waited for medical help, Mercy handed him one of the open bottles of beer that had half-spilled its contents onto the floor. In return he produced a packet of tissues from a coat pocket to use on her face.

'I'll report that fat bastard to the police,' he said as she carefully wiped the rest of the saliva off. 'We should press charges.'

'Thanks for defending my honour,' she said, checking her reflection in a mirrored wall and cleaning her face. 'But I should keep following Nick. This whole evening's been a bust otherwise.'

'Forget it,' he ordered after taking a swig of beer. 'It wasn't your fault it all went to shit. We'll try another tactic tomorrow.'

Medical staff arrived and began attending to Bill. Mercy moved away, wondering if she was ready to quit just yet. After all, she'd overheard that there'd been some problem with the Range Rover at a pub called the Ferryman. What was that about? Had Bob discovered the vehicle tracker they'd hidden underneath the chassis and mistaken it for a bomb?

More importantly, might the Long Needle still make an appearance?

'Hate to ditch you Bill,' she told him. 'But the night's still young.'

Then she dashed off in pursuit of the action.

# 49

Outside in the sleet, the young lovers placed several roads worth of distance between themselves and Spot's nightclub. Nick's groaning was incessant as they cut through quiet lanes to avoid the town centre. He pressed three bloody napkins to his nose as Roz led him toward the pub where Bob the Feet supposedly still was. She'd tried phoning him, but the useless old sod was no longer answering.

'Why's he at the pub anyway?' she cursed as they approached the roundabout down by the ferry. 'He's paid to drive us home.'

Nick moaned a word that could've been anything. She guided him underneath a bus shelter where she could inspect the damage.

'Let's have a look,' she said as she gently lifted the napkins from his nose, 'It can't be as bad as... oh Jesus!'

'Is it broken?'

'Not sure. But those cuts are bare deep.'

'I want it known... ' Nick uttered in what some might

have unkindly considered a whimper '… Bruno… he's on the fucking death list. Same as Victor.'

'*Shhh,*' she said, indicating a middle-aged couple waiting for the bus. 'We'll talk retaliation later.'

'He needs the hospital,' advised the pink-nosed woman of the couple, rotund in her big puffy coat, hat, and scarf. 'That won't heal untended.'

'Mind your own!' Roz blazed. 'I know what I'm doing.'

Roz did have some first-aid experience and knew she could attend to this if they could just get home to her kit. It was only as she reached for her phone again to call a cab that she saw that Bob was finally ringing back.

'You better have a bloody good reason for not collecting us, you clapped-out old ponce,' she said on answering. 'Where've you parked?'

'Cole Road,' Bob wheezed, 'near the bins. But, as I was telling Nick, I ain't turning the key. The Rover's been interfered with. It might explode.'

'Pick us up,' she hissed, 'before *I* fucking explode.'

'See for yourselves,' he cried in defiance. 'You know where I am.' Then, to her astonishment, he hung up.

Nick defended Bob, which was even more aggravating. Bob the Feet had always been more of a pet than an employee, one inherited from his dead dad, and he was sure he'd have a good excuse for his cowardice. Still holding the tissues to his nose, he searched for his phone with the other hand. A bus arrived and the middle-aged couple got on while they remained in the cold, his pocket search becoming more frantic. The pink-nosed woman took a seat inside and gave them a shitty look as the bus pulled away.

'I've left my phone in Spots,' Nick realised. 'Shit! What if the Needle tries to contact me?'

Typical, she thought as she searched for his number, that his obsession with this nuisance caller would be his first concern. A more urgent question was whether or not he'd deleted the incriminating footage of the gymnasium assault yet. She was prepared to bet that he hadn't. She called his number, praying that it had ended up in the hands of a friend.

'Rosalind my dove,' a voice answered. 'I've been wondering when you'd call.'

'Who's this?' Roz demanded.

'Mercy Tyler,' she was informed. 'We met earlier tonight but our conversation was rudely interrupted.'

'How'd *you* get this phone?

'Nick must've dropped it, the klutz. Probably around the time he was getting his face smashed in. How is he? I hope it doesn't sting.'

Roz looked over at Nick, the once-white napkin pressed to his face. He made a questioning gesture.

'It's your lady friend,' Roz replied.

'I'd be happy to return it,' Mercy was offering as Roz placed the speaker on.

'Who else is there?' asked Roz. 'Give it to Blaine or someone.'

'Your boys have all vanished,' they were told. 'I've just passed your mate Dogger who was being bundled into the back of a police van. Best place for him.'

'Where are *you*?'

'I'm heading towards a pub called the Ferryman.' It did sound like she was outside. 'I heard that your ride is there. Good job I've got this umbrella.'

Nick snatched the phone away with his free hand.

'Why you stalking me, Chrissy?' he spat into it.

'I tried explaining in the club,' Roz heard Mercy's tinny voice say through the speaker, 'we want the same thing:

justice for fathers. If you'll relax, let me finish a sentence and refer to me by my correct name, then perhaps I'll tell you what I know about the Long Needle.'

Nick's face, already drained from his injuries, went even paler. 'What's your game, Christopher?' he asked.

'Try again,' the voice insisted. Nick didn't understand so Roz grabbed her phone back.

'What's your game, *Mercy*?' she asked.

'There, that wasn't so hard, was it?' came the happier reply. 'I'll reveal all at the pub. Race you.'

Then she too hung up on them.

'Lippy bitch,' said Roz.

The Ferryman pub sits on the edge of a run-down street like the last tooth in an old man's mouth. With boarded up windows and graffitied walls, it appears as if it's been shut down. The stormy weather was causing the small triangles of England flag bunting that ran across the car park to flap in spasms of distressed patriotism. Nick and Roz arrived in an Uber that she felt should've taken them all the way home.

They entered the pub through a stiff door that emitted a resentful sigh as it opened. Roz hated the filthy place. Even on a Saturday night it was patronised by the usual old geezers and crack addicts. It was an insulting destination to have arrived at considering how much they'd both dressed to impress. They were wearing almost matching designer coats that she'd had to grab from the cloakroom on their way out. Around a pool table, a scattering of locals eyed them as they crossed through the bar. It burned to think that she'd spent so long trying to achieve her cool Viking hairstyle for the ultimate benefit of this shabby crowd.

Bob was sat alone at the bar with a pint of brown ale and his eyes glued to Sky Sports. He didn't notice them until they were standing beside him, and he was startled on account of Nick's battered face.

'You should've seen the other bloke,' her boyfriend said. He reached behind the bar and gathered cleaner tissues as they told Bob about the assault.

'You're supposed to be our driver,' Roz scowled, smelling previous pints on his breath. 'Why are you pissed?'

'What else could I do?' he shrugged, 'after that threat.'

'Threat?'

'I told Dogger all this on the phone,' he complained, puffing his cheeks in exasperation. He reached into the pocket of his anorak and produced an envelope. It was pink and spotted from raindrops. 'After dropping you lot off I parked up and went to the chippy,' he explained. 'I was in there for, what, twenty-odd minutes. Before coming in here for a harmless half-pint, I went back to the vehicle for my smokes. I found *that,'* he tapped the envelope which had been handed to Nick, 'underneath the windscreen wipers.'

Nick and Roz exchanged a look and then he peered inside the unsealed envelope.

'It's empty,' Bob shrugged after taking another slurp of ale. 'But that's all the warning I needed.'

'Fuck's sake,' Roz said after inspecting it for herself. 'It's Valentine's litter from the other week.'

'It's from your Needle fella!' Bob spoke as if they were both dense. 'You said he was going to give you something and there it is. There's no way I'd turn on the engine with that just sitting there in the window. He confessed to blowing up your dad's car,' he pointed to Nick, 'and now he's gonna do yours.'

'Someone's trying to freak you out,' Nick told him.

'You don't understand,' Bob said after wiping his moustache. 'That envelope was under the windscreen wipers... *inside the glass.*'

'Inside?' Nick blinked. 'You'd left my Range Rover unlocked?'

'Never,' he protested. 'As I told Dogger, I locked it, same as always, and there weren't no envelope inside then. And, when I got back, the Rover was still locked but that had appeared! I never saw it until I'd opened the door because of the tinted windows. Frightened the living shit out of me.'

'Someone could still be in there,' Roz said. 'Did you search the back seats?'

'Only the front,' he answered. 'It spooked me. I grabbed the envelope but it's pitch black in that lane and the inside is all shadows. I thought fuck this for a game of soldiers. Let it be someone else's problem. I've been here ever since.' He drained the last of his ale. 'Is the next round on you, boy? I'm out of cash.'

'Put your anorak on,' commanded Nick. 'Show us.'

The rain had lessened but it was still blowing a wild gust as they traipsed around the edges of the pub toward the dirt track that was Cole Road. Muddy puddles did their best to ruin Roz's high heels. As well as the bins there was a closed-up mechanics yard this end of the road and a line of garages that belonged to nearby flats. Cole Road was mainly used as an unloading dock for brewery lorries during the day and for selling drugs in the evening. They found the Range Rover parked in a dark spot, underneath branches that creaked in the wind.

'There she is,' Bob pointed at it, 'where I left her.'

'Why didn't you use the pub car park?' Roz asked as Nick circled his pride and joy.

'It was pissing down,' Bob said and pointed to the lamp-lit end of the street where the chip shop was. 'And I was going there, not the pub. After locking the car I ran to the chippy and stayed long enough for the rain to ease off. Then, I came back and found that envelope inside.'

'Did you lock it again?'

'From a distance, yeah.'

Nobody said anything but they all stepped away from the car, the charred spectre of Lawrence Neale on every mind. Messing with his car was the surest way to instil paranoia in Nick. Once they'd all backed far enough away, Nick pressed the button on the key. Lights flashed, the doors unlocked but nothing exploded.

'That was the easy bit,' Bob said. 'But who's gonna turn on the ignition?'

'You are,' Nick told him.

'Fuck right off,' replied his faithful retainer.

'Well, we can't leave it here,' Nick whined through his damaged nose. 'There's two bags of cocaine in the glove compartment.'

An irresistible idea struck Roz.

'Let's have Mercy do it.'

'Who's Mercy?' asked Bob.

'Some tranny that Nick went to school with,' she told him. 'She's coming to deliver a phone now.'

'Ray Tyler's boy?' Bob asked.

'That's the one. We could convince her to start the engine.'

'Great idea, babe,' Nick grinned for the first time since his assault. Even in these shadows his swollen face looked snooker ball red but at least he'd stopped bleeding. He resembled the devil, she thought, starting to like it. 'We'll say we're giving her a job.'

Close by in the dark, a throat cleared. The trio turned in

fright towards the malevolent black mass of the Range Rover.

'I don't much appreciate being called a tranny,' an unseen voice said, followed by a scraping noise. 'But at least your pronouns are finally on point.'

Roz saw the green jacketed half of a person's body crawling out from underneath the chassis. A small torch was turned on.

'And I've already got a job, thanks,' Mercy said, flashing the light directly into Nick's face. 'I'm a private investigator.'

# 50

When Mercy had first overheard Nick's phone call in the club, she'd assumed that the vehicle tracker that Bill had hidden under the Range Rover had been found and mistaken for a bomb. Later, as she'd approached the Ferryman, her umbrella protecting her from the deluge, she'd seen Nick and Roz pull up ahead of her and watched as they entered the pub. Instead of following them inside, she'd decided to explore the nearby streets. It wasn't long until she found the black customised Range Rover parked in Cole Road. The car exuded a silent menace as rain battered down on it. It did look like something that was about to go boom.

She removed her small torch from her handbag and studied the ground. The wheels on the passenger side were bumped up on a kerb and a storm drain underneath was attracting streams of rain. Other than that it was dry, which told her it hadn't been raining when first parked there. Since then, the weather would have washed away any tracks or muddy footprints leading towards it.

Folding away her brolly, she'd dared to get closer so she

could flash her light underneath. Then she'd dared a little more, each move making her feel more confident that there was nothing to fear from this slumbering SUV. Soon she was lying on her belly beside it, the muddy water soaking her jeans and jacket as she tried to identify Bill's tracker. To reach the mudguard, where she knew he liked to conceal them, she turned onto her back to get completely underneath the chassis. Soon her hands found the small device he'd purchased from Third Eye, removed it, and placed it inside her handbag.

Job done, she was keen to scuttle as far away as possible from the possible car bomb. However, now she was down there, torch in hand, curiosity demanded she search for signs of explosives. She was far from an expert on detonators, but she did have an idea of what belonged underneath an automobile and what didn't. She flashed her light around the chassis and saw nothing that led her to believe she was in imminent danger. Of course, there were other ways to rig a car to explode, including wiring the bomb to the ignition. But that seemed laborious for a vehicle parked in a street and if the petrol tank had been interfered with, she would've smelt it by now. Also, why would the Long Needle want to recreate Lawrence Neale's murder years later? The benefit of the copycat method had expired with Bobby McAlonan and there were simpler ways to execute a fool like Nick. No, she assured herself, this car was unlikely to explode; which was just as well considering she was lying directly beneath it.

She heard footsteps and so turned off her torch.

'There she is,' said a croaked voice. 'Where I left her.'

Mercy soon realised that this was Bob the Feet, using female pronouns to describe a car. He was with Nick and, on fast reflection, she decided that she might learn more by remaining hidden. That was how she overheard Bob describe a pink envelope found inside the car; just like the one her dad had handed to the Long Needle.

'Let's have Mercy do it,' she heard Roz suggest and so decided it was time to reveal her presence. Crawling out from under the vehicle, she turned her torch back on and took great pleasure in seeing their gobsmacked faces.

'Private investigator?' jeered Nick once she'd dragged herself out and was standing again. '*You?*'

'It's the family trade,' she replied, brushing wet dirt from her clothes. 'You of all people can appreciate that.'

'You're spying on us,' Roz pointed her finger like it was a pistol, 'which is suicidal!'

'Yeah!' agreed Bob the Feet, puffing himself up. 'You're fucking with the wrong crew.'

Bob was a short, unimpressive man with a face as lined as a walnut. Perhaps he'd been tough in his day. Unfortunately for him, his day was back in the previous century and now his attempts to intimidate her appeared comical. He stepped towards her and extended his own finger as Roz had been doing.

'And I tell you what else,' he cocked his head. '*This* here is your Long Needle!'

'Don't be daft,' Nick said.

'Stands to reason,' Bob persisted, twitching his moustache like a cut-price Poirot. 'It used its man's voice over the phone to fool you!'

She hadn't needed to hurt him. He was clearly just posturing in front of the others. But he'd just called her *it* and she was still agitated from her encounter with Dogger; could still feel the spittle on her cheek. So, as he came within her range, she grabbed him by the shoulders. She yanked him in for a hard knee strike into his stomach and then slammed him against the car door. He buckled to the wet ground as Mercy turned to the other two in a defensive stance, ready for them to rush her. Instead, they both stepped away, probably more in fear of the car exploding than of her.

'Don't dent it!' Nick cried.

'There could be a bomb in that, you silly bitch,' said Roz.

Bob sounded as if he was about to throw up. Mercy should have felt mild guilt at having used such a vicious move on an almost elderly man but the show of force had felt good, especially in front of Nick. She was even hoping he'd attack her next, as throwing her old bully to the ground was the stuff of her longest-held fantasies. But instead he was regarding Bob, still on his knees and coughing hard, with unconcealed disappointment.

'There isn't a detonator under there,' Mercy said as she moved toward the rear of the vehicle. 'And, there won't be one rigged to the ignition either. It would take too long to set up.'

'How come you're such an expert on car bombs?'

'I'm not,' she admitted, 'but I *am* becoming an expert on the man who you call the Long Needle. I've been investigating him since I was fourteen.'

Nick crossed over from the opposite pavement, emboldened by her assurances that his Range Rover was benign.

'Who is he?'

'I once overheard my dad hiring a hitman in his home office,' she explained. 'I never saw him but his voice was young. Dad handed him a pink envelope, identical to that one you're holding.'

'Bullshit!' Roz called over, still on the other side of the street. Mercy returned Nick's stare.

'Pink stationery like that is used by a gentlemen's club called the Never Setting Sun. Heard of it?'

'No,' he replied.

Picking himself up from the puddled ground, Bob held a hand out for some help. As Nick pulled him to his feet again, the older man admitted he knew of it.

'That's a posh club your uncle's a member of,' he wheezed. 'None of the firm could join because we all had criminal records. He loved gloating about that.'

'My dad was a Never Setter too,' Mercy told him. 'He even signed me up to be a member when I was a kid. Ironic, considering they don't allow women. But I've got it on good authority that their signature colour was pink. Dad handed one of their envelopes to the hitman in his office and said it was from an unnamed client. Inside were the details of who he wanted dead.'

'When was this?' Nick asked.

'About one week before your dad's Bentley exploded.'

Nick banged his open palm on the roof of his Range Rover. Then he spun around to face Roz who was watching from a sceptical distance, arms folded.

'Hear that, babe!' he appealed to her. 'This backs me up!'

'How come she's only telling us about this now?' Roz said, flicking her chin towards Mercy.

'I didn't know who they were fixing to kill,' Mercy clarified. 'And I'm still not sure it was your dad whose name was in the envelope. Also, I never heard the man referred to as the Long Needle until this Christmas when my dad called him that. He died later that night.'

'That's a week before I got my first call from him,' Nick nodded. 'He said that he was paid by my uncle to kill Dad. And that *your* arsehole dad,' he pointed the envelope at her, 'was the middleman.'

Bob had slunk away to lean against a far tree. He'd pulled out a packet of tobacco from his pocket and was rolling himself a smoke.

'I know about your anonymous calls from the hitman,' Mercy admitted. 'That's why I've come to you. We're looking for the same man. He killed both our fathers, so why not join forces?'

'Fucking Victor!' Nick roared, making them all flinch as if the bomb had at last gone off. He raised his fists to his forehead, staggered about and howled up to the clouded sky. 'He had his own brother murdered, a man worth ten of him. And *you,'* he pointed at Mercy, 'are the second person to tell me so.'

'Let me search the car for clues,' said Mercy.

'Keep your beak out,' Roz responded and strode over to the passenger door to search it herself. The interior light switched on and Mercy and Nick looked in the back seats. Bob was hanging back, puffing on his roll up. 'Check the boot, babe,' Roz said.

The thought struck Mercy that, if there was still an explosive wired in the Range Rover, the boot would be the ideal place for it. The back of the car faced away from the busy end of the street and if unlocked, rigging it would be a moment's work. Without hesitation, Nick opened it before either she or Roz had a chance to clear the area.

No blast followed.

'Well, well!' Nick cheered as he looked inside. 'Santa's finally been!'

'What is it?' Roz asked.

Mercy moved to see what was in that sizable space and was as stunned as Nick was delighted. There, illuminated by the car light, lay a military machine pistol with two cartridges resting beside it.

'A Skorpion!' Nick declared, reaching down to collect it. 'Exactly what I've been after.'

'That's the exact model you tried to buy from the Czechs,' Roz remarked, looking in. Nick pulled it out and felt the weight.

'It's the semi-automatic,' Nick grinned as he reached for one of the cartridges with his other hand, 'but it'll do the fucking job.'

'What job?' asked Mercy.

Nick didn't say anything but, as he made his first clumsy attempt to load the cartridge, Mercy suddenly realised she needed to get clear and fast. Negotiating with a moron she could handle, but a moron with a semi-automatic was too much.

'Babe...' Roz said, her voice nervous. 'Don't...'

Mercy heard the click of the cartridge connect with the gun and every nerve ending went into red alert. Then he turned a small lever on the side of the pistol grip and she knew the safety was off. She felt sick.

'What you calling yourself again?' Nick smirked as he turned his neck toward her. '*Mercy?* Well,' he pointed the gun at her, 'don't lie or you won't get none.'

'Don't even joke about it, Nick!' Roz screamed. 'If that thing goes off, its murder!'

'Don't run!' Nick commanded Mercy who, on sheer instinct, had taken several steps backwards without even realising. 'You've been asking questions, now it's my turn.' Her heart hammering, she opened her mouth to protest. 'Who keeps calling me? Keep on with your bullshit and I'll shoot you in the tits.'

Pure fear coursed through her.

'You'll be heard by the people in the pub!' she shouted

back at him. '*And* in the chip shop. And in that estate behind the garages. It would be insanity.'

'Who's paying you to follow me about?'

'Point it somewhere else, babe,' Roz implored him. 'This isn't funny and you're scaring the shit out of me too.'

Bob the Feet had thrown his roll-up to the ground and was hiding behind the tree. Nick's eyes hadn't moved from Mercy though. She saw how high the mere touch of a loaded weapon had made him.

'I came here at your request,' she answered in as steady a voice as she could manage. 'You're the one who left your phone in the club, and I offered to bring it. If you don't want to work with me, fine. I'll go. Hint taken.'

'This is some sick trick,' Nick growled 'and I know you're part of it. I told the man on the phone last night to approach me in the club. He doesn't arrive but then *you* appear, like a blast from the past, getting in my head. You were trying to distract me while someone else was fucking around with my motor. *Who do you work for?*'

An unseen phone rang. Mercy didn't immediately realise that it was coming from inside her jacket pocket.

'It's your phone,' she said, slowly fishing out the mobile with the silver skull-and-crossbones sticker on it.

'Is it a withheld number?' Nick asked, the gun still trained on her.

'No,' she answered, glancing at the screen. 'But it's not from your contacts either. Maybe it's him!'

'Put it on speaker,' he ordered. 'Turn the volume up high.'

Mercy accepted the call.

*'Mercy?'* a northern Irish voice crackled out. *'It's Bill. I'm sitting in a packed casualty ward and I can hear everything that's going on. Is he pointing a weapon at you?'*

'Yes I fucking am,' Nick shouted over.

*'Nick, this is Bill Mance, of Mance & Tyler Investigations. I was Ray's partner and a friend of your dad. We met many times when you were a lad.'*

'I don't know you.'

*'I was there that day at the Spoils, when you and your parents flew in by helicopter.'*

'So what?'

*'I'm who Mercy works for,'* Bill continued. *'She's my apprentice, of sorts. It was me who sent her into the club to follow you, no one else. I've placed a wire feed inside the lining of her leather jacket, which is how I can hear this and I'm recording everything you've been saying. You need to understand that, Nick. If you shoot her, I have a tape I can send straight to the police. You'll be a murderer, bang to rights. And the others will go down as accomplices.'*

'Listen to the man, son,' Bob appealed from behind his tree. 'For your own sake.'

*'But let her go unharmed and that'll be the end of it,'* Bill said in a reasonable tone. *'I don't like dealing with the police any more than you do. I'm a convicted felon so I'm happy to destroy the tape once she's safe.'*

'Why's this happening?' Nick's throat sounded sore. 'Who's paying you to follow me?'

*'Is he still pointing his gun at you, Mercy?'* Bill asked. *'Because I'll tell him everything he wants to know when I'm assured you're out of harm's way.'*

'He's starting to lower it,' Mercy said through tight breaths. 'But it's still in his hand.'

*'Once he's placed the safety on and handed the cartridge to someone else,'* Bill promised, *'I'll tell him the truth of things. We'll get this straightened out.'*

Nick seemed hesitant, but, after a beat, Roz took a cautious step towards her boyfriend.

'Let me hold that, babe,' she touched him gently on the shoulder. 'I won't let them take it from you.'

*'Would you feel safer, Mercy?'* Bill asked, as Nick handed the gun over to his girlfriend, *'if* she *was holding it?'*

'I guess,' Mercy said, considering Roz to be less insane than Nick. As the gun was handed over, she felt her entire body uncoil from the tension. Roz placed the safety on and, from behind the tree, Bob groaned with relief.

'Tell me what's going on!' Nick shouted.

*'Your uncle is worried about you, lad,'* Bill could still be heard as Nick strode over and tore his phone from Mercy's hand. *'After the Junior Bruno fiasco. He hired M&T to make some discreet enquiries about what's happening. But we don't know who your mystery caller is and neither does he. Sorry if we botched it tonight but Mercy is new to the job and it seems she wasn't ready—'*

On that deflating performance review, Nick turned the speaker off. He continued snarling into the phone about how he was going to get revenge for his dad's death and that Ray Tyler was a coward who'd betrayed a great man. Roz stood close by with the Skorpion aiming at the ground.

'Time you fucked off, I think,' she said, giving her gun wrist a tiny flick. Mercy had no inclination to do anything else. She zipped up her jacket and collected her handbag with the tracker still inside.

Before leaving, she noticed something on the ground. It was some litter that Bob the Feet had dropped. On impulse, she reached down, collected it, and placed it into her handbag.

Then she left without saying goodbye to any of them.

# 51

Mercy saw a mouse dashing across the carpet when she returned to her flat. She switched on the light as it disappeared underneath the sofa bed she slept on every night. She gave the sofa a heave, but the mouse had already vanished. They moved so fast and there were many escape routes around her studio flat, mainly behind her kitchen units. She dropped the sofa back down in frustration. The room had four humane mouse-traps in different corners. All were empty.

She removed the cushions from the sofa and unfolded the bed. Then she went to the bathroom to take her hormone medication and clean her face. Her mother had made her look pretty earlier today, but now she felt as though every rough edge had returned. She wiped a tear from the cheek that had been spat on; blaming her emotional state on too may gins. Then she returned to the sofa bed in her pyjamas as morose thoughts rattled around.

A loaded gun had been pointed at her tonight.

And she'd made a mess of her first big case.

Mercy had been living in this flat for less than a month

and it contained many things that had once belonged to her dad. There was his bicycle that she hadn't yet used, an old leather swivel chair from his home study, and, on the wall above the sofa, the framed picture of that signed football shirt. She liked football no more now than she had growing up, but she'd hung it in the empty space as a reminder to solve his murder.

Her head touched the pillow and she pulled the duvet over herself. She looked up at the ceiling and murmured, 'I need new traps.'

Minutes later, before her dreams could set in, she got out of bed and took her leather jacket from the bike handlebar where it was hanging. She folded it up and, for reasons she couldn't even explain, took it through to the cupboard in the hallway. She placed it on top of a Henry Hoover and shut the cupboard door. Only then was she able to sleep.

# 52

'I feel like I've been lashed,' Bill complained in a pained voice early next morning. He'd spent most of the night in a hospital with his back injury. 'I must've landed badly.'

Daylight cut into the room between the slats of Mercy's blinds. She used her free hand to fold the bed away again.

'Anyway, I'm home at last, soon to shut my eyes,' he continued through the phone. 'I just wanted to check in and say what a grand job you did last night. Well done for removing that tracker. Better to be safe than sorry.'

'A grand job? I heard you say that we botched it and I wasn't ready.'

'Depends how you view things,' Bill said, while she placed the cushions back onto the sofa bed. 'We wanted to learn more about the Long Needle, and I think we did.' Mercy crossed over to her third-floor window. She'd just heard a car pull up. 'The key thing,' he was saying as she peered down to the street below, 'from a business perspective, is that our client paid us to find out if his nephew was a danger to him and we established that yeah, he definitely is. You were there to witness Nick receiving a dangerous weapon from an unidentified party and we wouldn't have discovered that if you hadn't gotten so close. So don't feel bad, you acquitted yourself admirably.'

Mercy placed her fingers between her window blinds, opening them wider. Outside the house, a familiar car had just parked up.

'Sure, it was unprofessional to reveal the identity of our client,' Bill kept on with an audible wince. It sounded like he was trying to get settled on a bed. 'But Nick was pointing a loaded weapon at you, so what could we do? Victor will be pissed off that I involved you, but I'll explain that a thorough investigation requires a two-man team. And he knows that Ray left you half of the agency. You're a Tyler, not some random employee.'

Down on the street, a middle-aged woman in a black coat got out of the car and then a second person emerged from the passenger side. Mercy knew both of them, but was stunned to see them together.

'I'll phone him after I get some kip,' Bill was still saying, 'and send him the relevant audio. I'm interested to know where he'll take the situation from here.'

The two women were walking together towards her building. She wondered if she should tell Bill about their appearance here. He'd be just as troubled by it.

'Sleep tight, Bill,' she said instead. 'Oh, and thanks for sticking up for me last night. Appreciate it.'

The intercom buzzed just as their call ended. She'd already managed to make sense of the unexpected duo and seeing them together had confirmed her burgeoning suspicions about one of them.

'Miss Tyler?' said the crackling voice through the intercom. 'DCI Bracken. I'm here on police business. We've some questions about your whereabouts last night.'

'Sure, come up,' Mercy said as she buzzed them in. 'I've some questions for you as well.'

She was still in her pyjamas and the flat was a complete state. Wanting to greet them in something a little cooler than the girly pink top she had on, she fished out a black T-shirt from her laundry bin and wore that instead. It had Hauser and the Vultures on, some old goth band that her ex-boyfriend Carmelo had been a fan of. By the time they knocked on her flat door, Mercy was still scrambling around the place, tidying up and giving her hair a quick brush. The police had to knock a second time before Mercy eventually opened the door.

'Bracken of the Yard,' she smiled at the detective. 'Who's your friend?'

'Mercy,' Nina Markham nodded, holding her police identification open. It revealed her rank as Detective Sergeant. 'May we enter the premises?'

Mercy remained where she was, blocking the entrance and staring at the unsmiling Nina.

'Why, it's the Invisible Girl,' she said in an acid tone. 'Remember when you said you'd be my ally and you'd share information with me? Didn't mention this second job, did you?'

'I'm mentioning it now,' Nina said, placing her ID away.

'Have you mentioned it to Bill?' Mercy said. 'Because I'm fairly sure that he doesn't know you're still a copper.'

'Miss Tyler, this will be easier to discuss inside,' Bracken persisted. 'We *are* here to share information as well.' Mercy stood aside and permitted the policewomen to enter her abode. 'Are you here alone?'

'There's a mouse scuttling around somewhere,' Mercy

told them as she sat on the office swivel chair that once belonged to her dad. 'But he's the model of discretion.'

'Aside from the mouse?'

'Just me,' she confirmed and then pointed at the small two-seater sofa that was the only other furniture in the place. 'Take a seat. I'd put the kettle on, but I want to establish if you're friend or foe first.'

The two women remained standing. Bracken, especially, loomed. She was one of the few women Mercy had met recently who was taller than her. Nina was carrying a leather holdall over her shoulder and looked even stroppier than usual.

'Last night there was a violent disturbance at Jack Spot's nightclub in Woolwich,' Bracken began, 'involving Nick Neale and some other men. According to a statement Bill Mance gave to officers afterwards, you were in the thick of it. Can you confirm this?'

'Yep.'

'Why were you present?'

'Didn't he say?'

'He pressed charges against someone called Gary Bowsher for spitting at you in an attack. Do you support that?'

'If this Bowsher is the one they call Dogger then yeah, I very much do support it.'

'Mr Mance didn't inform police as to what either he or you were doing there though.'

'Just a standard Saturday night,' shrugged Mercy, and then lolled towards Nina. 'Sorry *you* weren't invited, DS Markham.'

'Where's the leather jacket?' Nina asked.

'Wanna borrow it?'

Nina glared back.

'In the cupboard over there,' Mercy pointed. Nina walked over and opened it.

'Are there any other potential listening devices recording our conversation in this place?' she asked, once the cupboard door was shut again.

'Not that I know of.'

`No Alexa? No webcams?'

Mercy shook her head.

'As you've surmised,' Bracken then continued, 'DS Markham has been working undercover within M&T Investigations for some time. Eighteen months to be exact. I'm her handler.'

'I hope we'll be compensated for the wages we've been paying her,' Mercy said, with a sulky swivel.

'She's been there under my orders as part of a covert investigation called Operation Greenwater.'

So that's why Bracken had been saved as OG on Dad's dodgy mobile, Mercy thought. He *was* a police informer! She swivelled her chair toward Nina.

'I clocked you the other night,' she told her. 'A kid on a bike saw you. So you weren't *that* invisible.'

'I was doing my job,' Nina replied, in a flat tone.

'I'm wondering why you were following me.'

'Are you?' asked Nina.

Mercy almost responded but caught herself. It wasn't the first time Nina had tried to use Mercy's blabbermouth against her and so this time she decided to let the silent seconds to tick by. It was DCI Bracken who broke the stand-off. She crossed over to the sofa and sat in the centre, underneath the framed football shirt. Nina meanwhile stepped backwards and placed her holdall onto the kitchen surface.

'The sole purpose of Operation Greenwater is to secure the arrest of Victor Neale,' Bracken told her. 'As you know, he's suspected of having been behind some of the biggest heists in Britain's history.'

'And he killed a copper,' Nina sniffed.

'The difficulty is that Mr Neale now leads an almost reclusive life and much of his business appears to be legitimate. Many of his accomplices are dead and he's already faced trial for his more famous crimes. He isn't an easy target to investigate.'

'That's why M&T was the pressure point,' Nina explained. 'Your dad specifically was one of the few people that Neale still conducted meetings with. We guessed that if there was anything dirty going on it would run through the agency. I needed to get close to Ray.'

'How close to him did you get?'

'It took me the best part of a year to gain his trust,' Nina continued, ignoring the insinuation. 'In those early months he kept giving me easy jobs – basic surveillance. But eventually he began involving me in his more complex operations and we became a two-man team. But whenever Neale contacted the agency, I was shut out,' she continued. 'Ray would visit the Spoils himself and I was never introduced. The only thing I knew was that Neale always paid cash for any rendered services – cash which M&T rarely declared.'

'If Mance & Tyler had been our principal target,' Bracken interjected, 'then their tax avoidance would've been enough. But Greenwater will be considered a failure if it results in anything less than throwing the book at Victor Neale once and for all. At the end of 2019 we almost had him.'

'You know that phone conversation that your dad overheard?' Nina asked. 'Barbara was gossiping and your dad overreacted.' Mercy confirmed that she knew about the incident. 'He went on a drunken bender immediately afterwards. Completely AWOL. Bill told the rest of us to carry on with our work, but I knew that I had to speak to him and find out what was up. I was concerned for him.'

'Oh, bless.'

'I mean it,' Nina replied. 'I'd grown fond of Ray and I know from bitter experience when's exactly the wrong time to leave an alcoholic alone. I understood enough to know that he likes to hit the bottle when upset. None of his local pubs would be open at that early hour so I went in search. His car wasn't at your mum's house and I visited a number of other addresses I suspected he might be at. I left messages but, as you know, he was forever changing phones. I ended up exploring some of the homeless spots close to the office, including that little churchyard that he'd been known to take a liquid lunch to on hot days. That's where I was when I got a call from him, asking to meet me urgently. His voice was dry, like he hadn't drunk a drop all day. "Neen," he said "I need to see you as soon as possible." I told him I was by St George's and less than ten minutes later his Porsche pulled up on the main road. He was bibbing his horn for me to get in and, when I did, said nothing. Not even hello. He just drove us away from Southwark as fast as he could. I asked what was up, but he didn't respond. He had some gadgets hooked up to his phone and, as we drove, he began playing me some conversations he'd recorded from my own phone. They were between the DCI and myself. Police business. Some of them dated back to the early months when I'd started working there.'

'Really?' Mercy asked, a rare sensation of filial pride swelling within her. 'He'd always known?'

'Greenwater had been blown for a while,' Nina confirmed. 'Ray had kept me there despite knowing full well I was undercover police. As soon as I heard that, I realised why I hadn't been making any progress and assumed the operation was a bust. He didn't speak as we drove,' she went on, 'not even a glance in my direction. Just made me listen to my own voice talking about what little I'd learnt that week. It was cold. I'd stopped asking questions or trying to lie and got scared. Understand, I didn't know if he was going to kill me. We drove to the top level of the multi-storey car park in Peckham where he stopped the car and at last acknowledged me. His face was deathly pale and I was sure he was about to get nasty. I flinched as he reached down into his side compartment, thinking he was about to produce some weapon. But it was just a bottle of Evian. What he said next astounded me. '"What d'you need to take down Victor?" he asked after taking a swig. "Let me help you nick him."'

Mercy considered this revelation. Bill had told her that her dad had always been staunch in his hatred of police informers. *Snitches get stitches.* That said, he'd just learnt about Sarah having been pregnant when she'd died. If he felt partly responsible for her death, then that could've been enough to make him finally betray his old mate.

'I told him what we needed,' Nina explained. 'Paper trails linking Neale's legitimate businesses to criminal enterprises. Documented evidence of his involvement in drug importation, prostitution, and armed robberies. Something that would earn a solid conviction. "He's not one leaving for paperwork about," your dad answered. "But I'll see what I can do." But what we really wanted was Victor on tape, admitting to being the head of a criminal conspiracy. Your dad went silent when I said that.

'"Victor's had people killed," he eventually said. '*Innocent* people.' I asked for details, but he went silent, as if already regretting the mention of murder. But over the next few days he produced some documentation linking the Meantime gymnasium chain to Maggie Neale's money laundering operation abroad. He told me about some minor crimes he'd witnessed in Victor's company, but nothing too exciting. He was careful not to give us anything that incriminated either himself or the agency. Next step; I asked if I could be introduced to Victor. I wanted to be taken down to the Spoils as someone who should be allowed to work his cases while Ray was away. Someone trustworthy. But Victor only wanted to do business with your dad or, at a push, Bill. He saw me as an underling.' She glanced toward her superior officer. 'We suggested another tactic.'

'Your father was persuaded to wear a wire,' Bracken said, 'He even suggested how we could get a confession. It was a tradition in the weeks before Christmas for your father to visit Victor alone in the Spoils. They drink together, play old songs, and reminisce. Your dad said that as the night wore on Victor would let his guard down.'

'That meeting was set for Sunday December 22nd,' Nina resumed in a heavy tone. Mercy knew the rest. Her father's dead body had been found in the river on the 21st.

'Greenwater was finished,' Bracken admitted. 'We decided not to shut down until after Ray's funeral as we knew Victor would be present. But that was when *you* stepped in and offered us another shot at him. Your story about the meeting you overheard as a teenager, as well as the voicemail message Ray had sent you, brought life back to a near-dead investigation.'

'I wish I'd known at the time,' Mercy said. 'I felt like I was talking to myself.'

'Far from it,' Bracken told her and nodded at Nina.

'Yesterday I called Third Eye Electronics,' Nina told her, 'and Kitty informed me you'd had a live feed sewn into the lining of your jacket. Why is that?'

'Victor has paid Bill to monitor his nephew,' Mercy replied without hesitation. Finally, the police were giving her investigation the attention it deserved. 'He thinks he's a danger to him. I'm assisting Bill.'

'Have you met with Mr Neale?' asked Bracken.

'The nephew or the uncle?'

'The uncle obviously.'

'No, Bill was summoned to the Spoils where he was given the task. He later involved me.'

'If you hadn't joined the agency,' Nina told her in unconcealed irritation, 'then I would've been the assist on that.'

'I doubt it,' replied Mercy. 'I have an existing relationship with Nick that Bill wanted to exploit. That's what I was doing last night. Engaging him in conversation, learning why he hates his uncle.'

'Why does he?'

'Someone introducing himself as the Long Needle has been phoning him up since New Year's Eve and telling Nick that he killed his dad on Victor's orders. I don't have a copy of the recordings we made,' she told them, 'but Bill does. You visiting him next?'

'No, Mr Mance is not to be told anything about this conversation and that's a police order,' Bracken informed her. 'As a founding owner of a business funded with Neale money, he's compromised.'

'How come you're trusting me?'

'We need you out of the way,' Nina said.

'There's a chance,' Bracken explained, 'that if you removed yourself from the agency then Bill would allow DS Markham to replace you. And she needs to be a lot closer to this than she currently is. She's a fully trained undercover operative which makes her better suited to the task of investigating a high-profile target than you are.'

Mercy's elation crashed. It felt like Operation Greenwater had just flipped her the finger. Everything about this conversation so far had been a prelude to giving her the shove. She watched Nina, her usurper, reach into the holder for some documentation.

'This is a legal warrant forbidding you from communicating with Bill or anyone targeted by our operation and revealing what you've been told. There are criminal consequences should you breach this order.'

'Withdraw from M&T,' Bracken ordered. 'Tell Bill what you like; that you're ill, bored of being an investigator, that you've simply lost your bottle. Recommend that Nina take your place in the Neale investigation. Mention that you've already told her everything.'

'But I can help more if I stay as I am,' Mercy implored. 'We're on the same team.'

'You'll receive official recognition of your role in Operation Greenwater once its concluded,' Bracken said, as Nina placed the papers on the coffee table. 'If you want recognition that is. Until then, comply or risk arrest.'

'Fuck that noise.'

'We could arrest you now. Interfering with a police investigation once you've been made aware of it is a serious charge.'

Mercy glared out of the window. How could she be ejected from her job just as she was getting the hang of it? The injustice stung.

'Miss Tyler!' Bracken then exclaimed.

Mercy turned back towards the women who were both staring at a tiny little crevice between her oven and the freezer. A tiny brown tail had just vanished into it.

'You *do* have a mouse!' the DCI said.

# 53

Sitting alone underneath a portrait of the Queen, Victor Neale was talking loudly on his mobile. He was in the restaurant of his club, the last traces of Eggs Benedict still on his lips. There were a handful of other Never Setters in the mahogany-walled room, many of whom were retired businessmen, trying to mind their retired business. But Victor had become so agitated by what his Head of Gyms was suggesting that his voice was making him impossible to ignore.

'The viruses of other countries are not our fucking problem,' he explained to his subservient. 'I didn't vote for this prime minister for him to shut down Meantime as soon as he gets in. The gyms stay open, end of. Now let me get back to my brunch.' With that, he cut the call, wiped his lips with a napkin and stared back at another pink-tied member watching him over a newspaper.

Once his plate was removed Victor was interrupted again, this time by Jayesh, the club manager. It appeared that he'd been hovering outside the room waiting for this moment. Victor often spent his Mondays at the club and a downside to that habit was that people knew when to accost him.

'I don't know if you're aware,' Jayesh began in a tremulous voice, 'but it's Norman Valence's seventieth birthday in a few days.'

'Good for Norman.'

'He's been a Never Setter for over three decades. Longer even than you. And he's been *almost* as generous in terms of charitable donations.'

'I know who he is.'

'He's made a request to celebrate in the private dining room with his sons and grandchildren tomorrow night.'

'And?'

'He has a granddaughter. She's seventeen.'

'He knows the rules.'

'He certainly does,' the manager flinched as Victor sipped his tea. 'But, considering how valued a member he is, he asked if an exception might be made. Other clubs such as ours have loosened similar restrictions and–'

'When was this club founded, Jayesh?' Victor cut in, placing the teacup onto the saucer with a small clatter.

'1953,' Jayesh answered. 'Coronation year.'

'Okay,' nodded Victor. 'And one of the first rules set down by those original members was that only one female is ever permitted to enter our club.' He indicated the portrait above. 'Her.'

'I'm aware,' Jayesh risked a laugh. 'Although in 67 years, Her Majesty hasn't yet graced us with her presence.'

'That's not the point,' Victor snapped. 'I became a Never Setter in the first place because I approved of the rules. No women, no convicted criminals; a place for respectable men, such as myself, to meet the like-minded. Now if Norman isn't happy, he can hand in his pink tie and find another club to grow old in. Or take it up with me.'

Jayesh bowed in response. 'God Save the Queen,' he smirked before exiting the room.

Once his table was cleared Victor reached for the suitcase by his feet. He clicked it open and produced the file with Bill Mance's report inside. He laid it on the table, placed on his reading glasses and looked again at the transcript of what his nephew had said over the weekend. It confirmed Victor's worst fears. Nick was telling everyone who'd listen that his father had been killed on Victor's order. Worse still, the Long Needle had, for some reason, provided him with a military grade weapon.

The threat was greater than he was originally told. When Bob the Feet, in an undignified attempt to worm his way back into his good graces, had told Victor about these phone-calls that Nick had been receiving, he'd thought it was a hoax. But now the situation was accelerating. Victor connected some earphones to his mobile and then listened again to the strange voice that Bill had caught on tape.

*'The serpent that stung thy father's life now wears his crown.'*

Was *that* what his hitman sounded like? Ray had never mentioned him being American, but then he'd withheld almost every detail about the assassin's identity. At the time, that disconnect from the killer had suited Victor. Ray was paid to take the risk and the buck would've stopped with him had the hits gone wrong. But now it disturbed Victor to realise how little he actually knew about this nameless hitman who could destroy him with a confession. He needed to reach out to this man somehow, to discover what he's playing at.

Bill was running out of mileage, Victor assessed as he continued through the file again. When they'd spoken yesterday, he'd complained about a bad back he'd sustained getting pushed over during the fight. He was useful for bugging phones, but he even had a criminal record for that. Sure, he could manage the agency into which Victor had invested so much laundered money, but he wasn't up to a job like this. He wasn't Raymond.

*'I am becoming an expert on the man who you call the Long Needle,'* he'd heard Mercy tell his nephew over the tape. *'I've been investigating him since I was fourteen.'*

Victor had been more impressed by Tyler Junior. She'd boldly approached Nick's gang in the club while Bill had been hiding outside. She'd had the presence of mind to pinch Nick's phone, pursued him to another location, beaten up Bob the Feet and kept her cool while a loaded gun was pointed at her. Chip off the old block.

He reached for his phone. This time, when the call was answered, he kept his voice lower.

'You in the office?' he asked his investigator.

'I'm working from home,' answered Bill, sounding like he was lying down. Typical.

'Alone?'

'Yep.'

'I think it's time we found our needle in the haystack,' Victor whispered.

'Agreed,' there were noises suggesting Bill was getting out of bed, 'before it's too late.'

'Contrary to my previous statement,' Victor confessed, 'I've more light to shed. Let's set up a meeting. Tomorrow, my club, dinner for two.'

'Sure,' Bill replied. 'What time shall I—'

'Not you,' he told him. 'Send Mercedes instead.'

# 54

Ray's vintage Porsche ripped through the country roads like it had been manufactured yesterday. The rear engine's sexy growl made up for the stiff handling and it was huge fun to drive this car through the small villages that led towards the Kent town of Whetstone. Mercy was approaching via the scenic route – under aqueducts and over fords – despite the town being only a 30-minute drive from her home had she used the motorway. The early evening was darkening as she raced along a clear road, keeping pace with a train packed with returning commuters on the other side of the valley. The radio was playing some absolute bangers, the speedometer climbed higher than was legal, and she was too energised to care. Despite the attempted obstruction of Operation Greenwater, fate had placed her back in the game.

That police order had left Mercy feeling dumped. To be forcibly removed from what she considered to be her case had sent her into a despondent funk. It had made her appreciate how much she'd taken to investigative work, how it had been the only thing giving her life meaning since returning from Spain. So when Bill had told her that Victor Neale, who'd barely acknowledged her existence before now, suddenly wanted to meet her for dinner, it had felt like a recently locked door had been reopened. Supposedly, he wanted to discuss the identity of the hitman with her. He had information, he'd told Bill, that he would provide exclusively to Mercy, but only in exchange for her information first. He wanted to quiz her about that day in her dad's office.

Bill had promised that she could reject the invitation if she wanted and he would go in her place. Mercy had considered it. Bracken had told her to step away from the case in order to set Nina up as her undercover replacement. She was doubtless breaking the law by not informing them of this dinner, but so what? Victor had specified that she – the daughter of his childhood friend – meet him in a social setting, an offer he was unlikely to extend to a stranger. So, if anything, Mercy thought as she entered the old market town, she was doing the police a solid by hearing what Victor had to say and reporting back. She was Team Greenwater even if Team Greenwater wasn't Team Her.

Whetstone was a short distance from Victor's home and was known to be one of the few places he ever left the Spoils for. She drove past a duck pond in the centre of the quiet town and looked for the location of the Never Setting Sun. It was in a pretty Georgian hostelry across the road from the covered market, and Victor's Rolls Royce with the number plate VIC III was parked outside. Two suited men were lurking nearby; Victor's security guys. She parked her dad's car further up the incline of the road, assuming that his old pal would recognise it. But would he recognise, she wondered in anticipation, what was underneath her mum's long black coat? She certainly hoped so.

Mercy was late because she'd visited Julie's house to inform her of where she was going, borrow from her wardrobe and get ready. As well as the coat, some discreet earrings and a quick spray of perfume, Mercy had requested a particular outfit.

'That's bad taste, darling,' her mother had cautioned. 'Even for you.'

Mercy had remained undeterred, especially after trying the item on. It was now concealed under the coat and she felt more feminine than she had in a long time as she walked towards the club in high heels. But, before heading up the stone steps to the main door, she continued towards the Rolls Royce. Standing beside VIC III in a chauffeur's cap, an ill-fitting suit and rolling himself some tobacco was a man whose presence here intrigued her.

'You've gone up in the world,' she greeted Bob the Feet as he licked his paper. Until she addressed him, he'd been pretending not to notice her, and she assumed he was still raw about being kneed to the floor two nights prior. 'How's Nick going to like it when he hears you're working for Uncle Victor now?'

'I play both sides,' Bob said with a sly wink. 'That's how I've survived so long.'

'Did Junior Bruno get the sack?'

'Too right,' Bob sneered, 'after that rumble in the club. Vic hates it when people get arrested over stupid shit. That's why he didn't trust Bill Mance for years.'

'You've done time though.'

'Not in this century. And I've performed vital services of late that have got me back in Vic's firm. He's a generous bloke when he's happy with you.' He flashed yellow teeth. 'Your old man knew that too. It's why you're here, innit? You Tylers do anything for cash.'

'If you say so.' Mercy reached into her handbag. 'By the way, you dropped something the other night.'

She produced a tobacco packet identical to the brand Bob was currently rolling for himself. He'd thrown it to the ground when Nick had threatened to shoot the gun and Bob had scarpered for the tree. It had caught Mercy's eye before she'd left the scene although she hadn't immediately known why.

'That's yours, right?' she said, offering it back to him. 'Golden Virginia.'

'Where'd you find it?' he coughed as he took it back.

'You tell me,' she replied. 'Are you in the habit of littering places with tobacco pouches?'

'If you see this as some sort of peace offering, you can fuck off,' he scowled as he pocketed the returned tobacco. 'And I'll say this; if the boss didn't want to meet you tonight then I wouldn't be as civil as I'm being. I should've beaten the shit out of you while I had the chance. You were lucky.'

'Understood,' Mercy nodded. 'I fear we shall never be friends, which is devastating to me. I'll leave you to your roll-ups. G'night Bob.'

She turned to leave, took a step away and then spun back around, karate-chopping the air in front of him. Bob cried out in fright and dropped his tobacco again. It amused her to see how quickly he could crumple at such a playful action. Behind her she heard clapping.

'I know who I'd put money on,' chuckled Victor, walking down the steps of his club and flanked by those suited men. He had on a black velvet-collared suit and a pink waistcoat and tie. Her dad had only ever worn his one pink tie when dining at this club. Victor's gammon head matched his waistcoat and he flashed a predatory grin. 'Mercedes,' he said as he offered his hand. 'How you've altered.'

Seeing him in the sweaty flesh pulled her up sharp. She'd become so excited by the thought of discovering more about the Long Needle, that she'd forgotten quite how much she detested this man.

'Call me Mercy,' she insisted. 'Everyone does.'

'Not everyone,' he replied with an apologetic tone. 'I heard you tell my moron nephew on the recording to call you Mercy. He didn't get it, did he? It must be annoying for you I imagine – being called Christopher or Chris,' his gaze dared her to look away, 'especially when you have to repeatedly tell someone. Disrespectful.'

'I don't love it.'

'Or Chrissy,' he added.

'Yeah, I hate that too.'

'Speaking of recordings,' he clicked his fingers. One of the suited men behind him stepped forward. 'Piper needs to search you for devices. Sorry, but you did have a microphone in your jacket the other night and I can't take chances. Alright if he goes through your handbag and gives you a pat down?'

She handed over her bag without complaint. Piper rifled through it and pulled out a number of objects, including a small pen that he unscrewed without apology. Bill had forbidden her from taking any of his gadgets with her for fear of the consequences should any be discovered.

'Splendid,' said Victor once his man had assured him that she wasn't concealing anything irregular about her person. 'Let's eat.'

Leaving his security guys outside, Victor walked her to the main entrance of the club. He held the door open and she stepped into an old-fashioned reception area where a gentleman in a tailored suit looked horrified to see her.

'Now, Victor,' he said, smoothly positioning himself

between Mercy and the rest of the club, 'unless your guest here is Elizabeth II then you know she isn't permitted.'

'Cool it, Jayesh,' Victor told him, holding up a palm. 'We can make an exception this time.'

'I'm not sure we can,' he protested 'considering our conversation yesterday. Norman and his sons are in the main restaurant celebrating his seventieth and we barred his granddaughter from joining them. To parade this lady past him now would be an insult.'

'Yeah, but there's a loophole,' Victor explained.

Mercy felt her spirit sink. She'd not considered that the Men Only rules of this club would also extend to guests.

'Remember Raymond Tyler?' Victor asked the man with discernible relish. 'He was a mate of mine and a member of this club during the nineties. Well, this is his only child and there's a tradition that the eldest son of any Never Setter is an honourary member here, right?'

'Well, yes but—'

'Good news!' he cheered, 'because Mercy was born Christopher Tyler. She's a man really.'

'Fuck you, Victor,' she said, as a shocked Jayesh studied her more closely.

'Don't be like that, Mercedes,' Victor winked. 'All you've got to do is sign in under your old name and it's sorted.'

'I'm a woman,' she asserted. 'And I'm not signing in under my old name.'

'Fuck off then, snowflake,' Victor shrugged. 'I'll give my business to another agency, shall I? Someone more robust.'

Jayesh had moved behind a reception desk as their exchange became more heated. She could tell that he wasn't about to stick up for her if he didn't have to.

'You want to find out who the Long Needle is?' she whispered, stepping closer to the old gangster, 'then you need to deal with Mance & Tyler. There's no other agency.'

'Old Bill and his tranny sidekick?' he laughed. 'I already know more about the Needle than either of you. So get over yourself and maybe you'll learn something.'

Jayesh had been tapping on an iPad as they stared each other out. He lifted his head up and addressed Mercy.

'Mr Neale is correct,' he told her. 'Raymond Tyler was a member here for a time. Under the rules, you're welcome to be our guest as long as you sign in under the name *he* gave you.' He produced a visitor's book and pen. 'That should settle things.'

Mercy breathed out. The level of fury she felt shocked her. Victor had invited her to his club so he could play this shitty trick. It made her want to kick his old arse in front of the whole restaurant – a feat she knew she was capable of.

However, there were other ways of hurting him and one was hidden underneath her coat. She needed to learn why he'd summoned her here and she had every intention of sharing her findings with Operation Greenwater afterwards. To leave now would be to relinquish her shot and so, as much as it grated, she'd let him win this one. She took the visitor's book from Jayesh's hands and signed in under what felt like a stranger's name.

'I haven't signed this name for five years,' she told Jayesh as her writing hand tried to form a long-discarded signature, 'so you might find it illegible.'

Once she'd filled in her address she slapped down the pen like it had been giving her cramp and asked to place her coat in the cloakroom. Jayesh shifted around from the desk and took it from her. Victor meanwhile had opened the glass door separating this reception area from the main restaurant and was shouting 'Happy Seventieth, Norman!' at an unseen someone.

A waiter appeared down the steps of a rather grand staircase to her left. Jayesh instructed him to escort Mr Neale and his guest to the Cecil room where their dinner would be served and a fireplace was lit as requested. On the walls leading up the staircase was a huge old map of the world with many countries coloured in pink to represent the glory of Britain's former empire. As Victor focussed his attention on Norman's birthday, she positioned herself at the foot of the staircase and a malicious smile crept onto her lips. When he finally looked in her direction, she enjoyed seeing his own grin vanish.

'I hope this inky dress is appropriate,' she said, resisting the urge to give him a twirl. 'Pink's not my colour.'

The waiter gestured for them both to follow him up the staircase, but Victor remained rooted to his spot, taking her in.

'My wife had a dress like that,' he murmured.

'It *is* hers,' Mercy smiled. 'Sarah gave it to Mum years ago in exchange for the red one she died in. As luck would have it, it fits me perfectly. Now, let's have dinner, I'm starving.'

# 55

Mercy had always known that her mother still had the dress that Sarah Neale had worn at her husband's 40th birthday. And she'd guessed that nothing would mess with Victor's head more than her wearing it tonight.

He was darkly silent as the waiter guided them up through the Georgian building and into the private dining room. There was a portrait there above a lit fireplace of a thin moustachioed man who Mercy didn't recognise. The waiter informed her, as he pulled out her chair, that this was Cecil Rhodes, the late-Victorian imperialist. Half-listening as he ran through a potted account of Cecil's achievements, Mercy didn't sit. Instead, she went over to the large windows that overlooked the street below.

Bob the Feet was sat inside the Rolls Royce, talking on his phone. Victor's security guards lurked nearby, and it seemed obvious that both of them had weapons concealed under their suit jackets. They'd positioned themselves between the club and her dad's car further up the hill. If she needed to make a run for it, they'd have no difficulty stopping her. Even though both Bill and her mum knew where she was, her situation was vulnerable.

Victor remained standing until she took her seat at their table for two. He nodded his approval when shown a bottle of wine and nobody spoke as their glasses were filled. The fireplace crackle and the glug-glug of the red wine were the only sounds. After placing menus in front of them, the waiter withdrew from the room, telling them he'd return shortly. The door shut, enclosing the two of them alone together in that small, flame-heated space. Victor stared at her with barely blinking, furious eyes.

'I bought that dress as a gift for my wife,' he growled, 'twenty years back, when I still loved the bitch. What the *fuck's* it doing on a walking travesty like you?'

'I'm wearing it as a tribute to Sarah, whose style I admired.'

'It should have been incinerated!' Victor shouted, slamming his open palm onto the table, disturbing the cutlery. The ferocity of his outburst was frightening, but she'd deliberately inflamed it, hoping the dress would trip him into talking about Sarah.

'What's your Mum's game?' he demanded, nostrils flaring, 'holding on to a dead woman's dress and then lending it to *you* of all people? It makes a mockery of Sarah's memory. She was the mother of my kids and you've insulted both them and me!'

'Technically, this dress belongs to Mum,' Mercy spoke in as calm a tone as she could manage. 'Sarah had swapped it for one of her own a short time before she died. She fell from the balcony wearing the red one Mum had lent her.' Victor blinked in surprise. 'You may not have known that,' Mercy continued, 'as you were out of the country at the time. But it was a distressing experience for

Mum who I believe has been keeping this out of respect for Sarah. And she had serious reservations about letting me wear it tonight so it's me, not her, who you should be angry with.'

'I *am* angry with you,' he jerked toward her as if to bite. 'I'm fucking livid!'

The door to the room half-opened. The waiter, returning to take their orders, heard Victor's volcanic rage and immediately shut it again.

'You're not wearing it as a tribute to Sarah,' Victor jeered, 'you barely knew the woman. You put that on to wind me up!'

'And you invited me to your all-male club,' she replied. 'So neither of us is averse to mind games.'

Victor turned his head to the fireplace, as if expecting it to take his side, and then looked back to her. He glared at the dress with a murderous expression. Then to her great relief, he emitted a short laugh through his nose and leaned back again.

'You're a cheeky cunt,' he said in a complimentary tone, 'like your old man.'

By the time the waiter had summoned up the courage to re-enter, things had cooled. Victor huffed as she ordered the only vegetarian option as her main course. He ordered the venison.

'I see you're driving Raymond's old car,' he remarked as soon as they were alone again. 'You appreciate vintage as much as he did?'

'It gets me from A to B,' Mercy replied, reluctant to admit that she'd fallen in love with the sleek sixties icon which made her feel like Emma Peel whenever she got behind the wheel.

'Bit of a magpie, aren't you? Driving Dad's motor,

wearing Mum's dress. I recall that you got into trouble as a kid,' he added with a long stare. 'Shoplifting.'

'If the infamous Victor Neale is about to judge me for some minor teenage theft,' she said, touching the stem of her wine glass, 'then I may pass out from an irony overload.'

'I'm not one to play judge and jury.'

'What about executioner?'

'I've killed a man if that's what you're asking,' he replied with defiance. 'It was manslaughter and I was let off in court. Aside from that, I'm an owner of some successful businesses and my only crime is having had criminal relatives.'

*He still thinks I'm bugged,* Mercy realised as she raised the glass. *He thinks Bill is recording this.*

'Blimey, this is nice,' she remarked after taking a sip of wine. 'What is it?'

'I don't drink any old piss,' Victor replied. 'Chateau Lafite Rothschild, 1970. Pricey.'

'In which case I'm glad you're paying.'

'Hard up, are you?' he asked, with real interest. 'Finding London expensive?'

'Very,' she nodded, understanding that this was why he thought she was here. Like Bob the Feet, he was assuming that all Tylers were motivated principally by money. 'Run straight, the agency provides enough for the rent and bills in my tiny flat,' she said, her eyes on the glass in an effort to appear coy, 'but, I don't know, there's hardly anything left to have fun with. I don't want to wear hand-me-downs all my life.'

*'Run straight,'* Victor repeated her insinuations back to her, 'no *fun* money. If I shut my eyes, I could be listening to your dad.'

She was unsure if that comment contained a dig at her

vocal depth, but she let it go and took another sip of the smoky wine. He continued his intense staring as she swallowed. He was being careful to not incriminate himself, so she'd have to broach sensitive subjects first. Outside it had started to rain.

'Bill and I are grateful for the work you've sent our way,' she proceeded in a quieter voice. 'I trust you're satisfied with our performance so far.'

'It's a start,' he replied after taking his own swig. 'But I still don't know whose calling my nephew and spreading lies.'

'We're all over that,' she insisted. 'Bill and I are developing a plan to root out and catch this midnight caller.'

'I never said I wanted him caught,' Victor glared. 'I want to know who he is.'

'Could you clarify that difference, please?'

'I don't want the police involved in my affairs,' he said as if she was stupid. 'I only wish to understand his motives. Then I'll settle things my way.'

On that sinister note, the waiter returned with their starters. Leek and potato soup for her, scallops for him. Mercy acknowledged the waiter as the food was placed in front of them. Victor did not.

'William played me your dad's last message,' he said once the door was shut again. 'That was tough to hear.' She dipped her silver spoon into the broth. 'In it, Ray was talking about some meeting that you spied on as a kid,' he watched her as she sipped, 'and he mentioned the Long Needle. Nick's anonymous caller also calls himself that.' Mercy swallowed. 'What's that about?'

'You mean, do I think that the hitman I overheard and Nick's anonymous caller are the same person?' A lorry could be heard trundling past outside in the otherwise quiet street.

'Is it the same voice?' Victor asked.

'No, Dad's hitman sounded English,' she told him. 'Although the American accent is probably faked.'

'Tell me what you know,' Victor said, once he'd bitten into his first scallop. 'Start in Dad's office. William gave me the gist, but I want your account.'

She obliged and by the time they'd finished eating their starters, he'd been given a complete rundown of her father's midday rendezvous with the hitman. She'd studied his reaction while describing the pink envelope that her dad had handed over on behalf of his client. She even remarked that the club napkins were exactly the same shade as that envelope, as was the tie hanging around his neck. They both knew that he must be the unnamed client her dad had been representing, but he genuinely seemed to have no idea who the hitman actually was.

'I knew this stuff already,' he complained as she finished speaking. 'Tell me something I don't.'

'Do you know why I was home that day?' Mercy said, resting her spoon in the finished bowl.

'You were playing truant.'

'Right,' she nodded, 'but why was I so scared of Dad catching me?'

Victor shrugged. Mercy had never told the police, or anyone, how she'd been dressed as she'd hidden behind the curtain that afternoon. It was an embarrassing, unnecessary detail so she'd generally omitted it from her statements.

'I was wearing a ladies' jumpsuit,' she explained, 'makeup and clip-on earrings. I'd been dancing to a Kylie song like I was auditioning for Stars In Your Eyes and looked like what I was; a girl.'

'Jesus,' Victor raised his eyebrows. 'No wonder you hid. Ray the Rottweiler would've gone berserk if he'd caught you dressed like a bird.'

'Quite.'

'He'd have beaten the crap out of you.'

'I doubt that,' she replied, trusting that she knew her father better than he did. 'He never laid a violent hand on me in his life. But yeah, I was scared.'

The waiter returned and removed their starter plates. Victor asked for some club stationary and a pen as the waiter was backing out of the room, then turned his attention back to her.

'Frankly, I don't care if you were dressed as Dame Vera Lynn. That's not useful information.'

'See, I'm not so sure,' she replied, bracing herself for another confrontation. 'Because I've always been under the impression that there wasn't a soul who knew about my little Kylie outfit. But I recently discovered that your Sarah had been in possession of the fact.'

'What crap.'

'A friend of hers told me that she'd been gossiping about how I was transgender.'

'Friend?' Victor squinted his eyes. 'Sarah didn't have any friends.'

'I'm not going to divulge my source,' Mercy told him. 'But does it make sense to you? How would she know about my one attempt at teenage cross-dressing unless she also knew about the meeting?' Victor went silent. 'Dad's voicemail proves he was aware I'd overheard the conversation,' she continued. 'Maybe he told her about it?'

'Why would Raymond,' he cried in outrage, 'be telling *my* wife anything about anything?' She tensed her body, ready for another explosion.

'Maybe they had some kind of secret relationship that you weren't aware of.'

'Was she fucking him?' Victor demanded.

'I've no idea,' she answered. 'But, aside from me, they were the only two people there that day who could've told her about it – Dad or the Needle – so it sheds new light on her role in this.'

Victor's clenched hands had been resting on the white tablecloth during this exchange. Otherwise, he was still and when he spoke next it was with a low, uncontained hatred. 'I wouldn't put it past the bitch.'

The waiter returned with the requested pad and pen. The paper was pink. Victor had withdrawn into himself as it was placed next to him and the waiter withdrew. Rain pelted down outside.

'I've only been a private investigator for a week,' she spoke carefully, wary of his sudden introspectiveness, 'but I know that discussing marital infidelities with clients is one of the toughest parts of this job. So I ask this next question purely in a spirit of professional detachment and in the interests of the case. Do you know if your wife *was* sleeping with anyone else?'

His eyes were fixed on the fireplace. She recognised pain in them and might have felt pity had he not been who he was. He opened his mouth a lot, even when not speaking, like a man with a constant thirst, and she sensed his tongue moving inside even when it was shut. She imagined that his every thought was a conflict between shrewdness and rage and wondered how her dad had handled him so well.

'There were rumours,' he eventually admitted.

'You hired M&T to look into those rumours,' she said. 'Bill told me that you didn't trust Sarah much. You were worried about her drug habits and the company she kept.'

'She had mental health issues,' he snapped. 'Even before I met her, she'd tried to take her own life. People forget.'

'You were worried for your children,' Mercy encouraged him. 'It's only natural you'd want to know what was happening while you weren't there to protect them.'

'Right,' he nodded. 'Your dad found out that she'd slid back into drugs. And that my own brother had been supplying her with the junk. I was gutted. And then Bill sent me a recording of her therapy session where she was babbling incomprehensibly. He thought she was saying that Lol was raping her. I didn't believe it,' he snorted. 'If they fucked, *she* was up for it.'

'Why do you think that?'

'She told me she loved him.'

'She confessed?'

'By accident,' he avoided her eyes as he spoke. 'I received a text from her one night while I was in Antigua, meant for someone else.'

'Was this text unambiguous?'

'It's hard to talk about,' Victor winced. 'I'm a proud man.'

'I understand,' she nodded and waited for him to proceed. Only the fireplace and faint light from the windows gave any illumination. Half of his face was concealed in shadow as he brooded on these past betrayals.

'Four words,' he whispered. *'Lol, I love you.'*

'Lol?' she clarified, 'as in your older brother?'

'Yeah, my brother!' He suddenly convulsed. 'That's what everyone knew him as.'

'Yeah, but...'

'If you're about to tell me it stands for *laugh out loud,'* he warned, 'you can fuck right off. Because that's what she said when I confronted her. Can you believe the nerve? Trying to gull *me* of all people? With my own flesh and blood and then talking that shit? Like I'm some two-bob moron who'll believe any old bollocks?'

'You're very angry with her,' Mercy said. 'How do you feel about Lol?'

'How d'you think?' he snarled. 'My brother carrying on with my wife! *I wanted to kill—*'

They were interrupted by the main course. The waiter walked in backwards carrying the trays and, on impulse, Victor lifted a napkin to his mouth. The plates were placed in front of them. It was an unfortunate interruption just as he was about to admit to a motive for ordering a hit, but it gave her a chance to think.

Lawrence Neale had been a violent sexual abuser, as well as an ugly man. Nothing about him suggested that he was someone a refined woman might fall in love with, but, Mercy reminded herself, Sarah had willingly married Victor, who was also a walking horror show. The human heart was perverse, so she supposed anything was possible. But what if her real lover had said something funny and she'd accidentally sent the response to Victor? She remembered the photo from the birthday celebration. Sarah laughing uproariously at whatever her dad was saying.

The waiter set about lighting more candles as the rain continued to patter. Victor reached for his pen, but it was too dark to see what he was scribbling.

'Did you ever confront Lol about it?' Mercy asked once they were alone again.

'By phone,' he murmured while concentrating on what he'd written. 'He denied it but still managed to call my wife a slag.'

'How soon was this before his car exploded?'

Victor looked up from his pad, surprised by her bluntness. He scrunched up the piece of paper and tossed it into the flames.

'Two weeks later he was dead,' he said as he watched the paper burn. He began scribbling again, ignoring his hot food.

'How might one go about hiring someone like the Long Needle?' Mercy then asked, taking a fork to her mushroom risotto.

'Why you asking me?'

'You're a businessman,' she said, before taking a bite. 'And his doesn't seem a very stable business model. No one knows who he is and we've no clue how to contact him.'

'Your dad knew how to contact him.'

'Yes, and I'd love to understand how,' she said, chewing.

Victor rested his pen down and looked up. He smiled before reaching for his cutlery and she was astonished at how quickly he could alter his mood.

'Change of subject while we eat,' he said, cutting into the venison as if it was his latest victim. 'Does the name Yulia Ilyinskaya mean much to you?'

Mouth full, she shook her head.

'She was a Russian professor of nuclear physics working in Cambridge,' he continued 'who was poisoned in 2001 with a rare chemical nerve agent. They called it the Russian Teapot Murder.'

'I've seen a documentary,' Mercy remembered after swallowing her food. 'She was poisoned at a tea party in her own home. The Russian government did it.'

'That's never been proven,' Victor chewed as he spoke. 'But it's what MI6 thinks. She'd arrived in Britain decades earlier as part of a spy swap and was a vocal critic of her country. The security services protected her for years but that had eased off. By the time of her death, she was just some old woman teaching undergrads at a university who held weekly tea parties for favoured students. But the autopsy found that inside her stomach was a nuclear chemical poison that only three countries in the world could produce. One of them being Russia. It was a major international incident, especially considering that three other British citizens died drinking from the same teapot.'

Mercy reached for the wine bottle and poured herself a tiny amount, confident it wouldn't push her over the limit.

'And, as with other state hits that have taken place on British soil,' Victor continued, 'our government did fuck all about it because they're shit-scared of Moscow. Thing is,' he continued, not thanking her as she poured him a more generous share, 'it wasn't what it looked like.'

'Are you saying that this was our man?' Mercy asked. 'If that was true, which I doubt, how would you know about it?'

'I learnt the tragic truth about poor Yulia in this very room some time after her death. There were only three of us present. Myself,' he indicated the wall, 'good Cecil up there, and another Never Setter sat right where you now are. Martin Bertsmouth. I don't mind telling you his name because he died of heart failure years ago and, in my book, it's okay to grass on someone if they're too dead to care. He's the one who first told me about the Long Needle.'

Mercy placed down her fork and swallowed.

'Bertsmouth talked too much,' he went on. 'I hadn't known him long, but he was forever trying to impress me with stories about what a player he was. But he was just a toupee-wearing, corpulent fool who ran an office cleaning company and cheated on his wife whenever he could. On learning that I was leaving the country for a spell he asked to have dinner with me. I assumed he wanted money, people invariably do. Instead he told me about a pickle he'd got himself into with a teenager who was in the same class as his daughter. Jenny was, by his description, a mousey sort who'd been visiting the Bertsmouth home ever since she was a kid. Turns out, dear old Martin had been secretly coercing her into sex since before she was legally allowed. I can see from your face, Mercedes, that you're as disgusted with him as I was.

'Seasons pass and she goes to university, safely out of that pervert's way. Then one day, out of the blue, he receives a letter from her in which she calls him a rapist. *Tell your family,* her letter said, *before I do.* Well, I began to suspect what Bertsmouth was driving at. Like every other peasant in the land, he was under the impression that I'm some Godfather type. He wanted the girl rubbed out and thought he could speak to *me* about such a thing. I blew my top!

'*"I wouldn't involve myself in your seedy problems, Bertsmouth,"* I told him. *"Be a man, tell your wife and don't shag any more kids."*

'But he then told me she was already dead. This drama had all taken place before I'd even met him. He'd taken to the internet – using the PC in his work office, would you believe – and made discreet enquiries into how to hire a hitman. He claimed he'd concealed his identity, but I doubt that someone like him would have the nous to do that effectively. After a few false starts and unexpected turns, he found himself on a private forum called Needlework Productions. Deep, dark web. In a coded way, he began discussing business but then chickened out, shut down his computer and rethought his actions. Next day a young man appeared in his office, the same one the computer was in. Early twenties, dark complexion, wearing a business suit. He claimed to represent a production company called Needlework. Bertsmouth took a slow moment but, when the penny dropped, he almost jumped out of the fourth-floor window in fright. But the young man assured him that everything was fine. And that he could solve the problem that Bertsmouth was alluding to online.

'They went for a lunchtime walk along a canal and Bertsmouth explained, in a less coded way, who the girl was and what he needed. *It won't look like what it is,* he was assured by the man. But he shocked him when he named his price. It was steep, too steep for Bertsmouth. But, desperate to silence the girl, the arsehole made the deal.

'Less than a fortnight later, Bertsmouth read about the Russian Teapot Murder on his morning commute. Like the rest of the world, he assumed it was a spy thing. The paper claimed that this incident could have damaged our relations with Russia to the point of another cold war. But Bertsmouth turned the page to read about the cricket. Hours later, he received a tearful phone call from his daughter, asking him if he remembered her old school friend Jenny. Bertsmouth felt sick, assuming he was rumbled. But his daughter told him that Jenny was a physics student at the college that Ilyinskaya taught at.

*'"And guess what Daddy, she drunk from the teapot. Jenny's dead"!*

Bertsmouth described the relief washing over him, even as his daughter was blaming Vladimir Putin.

'"*Thank you, Russia,*" the idiot thought, "*much obliged!*"

'Then a mysterious package arrived at his work. Inside there was a teapot and a business card from Needlework Productions with details of an offshore account for immediate payment. Bertsmouth was so horrified his wig span.'

Victor couldn't contain his laughter anymore. Mercy was fascinated by how much his mood had lifted during the telling of this vile story. In contrast to the acute discomfort he displayed when discussing his own troubles, he seemed to be relishing every detail.

'That's more than a little unbelievable,' she told him. 'For one thing, how did the killer get radioactive poison? They don't sell it in Boots. And it's a bit of a coincidence that Jenny would've been having tea with someone on a Russian hit list.'

'Only if she *was* on a Russian hit list,' Victor shot back. 'But one of the biggest mysteries surrounding the death of the professor was that all her links to Russian intelligence were old news. She hadn't been relevant in over a decade and it's only the rare poison that speaks of a state hit. But nobody would go to all that trouble to kill young Jenny, so nobody suspected she was the real target. Which was exactly what Bertsmouth had paid for, although he'd just wanted something simple, like a fake overdose, or for Jenny to be shoved in front of a train. He hadn't expected it to trigger a diplomatic incident. He spent the following months trying to duck payment, arguing that he believed that the Russians *had* smeared the inside of the teapot. He actually *hung up* on the boy, telling him he'd call the police if he kept bothering him.

'Days later, he was having a liquid dinner in this august establishment,' Victor continued after pouring the wine dregs into his glass. 'He called a cab firm to take him home and a car pulled up, telling the doorman that he was here to collect Martin Bertsmouth. Too inebriated to check, Bertsmouth bundled into the back of the cab and found himself kidnapped. Up popped a young teenage girl who had been crouched in the passenger seat and she pointed a gun at him. He described her as about nineteen, pale-skinned, with short, white hair. Doors locked, driving at a crazy speed down a series of winding country lanes, the driver accused Bertsmouth of owing him twice the amount they'd initially agreed upon. *"Radioactive poison is expensive,"* he was told once they'd pulled over in a dark byway, *"especially at short notice."*

'"*I never asked you to do that,*' Bertsmouth pleaded.

'"*Our research revealed that your target took regular tea with a former enemy of the Russian state,*" the girl said. *"It was the perfect cover."* Then the girl explained that she'd befriended Jenny and had even given her the teapot to take it to the party with her, the poison smeared inside! I mean, come on, it was audacious, we'll say that for them. But Bertsmouth didn't agree, he thought they were maniacs. The old fart sat across from me,' Victor indicated Mercy's seat, 'fucking quivering. If he couldn't pay up soon, he was dead, that's what he said to me. So he wanted to know if I'd ever heard of Needlework Productions, did I have any influence over them? I said, no, course I haven't, but if you find out who they are, let me know. I might have some work. And unlike you I *can* pay.' he winked as he shovelled the last cut of venison into his mouth. 'I was joking obviously. But *he* was shitting himself. Wiping every glass with a napkin before he drank, convinced that the rims might be poisoned. And the cheeky sod reasoned that, because we both wore the pink ties of this club, I was obligated to help him. I'd no intention. Bertsmouth's problems were his, I had my own.' Victor wiped gravy from his lips and then flung the napkin down onto his finished plate. 'So I told him to fuck off and left for Antigua soon afterwards. You not eating that risotto?'

Mercy shook her head. He leaned over and took her plate, replacing it with his. She was revolted by his story on behalf of Jenny, the professor and the other students who'd died as collateral damage. But, she had to admit, the account slotted in well with the image she already had of the Long

Needle. Young, dark-skinned, and with a female accomplice. What's more, during the telling, something astounding had occurred to her. She was developing a wild suspicion, one even more fanciful than anything she'd heard tonight.

'The upshot,' Victor admitted after making short work of her risotto, 'is that I'm the one who told your dad about the pair, just as Bertsmouth told me. Raymond worked out how to contact them, but then he was a bloody good investigator. Will you and William be able to sniff them out too? We'll see.'

'Why did you tell Dad about these people, Victor?' she asked, as he shovelled the last of her main course into his mouth.

'Dunno,' he shrugged, the sound of cutlery scraping on his teeth. 'Making conversation.'

'Did Dad ever interview Martin Bertsmouth about how to find these assassins?'

'Impossible. Soon after he spoke to me I was informed that Bertsmouth had died of a heart attack.' Victor grinned. 'Which is how you'd expect someone with his high blood pressure to go.'

The door to the Cecil Room opened again. Two waiters entered to remove their plates and ask if they wanted dessert. Mercy told them she was full while Victor ordered a sticky toffee pudding with custard. She considered what she should be asking him before their evening was concluded.

'When I was a kid,' she said once they were alone, 'shortly before the Long Needle day, dad's car engine was vandalised. We'd returned to it after one of my karate lessons and petrol was flowing everywhere. The rubber on the manifold had been slashed with a blade. What do you know about that?'

'Your dad had gambling debts,' Victor said, leaning

back, his white shirt straining from almost two dinners. 'Raymond owed the McAlonan boys fifteen grand from losing in their rigged casinos and they were getting heavy. That would've been a warning – pay up fast.'

Mercy recalled how her dad had been in the months leading up to the hitman meeting. Sleep-deprived, evil-tempered, always drunk or hungover. Owing some car-exploding gangsters £15,000 might do that to a person, she supposed.

'I paid it for him,' Victor said, picking up the discarded pen and writing something down. 'Anything for a mate.' When he'd finished, he beckoned for Mercy to lean closer so she could read his spidery handwriting against the flames. 'But even a mate,' he said, 'has to repay me somehow.'

***Raymond hired the hitman on my behalf . I paid £150,000 all in***

He scrunched up the page and threw it into the flames.

'Which was a lot of money in those days,' he said, as they watched it burn. 'But here's the most crucial information.'

'Okay.'

'Ray refers to the guy as *the Long Needle* in your voice-mail,' Victor whispered, 'but that was his name for both of them, the boy and girl. He was speaking plural.'

'Was he?'

'The Long Needle isn't a *who,* it's a *where*. An address. He never told me what it meant but, if you find that location, you'll find his killers.'

# 56

It was minutes to midnight by the time the two of them left the club. They were the last diners to vacate and, as they came down the wide staircase, Victor's suited security guys were sitting in the otherwise empty bar. They downed their respective whiskeys and headed out through the main door ahead to summon Bob from wherever he'd parked the Rolls Royce. Jayesh helped Mercy on with her coat while carefully avoiding the use of either her name or pronouns. He'd hoped she'd had a pleasant evening at the Never Setting Sun but didn't add 'come again soon.'

It saddened her to think that, in an earlier time, her dad had wanted her to join this very conservative club. It illustrated what sort of child he'd expected her to be. This was an exclusively male world constructed of pompous after-dinner speeches, table clapping, archaic jokes, sly winks, God Save the Queen, golfing weekends without the wife, backscratching, secret handshakes and other signifiers of brotherhood. Regardless of gender, she would've struggled to share the values of the place and people. Now that dinner was over, and that she'd learnt everything Victor was prepared to tell her, she felt glad to be leaving the suffocating, imperial-themed atmosphere.

Outside in the quiet lamp-lit street, Victor stood on the pavement in his thick coat as he waited for the Rolls Royce to come and collect him. The roads were still wet, but the rain had ceased. A stillness had descended on the small town and hardly any cars passed by. A fox trotted across the road further up the hill, ignoring them.

'Vermin,' Victor said as he lit up a cigar and offered one to Mercy as she buttoned up her coat. She refused the cigar but went in for some final probing before they went their separate ways.

'Do you think someone has hired this hit couple to kill you?' She watched Victor exhale some smoke instead of answering. 'And that they're manipulating Nick into doing the job for him.'

'There are *lots* of people who want me dead,' he shrugged, keeping his eye on the corner around which his chauffeured car was scheduled to turn. 'For a myriad of reasons. But who'd hire the Long Needle? For one thing, they're not fucking cheap.'

'What do *you* think is happening?'

'They want my attention,' Victor said as the smoke surrounded them both. 'And my business. This pantomime with Nicholas is an advert aimed at me.'

'The hitman wants you to hire him again?'

*'Again?'* Victor's head sharp-turned toward her. 'Careful, Mercedes. I never said I hired him!'

He sucked on his cigar and she realised she wasn't going to get much else out of him tonight. And so, as VIC III appeared around the corner, she said goodnight and told him she'd be in touch. Bob the Feet pulled the car up and, with the engine still running, got out of the driver's seat in his little grey hat to open the passenger door.

'I haven't finished smoking yet,' Victor told his unctuous chauffeur before turning back to Mercy. He flicked some ash, letting it fall by her high-heeled shoes. 'There is no Mance & Tyler without Victor Neale, and there never fucking has been. I've been funding your lifestyle since the dawn of time,' he moved forward and spoke in her ear. 'It was my money that paid for your education, your family holidays, that car over there, and your mum's prettier dresses. Fuck, I probably paid for your sex change.' The smoke in her face was as obnoxious as the man responsible for it. She tried not to flinch. 'Get me the sort of results that your dad did,' he continued, 'and the money will still flow. But don't let me catch you wearing my dead wife's clothing again. That's taking the piss and you know it. Next time we meet I want you looking professional. That means trousers.'

Mercy coughed but kept her eyes locked with his. She felt an urge to snatch the cigar from his mouth and snuff it out on his forehead.

'Next time,' she replied instead, 'you're going to need another fat envelope stuffed with cash. Bill and I are closing in on this guy and we don't work for free.'

'Spoken like a Tyler,' he said after releasing a new plume of smoke into the air. 'But that pokey agency doesn't survive without its benefactor. Raymond understood that which is why he rarely let me down. Now fuck off and call me when you've got something.'

Victor turned away, cigar in mouth, and asked Bob what had taken him so long. Dismissed, Mercy began walking back up the small incline of the hill towards the Porsche. She checked her phone and saw that she'd missed several anxious messages from Bill asking how it was going, as well as some from Nina demanding to know where she was. She decided to reply to Bill as soon as she got home but would let the Detective Sergeant wait until morning.

Her car was parked outside a quaint one-screened cinema showing only *Little Women.* She was a few feet away from it and reached into her handbag for the keys. That was when the peace of the night was disturbed by a sudden blast of high-volume hip-hop coming from behind her down the lane. She turned to see where the music was coming from. Victor was still outside the Never Setting Sun, finishing his cigar. Bob the Feet was closer to the Rolls, as were the two security men, all of them spotlighted underneath the lamp-posts. They were all looking across the road toward the entrance of the covered market from where the thumping bass notes were booming. From what Mercy had seen of it, the interior of that market area had been concealed in shadow. It would make a good spot from which someone could watch the outside of the club.

The track reached an even more confrontational pitch. She could hear Victor asking, *"fuck's that"*? over the noise. Lights in the windows above the shops were switching on and faces appeared, clearly asking the same question.

A headlamp beam came from the market entrance and Victor raised his hands to get a better look. Then the front of a familiar murdered-out Range Rover with black alloys poked into view. Mercy realised what was about to happen.

'I swear, boss,' she heard Bob plead as he turned toward Victor. '*I* didn't tell him where we was.'

Victor gave an unheard instruction to the security men. One of them crossed the road to approach the driver side of the Range Rover. Victor stayed where he was, puffing on his cigar.

Piper tapped on the black-tinted window, his other hand

inside his suit jacket in a warning gesture. Dead seconds passed.

'Turn it down, Nicholas,' she heard Victor shout over the music. 'This is a respectable area.'

A roar of engine and a tyre screech answered him. The Range Rover pulled out of the market entrance, leaving Piper behind. It swerved into the street, pulling up beside not Victor, but instead the Rolls Royce against which Bob was leaning. The other security man reached into his suit jacket too as Mercy edged backwards. Because of the tinted windows it was impossible to see who the driver was, but she heard Bob speaking to him. He seemed relaxed considering the aggressive behaviour of the vehicle.

That was when the quiet town of Whetstone exploded. Even before she heard Bob's scream, she watched his entire body go into a spasm of panic and her own jumped. The nearby security guard pulled out a gun but the shots that shattered through the night were not his. Mercy almost fell over backwards in shock as she watched the security man drop his weapon as a rattle of bullets hit both him and the chauffeur. Bob fell back onto the bonnet of the Rolls Royce as its windows smashed around him.

*It's the Skorpion!* her mind shrieked.

The vicious machine gun that Nick had been given on Saturday night had just cut through two men and a car. Now Victor was running in *her direction!* She turned from him and raced toward her dad's Porsche, aware that it wouldn't shield her from the Skorpion spray, so she needed to drive clear of the scene fast. Before she reached the car door she heard more gunshots from behind and screamed. She ducked down behind the passenger side of the Porsche and looked back toward the killer SUV.

Piper was stood in the middle of the street and had

begun shooting at the back of the Range Rover. The black glass of the rear windows could be heard shattering, but the vehicle switched into reverse and hurtled backwards into Victor's last remaining bodyguard. He fell on impact and the back wheels of the Range Rover proceeded to run him over. She could hear the crunch of his body from where she was.

'Drive!' Victor commanded as he too reached the burgundy Porsche. 'Get us out of here, you gormless bitch!'

'Piss off Victor,' she shouted, dodging away from a man who might as well have had a target marked on his head. 'Save yourself!'

The Range Rover was disengaging from Piper's body as she darted around to the driver's side of the Porsche and tried to force her keys into the old door lock. Victor followed, grabbing her by the arm.

'You work for me, Tyler!' he hissed as he pulled her towards him. 'Give me the keys!'

She elbowed him away and unlocked the door. But before she could get inside he grabbed her from behind and tried to prise her out of his way. They were wrestling with their backs to the scene of violence as the pulsing hip-hop drew in closer behind them.

Then, in a moment that was as terrifying as any that had preceded it, the music was cut. A car alarm was sounding. They turned to see the Range Rover facing them. Pausing before the pounce.

'I'm your blood, Nicholas!' Victor roared at the driver. 'I'm your *kin*!'

His arms still locked around Mercy's body, he somehow summoned the strength to heave her around into danger's path, attempting to make a human shield of her. She looked at the black-tinted windows of the car facing her and sheer fear overcame her.

'Shoot her if you want,' Victor continued to appeal, 'but *Neales don't kill Neales!*'

Years of martial arts training kicked in. Victor may have been a heavy man, but she performed some swift foot moves, pulled Victor into her hip and then threw him over so he landed hard in front of her. She'd executed this basic throw during countless classes, but this was the first time her opponent had crashed onto concrete ground and not a padded floor.

The Range Rover revved loudly. Mercy moved and within seconds was behind the wheel of her car with the keys in the ignition.

It stalled.

*'Fuckfuckfuck,'* she cried, her hands shaking now as she attempted to start the vintage car again. *'Please wake up!'* she shouted, trying again.

She couldn't keep herself from glancing up at the unfolding scene. She saw Victor trying to stand but he was too out of shape to be quick about it. The Range Rover crawled forward, manoeuvring around Victor's fallen body so the window to the driver side lined up with him.

On the second go her old Porsche revved back into life. Mercy clicked the gearstick straight into reverse and the Porsche bolted backwards. The slight incline of the road wasn't helping to speed her escape, but she didn't feel safe performing a U turn this close to the shooting. From Mercy's reversing perspective the image of Victor staggering to his knees was becoming smaller and harder to hear but she could tell he was pleading for his life.

'You've been told lies, son,' she heard him say. 'I loved your dad like a—'

Mercy was ready to perform a three-point turn when the driver's door of the Range Rover flung open. And in that moment, just before she put the car into first gear, she saw Victor's face change. Due to the angle she was at she still couldn't see who the driver was, but it was obvious that Victor could. Shock cast across his face.

'What the fuck's this?' she heard him demand of the driver.

However, any further enquiry was interrupted by a deafening trail of bullets cutting through Victor from head to legs. Mercy screamed again and ducked down from the horror.

Self-preservation stopped her from freezing. Victor might have had been the target, but she was still a witness. Her foot hit the accelerator and she turned in one swift move, knowing the bleak truth that the Range Rover's powerful engine would easily outclass the old wheezer in the back of her Porsche. But, before she completed her getaway, she glanced in the rear-view and saw two things get thrown onto Victor's bloodied body. It was the Skorpion gun she'd had pointed at her on Saturday and its presumably now empty cartridge. The door to the Range Rover slammed shut after disposing of them.

Relief coursed through her like the blissful shot of a first drug. Suddenly secure that her life was no longer in immediate danger she remained where she was and watched as the unseen murderer turned the Range Rover in the street, revealing the rear window that had been shattered by gunshots. She strained to see who the driver was through that exposed section, certain now from Victor's reaction to seeing the driver that Nick Neale had not committed this massacre. But it raced off in the other direction, away from the carnage it had created. An assassination that looked like something it wasn't.

Her heart was hammering as she surveyed the scene.

Terrified faces with phones looked down from the windows above the shops, filming and making calls. Someone, somewhere was screaming.

She released the clutch and started driving slowly past Victor's riddled corpse and then on towards the bullet-sprayed Rolls Royce. Against the front wheel on the passenger side was Bob the Feet's leaking body that had curled into the foetal position, his little chauffeur's hat on the ground beside him. Broken glass spread out on the street below him like a bed of stolen diamonds.

The doors to the Never Setting Sun opened and she saw a horrified Jayesh poke his head out, looking as though he thought the British Empire had fallen outside his club and all because he'd admitted a woman. One security guy appeared to be still alive and groaning on the pavement. She should stay and help but ambulances were surely coming. And besides....

*... the real killer,* she fastened her seatbelt, *is getting away!*

The Range Rover had taken the first exit at the duck pond so she pressed her foot down and sped off in its wake. He was heading for a motorway exit. Hopefully she could get a clear look at the driver through the shattered glass before that. The roads were tricky and wet so it would be hard for the killer to really open his engine just yet. Ahead of her she saw the Range Rover's backlights as it drove underneath a viaduct.

*Once I see a face,* she told herself, accelerating her much more delicate vehicle, *I'll back off.*

The Porsche's needle rattled above 60mph, a dangerous speed for the roads she was driving through. Ahead of her the Range Rover pulled up sharp at a crossing, giving her a chance to catch up. She saw a motorbike pass in front of it and then the killer drove on, oddly considerate behaviour considering what he'd just done. Another clue that this wasn't Nick. He would've just charged through.

Her chest was playing like a painful accordion and gunfire still rang in her ears. The Range Rover was approaching the motorway slip road and then he'd been gone. Knowing that it was now or never, she pulled into the other lane to see if she could view him from a side angle. But, as she did so, she was caught in the flare of some oncoming car lights. Tyres shrieked as she veered back out of its way, the old steering wheel locked and the Porsche skidded through the wet lane and off the road. The car hurtled toward oil-black trees, her lungs not even given time to scream before impact.

# PART VI

*Needle Drop*

# 57

Nobody would believe her after his arrest, but Roz Stern had been considering dumping Nick anyway. He'd been unbearable to live with since receiving the submachine gun on Saturday, not to mention learning that his uncle had sent those people to spy on him. In fact, his continual coke-fuelled rages about how he was going to destroy Victor were so aggravating that she'd begun taunting him.

'Do it then,' she'd dared him on the previous day. 'Kill your uncle and shut up about it.'

He'd been describing how he was going to break into the Spoils using some secret tunnel that his dad once told him about and shoot Victor in his bed.

'But can I trust you not to grass on me?' he'd added. '*That's* the question.'

'Babe, are you joking? You've been telling *everyone* about this for *weeks*. You've been grassing on your own self.'

Later, after one of their more intense workouts, Nick calmed down and went for a shower. That's when his phone started ringing with another withheld number. She snatched it up.

'Hey Nicky Boy,' the gravelly American voice said, 'today's the day. You asked for proof of your uncle's guilt and I'm delivering it tonight. Be home.'

'You step one foot inside this building,' she warned, 'and you'll leave in an ambulance. Stop winding my boy up!'

'Rosalind,' the voice replied. 'I've heard so much about you. But I *am* visiting tonight with hard evidence that Little Neale had Big Neale murdered. I'm talking *incontestable.* So, tell your boy to wait in, or you'll miss me. I'll be there sometime between ten pm and the early hours.'

He'd cut the call just as Nick was emerging wet and naked from the bathroom with a dim expression on his face.

When she'd given her statement to the police on the following morning, she'd repeated the words the caller had used to the best of her memory. Sat inside the colourless interview room in the station, a tall police detective named Bracken had repeatedly grilled her about Nick's whereabouts that evening and her story hadn't altered once. She'd explained that they'd been inside the flat the whole time, waiting for the visit and that Roz had been watching TV and smoking some of the weed that had been found during the raid. Around eleven, she'd gone to bed. No, she told DCI Bracken, Nick had not followed her into the bedroom but had remained in the living room, high as a kite and practising with some nunchucks how he was going to attack their visitor. Roz had fallen into a deep sleep from which she hadn't woken, until the armed police had battered down their front door at one in the morning. Nick had been beside her and seemed as shocked and confused as she was when four officers had surrounded their bed, pointing light firearms at them. Nick had been subdued, cuffed, and bundled out of their flat. The last she'd heard of him was a high-pitched cry from the corridor of their apartment building.

*"Call Mum!"* he'd shrieked.

# 58

The first news reports of the slaying had been broadcast at around two am. As was often her habit, Barbara had been awake in her kitchen, smoking and listening to LBC. She enjoyed a cigarette around that hour as Bernie was in bed and so she needn't worry about the effect her smoking might have on his lungs. Despite the cold night she was sat beside an open window, gazing out at her garden and enjoying the peace. She liked these solitary hours, when she did her best thinking.

She'd been quietly planning her husband's funeral as she drew on her cigarette, wondering what old faces she could expect to attend and offer condolences and who she wouldn't hear from. The doctors claimed that Bernie might still have years ahead of him, but she'd known slow deaths before and recognised how they could suddenly accelerate on the unprepared. She'd barely been listening to the radio until the mention of Whetstone, Kent, snagged her attention. She knew the place, having driven through it on the way to Victor's home back when he'd been more sociable.

Whetstone was a Britain in Bloom contender several years running, all cream teas, cobbled lanes, and a nearby deer park. Not the sort of place from which you expect to hear reports of a gun massacre.

*"Three men shot at point blank range, one run over by a car."*

The victims were not named, but Barbara knew in her heart that Victor would be involved. He belonged to some old club there, she'd been told. To learn more, she took to social media and found video footage of a black Range Rover racing through a town road. To her horror, Ray Tyler's lost Porsche was pursuing it.

Eventually, after searching through many news outlets, a BBC broadcast shed some light. The notorious businessman Victor Neale was thought to be among the dead. Barbara raised a hand to her mouth and considered waking up Bernie to tell him.

Her mobile rang. It was her best friend, Maggie 'the Cleaning Lady' Neale calling from Nevada. Lol's widow sounded completely hysterical.

'They've arrested Nick!' Maggie was screeching. 'They think he shot Victor!'

'Why on Earth do they think that?' asked Barbara, although it made immediate sense. Frankly, her friend's moronic son had been an agent of chaos ever since birth. 'Your Nick wouldn't hurt a fly,' she said anyway.

'I don't know what's going on, Barb,' cried Maggie. 'I've called my lawyer and I've shaken the friends we still have on the force but there's not many these days and I need facts. Can you sort things for me? I'm *stuck* over here.'

Barb sat up straight, extinguished her cigarette and shut the window with her free hand. If there was one thing she prided herself on, it was being there for a mate in crisis.

'Leave it with me, Mags,' she promised. 'I'll get to the root of things.'

But as soon as she hung up she wondered what she could actually do. Not much on her own. And so, with no consideration for the smallness of the hour, she raised her phone again and called Bill.

# 59

That same hour Nina Markham had been driving her family hatchback, with her son's booster seat in the back, toward the Whetstone crime scene. An eyewitness had immediately identified Victor as one of the dead. So, as head of Operation Greenwater, DCI Bracken had been appointed as Senior Investigating Officer and sent Nina to Kent to present herself to the DI running the scene.

'Sorry it's ended like this, Nina,' Bracken had said. 'I appreciate that you had more reason than most to see him in cuffs.'

*But on the plus side,* Nina thought as she parked close to the flashing blue lights of the murder scene, *the prick finally got justice.*

The high street had been cordoned off all the way down to the duck pond, as had the covered market out of which the murderous Range Rover had emerged. Sharp winds whipped through the provincial lanes, causing the crime-scene tape to hum like hornets. National news stations were already reporting to camera close by as Nina presented her badge and was ushered through the cordons to DI Aston and the techs.

Ahead of her she recognised the Rolls Royce with the number plate VIC III. While the back half had been untouched by the ammunition burst, the front looked like it had co-starred with James Caan in *The Godfather.* A team of boiler-suited techs were overseeing two fallen bodies and processing every piece of surrounding evidence. Ballistic experts were inspecting holes dotted along the long bonnet and a gun was getting bagged. Blood sprays and shattered glass were being photographed beside the written-off car and across the street. White-coated professionals worked hard and fast underneath large flapping shelters erected to protect the scene from an evidence-destroying shower of rain.

Despite the early hour, DCI Bracken had insisted that Nina was essential to the crime scene. An eyewitness had revealed that Victor Neale had spent the evening having a private dinner with a transgender woman who had subsequently fled the scene in a vintage burgundy Porsche. *Jesus,* Nina thought when told. The tabloids are going to gobble that up. What an absolute circus.

Mercy was now wanted in connection with this crime and was suspected of having conspired with the killer. It made Nina angry; she'd presented her with that legal warrant to avoid this very situation. Until now she'd respected Mercy. But Operation Greenwater, to which she'd committed the past eighteen months, had just perished in the street with Victor. Although she still knew little about Mercy's involvement, she couldn't shake the feeling that Ray's meddling daughter was somehow responsible.

As Nina approached the spot where the first two corpses were lying, she braced herself for the possibility that she might recognise one of the as-yet unidentified victims. Because if Mercy had been present tonight, then so might Bill Mance have been. Was she about to identify his body among the dead? The savage image of a bleeding Bill, shot dead at point blank range, flickered without consent through her mind's eye as the techs parted for her to get a better look. To her huge relief, neither of the corpses were him. When Ray had been found dead, she'd felt like her undercover work had made her somehow complicit. She was grateful that she didn't have to endure that guilt twice.

'I don't recognise him at all,' Nina informed an officer when referring to the suited man who'd been run over by the car. 'This one is familiar,' she said, indicating the older man in the chauffeur's uniform who'd received four vicious shots from his face down to his groin. 'But it's hard to tell like that.' She looked further up the street toward the third body over which another flapping canopy had been erected. 'I take it that's the main man over there,' she said.

They were dusting the submachine gun that had been discarded beside Victor's body as she approached with her ID out. DI Aston, a middle-aged, broad-shouldered copper with a northern accent had been addressing the forensics team but broke away to speak to her.

'You're the Greenwater UCO?' he said over howls of wind. 'I haven't had a chance to read the case file, but it seems your operation is redundant now.'

'Tell me about it,' she agreed, looking over at the slain body of the man they were processing. In the dark, his blood was the colour of blackberries. Victor Neale, who she'd loathed above all other humans for the best part of two decades, the scumbag who'd destroyed the lives of her family as well as many others, and who, until tonight, had always gotten away with it. Now here he was with police in protective masks poring over his still-warm body. Had she been here alone with Victor, she'd have spat on his corpse.

'That man killed a police officer,' she said, gazing at the dead criminal.

'I know who he is, Detective Sergeant,' said Aston.

'The officer was Shaun Kirby,' she added, knowing it was unprofessional to bring this up. 'My older brother.'

One of the boiler-suited techs turned their head toward her. The rest kept working without missing a beat.

'I didn't know *that,*' admitted Aston. 'Is that why Bracken sent you down? To take one last look at the cunt?'

'No,' Nina said, and snapped out of the withdrawn state that had taken hold since seeing her brother's killer. 'It was to see if I could identify the other bodies – which I can't – and to find out more about Mercy Tyler's involvement in all this.'

'You mean Christopher Tyler.'

'She's called Mercy, sir.'

'That's not the name she gave when she met the victim tonight,' he pointed over at the building outside which the shootings had taken place. 'Our main eyewitness, a Mr Thakkar, told us she signed in as Christopher.'

'Well, I don't know what that's about,' Nina said, becoming more confused by Mercy's erratic behaviour by the second. 'But I developed a relationship with her during my UC work and Bracken wants me to interview her once she's been apprehended.'

'We've got her,' he told Nina after blowing his nose, 'she crashed into some trees after leaving the scene.'

'Is she okay?'

'Yeah, but the car's a write-off. She claims she was following the Range Rover, wanting to see who the driver was,' he added with a cynical tut. 'She's not been charged yet.'

'Where's Miss Tyler now, sir?'

'Queen Mary's Hospital, Sidcup. She's sustained only minor injuries and they'll be taking her to Marlowe House soon though if you want to sit in on it.' He blew into the handkerchief before continuing. 'Apparently they're having trouble shutting her up.'

THROUGH A LIVE LINK at Sidcup police station, Nina watched Mercy's witness interview, which had been underway for over an hour. Beside her in the observation room sat a constable, sipping black coffee from a paper cup. He'd been filling Nina in on what she'd missed and seemed amused by the chaotic turns that Mercy's statement had taken.

*'I don't know* where *they obtained the chemical poison,'* Mercy babbled through the speaker. *'But if you investigate the victim Jenny you may find she has links to this Bertsmouth character. Seriously, it's worth checking out.'*

'Why's she talking about poisoned teapots?' Nina asked as they watched the monitor.

'She's suggesting a link between the Yulia Ilyinskaya poisoning,' the officer replied with a half-laugh, 'and what happened tonight. Look how cross the DS is getting.'

The interviewing detective did look agitated as Mercy related her earlier conversation with Victor. It seemed like this wasn't the first unlikely avenue her story had gone down.

*'Tonight's massacre is* not *what it looks like,'* she was insisting.

Nina had expected Mercy to look more drained, after her long ordeal tonight. But instead, she was gesturing with her hands excitedly, as she described the *modus operandi* of the hitman and his apparent girlfriend. Mercy was wearing a blue evening dress and her make-up was holding up well considering all she'd been through. But Nina wondered if she realised how inadvisable it was to be saying all this without a lawyer present.

'She's defending the nephew,' the constable said. 'But it stinks. You know, she went to the same school as him. Suggests to me that she's an accomplice who lured the victim into the open.' He took another slurp from his coffee.

'They aren't *friends,*' Nina said with some authority. 'She told me that Nick used to bully her.'

By the time she'd got to Sidcup station, Nina had heard that Nick Neale had been arrested. His girlfriend was his alibi but she couldn't swear that he hadn't left the flat while she'd been asleep. The Range Rover was missing and the door to the garage had been locked from the outside. Surveillance cameras overlooking the garage had been deliberately cut prior to that evening.

'You've seen the footage,' the officer persisted. 'The killer made a point of attacking everyone on the scene except for your mate in there. It's dodgy.'

*'This may sound mad,'* Mercy continued on the small screen, *'but I think I've met the contract killer. And I can give you a decent physical—'*

Just then a tall grey man in a blue suit entered the interview room. Nina knew him as the M&T lawyer she'd last seen at Ray's funeral. He immediately tried to stop Mercy from speaking further and insisted that the interview be concluded if she wasn't about to be charged with anything more than being over the limit behind a wheel.

'I need to make some calls,' Nina said to the officer. 'But

if she gets released, let me know immediately. The SIO wants me to speak to her in a less official capacity.'

Out in the corridor, Nina yawned and reached for her phone to text her ex-husband. She apologised but told him it was unlikely that she'd be back to collect Kyle in time for the school run tomorrow. As inconvenient as that was for him, she doubted that Ian would mind. He'd hated her involvement with Operation Greenwater ever since she'd agreed to go undercover. Her obsession with busting her brother's killer, he felt, had been among the reasons that their marriage had deteriorated.

As she approached the front desk she heard a highly-strung but familiar voice berating the night staff.

'It's a *disgrace* that my daughter has been held without representation,' said Ray's widow, who'd obviously arrived with the lawyer. She was wearing a long coat and was as animated as Mercy had just been. 'She's a victim in this and you're treating her like a suspect,' Julie Tyler insisted, 'and that... yeah, I'll say it... feels like prejudice!'

Nina hesitated before stepping toward Julie. They'd only met at the funeral where Julie regarded Nina with unconcealed distrust and so the imminent revelation that she'd been an undercover cop was not going to land well.

'Hey Julie,' she eventually said, catching the ranting woman mid-breath. 'Can I have a word?' Julie turned, looking surprised to encounter someone who knew her name.

'Oh,' she said, after some rapid blinks. 'I didn't expect to see you here.'

'I've been checking in on your girl,' she explained, registering the confusion on Julie's face. 'And she *was* informed that she didn't need to speak to anyone until her lawyer arrived, so the police here haven't crossed a line.'

It had been days since she'd revealed her police identity to Mercy, and Nina had wondered if she'd broken the law by telling anyone else about it. But it was clear from Julie's reaction that she didn't know.

'Listen, there's something I need to tell you,' she beckoned Julie away from the front desk. 'And it might easier for us both if we find somewhere more private.'

Julie became still. Then she reached into her coat pocket and pulled out a packet of cigarettes. 'Let's go outside,' she said in a duller tone. 'I'm gasping for a fag anyway.'

The night was at least dry as they left the police station and stood on the pavement outside the shut Costa next door. They buttoned their coats against the cold and Julie stood downwind so as to not blow smoke in Nina's face. Strong gales messed with her blonde hair as she waited to hear Nina's confession.

'Here's the thing,' Nina began as a night bus passed by. 'I want you to know that I was behaving in a professional manner. It was nothing personal—'

'If you were fucking my husband,' Julie interrupted with a marked impatience, 'spit it out. It's hardly the first time I've heard it.'

'What? Jesus no.'

'Don't kid yourself it would've lasted,' Julie persisted before taking another long, bitter drag. 'He got bored easily.'

'Trust me, it's nothing like that. Ray always behaved like a gentleman,' she added, choosing to ignore the time he'd touched her leg in the Blue-eyed Maid. 'But I've been misrepresenting—'

'Bill!' Julie called out, looking over Nina's shoulder toward the police station. 'Over here!' Nina turned to see the large figure of Bill Mance in his waxed canvas coat striding up the steps towards the station in a tremendous hurry. He looked over and cried out to Julie as she went to him. 'I'm glad to see *you* at least!'

'Mother of Christ,' Bill said as he hugged his best friend's widow. His face looked distraught. 'I'm sorry, Jools. I never would've sent her into that situation if I'd had *any* inkling—'

'It's not your fault, darlin',' Julie assured him. 'Maggie's boy is a fucking psycho. I hope they send him down for life.'

Bill glanced over Julie's shoulder.

'Nina?' he exclaimed as she came forward. 'Did Barb wake you too?'

'No,' she replied. 'I've been here awhile. Listen Bill, before we go on, there's something I need to admit to.'

'Is it that you're still a police officer?' Bill said. Julie released herself from his embrace and turned back to Nina with a shocked expression. 'Because I know that already.'

'Since when?' Nina asked.

'Mercy told me,' he explained. 'Probably less than an hour after you told her.'

# 60

Word came through that the police had located the wanted Range Rover. It had been found abandoned and unlocked round the back of the Ferryman pub in Woolwich, close to Nick's home. Bill informed them that this was where Mercy had tracked him to on Saturday night and where Nick had received the Skorpion machine gun.

'We'll make our audio recording available to *your* lot,' he told Nina with some edge to his voice. He and Julie were sat opposite her in the otherwise empty police canteen, waiting for Mercy to be released.

'I know Victor was rough and ready,' Julie said, tapping another Silk Cut out of the packet. 'But he wasn't *that* bad. Lol was the problem.'

With considerable restraint Nina elected not to reveal that her brother Shaun had been the young policeman who'd been stabbed to death on the grounds of the Spoils. Or how her mother had never fully recovered from his loss and the shocking injustice of the trial. As a teenager, Nina had experienced nightmares involving Shaun's final moments. She'd dreamt of Victor leaning over her, stabbing her in vital organs as blood rose in her throat, preventing her from screaming. Her family had been mortified when she'd decided to follow in Shaun's footsteps and become a police officer. They were certain she'd fall victim to the same crime, perhaps even to the same criminal.

Julie went outside for another smoke and Nina was grateful for that. Some silent moments passed between her and Bill during which she wondered if anyone had told her mum about her son's killer yet.

'D'you think Ray was murdered,' Bill asked with an uncontained contempt, 'because Victor discovered he was *your* informer?'

Nina was stunned by such bluntness from a man known for his tact. She held his stare.

'Do you think Ray was murdered?' she asked back.

Before he could reply, Nina sensed someone entering through the door of the canteen. Nina herself turned to see the M&T lawyer walking in and Mercy following, her coat folded over her arm and looking more tired than she had on the interview monitor. Bill seemed immediately rattled by her appearance, his expression was stunned.

'Mercy,' he said. 'My god, what a nightmare this has been for you. Your mum's outside,' he spoke like she was a child, 'to take you home.'

'Yeah, whatever,' replied Mercy in a truculent tone.

'You must be exhausted,' he continued. 'We can talk about what happened in the morning.'

'I'm not talking with you anymore,' Mercy said to him. 'We're done.'

Her comment sent a jolt through the room. Nina turned to Bill for his reaction. He looked stricken.

'You've asked to speak to me, DS Markham,' Mercy then

said, turning her attention towards Nina. 'We can chat on the way home if you want. I've a feeling I'm going to need as much police protection as I can get from now on.'

'Protection from who?' Bill asked. Mercy ignored him.

'I'm parked round the back,' Nina told her and crossed the room toward both Mercy and the exit. 'Put your coat on, you'll freeze in that dress.'

# 61

Apart from Barbara, nobody went to the M&T office on the following day. Robbie was working from home, but the others hadn't contacted her to explain their whereabouts, which was odd. Barbara had been sending emails and making calls, trying to make sense of what was going on with Maggie's stupid son who was still in custody. Then, at about three in the afternoon, she received a text.

**Contact the Cleaning Lady,** Bill said, referring to Maggie. **I need 100G fast. It's for her son. Tell Vegas she'll get it back but I need it in my account asap.**

Barbara frowned. She wondered if someone had stolen Bill's phone and was taking the piss. Another text appeared.

**that's 100 grand FAST! Tell her it'll save him but no time wasting. DO IT**

Right, this definitely wasn't Bill. He'd never spoken to her like that, and he certainly wouldn't discuss that kind of figure in writing.

**Do not tell the others,** another text declared. **Nina is police!**

What on Earth was happening?

**MERCY IS NOT OUR FRIEND. EXPLAIN LATER BUT WE NEED THAT MONEY ASAP**

'Jesus wept,' she said to nobody.

# 62

The Fitbit that Roz had been wearing as she'd slept on the night of the massacre had established that she hadn't been inside the Range Rover. But no such evidence protected Nick. His phone had been in the flat too, but an unfamiliar burner had been found in the killer car. This phone had made and received calls to the number used by Bob the Feet and the last text it had sent had been minutes before the massacre.

**On way. Nick.**

Nick hadn't been charged yet, but it seemed a matter of time. CCTV couldn't identify the driver because of the tinted windows, but the car had been dumped in a blind spot near their home so it looked bad. Blaine, Dan B and Dogger had all been picked up. Their DNA was all over the car seats from the weekend. But Blaine at least had a cast iron alibi and so had been released around the same time Roz had. He'd given her a lift back from the station and they'd spoken about what had happened during the short drive. The news that Bob the Feet was among the less-publicised dead seemed to interest him.

'Is that why Nick shot him?' he'd asked as they'd pulled up outside her home. 'Betrayal?'

'Nick didn't shoot anyone,' she'd said with the same conviction she'd told the police. 'He was with me.'

'Cool,' said Blaine, offering her his fist to bump by way of goodbye. 'I respect your loyalty.'

Ever since her mother had died of cancer, Roz had had little contact with the rest of her family and her best friend Aida was visiting family in Ethiopia. There was no one else she wanted to see who wouldn't get on her nerves and so all she longed for now was to get high and pass out. But the police raid had cleaned them out.

She tried to sleep but it was impossible. Unused to drifting off without narcotic aid, her mind was whirling. She was furious with Nick for not listening to her about Bob the Feet, for buying that stupid gun, for his obsession with his dead dad, and for telling everyone he was going to kill his uncle. And, if she were honest with herself at the very least, Roz believed that he *had* done it. If Aida were here she'd rightly scold her for not having chucked him sooner. But how could she chuck him now? It would make her look like a fair-weather bitch, the sort of person she'd always despised.

It was on that weighted thought that the buzzer to her building rang. She picked up the receiver and looked at the small monitor, expecting to see more badge-wielding detectives or, worse, journalists. But, amazingly, it was someone she wanted to see even less.

'Hey Rosalind,' said the infuriating face of Mercy Tyler. 'Remember me?'

'What d'*you* want?'

'I heard you'd been released pending investigation and thought I'd pop round to see how you are.' Mercy's head cocked to one side in an expression of faux concern. 'How *are* you?'

'Fuck off,' Roz said. 'You think I'm going to talk to you of all people? You've probably got another microphone under that tracksuit. Do one, love.'

'If you're not in a chatty mood that's fine,' Mercy spoke quickly before Roz could hang up. 'I've got a better idea.'

'What?' Roz asked, suddenly wondering if Mercy might have drugs on her.

'I was wondering,' Mercy asked, 'if you fancied a fight?'

MERCY barely even saw the cross-kick coming as it impacted hard against the side of her body. She swore loudly as she staggered away, angry with herself for having failed to block another strike. She was already hurting from Roz's previous attacks and this was only round three.

'Fuck you, Rosalind,' she panted through her gum shield, bobbing away from the fast follow-up punch and trying to concentrate on maintaining balance and keeping her gloves raised. 'Give me a chance to breathe.'

Ever since learning that Nick's girlfriend worked as a Muay Thai instructor Mercy had been keen to see how she'd acquit herself against her in a fair contest. The answer, she realised, as another powerful kick forced her to drop down onto the canvas, was not well.

'Rosalinds don't kick like that,' her opponent spat as she circled the ring. 'I'm Roz!'

She was jabbing the air as she spoke, not conserving energy between rounds like many fighters would. Her face was a fierce-red, her hair pulled back tight, and her abs pulsed as she breathed. Her gum-shielded mouth puffed out like a scuba diver as she waited for Mercy to get up again.

Mercy had discovered that since getting the sack from Victor's gym, Roz had found work at Fight Hub in Woolwich, and so she could secure them a ring session at short notice. They only had half an hour to spar in, but it was obvious that the activity was an even larger release of tension for Roz than it was for Mercy. Sometimes referred to as the "art of eight limbs," Muay Thai was a perfect combat sport for someone like Roz who was all attack, all the time. Elbow punches to the head, knee strikes to the stomach, leg kicks to the thigh; a full-on assault. Mercy had a lot of experience in martial arts over the years, but she always fought defensively. However, she'd been getting her arse kicked ever since she'd stepped into this ring, and it was time to regain some dignity.

Round Four. Again, Roz came in fast and hot. But this time Mercy was more familiar with her moves and was able to pre-empt. After avoiding several of Roz's savage strikes, she kneed her hard in the stomach and then used an adrenalin surge to pummel Roz until she fell against the ropes. It was the only round of the six they fought that Mercy won.

Afterwards they sat beside each other on the slatted bench by the lockers and watched the kids' class warm up on the raised platform. They didn't speak as they removed the gum shields and swigged from their water bottles. Mercy's body already ached from the car accident and it had perhaps been a mistake to fight before those injuries had properly healed. She'd be suffering even more tomorrow. Despite that, the contest had been a valve through which to release all the pressure that had been building up within her. The experience of being almost caught in the crossfire had shaken her more than she was trying to show, not to mention the dark conclusions she'd been drawing ever since. Working off some adrenalin felt like a necessary discharge.

'Sorry for getting your name wrong,' she finally said as she unwound the wraps from her now ham-like hands. 'I get how annoying that is.'

'Not even Mum called me Rosalind,' the winner told her as she spat into a tin bucket.

'Really?' asked Mercy, releasing her hair from the ponytail she'd tied it back in. 'So how come your personal trainer card at the gym read Rosalind Stern?'

Roz side-eyed her. 'The one person who called me Rosalind was Victor,' she explained. 'I only met him a few times, but he had this habit of calling everyone by the long version of their names.'

'Yeah, I noticed that,' nodded Mercy. 'A weird affectation.'

'He got me the job at Meantime back when he and Nick were still getting on. Arranged it himself, referred to me as Rosalind to the manager and it got stuck on the company database. But I hate it and will hurt anyone who calls me it.'

'As I just discovered,' Mercy winced.

'That's why I told the police I think it was Victor himself who made those calls to Nick,' Roz added, after drinking more water.

'Excuse me?'

'I spoke to the Needle when he phoned before the murders,' she added, staring at the ring where heavily padded children were learning how to fight. 'The American accent was fake as fuck and he called me Rosalind. To me, this proves that Victor was behind it all. The cops don't care, they thought I was talking shit to divert attention from Nick.'

Another spit.

'I don't believe that Nick killed his uncle,' Mercy told her after she'd opened the locker behind her and removed her sports bag. 'And I'm close to proving who the real killer is.'

'Hark at Jessica Fletcher.'

'Take this,' Mercy reached inside her bag and produced one of her *Ask for Mercy* business cards. 'The police don't care for my theory. But, if I'm right, it'll clear Nick's name and save him from a life sentence. Not that I give a flying fuck if he rots in jail forever, you understand. But I *do* want to uncover the truth so our objectives align. If you learn anything useful,' she handed Roz the card, 'tell it to me.'

Roz inspected the card as if she was considering throwing it in the spitting tin.

'I'd love for you to prove Nick's innocence, as it goes,' she murmured before placing it in her bag. 'It'll make me feel better about chucking him.'

# 63

Outside her boss's building, Barbara recognised Robbie Ingleton's bullet-grey mountain bike chained to an iron fence. She'd not expected their data expert to be here too and was immediately worried what Bill might be saying to other people. He'd contacted her the previous evening, using a landline, and had sounded even more highly-strung. It was always Ray who'd been the dramatic half of the partnership, forever in debt, ducking someone, demanding favours from someone else, and trying to solve both his personal and financial problems through increasingly desperate schemes. Traditionally, Bill was the rock, so it was disturbing to hear how manic he'd become as he called from the office phone. He reiterated the importance of secrecy, despite using an open line, and the urgent need for £100,000 that he thought Maggie could make appear overnight into his business account. He gave dark hints as to what the money might be for.

'Mercy is turning on us,' he'd said in a grim tone, 'or

rather, against *me*. There's a growing chance that she'll talk to someone about where the money's been coming from.'

'You mean Victor's payments?' Barb had asked. 'So what, it's not illegal to hire detectives.'

'Come on, Barb, we both know there's more going on than that. It was all Ray, you understand, none of it was me. I'm clean, always have been. But getting caught up in that shooting seems to have frazzled her brain. She's threatening to sell her story to the tabloids.'

'I hate to say I told you so.'

'She'll screw everything up. All we've built unless we... nip it in the bud.'

'Nip what in what?' she asked, unsettled by his vague language.

'I can't say over the phone, but there's a man who can help. Have you asked the Cleaning Lady for the money yet? Because he's not cheap, this guy.'

Barbara didn't reply straightaway. Mercy had been wittering on about some hitman that her dad was involved with, but surely Bill couldn't be talking about that. The thought was monstrous.

'Why d'you want this money, Bill?' she enquired in a stern tone. 'It's a large sum to ask for without explanation.'

'It's to help Maggie's family,' he insisted, 'sort of. Mercy wants to reveal secrets to the police about Nick's dad and we've limited time to contain them. Make sure to tell Maggie that, send her another email.'

'She's got a lot on her mind at the moment.'

'Same here,' he replied. 'Look, I don't mean to scare you but this is urgent. Also, don't go to the office tomorrow morning. Meet me at my place. Nine thirty.'

So at exactly 9.29 Barbara was ringing the buzzer to Bill's apartment, hoping his paranoia hadn't worsened. To her astonishment, Maggie Neale had already responded during the night and expressed a willingness to move the money, if it guaranteed her son's release. She wanted more details – fair enough – but it had surprised Barb that she was even considering it. The world had gone mad.

'Come in,' Bill smiled, opening the door to her once she'd walked up to the second floor. 'Sorry for dragging you across town, but you'll understand why in a moment.'

She'd only visited Bill's home a few times, and usually on errands. The hallway was sparsely decorated and lacked a woman's touch. Bill's behaviour now contrasted with his earlier messages. He was warm and hospitable as he took her anorak and hung it on a stand next to Robbie's cycling helmet and his coat. He motioned for her to follow him through, but Barb wouldn't budge. She had something she needed to say in private first. She'd been rehearsing how she was going to phrase her concerns during the bus ride over.

'I don't know what's occurring,' she began, craning her neck up to the tall man in the cramped space. 'And honestly, I don't want to know. But before you do anything you'll regret forever, I feel duty bound to remind you that Mercy is Ray's child. Your best friend's kid! And it would be a sin to harm her.' Bill opened his mouth, but she kept speaking. 'Don't get me wrong. I dislike the insufferable smartarse as much as you do. But this... Bill... is too far. If I've misunderstood what the money is for, then I humbly apologise... but if I haven't... then what the fuck are you playing at, son?'

A sound from behind the nearby door disturbed her. She couldn't see who was in there but cringed to think that Robbie must have heard all that. When the person emerged into the hallway, holding a mug of tea, Barbara was even more shocked.

'Why Mrs G,' blushed Mercy with her other hand

resting on her heart. 'That's the sweetest thing I've ever overheard anyone say about me.' Barb looked from Mercy, who still had her jacket on, back to Bill. 'I mean, not when you called me an insufferable smartarse,' Mercy continued, 'but you trying to talk him out of putting out a hit on me. Honestly, I could well up.'

'What's she doing here?' Barb spluttered. 'You said her brain had frazzled.'

'That wasn't true,' Bill admitted in the embarrassed manner of someone excusing themselves from a poor joke, 'and we haven't fallen out. But we do want someone to think that we have. Sorry about the misleading messages, but there's a chance the agency phones and email addresses are being hacked. In fact, Robbie's here now lowering the security on all our communications to increase that chance.'

'You expected me to gossip about you?' Barbara asked, hurt.

'Not at all,' he assured her. 'I've never doubted your discretion. But we do want any nosey parkers to think I plan to kill Mercy, even though – obviously – I wouldn't dream of it. In fact, she stayed on my sofa bed last night so we could talk our plan through. The emails I asked you to send are props to create the illusion that I want her dead. Even the police are under the impression we're in conflict.'

'It's to entrap a killer,' Mercy said, handing Barbara the hot cup of tea. 'This is yours, by the way. One sugar?'

'What killer are you on about?' Barbara asked, ignoring the tea. 'Not this Needle person again?'

'Needle *people*,' Bill said, pointing toward the more spacious living room. 'Come through and I'll talk you through it.'

Robbie was sat on the sofa working on his laptop and he

barely acknowledged Barbara's entrance. His feet were up on a pouffe and his socks didn't match. Bill had erected a large whiteboard against the far wall and it was covered with photographs, notes and pinned documents all pertaining to Victor's murder, Nick's arrest, and the assassins they were apparently trying to ensnare. Mercy asked if she'd ever played her the recording of her dad's final words, or told her about the afternoon she'd overheard her dad talking to a hitman.

'Only a million times,' mumbled Barbara, parking herself on the far end of the sofa. She should've been relieved that Bill wasn't going to do anything crazy after all, but felt raw about their deception. Nobody liked being lied to, it felt like they were smirking about her behind their hands. The tea felt bitter as she sipped.

'As we now know,' Bill said, standing by the board, 'Nina no longer works for us. It transpires she was an undercover cop investigating our agency. Which is a bit of a kick to the bollocks, but there we are.'

'Despicable,' Barbara contributed. 'Taking our pay, acting like one of us. You worked with her the most,' she turned to Robbie. 'Did you suspect anything?' He shrugged and focused on his laptop. 'A fine bunch of sleuths we turned out to be.'

'However,' Bill continued, 'it was Victor, not us, who the police were investigating.' He indicated the pinned front page of yesterday's Sun, which showed a photo of the crime scene. **VICTOR NEALE GUNNED DOWN IN STREET,** the headline read.

'Before he died,' Mercy said, moving toward the only armchair in a slow, jerking motion, 'Dad was providing Nina with details about Victor's criminal activities. He was a police informer.'

'Rubbish,' Barbara cried. 'Ray was no more of a grass than I am.'

'It's true,' Mercy winced as she lowered herself into the chair. She'd removed her jacket by now and was rubbing her sides. 'He overheard you talking about the day Sarah Neale had died. Soon afterwards he went to the police. Let me confirm something; did you inadvertently reveal that Sarah had been pregnant at the time of her death?'

'What's that got to do with anything?'

'We're working on a theory,' implored Bill, 'and Sarah's pregnancy might be relevant. Please answer.'

'Yes then,' Barb huffed. 'Ray would've heard me mention that Sarah was pregnant.'

'Who do you think the father was?' asked Mercy.

'I wouldn't care to speculate.'

'Would you be surprised to learn that Victor himself thought his older brother had been sleeping with his wife?' Bill then asked.

'There were rumours,' Barbara admitted.

'And yet the minute Dad learnt from you that she was pregnant he had a meltdown. That was the catalyst for his betrayal of such an old friend.'

Barbara shrugged.

'Perhaps Victor was mistaken about who'd been cuckolding him,' Mercy suggested, 'to use an old-fashioned term.'

'You think Ray was the daddy?' cried Barbara, and then turned to Bill. There followed a pause in which the only sound was the quick *tap-tap-tap* of Robbie's keyboard. 'But he was Victor's mate!'

'I loved the man,' Bill eventually said, 'but Ray would steal the food from your plate if you left it unattended for long.'

'How would it have happened though, Bill?' Mercy asked him. 'Victor had hired M&T to keep an eye on Sarah, right?'

Barbara watched her closely. She thought Mercy seemed unphased by the suggestion that Sarah's unborn baby might have been her half-sibling.

'Ray was working the night shifts,' Bill told them. 'And would often report that she was having early nights. I suppose there's a chance he'd somehow instigated an affair and, well, would be in bed with her.'

'What were his reports like?'

'Early on, he provided Victor with evidence that Lol had approached her and was sexually harassing her when he could.'

'Lol *was* an awful sex pest,' Barbara interrupted, 'so that I can believe. But what's this got to do with the recent killings?'

'Victor hired my dad to broker the original hit for him,' Mercy explained. 'He confessed it to me over dinner. But he never confirmed who the target of the assassination was. And, considering that Lawrence died in a car explosion a week after Dad's meeting, it could be assumed that he was the target, what with his predatory behaviour towards Victor's wife.'

'Bobby McAlonan blew Lol up,' Barbara exclaimed. 'Common knowledge!'

She looked to Bill for some support, but he was staring at the whiteboard. He seemed fixated on a group snap taken at Victor's fortieth birthday. Ray could be seen in the photo with his arm around Sarah Neale wearing the blue dress.

'Okay, I'm starting to think that you and everyone else are right about that,' Mercy conceded. 'But, if so, who *was* the target? During the meeting Dad was shown who it was against his will. Then, once he thought he was alone, he broke down in tears. He wouldn't weep over a scumbag like Lol. But Sarah?'

'If it had been her name inside the envelope,' Bill said, moving his eyes from the photograph, 'and he'd been sleeping with her, then that might explain his tears.'

'Not necessarily,' Mercy replied with a trace of a rebuke. 'She was an innocent mother of two and he'd just handed over her death warrant. My opinion of his morals are low, but even I can imagine that this may have upset him, even if he wasn't fucking her.'

Barbara was horrified by the discussion. Ray Tyler arranging the murder of Sarah Neale? Was she dreaming this?

'It scans though,' Mercy said, pointing at the corner of the board where a timeline had been pinned, 'with or without the affair. M&T prove to Victor that his wife is back on drugs and is sexually involved with Lol. A text is sent to Victor that appears to confirm his suspicions that she's fucking someone. He wants her dead, but, because it's Sarah, he can't use one of his usual boys. So, he outsources the job to this young baby-faced killer that Martin Bertsmouth told him about. Dad's in terrible debt at the time and Victor clears it in return for him tracking down the killer and arranging things. For the same reasons we did, Dad thought the target was Victor's brother. By the time he realises his mistake, it's too late, wheels have been set in motion. A week later Lol's car exploded with him inside. But that was just a coincidence. The real hit took place a month later at a garden party held at the Spoils.'

'Sarah wasn't assassinated!' Barbara cried. 'I was at that party. We all saw her. She climbed on that balcony edge of her own volition. Every woman present called out for her to not to do anything daft and then she stepped off anyway. It was suicide, nobody pushed her. You're making shit up, the pair of you!'

Barb had become more agitated than she'd meant to, but she wouldn't apologise for it. Their speculations were in poor taste.

'It's hard raking over old stuff,' Bill said. 'But if we're right, these killers have been getting away with this for decades. Considering that Ray had become a police informer, these people had a motive to kill him. Plus, they could've killed Victor and framed Nick. It's far-fetched, I grant you and please, tell us why you think we're wrong, so we don't go down any dead ends.'

'For one thing,' Barbara reminded him, 'there weren't any men at the garden party. It was ladies only.'

'I spoke to Kittichai McColl,' Mercy then said. 'She told me that among the catering staff that were there that afternoon were a young man and woman who vanished before the police arrived. Do you remember either of them?'

Barbara had actually forgotten that Alan's Thai wife had been at the garden party. But now she recalled other details such as the waiters who'd been serving prosecco as they'd arrived. It wasn't so much them Barbara remembered, but their later absence. She'd been refilling everyone's glasses herself, complaining that *you can't get the staff these days.*

'Why would a grown woman, with a baby inside of her, throw herself off a top floor balcony?' Barb argued.

'I managed to get a look at her toxicology report,' Bill said. 'And her bloodstream was a cocktail of different substances. She had a history of drug abuse and it was all accounted for on the premises. But it's not impossible she was fed something.'

'According to Kitty,' Mercy revealed, 'Sarah was lucid the

night before she died. Happy, healthy, and not under the influence of anything. Now, I've encountered enough addicts to know that this doesn't prove she was unwillingly drugged on the following day. But it does add credence to the idea that her destruction was orchestrated. If someone with a gun was in her bedroom, blocking all other exits and threatening to shoot, she might have headed for the only available escape route. Especially if she was high.'

'If her killers were disguised as caterers,' Bill contributed, 'feeding her substances would've been easy. Just because you didn't see anyone up there, Barb, doesn't mean she was alone.'

Barbara tried to make sense of what they were telling her. If they were right, Ray would've learnt from her that he'd colluded in the death of his own unborn child. She fell silent.

'How's it going, Robbie?' Bill asked their data retrieval expert. 'Found anything related to Needlework Productions?'

'Outside of sewing sites, no,' he said. 'Though, if this Bertsmouth had stumbled onto the forum in the early part of the century, I was unlikely to. I've established that his daughter *did* go to school with one of the Teapot victims though.' As far as Barbara was concerned he may have been talking in Arabic. 'Still can't find an address called the Long Needle though, if it is an address. Where did you say it might be again?'

Mercy reached into her bag, which was resting beside the armchair. She pulled out an old exercise book.

'Claudia Beech told me that Dad met our man in different places,' she said flicking through the pages. 'I jotted them down after chatting with her. Here we are. Camden,

Kings Cross, Little Venice and Limehouse. It seems Dad went all over the city to meet the guy.'

'The electoral registers in those areas might reveal something,' Robbie said, returning his attention to his computer.

'Thanks Robbie,' Mercy said, still searching through her exercise book. They were all ignoring Barbara by then. Robbie engrossed in his online search, Mercy in her book, Bill still staring at the mess he'd made on the whiteboard. It was like they were all trying to solve the same puzzle through three different methods.

'Victor thinks the Long Needle is a place,' Robbie said, looking up at Mercy. 'But Claudia said he moved around a lot. What if it's because he's always meeting the guy in churches?'

Mercy briefly looked up from her book. 'How would that work?'

'Every district has one and they're pointy. Like a needle. Maybe Ray used to meet him inside one to do business. Sat beside each other, pretending to pray, swapping envelopes.'

'Good thinking, Robbie,' Mercy said. 'We should look into it.'

Barbara was getting cheesed off with all this "*Thanks, Robbie*" and "*Good thinking Robbie.*" As if he was the most valued employee. She took after her dad in that way, thought Barbara. Ray used to play favourites too.

Barbara cleared her throat.

'It could be a mobile home,' she suggested. Nobody looked up from what they were doing. She wondered if they'd heard her. 'Like a caravan,' she added. The tapping on the keyboard slowed.

'You think this six-figure hitman lives in a caravan?' asked Robbie.

'I didn't say caravan,' she shot back. 'I said *like a caravan*.'

'Actually,' Mercy looked at her, 'that's quite clever.'

'I could've done without the actually, actually.'

Mercy picked up a pen and started writing in her exercise book. 'Forgive me,' she smiled. 'It's *very* clever. Nice work, Mrs G.'

'You're welcome,' Barbara said, and sipped her tea.

# 64

The M&T team spent the rest of the morning going over their plan. Once she'd got used to the idea that these killers existed, Barbara began to feel good about helping to catch them. She'd promised Maggie that she'd do everything she could to free her son, and rooting out this hitman worked toward that end. However, and she felt a disloyal friend for thinking it, she wasn't as convinced of the boy's innocence as Bill and Mercy seemed to be.

'Nick's been arrested and it doesn't look good for the lad,' Bill addressed the room at one point, as if rehearsing for a courtroom appearance. 'Our theory is that he was framed. The killer was driving his car and used a gun that Mercy witnessed him receiving on Saturday night, an encounter we have on tape and have shared with the police. Nick's girlfriend is his alibi, but it's not solid. So, unless, a CCTV shot of the driver appears or some forensic evidence acquits him, Nick's only real chance is if we find the actual culprit. Otherwise, they're going to throw the book at him.'

'And, although prison is probably the best place for

him,' Mercy said, groaning as she moved, 'we need to bring the real killers to justice.'

'My sentiments exactly,' Bill agreed.

But, for all their outward expressions of unity, Barbara was noticing a tension pass between Mance and Tyler. Their every exchange seemed keen to communicate, especially to each other, that their rift had been mere pretence. And yet, for some indiscernible reason, she couldn't quite believe that it was all happy families now. Ray's daughter was watching Bill closely, particularly when he wasn't watching her.

'Remind me,' Mercy asked him at one point. She was by then standing close to the door, her jacket in her arms. 'What's Nick's girlfriend called again?'

'Rosalind,' answered Bill.

'Is that so?'

'Rosalind Stern, personal trainer,' Bill checked the whiteboard where a small business card was pinned underneath her picture. 'It says so on this card you collected from the gym.'

'Of course,' Mercy replied, but in a strange tone. Bill sensed it too and asked if there was a problem. 'I just forgot,' she assured him. After that she excused herself, went to use the bathroom and was gone for a long time.

At lunchtime Robbie volunteered to cycle to a nearby deli to fetch sandwiches. Barbara, who'd been gasping for a fag all morning, asked her boss if she could go out onto the fire escape that was accessible via his kitchen. The day was spitting but she was sheltered underneath the iron staircase and took her first overdue puff. Long droplets of accumulated rain fell from the railings above her as she surveyed the soggy series of back gardens it overlooked.

'Mind if I join you?' Mercy asked as she too stepped out

onto the fire escape. 'Bill's on the phone to the police. They're scheduling a second interview with Bracken about our surveillance of Nick. I've already been over it countless times so I daresay she's sick of my voice.'

Barbara had already made out an invoice from M&T Investigations to Victor and placed last week's date on it, just in case they tried to bust them for not declaring cash. She offered Mercy one of her cigarettes.

'Thanks, but no,' she replied. 'Just needed some air.'

The two women stood beside each other, staring over Denmark Hill like guards on a battlement. They could see Robbie's cycle helmet as he darted through a fenced off alleyway toward the deli. Silence descended, but, to her own surprise, it was Barbara who broke it.

'You're right not to touch them,' she said, flicking ash over the railing 'These bloody things have done for my Bernie.'

'My parents both smoked,' Mercy said. 'I grew up in a fug of tobacco. Maybe that's why I could never see them straight.'

It was chilly and Barbara wished she'd put on her anorak before lighting up. She was envious as she watched Mercy pull up the zip on her leather jacket and button the poppers.

'What brand did Bill smoke?' Mercy asked, 'before his e-cigarettes?'

'Silk Cut,' answered Barbara, indicating her own packet. 'We all did, including your dad. It was the M&T fag of choice.'

'Not Golden Virginia?'

'Bill smoking roll ups? I shouldn't think so.'

'Who smoked that then?'

Barbara inhaled and felt her inner drawbridge pull up

again. She was just starting to feel comfortable around Mercy but these incessant questions created distrust.

'He drove me home once and I saw inside his glove compartment,' Mercy explained. 'There was an empty packet of Golden Virginia in there, which struck me as weird considering he vapes now.'

'That doesn't tell us so much about *him*,' Barbara exhaled smoke, 'as it does about *you*. Rifling through people's glove compartments? You're worse than your dad.'

They continued chatting in a stilted way before Mercy went back inside again. As she lit up a second cigarette, Barbara wondered what she should make of this curious person now. Since they'd last spoken Mercy had positioned herself at the centre of a number of terrible events – the fight at the club, the appearance of the gun, the massacre at Whetstone. Those experiences seemed to have knocked some wind out of her. She seemed less cocksure now and more inclined to withdraw into her thoughts. Investigative work was taking its toll, which wasn't surprising. Over the years M&T had employed several people who hadn't lasted more than six months. She wondered how long it would be before Mercy quit.

Barbara extinguished her cigarette and returned to the kitchen, shutting the door behind her. Mercy was sitting on a stool at the narrow kitchen table. She was alone and in the reduced light looked utterly miserable. On the table her fingers were examining something small that Barbara couldn't see.

'What's up?' Barbara asked her as she edged a little closer. In another room she could hear Bill's murmuring phone conversation. The younger woman said nothing for a moment, but her posture was slumped. 'Are you crying?'

'Nah,' Mercy replied, raising her head up. Her eyes were wet but her cheeks still dry. 'Just thinking.'

Barbara felt a rare pity. In Mercy's hands she saw a small Union Jack magnet that she'd pulled off the fridge. She was studying it in a manner that suggested it contained all the mysteries of the universe. The magnet was identical to the one on the small mini-fridge in the M&T office.

'I knew I'd uncover bad stuff about him...' Mercy said '... but I hoped I'd find some good too.'

'Oh dear,' Barbara said, guessing who this was about. She pulled out the vacant stool beside her and wondered how to go about comforting the daughter of a man who'd been revealed as having had some extremely dark sides. She'd wanted children of her own once but wasn't well practised in moments like this. Mercy's enquiries into her dad must have finally cracked her shell.

Barbara's own father had run an East End protection racket back in the fifties. She'd spent most of her life sticking up for him and other similar men and only in later life questioned the value of her defence. But she'd never imagined that Ray could have plumbed such immoral depths as the ones discussed this afternoon. If it turned out that he'd had a hand in Sarah Neale's death, then that would truly shatter her image of him. No wonder Mercy was struggling not to cry.

'All I wanted,' Mercy then said, her throat dilating with emotion, 'was *someone* to admire. Was that too much to ask?'

Barbara put her arm around the girl's shoulders. 'I know how you feel, love,' she told her. 'My dad was a bastard too.'

From the other room they heard Bill finishing his call and then shouting through that their lunch had arrived. Mercy's leather jacket felt cold to the touch.

# 65

Somewhere across the otherwise quiet marina, a ukulele could be heard playing *Maybe it's because I'm a Londoner.* Mercy scanned the many narrowboats that were docked at Limehouse Basin for the one she'd been searching for. One that, according to the Inland Waterways database, belonged to a Julian Kistler.

She'd risen early and already scoured Battlebridge Basin in Kings Cross and the South Dock in Rotherhithe. These were the other locations featured in the boat's recent mooring history. She'd hacked the database using methods that Robbie had been teaching her and learnt Kistler's name doing that. Inside her handbag was the GPS tracker that she'd liberated from underneath Nick Neale's Range Rover on Saturday night and, if she were successful, she planned to somehow attach it to the boat.

She had a short time to inspect Limehouse before her appointment with Bill. She hadn't shared what she was doing with him because she knew now that, although they shared the same goal, they did not want the same results. Bill was busy making every underworld contact he'd ever known aware of how threatened he was by the news story that had appeared online that afternoon, allowing her some time to follow her own leads. Her phone had been buzzing for the past hour, but she ignored it. It was either her mother having conniptions or more journalists wanting a follow-up interview. Frankly, traipsing around the docks of London looking for a particular boat was a welcome distraction from the fires that were blazing elsewhere.

Seagulls circled and squawked above as dusk began to settle. Mercy stalked the perimeter of the north bank marina, squinting to read the names of narrowboats moored on jetties far from the edge. She read Blue Breeze, Luna Papier, and The Cormorant, but not the name she'd come for. She approached the entrance to the marina only to find it locked and only accessible via a code she didn't have. However, there was nothing preventing her from stepping over the low chain link bollards that formed an ineffectual barrier and jumping down. In her right hand was an empty Amazon package that she'd pretend to be delivering if questioned.

Once on the platform she began exploring each of the jetties, reading more narrowboat names. Sir Galahad, Uptown Girl, Miss Gwendoline. There were few people around and lace curtains were drawn over most of the boat windows. Occasionally, she'd pass someone attaching water or electricity leads to the plug posts in between each boat. She nodded to one old man tending to his boat plants. He wished her a good afternoon.

Children's laughter could be heard along the same jetty where the ukulele was playing, along with the soft sound of wind chimes. As she explored, she scanned more boat names – Soggy Bottom, Knot So Fast.

*"I getta funny feeling inside a me,"* the ukulele player was

singing. And that was when she saw the words written along the cabin side in faded green letters.

The Long Needle.

The sight made her freeze. Ever since Barbara had uttered the words "mobile home," Mercy had known that she was looking for a boat. Kings Cross, Camden, Little Venice – all places with canals running through them. And so, when she'd discovered the existence of a narrowboat bearing that name, she'd been certain that here was her man, threading his way through the waters of London.

The ukulele ceased playing. Mercy looked up at the trio sitting on the long thin boat who were all staring back at her. Two cute little girls and a woman in a woolly hat holding the stringed instrument, clustered together on the deck seating. Hardly what she'd expected to find. For a shaky moment, Mercy thought she'd got it wrong. This couldn't be the home of an ice-hearted killer because ice-hearted killers didn't have cute children, ukuleles, and solar panelling. The woman in the woolly hat was smallish and wearing a baggy white top with Be Kind emblazoned across it. Externally, she posed all the threat of a primary school teacher.

And yet.

When Mercy looked into the eyes of this wan woman in her mid-thirties, she clocked surprise, recognition, and suppressed panic registering at once. *She knows me!*

'Hey,' said Mercy.

'Hey back,' replied the woman. 'Can I help you?'

'Yeah, I'm looking for Julian Kistler,' she nodded toward the shut doors of the cabin. 'He in?'

The children either side must have been around six or seven and they looked up to the Be Kind woman as if wondering why she wasn't immediately answering so simple a question.

'Who's asking?'

'My name's Mercy.'

'What business do you have with Julian?'

'I think you know.'

'Excuse me?'

'It's a little sensitive,' Mercy said, glancing toward the girls. 'Are you his wife? Are these his children?'

'That's none of your business,' the woman responded. She had a light Welsh accent and extremely pale skin. She was just about old enough to have been the missing caterer from Sarah Neale's fatal fall and the girl who'd helped kill a young physics student for Martin Bertsmouth. In fact, back then she would've been around the same age as poor Jenny.

'Do you ever ride a motorbike?' Mercy asked. 'In the Lewisham area?'

'Now look,' the woman said, handing the ukulele to the older girl. 'If you've come to start trouble, you can leave now. You're frightening the kids.'

The girls, who hadn't seemed frightened until then, became a little distressed. It unsettled Mercy, who'd imagined confronting the Long Needle many times but had never factored children into the scene.

'What I'm about to say might upset you,' Mercy persisted, hoping to be heard even from inside the cabin. 'But I think it's important you know what kind of man Julian is. I'm sorry to say, he's kind of a player.'

'Okay, that's enough,' the Welsh woman said even louder. 'I don't want to hear it. Leave!'

'He asked me out on a date once.'

'You are not allowed to be on this jetty and I'm calling marina security.'

'He hacked my phone and misrepresented himself.'

'Must you do this?' the woman implored. 'In front of the kiddies?'

'We went on a date,' Mercy continued, looking at the floating cabin and imagining him inside listening. 'On Valentine's day.'

'Everything alright, Meredith?' asked a male voice from behind her. Mercy turned, hoping it would be her man, but instead saw a heavy guy with a grey beard and a blue cap standing by a plug post. Behind him, a large woman in a pashmina was on another narrowboat, ready for a confrontation.

'This woman's being a nuisance, Alf,' Meredith replied, holding Mercy's stare. 'Talking absolute rubbish.'

'Only he didn't call himself Julian that night,' Mercy went on, 'he was pretending to be someone called Jamal.'

'She's crazy,' Meredith told Alf in the cap. 'And she's not supposed to be on the marina.'

'Right you,' said Alf, stepping forward and pulling in his stomach. 'Hop it. You're disturbing my kids and bothering my friend.'

'Here's what I *think* happened,' Mercy spoke to the man as if he was invested in her theory, 'somehow your Julian learnt about my police statement describing how I'd overheard him conspiring in murder years ago.'

'Are you on drugs?'

'I'd mentioned *the Long Needle* in my statement,' she pointed at the side cabin, 'and he needed to find out whether or not I could identify him. He hacked my phone, discovered I have an Uber account and somehow appeared outside my door one morning, posing as a cabbie called Jamal.'

'Who are we talking about?' asked the pashmina on the opposite boat. *'Julian?'*

'If that's his real name, yes,' Mercy nodded. 'So his face appeared on my phone and we had a conversation during the journey in which he made a point of turning to face me. I didn't recognise him which, on hindsight, probably saved my life.'

The doors of the neighbouring narrowboat opened. Another bearded head popped out. 'I've called security, Meredith,' he called over. 'They're on their way.'

'But that wasn't enough,' Mercy continued, watching the little lace curtains on the Long Needle. 'He needed to know what I knew about the conspiracy I'd overheard. That's why he insisted I go out on a date with him that night. I hate to say it Meredith, but your man was quite pushy.'

'Girls,' the woman in the pashmina called over from her boat. 'Come to mummy. This isn't our business.' The two children remained where they were, staring at Mercy.

'I ended up telling Jamal *everything* I knew about the deal he'd done with my dad. Thing is, back then I had it all wrong.'

'You sound delusional,' the Welsh woman told her.

'See, I thought the Long Needle was a person,' she addressed the cabin, 'whereas I now know it's your boat.'

'There's nobody in there,' Meredith scowled.

'Also, I wrongly told you that Lawrence Neale was the target of the assassination,' she raised her voice. 'I now realise it was actually Sarah Neale who you killed. No wonder you let me live, I was miles off!'

Alf reached over to the Long Needle and beckoned his children to join him on his side of the jetty. Meredith remained standing in her baggy top, glaring at her with an expression that was anything but kind.

'But there was only one snag,' Mercy held her stare. 'The fake Uber profile you'd created had your photograph on, plus the make and registration of the car you'd driven. Hence the fake mugging you performed.'

'Here we are,' said the man in Knots So Fast, pointing to the entrance of the marina. Two uniformed security guards were trotting down the planked path towards them.

'You were his getaway rider, weren't you, Meredith. What hurt the most after I'd beaten him up? His head or his pride?'

'Right then, what's all this?' asked the first security person to reach the Long Needle. 'Who's the troublemaker?'

'Not sure,' Mercy replied, noticing that these were private security not real police, 'he seems to go by different names.'

'*She's* trespassing,' Alf informed the guards with his daughters in each arm.

'And talking a load of S H I T,' added Meredith.

'Julian's a screenwriter,' Alf said, trying to console his daughters. 'Not a hitman.'

With that, he went to return the crying children to his own boat, but Mercy called him back. She reached inside her handbag.

'Before you go,' she asked, stepping away from the encroaching security men. 'I have a photofit that I had made at a police station the other day. It's of the man I went on this date with. I'm wondering—'

*'Make her fuck off!'* Meredith screamed. Everyone turned in surprise at her sudden ferocity. 'She's on private property. We pay a lot of money for these moorings, and I don't expect to be *harassed* like this. Take her away!'

One of the security men grabbed Mercy by the arm and tried to pull her back down the jetty. The family disappeared into their brightly painted boat and shut the doors after them. The man in Knot So Fast shook his head as she was tugged away.

But Mercy already had the answer to the photofit question from Meredith's hysterical reaction. Julian Kistler *was* the man she'd gone on a date with. There was just one bit of business remaining.

'It's over, Kistler,' she called over to the boat. 'I'm bringing you *and* Bill to justice even if it means destroying the agency. You're both going to jail!'

Then she allowed the security men to escort her away from the Long Needle and out of Limehouse Basin.

'You're nothing but a psycho!' Meredith was shrieking louder than the seagulls as she went. 'A fucking *fantasist!*'

# 66

The first legitimate news outlet to carry the story of Mercy's betrayal was the London Crier. That felt strangely apt to Bill. It was that publication, with its twee town crier logo, that he'd sold his soul to over a decade earlier. And, of all the phone hacks he'd been arrested and charged for, it was the one he'd performed for that paper that he was the most ashamed of.

Lucy Stafford, a pretty young teenager from a respectable family had gone missing in 2009. It had become national, front-page news. Matt Wren, who was Bill's contact at the Crier, had made it clear that any information relating to the disappearance he could provide via "the dark arts" would receive generous remuneration. Bill immediately set about employing the same skills he'd used to spy on celebrities, sportsmen, and royals in order to tap the voicemails of the whole Stafford clan, including the phone of Lucy herself wherever it and she were. Later, while contemplating his actions from the inside of a prison cell, he'd been horrified by his transgressions. But at the time he'd deluded himself into thinking that he was contributing to the investigation in ways in which real detectives were unable to do. He was a force for good, he'd assured himself, as he'd deleted private messages on Lucy's phone to make room for more illuminating calls.

Soon after Lucy's drowned body had been found in a disused water tank, Bill's illegal activities had also surfaced. He'd given the Stafford family false hope; the activity on her phone had suggested she was still alive when in fact she'd been dead for weeks. It was only then that the self-disgust had overwhelmed him. He'd suffered a panic attack at his family home when the police had arrived to arrest him.

Now, as he studied the story that had appeared on the Crier website, he wondered if he could endure such disgrace again.

**WHETSTONE MASSACRE UPDATE: PRIVATE EYE ACCUSES OWN DAD OF MURDER CONSPIRACY, writes Matt Wren.**

Yes, he thought as he reread the article that placed M&T at the centre of a criminal empire, after that he could endure anything.

Mercy had contacted Wren soon after leaving Sidcup police station to offer him an exclusive interview about the corruption she'd discovered at her family business. Considering she was fresh off the Whetstone crime scene, the journalist must've bitten her hand off for the scoop. He and Mercy had discussed the plan beforehand, but she'd only told him she'd done it after it was too late. But, the more he considered her move, the more he accepted its necessity. Their original plan to trap this still unnamed hitman remained sound, although it relied on her finally giving him access to those remaining numbers she'd been withholding from her dad's secret phone.

He crossed over to the one filing cabinet in his office. An

anglepoise lamp lit that corner of the room but otherwise it was dark. Bill had been at work for hours and the evening had drawn in. He was thinking of the one remaining task he had to perform before this was over. He bent down, opened the bottom drawer and pushed back the files. Underneath was a small handgun he'd purchased for this last purpose only.

The gun was heavy as he pulled it out and he took it closer to the light. It was a Glock 42 and it was already loaded with a round of live 9mm ammo. He'd purchased it the previous Friday from the same arms dealers who'd refused to do business with Nick. Bob the Feet had given them their details during an interview in his Nissan the day after Victor had summoned him to the Spoils. Smoking one of his smelly roll ups with the window down, Bob had provided useful intelligence about Nick. It was amazing what a weak man will tell you if you paid for his lunch, ale, and tobacco. Bill had promised Bob that he'd get him back in with Victor and had soon secured him the chauffeur's job that Junior Bruno had vacated. On grim reflection, that had been lucky for Bruno and decidedly unlucky for Bob.

Now that Bob the Feet was dead there was little trace of their former dealings. The only misstep that Bill had made was when he'd driven Mercy home and asked her to open his glove compartment to show her the pink envelope that Victor had handed him. But he doubted that Mercy would've registered the Golden Virginia packet.

The door to the outer office could be heard opening. Mercy was arriving later than scheduled. He placed the gun inside the desk drawer and shut it again. Despite it being outside working hours he was wearing a business-like shirt and tie. It always made him feel strong to be presentably dressed and he needed strength for what was going to happen if Mercy's plan worked.

'Bill?' she called out as he heard the door shutting behind her. 'Why's it so dark?'

'In my office!' he shouted through. 'I've been here hours. It got darker around me, and my eyes adjusted. Turn a light on and join me for a drop of whiskey.'

On the desk already was an unopened bottle of Glenfiddich and two tumblers.

Through the open door he saw the outer light switch on, giving him a rectangular view of the kitchenette. Into that frame stepped his goddaughter, wearing her dark green leather jacket. The jacket had been debugged and sewn up again and M&T had handed over the relevant audio to the police as requested. Mercy's conversations with Nick, if played to a jury, could be enough to send him down for life. Good, Bill thought, as he sipped from the tumbler. Another shit well and truly flushed.

'How did your police interview go?' Mercy asked as she lightened his office via a dimmer switch. 'Do the cops still think we hate each other?'

'I made it clear that we weren't communicating anymore,' he replied as he poured a dram into her glass. 'And I refuted your version of events. So, if the Long Needle has any police connections, that's what he'll learn. What've you been doing?'

'Not much.'

'Hey, take a look at this.' He pointed at the computer screen on his desk. 'You're famous.'

Mercy placed her handbag on the seat of the client chair and came around to the view the screen. The photograph accompanying the article was taken from her Facebook profile. She was in a Spanish bar with a Mojito in front of her, flashing that Tyler smile. Her tanned arms displayed the feathery tattoos that the British winter had compelled her to cover up. Bill thought she looked fantastic.

'What a heartbreaker.'

'My ex took that,' Mercy told him as she unzipped her jacket. 'I guess it's not appropriate to look so cheerful in a story where I'm accusing my father of death-dealing, but I thought, fuck it, why not? It's important to look your best, even when betraying the family name.'

In the exclusive interview with the Crier, private investigator Mercy Tyler – "*the last person to speak to Victor alive*" – was making outrageous claims. According to Mercy, infamous "businessman" Victor Neale had confessed that he'd hired a hitman to kill a member of his own family. Furthermore, her dodgy detective dad had brokered the deal. It was hot, unsubstantiated stuff and included a description of the meeting she'd overheard as a teenager. The Crier made clear that she'd presented no evidence for these assertions but heavily implied that the unnamed family member must surely be the more famous Neale brother, Lawrence. Perhaps to legally cover himself, Wren had hinted that his source – "born Christopher Tyler" – was perhaps an unreliable one. Reference was made to a "difficult" background, her "alternative" lifestyle, and "sensational" story in a way that suggested he knew his readers might have concerns about her credibility.

'This has always been a tacky paper,' complained Bill as they read it together.

Mercy returned to the client side of the desk, looking exhausted. He could imagine what she'd been dealing with today.

'Mum's ignoring my calls now,' Mercy sighed as she sat down.

'She'll understand your motives in time.'

'Uncle Den called though. First time I've heard from him since the funeral. He berated me for slandering his brother, told me I've broken Nana's heart. He said – and I quote – that I've "disgraced the family once again." I love that *once again,* don't you?' Her voice was bitter. 'Classy.'

'Fuck Dennis,' said Bill, handing her a glass of neat whiskey, 'he was a shitty brother to Ray and a worse uncle to you.'

She took the tumbler from him, chinked his glass, but didn't return the smile. Compared to the bright, holiday spirit in the photograph, Mercy looked beaten down by the events of winter. He felt anger at the mess she'd been drawn into. None of this was her fault, and yet she'd shown such guts in trying to make sense of it. He admired her idealism and felt sorry that his own had diminished.

'I spoke to Nina Markham earlier,' she said, circling the glass in her hands. 'Relax, I didn't say anything to contradict your statement. But she had an update on Philip Papatonis. He's out of his coma.'

'I don't know who that is,' Bill said, sitting opposite her.

'One of Victor's security guys. The one the Range Rover reversed into and ran over. They called him Piper. As well as the concussion he's got two broken legs and a serious pelvic fracture. They doubt he'll walk again.'

Bill took a much deeper swig of the whiskey and closed his eyes for a second. It was delicious and smoky. Good stuff.

'Those are nasty injuries,' he said, reopening his eyes. 'But if he was working for Victor then he was probably a scumbag.'

'*We* were working for Victor,' she reminded him.

He didn't like the way she was looking at him. Not for

the first time, he couldn't get a read on where her head was. He decided to move things along.

'Did you bring the burner?'

She reached into her jeans pocket and produced the phone that she'd found inside the office mini-fridge. 'As promised,' she said, resting it on the desk. 'I've already identified most of the contacts on there and its quite the array. As well as Operation Greenwater, there are tabloid hacks, side-chicks, some Neale associates, a drug dealer, and a local knocking shop. I've run checks on them all but none fit the bill of the man we're looking for. One number sticks out though.'

Bill had taken the phone and was flicking through the contact list. Most were saved as two letter initials, but he could tell who they were at a glance.

'You could've saved a lot of time and energy if you'd handed me this earlier,' he remonstrated after clicking on one unidentified number saved as SJ. 'This is Sonny Jago, a debt collector from Peckham. He was in prison for most of the noughties so he's not the man you overheard in the office.'

His thumb hovered over a particular contact labelled as JK.

'That's him,' Mercy told him. '100%. Robbie says the number is still active and, aside from Claudia, it's the only one Dad phoned in the last week of his life. And he phoned it several times.'

'JK?' murmured Bill.

Mercy nodded. 'He's definitely our man.'

She seemed very sure, so he jotted down the number and returned the burner. He placed his hand onto the landline phone and exhaled.

'You didn't tell Nina about this, did you?' he checked,

before lifting the receiver, 'because cops would scare him away. I won't.'

'This is ours,' Mercy promised him. 'The police can't entrap a person like we're going to. Besides, this is personal, right? We both want to nail the bastard who murdered Sarah.'

'Sure,' Bill said. 'And, of course, the bastard who killed your dad.'

'If you say so.'

Bill hesitated. She'd hardly blinked since sitting down and he knew there was a problem. Together they'd planned this trap, but it was only now, as he was poised to make a deeply incriminating call, that he began to question who the trap might really be for.

'If footage of my dad's death came to light now,' she said casually, 'and it revealed that the coroner's report was accurate – that he'd just drunkenly tripped and smashed his head open before plunging into the river – I'd be so relieved. Case closed, that was that. But, if it transpired that he *was* murdered, then let's be honest,' she looked down at her swirling drink, 'fair play to the killer. He had it coming.'

'Mercy!' Bill exclaimed. 'That's an awful thing to say about your own father.'

'Even if your father is Ray Tyler?' she looked up at him. 'I mean, I knew he was dodgy but come on, this whole investigation has been a series of horrendous revelations. Imagine owning a thing like this,' she held up the burner, her voice growing hot, 'so full of seedy contacts that he felt the need to hide it inside a secret compartment. Especially *that one*,' she pointed at the one he'd jotted down, 'I mean, who *was* my dad? Just a servant of evil, as far as I can make out.'

Bill was unsure how to respond. Should he defend his former friend, or admit that he agreed with every word?

'Same goes for Victor Neale,' she continued in a steel-tipped tone. 'Whoever riddled his body with bullets – whether Nick, the Long Needle or someone else – they lightened this world. There are a hundred reasons to celebrate that man's death but, for me, top of the list is his treatment of Sarah. I know you agree.'

His hand was still rested on the desk phone and a muscle in it twitched. He commanded himself not to panic.

'She was a lovely woman,' he said carefully.

'By all accounts,' Mercy nodded. 'Kittichai McColl talked about her like she was the only kind soul she'd met since arriving in England. She was with Sarah in the Spoils on the night before she died and told me that she'd seemed happy then. As if she were in love.'

'Really?'

'Yes, that's the main reason I don't believe that she took her own life. I think she had quite a bit to live for. Perhaps she was planning on leaving Victor for someone else.'

'Perhaps.'

'Perhaps the real father of her baby even?'

Bill said nothing.

'But, because of the machinations of three men,' Mercy raised her hand and counted them off, 'her husband, my dad and *that* piece of shit,' she indicated the phone in his hand, 'she was robbed of that happy future. It makes you livid to think about, doesn't it?'

'It does.'

'What a trinity of shitheads,' Mercy swore. 'Justifiably, two of them are now dead. First my dad, who brokered her murder, then Victor, who'd ordered it. So that just leaves one remaining. The man we're about to phone is the only one still alive who hasn't been punished yet.'

Bill's mind flicked to the handgun hidden inside his desk drawer. 'Mercy... I'm not sure what...'

'Why are you waiting, Bill?' she challenged him. 'Don't you want to get that bastard too?'

He stared back, astonished by her implication. There was a searing quality about her, she seemed to sense his every dirty secret. For a brief moment, he wondered if he were dreaming her. He opened his mouth to defend himself.

Then shut it again. And, without saying anything, he lifted the receiver and dialled. Her eyes were locked on him as he waited for the line to ring. In those dead seconds one urgent thought pulsed through his mind. *I'm about to speak to Sarah's killer.* His heart rate had quickened and he thought again of the morning he'd been arrested for phone hacking. He'd sensed a similar tightening in his chest.

'Please leave a message,' a voice then said, '*Beep.*'

## 67

'This is Bill Mance,' he spoke into the receiver, sounding as awkward as he had delivering her dad's eulogy, 'perhaps you've heard of me.'

Mercy had noticed he'd been drinking more than was normal for him and saw sweat on his hands. She wondered if he might pass out.

'I'm the business partner of the late Mr Tyler. He gave me your number,' he said, avoiding her eye. 'Anyway, I've run into a problem and I'm hoping you might help. I can't go into what over the phone, but it's a family matter, very sensitive. There's an unwelcome,' he paused and looked over at her, '*element* in my life that's threatening my agency and my liberty. It's your problem too. Take a look on the Crier website for context.' He turned his whole body away from Mercy. She sipped her whiskey. 'I know you don't work for free,' he whispered. 'But I have funds and can prove it. We have to act fast, and it can't look like what it is. I believe that's your specialty. I'm calling from Nadgett Street,' he continued after another short breath. 'I'll be here until morning. Call or meet me here tonight. No fucking about.'

He slammed the phone down but continued staring at it. It seemed he couldn't lift his eyes just yet.

'Well done,' she said to him. 'Now we wait.'

'There's no need for you to stay,' he replied, pretending to shuffle some papers. 'I can deal with him.'

'Bill, you've just ordered a hit on my life and impressed upon the assassin the need for urgency. Don't you want to keep an eye on me? Make sure I'm safe?'

'Of course!' he protested. 'I'm not going to let any harm come to you!'

'In which case, we'll stick together for now,' she raised her glass to her lips. 'Drink your drink.'

The light ticking of the office clock was all that could be heard for some minutes. Bill knocked back the rest of his glass. As he sat down again she recalled the moment in the police station when she'd walked into where he was waiting. He'd gawped at her like she'd been resurrected. She realised then that Sarah's blue dress which she was wearing had as potent an effect on him as it had had on Victor.

'Did you love her very much?' she asked. Bill reached for the bottle to top his own glass up. Hers was still only half-drunk.

'My Moira?' he replied as he poured. 'Well, it wasn't a perfect marriage by any stretch, but we had our moments.'

'I think you know I'm not talking about Moira.'

He leaned back in his chair with his full glass in both hands and she felt his attitude alter. The awkwardness dropped away.

'Who *are* you on about then?' he asked. 'You've got something to say? Say it. Make your charges and give me a chance to refute them.'

Mercy straightened up.

'Okay,' she said, resting her unfinished glass next to it.

'Let's get into this. What did you mean when you told Victor that you'd known what I was for decades?'

'Excuse me?'

'The interview with him at the Spoils that you played me in your car,' she elaborated. 'Right at the start of that audio Victor called me a fantasist and then claimed that I think I'm a woman. And then you said, *"I've known what she is for decades."* The phrase stuck out somewhat. What did you mean by it?'

'Is that what's bothering you?' Bill almost laughed. 'Mercy, I was just trying to gain his trust. You know, speak his language. I'm sorry if I caused offence.'

'I wasn't offended,' she insisted. 'In fact, I appreciated your use of female pronouns. You weren't speaking his language *that* much. But I do wonder if there is more to your remark. I've always assumed that nobody knew that I was trans when young, but lately I'm realising that wasn't true.'

'I wouldn't say I knew that you were transgender exactly,' he shrugged, 'but you were an effeminate child. That's all I meant.'

'Sure,' she smiled, and reached for her tumbler again. 'I suppose I was a pretty queer kid. And an observant man like you would pick up on that.'

'Right,' he said, watching her take another sip.

'So it had nothing to do with the fact that you'd been monitoring my family home on the day the hitman visited?'

'Excuse me?'

'June 7th, 2004. That was the day I bunked off school, dressed up in make-up and a modified jumpsuit, and spent the afternoon dancing around the house to pop songs. You saw all that.'

'Absolutely not!'

'I'm not accusing you of spying on *me*,' Mercy clarified.

'You were spying on Dad. You just happened to see me in all my amateur pop glory while at it.'

'Where are you getting this from?'

'Kittichai knew that I danced around as Kylie. I only did it once. She said that Sarah told her on the night before she died. So how did Sarah know? Because you told her. Because of the affair you were having.'

'An affair with Sarah Neale?' he tried to laugh. 'Why, I should be so lucky!'

'The afternoon before,' Mercy went on, 'specifically Thursday the 6th of June, Mum received a surprise visit from Sarah. I came home to find them nattering over tea and cake. She'd asked to borrow a dress, Mum's summery red one, for the fateful garden party that Sarah was organising for her sister-in-law. In return she lent Mum her blue one, which is how it ended up in our house. This meant that Mum had to go upstairs to fetch the red dress. While she did, Sarah would've been able to go into our kitchen and unlock the side door, allowing you access to the house while they continued chatting in the front room.'

'Ridiculous.'

'You were probably still in the house when I returned from school. Sarah seemed tense and she wouldn't let Mum go to the kitchen to fill the teapot again. Eventually her phone buzzed and she pretended it was Victor calling her from abroad. But it was you, telling her that the coast was clear.'

'Pure conjecture.'

'It wouldn't be difficult for you to bug Dad's office, although it took me a while to figure out how. First I thought the fridge itself was wired for sound, or maybe you'd even placed a device behind the football shirt in the picture frame. But now I realise that neither of those options would've done. The bugs would be too hard to put in place and then remove again. You can't leave a device *in situ* to be discovered later, especially if the person you're spying on is also in the trade. You'd need something simpler.'

She reached into her jacket pocket and pulled out two identical Union Jack magnets. One of them had adorned the mini-fridge that was once in her dad's home and the other was from Bill's kitchen. It had been used to hold the photo of Victor's birthday to his fridge door.

'Swapping a fridge magnet with one that is bugged would be the work of a moment and, considering that you were invited to drink in his office every second Sunday, it would be easy for you to swap them back again. I've opened both of these up and, although I didn't find a listening device, the one in your home fridge had been tampered with before and could be used again. Presumably you're keeping it around in case you ever needed to employ a similar trick. It's clever, I'll give you that.'

'This is delusional,' he said. 'And it makes me sad. I'm not in the habit of spying on my friends and I'm sorry you think so little of me.'

'Remember when I visited this office a couple of weeks ago? I sat in this chair and told you I'd overheard Dad with the person I thought was called Long Needle. You acted like you didn't believe a word of it.'

'It was a little far-fetched on first hearing.'

'The only thing that caught your attention was when I mentioned the mystery client's envelope, and that it was pink. I didn't understand the implication of that colour at the time. But you did.'

'Yes, that's when I started taking you seriously. I knew that pink was associated with The Never Setting Sun, which linked it to Victor.'

'But you already knew that Victor was involved,' she asserted, 'and you knew about the meeting because you'd heard every word of it. But you hadn't *seen* anything because your bug in the office was audio not visual. That's why you didn't know about the secret compartment in the fridge or what colour the envelope was until I told you. It's why you still don't know what the hitman looks like.'

Bill shook his head.

'You saw *me* though,' she continued. 'Somehow. And if you didn't see the hitman, that means you were staking out the rear. I can only imagine that you used the electricity pylon that overlooks our back garden. There were always men climbing it in high-visibility coats.'

'Now Mercy,' he said in a patronising tone, 'listen to what you're saying. D'you honestly believe I'd have the ingenuity to pull a stunt like that?'

'You put a live feed inside my jacket,' she replied. 'And when we visited Third Eye, Alan waxed lyrical about your "creative solutions." So yes, I can believe it. And it must have been pretty annoying when you saw me return home and almost mess everything up. I'm dying to know, was it you who phoned the landline minutes before Dad arrived home? It scared the shit out of me. I'd been happily dancing around the kitchen and the dining room – both of which are visible from the pylon – when suddenly it rang. You knew he was returning home. Were you warning me?'

Bill's eyes looked away – a sharp movement as if he'd been accused of having seen her naked.

'Because if it *was* you who phoned the house, I should thank you. If you hadn't alerted me, then Dad would've walked in on me dressed like that, which was not a conversation I was ready to have at fourteen. In fact, you saved me from discovery *twice*. Once the meeting was over Dad remained in the office and I could sense him edging closer to the curtains, ready to let in some light. But you called his phone, pulling him out of there. So,' she raised her glass, 'cheers for the rescue.'

Bill mumbled something barely discernible. Did she imagine it, or had he just said *you're welcome?* Mercy should've felt something, an anger to match that which she held for her dad. But she felt a different sensation, like she was talking to the most interesting person she'd ever met.

'Why were you spying on our home?' she asked.

He said nothing but he'd stopped denying it.

'Then let me tell you what I'm currently working with,' she continued. 'Victor told me that while he was in Antigua he'd received a text from Sarah that was clearly meant for someone else. LOL, I love you, it read. He assumed, not unreasonably, that the Lol referred to his brother Lawrence. But I think LOL stood for 'laugh out loud' and was just a response to something funny her true lover had texted her. She would have realised her mistake, instantly of course, and would've contacted her other man in a panic, especially if he was a private investigator who might be in a position to look into it. According to his own account, Victor didn't confront her about any infidelity, although he spoke to both Lol and his wife about it. As the real lover in question, you must have been on high alert. Victor spoke to Dad and, without telling him who the target was, hired him to find and secure the services of the same hitman Bertsmouth spoke of. You realised something was up and needed to know what. And whenever Dad had stuff he wanted to keep secret from you, he'd do it at our home rather than in the office. So, using Sarah to help gain access, you bugged chez Tyler to learn what was being discussed in secret. How am I doing?'

Another silence he was prepared to hold. The air between them felt dense with pressure. She didn't like the way he kept glancing toward his desk drawer.

'You heard the same conversation that I did. A hit being arranged and Dad not knowing who the target was until shown the contents of the envelope. Knowing what you did, you must've been concerned that it was Sarah who Victor wanted dead. But then, just a week later, Lol's car went kaboom, which seemed like the answer to the question. A hit that didn't look like what it was. Especially to you, knowing that Victor mistakenly thought that Lol was her other man. Lawrence was dead but Sarah was safe. Is that what you assumed?'

Bill laughed, but quietly. To himself.

'What's so funny?'

Then he laughed even louder. Mercy leaned closer.

'Because she'd never be safe, would she, Bill?' she prompted him. 'Not from Victor. You know that now.'

Abruptly, his laughter stopped and he rubbed his face.

'I had my bags packed,' he suddenly declared.

'Okay.'

'I didn't *assume she was safe!* We were going to leave the country because we both knew she'd never be that. She was going to elope with me after the garden party. And here's the joke.' He shook his head and exhaled. 'I was on my way to the airport when I heard she'd killed herself!'

# 68

*'I'd written a note to Moira,'* his voice rattled through the car speaker, *'apologising. Sarah and I were off to Brazil, using funds we'd stolen from the Costelloe loot* and *M&T's annual profits.'*

Parked further up Nadgett Street, Nina listened in astonishment to the voice of the man whose agency she'd been working at for the past eighteen months. She leaned forward in her seat and peered up at the M&T office windows. But the blinds remained shut.

*'Of course, it meant abandoning her other kids but we had no choice,'* Bill continued. *'She couldn't go on as Victor's wife and he'd never grant a simple divorce.'*

Bloody hell, Nina thought, as he was confessing to an extra-marital affair with a gangster's wife. And I thought he was the boring one.

*'But it never occurred to me that she'd been murdered,'* he added. *'Not then. Like you, I thought that Lol's explosion was the result of your dad's meeting. And Sarah was...'*

It sounded like he was becoming emotional. Was he crying?

*'I'd pressured her, you see, into leaving. Knowing that she had this history of self-harming and severe depression, I badgered her to leave her kids. So when she fell I....'* there was a heart-breaking pause on the line, *'I believed it. And I blamed myself.'*

When they'd laced the leather jacket with a brand-new mike feed, one that Nina could listen in to from a reasonable distance, Mercy had told her it was to catch the contract killer. She'd outlined her plan about summoning him under false pretences and asked if she could have an unofficial police backup waiting in the wings. She'd never told Nina her suspicions about Bill. But, so far, he'd only confessed to an affair and some attempted fraud. He hadn't even really admitted to bugging the Tyler home yet.

*'I managed to intercept the note that I'd written for my wife before she read it,'* his miserable voice was saying. *'And I grieved for Sarah in secret.'*

On Nina's lap rested her two-way police radio and she was ready to call this in if things got violent, or if the hitman arrived. But for now, she was too engrossed in Bill's story.

Behind her, she'd failed to notice a white car drift past, slow enough to see her face.

# 69

'How did the affair begin?' Mercy asked. 'Was it like *Vertigo?*'

'I'm not sure,' he replied, 'I've ever had vertigo.'

'No, I mean the film with Jimmy Stewart. He's a private detective – like us – and he's following this wealthy wife around who's played by Kim Novak. She tries to kill herself, he intervenes, they have an affair. Is that how it was with you and Sarah?'

Bill took another sip from his whiskey and seemed to give the question serious thought. She wondered if he'd ever told another soul about this before.

'No,' he said at last. 'It was nothing like *Vertigo.*'

'Where did you fuck?'

He shot her a disapproving look.

'She got pregnant, right?' Mercy shrugged. 'And you were supposed to be tailing her in the afternoons. Did you rent rooms or do it in the Spoils?'

'It wasn't like that,' he protested, 'at first. Tailing her was obviously difficult because she knew Ray and myself, so we kept a tracker under her white convertible. However, one afternoon she discovered it while retrieving a football from under the chassis. That day she drove close to a nearby wood, parked up in a secluded spot and left the car. I couldn't tell what was going on, so I approached for a closer look. As I neared her Mercedes Benz, I found it parked at a weird angle and her doors were wide open. I thought that she'd been abducted at gunpoint by one of Victor's rivals, so I rushed over in a panic. That was when she stepped out from behind a tree. *Fancy seeing you here,* she said.'

'You were busted,' Mercy smiled. 'Good.'

'She had every right to be angry with me,' he agreed. 'But I was so ashamed at having been found out, I practically dropped to my knees in apology. I mean I didn't even *like* Victor, and she was... well, I'd heard the therapy session so I knew she had enough demons in her life without me joining their ranks.

'We went to a café and I confessed to everything, including the bugs. She cried and I was distraught. She told me how she'd been treated at the hands of both brothers and I swore I'd help, that I was on her side from there on. Soon I was filing erroneous reports to Victor and giving her loads of space. After some weeks, I reported that she'd been to see a movie on her own. I didn't mention that I saw it with her, or that we'd held hands in the cinema.'

'Romantic,' Mercy nodded, 'like *Vertigo.*'

'So yeah, things got intimate. I'd loved her since...' he sighed, '... since our first meeting. I still can't believe she ever returned that love but, well, it happened. And then she fell pregnant.

'I was delighted to hear it. I'd always wanted a child of my own. And for her to be the mother... well, that was something. But around that time was when Sarah accidentally sent that text to Victor instead of me. And after eavesdropping on Ray's conversation I knew a hit had been arranged, which accelerated our elopement plans. When Lol's car exploded, that caused me to rethink. I didn't assume she was safe, but I thought we had more time. And so we decided to leave it until after the garden party. What a mistake that was.' He shook his head and stared at his glass. Then his brow creased. 'We weren't laughing at you,' he said.

'I'm sorry?'

'When I told her I'd seen you dancing around as a girl. I told her that I'd never seen you looking so happy and honestly, I hadn't. You looked wonderful.'

Despite the loaded situation, Mercy was grateful. She wished he'd said it earlier in life.

'You thought that Sarah had committed suicide,' she continued, holding the line, 'but it was only recently that you discovered it was murder. How?'

There followed the longest pause. He hadn't confessed to anything major yet. Nothing worth involving Nina for. But they'd reached the precipice of his truth and she considered what he should do next. He needed to stop talking. It was his only real move. He couldn't lie his way out of this and nor would he. That would insult them both. But he should definitely plead the fifth. That's what she'd do, she reasoned, if she were in his position.

His eyes glistened in the dark. On his desk was a box of tissues he kept there for his cuckolded clients whenever they turned emotional. He took some to use on his own eyes.

'I thought it'd be just another Monday when I walked into this office that morning,' he spoke in a quiet voice. 'But instead I found him raging at Barbara. When I tried to make sense of the scene he stormed off, leaving me to deal with her. I tried to quiz Barb, but she didn't seem to understand what she'd done wrong. I got the truth from Ray later.

'I'd waited in the office after work, guessing that he'd return. Sure enough, at around eight o'clock, he bumped the door open and entered carrying a full plastic bag from the off-license. He was surprised to see me.

'We sat on the sofa out there. I told him I was worried about him and expressed concern about his drinking. He was guarded at first, but crying. I patted him on the shoulder. *There there, it can't be that bad.* Then he looked at me with red eyes and told me that he'd learnt that Sarah had been pregnant when she died. I already knew that, but acted surprised. And that's when he told me something I didn't know. That he'd arranged her murder.

'He confessed to everything. How he'd brokered a hit for Victor, thinking that the victim was Lol. He'd been shocked to learn that Sarah was the true target. But he'd done nothing to prevent it.

'He whimpered all that, oblivious to the rage building in me. Until then I'd not entertained the idea that she'd been murdered, but the reality of it came crashing in. Of course she hadn't jumped of her own accord!

'And your dad expected sympathy from me! Poor Raymond and all his bottomless secrets. Poor Ray and his regrets. As if *his* rotten guilt was the true tragedy. That's when I attacked him.'

His face was wet and angry. By contrast, when Mercy spoke next, it was with more composure.

'Bill,' she asked, 'did you kill my dad?'

He used the tissues again and exhaled.

'Oh Mercy,' he said with a choke, 'I never meant to.'

# 70

There, thought Mercy, shutting her eyes. The case solved.

He'd said it. She'd made him say it.

She'd won.

Now how could she make him unsay it?

'We'd never fought before, not even in a playful way,' he continued, 'and he wasn't expecting it.'

She opened her eyes again and felt the tears follow. He was pointing to the outer office.

'We were on the carpet, I was on top, strangling him.' He lifted his big hands to act it out. 'Like this. If I'd wanted to kill him, I could've done it there. I almost did. But I loved your dad, Mercy. I couldn't bring myself.'

'Besides,' she observed, loud enough for her jacket to catch, 'he hadn't told you who the killer was yet.'

'Yeah,' he admitted. 'I needed him alive. So, I released his throat and crawled off him. He lay there coughing on the office floor as I slumped onto the swivel chair. Eventually, I got him a glass of water.

'"*Mate,*" he pleaded after I'd told him that I was the baby's father. "*I'd no clue.*"

'I demanded to know who'd killed her. Ray told me he didn't know his name and I called him a liar.'

Mercy's body shook inside her jacket. Should she warn him about the policewoman listening outside? Was there still time for that?

'Your dad wanted to atone. He told me he'd get in touch with the hitman if I wanted, that he'd set up a meeting in Greenwich. And that he'd help me kill him.'

'That was the midnight meeting he went to after leaving Claudia's,' Mercy said. 'He told her that someone wanted to kill *him* that night.'

'He knew there'd be consequences for letting me down,' Bill confirmed 'so I guess he was pretty shit up.'

*Why don't you deny it?* Mercy wanted to scream at him.

'He was going to meet his contact around midnight, close to the Cutty Sark. I was loitering around the entrance to the foot tunnel. As soon I'd see Ray pat his contact on the shoulder that was my signal that here was the man who'd killed Sarah. The Judas kiss. I'd wait until the right moment, grab him from behind and drag him into the shadows where I was going to break his neck and dump him in the river. Ray was going to help. It was the price he'd agreed to pay for my forgiveness.'

'What went wrong?'

'I saw a car pull up outside the Gypsy Moth pub and Ray got out alone. He was supposed to wait there until his contact appeared. But he started walking straight toward me, breaking my cover. The weather was filthy and he was shaking his head. "It's off," he said as he drew near. "He's not coming." I was furious. His phone had been off all night so I knew he must have spoken to this guy in person. I could smell booze on his breath, making me angrier. I told him he was contemptible.

'"I've my family to think of," he complained. "He'll have them killed if I fuck with him. He knows where my son lives in Barcelona. He said his friend will kill Chrissy if anything happens."'

Mercy squinted. She'd suspected that the hitman had been driving the cab that had taken him from Claudia's house to the meeting in Greenwich. He must have dumped him at the spot after making the threats. But was this the real reason Dad hadn't delivered him up? To protect her and Mum? Or was that just more bullshit from a man who swum in it?

'I told him he'd already destroyed his family,' Bill continued. 'After all, why were you transitioning in another country? I don't think you were ashamed of who you were. You were ashamed of who *he* was.'

This stunned Mercy because it was absolutely true. She'd moved to Spain to get away from him. It had nothing to do with being trans. In fact, after transitioning, she'd only returned to Britain after learning her dad was dead. How had she not realised that about herself before?

'I told him that you'd overheard his first meeting with the hitman and that was why you hated him. That hit him hard. We were both soaking from the storm and shouting in each other's faces. At some point he pushed me backwards and I stumbled to the wet ground. Then he ran off towards Deptford.'

*"I understand why you turned against me..."* Mercy remembered him saying in his message that must have been made mere minutes after this confrontation. *"I get that now."*

'I'd lost him,' Bill moaned, 'for a while. So, I returned to my car and turned on my scanner. Ray had switched his phone back on for the first time that night. So, I tracked him through the rainy streets until I got a clearer read on where he was and then I approached on foot. Mercy, please, I had no intention of harming him. But he kept fighting back and wouldn't tell me what I wanted to know. We were down by those old steps into the river. He tried to punch me but was too drunk. I shoved back harder.... He fell. Slipped on the stone. I'm sorry. If I could take it back, I would. He was my only friend.'

Her dad's death had been clean. He'd cracked his head open and drowned in the Thames, making it easy for Bill. Ray Tyler, accommodating his mates until the bitter end. She ignored his apology.

'It was you who's been phoning Nick, wasn't it?' she then said. 'The caller only began introducing himself as the Long Needle after I'd played you Dad's voicemail message. But you wanted revenge on Victor and were hoping that by winding Nick up, he'd do it for you.'

'No, I was trying to get Victor to contact me,' he replied. 'After Ray, he was the only other person who might know the identity of the hitman. But, aside from the funeral, I couldn't get close. He wouldn't take my calls or acknowledge any existing relationship beyond Ray. But I knew if he thought the hitman was a danger to him, he'd tell me who he was. So I created a situation where he'd summon me to the Spoils and tell me everything.'

'Did you want Nick to kill him though?' Mercy asked in a clear voice. 'Or was it always the plan that you'd do it yourself?'

'Oh, believe me,' he straightened. 'I very much wanted to shoot that bastard.'

'Bob the Feet granted you access to Nick's car so you could plant the Skorpion,' she said, 'and we got him on tape saying he wanted to kill his own uncle. A nice little stitch up.'

'I'd no idea that the numpty would point a loaded weapon at you, love,' he implored.

'So the police now have an audio of Nick receiving the murder weapon,' she continued, 'inside the murder vehicle and boasting that he was going to kill his own uncle. And when Victor asked to see me at his club you had your chance. He'd be out in the open. Better yet, I was able to learn everything he knew about the Long Needle beforehand. Is that why I was spared in the massacre? So later on I could still tell you everything I'd learnt over dinner.'

'Christ, is that what you think?' Bill said. 'Mercy, you're like a daughter to me. I'd never hurt you.'

Mercy felt as though her heart was exploding. She wanted to reach out, grab his hand and admit she was betraying him, to apologise for turning his tricks against him.

'I'd turn a gun on myself,' he insisted, 'before I'd ever turn it on you. I deliberately didn't strike at Victor outside his club until after you'd walked away. When he tried to use you as a shield I almost abandoned the whole venture and let the bastard live. I swear, there was never a single moment when I considered harming you.'

'Bill, you've killed four men,' she reminded him, 'and hospitalised a fifth. You're a seriously dangerous man.'

'None of those men were saints,' he defended himself. 'Including your dad. I'm not lying when I say that his death was more accidental but even so—'

The phone rang.

'That'll be for you,' she said.

Bill breathed out and then rubbed a hand quickly over his face. Then he reached over and answered it.

'M&T Investigations,' he said. 'Bill speaking.'

A pause.

'I can hear you breathing,' he whispered. 'I'm alone.'

Mercy heard a faint voice speaking on the other end. She stood to better hear it, wanting to know if it was the same voice as she'd heard from behind a curtain at the age of fourteen.

'That's right,' Bill said to the caller. 'I'm serious.' He turned his head to Mercy.

'No,' he said, looking at her with a distrustful eye. 'I was not aware of that.'

Mercy heard the caller's soft voice continue.

'I see,' Bill said. 'Yes, that is difficult.'

He shifted away again.

'No need for a pen,' he assured the caller. 'I've a good memory.' He nodded as she heard the voice continuing. 'Uh huh, uh huh,' he murmured. 'Got it,' he said when the voice stopped. 'How will I recognise you?'

The caller appeared to have hung up. Bill stood with an expression of intense concentration on his face.

'Is he coming?' Mercy asked. Slowly, he raised a right-hand finger to his lips.

'Oh yes,' he said but immediately contradicted that with a shake of the head. 'He's on his way.'

His left hand reached down for the desk drawer and slid it gently open. From inside he produced a small gun.

She jolted backwards.

'He'll be here shortly,' he was saying as Mercy tried to compose herself. 'You and I should wait here until he does. Won't be long.'

Perhaps she was getting used to the occupational hazard of being threatened by a gun, but she felt cooler now than she had when Nick had brandished his. Or perhaps it was because she'd believed Bill when he'd said he'd never harm her.

'Before you do anything stupid, I need to tell...'

'It's fine, everything's fine,' he interrupted with a finger to his lips. 'Let's you and I have another glass,' he winked. 'Top up?'

He reached over with his free hand and gently patted her leather jacket, searching. He stroked over the wire that she'd told him the police had removed. He removed his hand and looked furious. She understood why her dad had been so scared of him.

'Until our man arrives,' he said stepping away with his gun pointed at the floor, 'let's stop talking. I've said too much for now.' He gestured for her to remove the jacket. 'We'll listen to some music.'

'Sure,' she said, remaining where she was as he tapped the keyboard on his PC. 'You've told me enough.'

It seemed like he understood what she was communicating. He'd be mad to shoot her now and she didn't think he was that.

'Get comfy,' he said and again mimed the removal her jacket. 'I insist.'

Slowly Mercy took it off and draped it over where she'd been sitting. Bill turned the volume up loud.

'Tina Turner,' he said with a conversational air. 'Gotta love her.'

Nutbush City Limits was now the only sound the jacket could be picking up. He pointed toward the door. Mercy wondered if she should call out now while the jacket might still hear her.

'Go through,' he mouthed.

Once they'd both stepped through to the outer office, Bill shut the door between them and the jacket. Then, gun in hand, he strode over to the front window next to Barbara's desk. The blinds were down and the lights in this office were off. He edged close to the window, placed his fingers between two slats and inched them open.

'He came here,' Bill seethed as he peered down onto the street, 'just now. But something put him off. *You fucked it.*'

'So what, it's my fault he didn't turn up?'

'That's Nina out there,' he said, tapping the window-pane. 'He clocked her. Told me that I'm under police surveillance. You're bugging me.'

'She wants Sarah's killer,' Mercy said, 'just like us.'

'I don't want him *arrested!*' he burst out in anger, tapping his chest with the gun muzzle.

'Cool it, okay?' she said, placing her hands in the air. 'I know how much you hate him, but this is London, not the Wild West. You couldn't possibly have expected to get away with this carnage for long.'

'I *was* getting away with it!' he spat. 'Until you *betrayed* me.'

'Lower the gun,' she told him.

He sagged and rested the weapon by his side. 'I didn't buy it to use on you,' he said, looking at the closed blinds again.

'I'm more concerned that you're going to use it on yourself.'

He turned back to her, and she saw from his face that he might actually consider that if cornered. This was a man who'd been to prison once and had repeatedly sworn that he was never going back.

'Nina is off-duty,' Mercy explained after Bill had rubbed his face again in agitation, 'but she'll call it in as soon as the man arrives.'

*'He's not going to—'*

'What *is* he doing?' she asked. 'He agreed to meet you somewhere?'

'The underground,' he told her. 'A tube station, before it closes. I'm not telling you which one, but I could still make it if weren't for that copper out there.'

'Listen, if I scream out for help, the police will have you surrounded within minutes.'

'Then it's over. He'll have gotten away.'

'Not if you don't want him to,' she replied. She went back into his office where the jacket was. When she came out again, she held out the photofit she'd previously had Nina arrange for her.

'This is Julian Kistler,' she said, showing him the handsome mixed-race man who'd called himself Jamal on Valentine's Day. 'I'm fairly certain that he's the JK that just replied to your call.'

'How do you—'

'He's about ten years older than me, lives on a narrowboat called the Long Needle, and he's a tricky fucker. Watch out for him.'

'I don't understand...'

'He's got a female accomplice. A small pale woman, Welsh accent. I'll wait until the end of the next song before screaming,' she whispered, seeing his confusion. 'That should give you a good head start.'

Dumbly, he took the photofit from her.

'Do it for Sarah,' she told him.

# 71

Nina hadn't heard any talking since the music began and was certain that something had gone very wrong. She couldn't imagine that they were just sitting together listening to Tina. No, there was a strong chance that Mercy's life was in danger and the two-way radio was in her hand. She'd been on the verge of calling it in ever since Bill had admitted to being the true perpetrator of the Whetstone gun massacre. This was a major bust and it was *all hers.*

But, if she did that, the Met would be all over the place in minutes and the contract killer would never arrive. Arresting Bill would have to wait. The second song was entering its final chorus when, through the speaker, she heard Mercy screaming.

*'Help! He's got a gun!'*

She drew the remote up to her lips and called in the situation immediately. Southwark, Nadgett Street, armed hostage situation, all units. Then she grabbed the firearm she'd brought with her and got out of the car.

She moved toward the building, still providing information into her remote. She remained on the opposite pavement, ready to shield herself behind parked cars should Bill come out shooting. There was a fire exit to the building and, from her vantage point Nina had a good view of both that and the main door. But there was a chance he could escape via the Chinese takeaway below. Her heart rate was jacked as she looked up to the windows. The blinds suddenly lifted and Mercy was visible in her leather jacket. She was banging on the glass pane, but Nina had left the receiver in the car. There was no sign of Bill.

Sirens could already be heard approaching from the direction of Southwark police station. Mercy lifted up the windowpane and shouted down.

'He's not here,' she called down. 'I'm safe!'

'Which exit is he coming out of?' Nina shouted up.

'He's already gone!'

She could tell by Mercy's body language that she was not being held at gunpoint. So, her own weapon raised, she crossed to the main M&T doorway and used her old key to gain entry to the building. Kicking it open, she checked the corners before running up the stairs to where she could hear another song - Street Life by Randy Crawford -starting up. When she reached the first landing she called up again, aware that this could be a trap. The M&T office was on the top floor and she heard the door open. Light entered the dark stairwell.

'He's jumped out the back window,' Mercy's shaken voice called down. But something about her tone felt wrong. This was bullshit.

'An armed response unit is going to be here in seconds,' she called up. 'If you're still up there, Bill, you need to surrender now.'

'I'm not a hostage,' Mercy insisted, stepping out of the office and into Nina's view. 'See.'

Nina radioed in that this was no longer a hostage situation but that an armed and dangerous man was at large.

'Show me where he went,' she commanded as she pushed past Mercy and into the main office. She scoped the place to ensure he wasn't still there. The place stank of whiskey, reminding her of Ray. Inside the smaller office was a tight little window that Nina had never seen open before. It was usually obscured by box-files now scattered to the floor. The whole frame had been detached.

'It leads to some outhouse roof,' Mercy told her as Nina climbed onto the cabinet to look through. Once up, she peered down onto the dented platform of corrugated iron below. 'He jumped down and then into next door's garden. I think. Everything happened fast.'

From the front they could already hear the sirens of the armed response unit arriving. Nina stared at Mercy as she radioed in that the armed man had escaped via the back of the building. His name was William Mance and he was wanted for the murder of Victor Neale, among others.

'This would've taken assistance,' Nina indicated to the tight space from where the window frame was removed. 'And he's a big man. Did you push him through?'

'I was held at gunpoint,' Mercy answered with a steady eye. 'Frightened for my life.'

Exasperated, Nina walked back through to the main office window so she could communicate better with the armed response.

'Turn that fucking music off,' she snapped at Mercy.

# 72

Flashing blue lights and piercing sirens tore through the streets of Southwark. Another armed response van raced past Bill as he hurried through a crowded pavement in the opposite direction. From his coat pocket he'd produced a white surgical facemask, much like the ones people had been wearing in recent days. He placed it on with his free hand as his other sweat-soaked palm continued gripping the concealed gun inside his coat pocket.

He'd been a policeman once. That fact seemed obscure now, as the full force of the Met was co-ordinating against him. What a haphazard life. Now he was a killer on the loose, responsible for a massacre and the death of his best friend. He was unlikely to survive the night unless he surrendered to the authorities immediately.

But how would he avenge Sarah if he did that? The thought was all-consuming, so he kept striding toward where he parked his car.

When Mercy had suggested to Bill that, with her help, he might make the rendezvous with Sarah's killer after all, he'd assumed she was declaring herself his ally. As she helped him remove the frame to the smaller office window, which he had no intention of exiting through, it seemed like she was supporting him in his quest for vengeance and was even prepared to conspire in it. But after he'd actually exited the building via the Chinese takeaway, seconds before Nina had been alerted to his loaded gun, it occurred that her real plan might have been to condemn him to Death by Policeman. If an armed copper were to confront him on these streets, they wouldn't fuck about. He'd be shot dead. Maybe this was *her* revenge for Ray's murder.

Yeah, she'd completely fucked him, his racing mind screamed, as he ran along a row of railway arches.

By the time he'd unlocked the garage where his car was parked, he'd regained mastery of himself. Whatever Mercy was up to it didn't alter the fact that he was in serious danger and needed to make a life-or-death decision. His number plate would be in the system already so he wouldn't get far. He'd been successful in evading the police in Nick's Range Rover, but that hadn't involved anywhere near as much traffic. As his Nissan crawled up Tooley Street he considered ditching the car somewhere discreet and then vanishing. In three decades of investigating missing person cases he'd developed a decent understanding of how a person might effectively disappear, and they didn't all involve self-destruction. He'd tracked several missing people down to foreign locations where they'd been living under new names and he'd learnt from all their mistakes. Back in Denmark Hill he had a fake identity passport that he'd acquired years before, but he couldn't risk going back there. The police could be at his home already.

More urgently, it was twenty minutes until the ten o'clock rendezvous. The man he'd just spoken to on the phone, who'd had the same cold voice that he'd heard in Ray's office years earlier, had just arranged to meet with him on the Circle line. Bill had been instructed to catch the underground train that would be passing through Tower Hill close to the hour. They'd discreetly discuss business as the train performed its eastbound rotation. The plan was for them to separate when they were done. But Bill had his own plan.

At last the traffic cleared and he turned his car left onto Tower Bridge. The station was just on the other side of the north bank. The Tower of London was floodlit as he crossed the river. The ancient palace struck him as fitting backdrop to this, his final murder. Consequences were pushed to the back of his mind. He'd done prison time before, but this time it would be for an action he could live with.

Once over the bridge he dumped the car and was soon running to the tube station with time to spare. A hooded busker asked him for change as he dashed for the escalator. But he ignored her and her little ukulele.

Down on the eastbound platform the clock told him he still had minutes before the right train arrived. He stalked the length of the platform, scanning faces for anyone who resembled Mercy's photofit. There were less than a dozen people down there, but it was a long platform. He passed an overweight man in his sixties, a cluster of women wearing burkas, a ginger teen swigging from an energy drink, and two girls snogging in front of a tube map. He made a brief study of each as he moved toward the far mouth of the tunnel. Nothing.

*"See it, Say it, Sort it,"* advised a recorded voice through the tannoy. Bill looked up at the ceiling to see cameras pointing in every direction. This was an insane place for a fugitive to have come.

'Mr Mance!'

He looked about, unable to identify who had just called out. The station hissed with the sound of electricity and working metal, but the light was unflinching.

'Over here!' he then heard from over the tracks. 'You're getting on the wrong train.'

It was then that he saw the man standing in plain sight on the westbound platform. He was of medium height and wore a blue sweater with its hood up and white trainers. He looked about forty but carried himself in a boyish manner, standing with his feet apart and both hands hooked into jean pockets. He resembled an urban magician. Crucially though, his face matched the picture that Mercy had given him, and a heat roared through Bill's body. Here, at last, was the murdering little shit.

'We're supposed to be meeting on the *eastbound* train!' the man shouted, cupping his hands over his mouth and standing on tiptoe.

'This *is* eastbound!' Bill shouted back at him.

'Say again?'

'I'm eastbound!' Bill repeated, snapping off his facemask. '*You're* on the wrong platform.'

'Am I?' the man looked confused and checked the signs on his side. 'So I am!' he chuckled, shaking his head. 'Honestly, what am I like?'

An old Indian man was eyeing them from the third platform beyond but beside that every Londoner down there was ignoring their exchange. The low rumble of an approaching train could be heard.

'Lucky you said so,' he raised his voice. 'I was just about to get on this one.'

'Don't!' Bill commanded. 'Stay there.'

'Are you coming to me,' asked the man as the lights from the tunnel got nearer on his side, 'or am I coming to you?'

'Don't move, alright!'

The surging sound grew louder. Bill felt the weight of his concealed weapon inside the coat.

'I'm looking forward to our chat,' the man grinned like a holy fool.

*'Mind the gap,'* crackled the tannoy, *'between the train and the platform.'*

'I want to tell you how I *do for them*,' the man called just before the westbound train emerged from the far side of the tunnel. The noise was thunderous and it was hard to hear what he was saying. Bill cupped his ear.

*'I want to tell you how I killed Sarah!'* the man shrieked before a wall of public transport separated them.

Bill stepped backwards. Had he heard that right? The scraping steel was deafening as the train slowed. From between the windows he could still see the hooded man grinning at him through the train's artificial light. He's fucking taunting me.

*"Mind the gap!"*

His mind scrambled as the doors to the westbound train opened. If I give chase now, I'll lose him. But if I remain where I am, and he gets on, my chance will be lost.

People were alighting but the hateful individual remained on his platform, holding Bill's stare. He doesn't know about my concealed carry though, Bill reassured himself as his grip tightened around it. And it was powerful enough for him to make the kill shot from this distance. If he stays where he is, Bill thought, waiting for the train to move on, I'll shoot the bugger like it's a fucking western, chuck the gun once he's hit the ground, and then get on my knees with my hands behind my head. A life sentence is a small price to pay.

The beeping of the train indicated that the doors were about to shut. Bill prayed that the man wouldn't trick him and jump on board at the last second. But the doors closed with him still on the platform. As it was pulling out, Bill looked up to see what time the eastbound train would be coming in and realised that he had about one minute to make the shot before they were separated again. That would be enough.

'I spied on her,' the man on the opposite platform resumed once the train had pulled away, 'for weeks. I overheard you and her making plans. You were going to elope, Mr Mance. And both of you married to other people! I was scandalised!'

The man had moved down the platform toward the tunnel mouth. Bill positioned himself directly across from him. He prayed that the weapon wouldn't jam as he fired.

'I *used* that, Mr Mance,' the man told him with raised eyebrows. 'After I'd entered her bedroom and gave her my sweets.'

He *had* drugged her. Bill's feet crossed the yellow line by the platform edge.

'I told her I was your friend,' the man cackled. 'That I was helping you both and you were outside waiting to whisk her away. I pointed at the balcony and said *he's out there!*'

Bill became paralysed with rage. He stared at the man, never hating anyone more.

'She went out to look for you, Mr Mance,' the fiend was giggling. 'Then I pointed my gun. She probably thought you'd catch her!'

A dragon roared inside Bill's ears. Unable to prevent himself anymore he produced the gun from his coat pocket.

"*Watch out!*" someone further down the platform screamed. His target didn't flinch.

'And another thing...'

*WATCH OUT!* Too late he realised that the warning was for him. His back buckled under an almighty blow from behind and he fell forwards onto the tracks.

'...I had an accomplice!' were the last words Bill heard before his every sense was annihilated.

# 73

'That's Bill's car!' Mercy told Nina, pointing at the abandoned Nissan. *'Fuck!'*

Any hope they may have been harbouring that Bill was not the man they'd heard described over Nina's police radio was dashed in that moment. The car was parked on a double yellow line in this built-up area. Nina had been busy looking for a place to park her own car, but as soon as it was pointed out she emitted a deep sigh.

'Shit yeah,' she agreed as they passed the people gathered around it. It was blocking access to the rear of a pub. 'You wouldn't leave it there unless you were never planning to return.'

Back in Southwark, Mercy had been selectively describing what had passed between her and Bill. She'd informed the police that he'd claimed to be heading for a meeting with a hitman which was to take place in an unspecified tube station. She hadn't mentioned that she'd given him a head start, although she was getting the strong sense that Nina suspected her of aiding and abetting.

They'd been together when the report came through, an incident at Tower Hill station on the Circle line. A man had been pushed onto the tracks in front of the eastbound train. Eyewitnesses reported that a smallish woman in a hoodie had approached him from behind with a fire extinguisher she'd freed from the wall. She'd struck him as he'd been engaging in an altercation with a man on the opposite platform and then dropped the extinguisher and immediately fled the scene. The victim was reported to have been brandishing a gun as he'd fallen.

Following in the wake of speeding police cars, Nina and Mercy had arrived on the scene minutes later. Mercy had insisted that she might be able to identify the perpetrator, so Nina had agreed to take her.

'Have they got anyone yet?' Mercy asked after Nina had parked up. She hadn't understood the call signals she'd been hearing on Nina's radio but had got the impression an arrest had not yet been made.

'CCTV shows the hooded woman running up the eastbound escalator,' Nina told her after briefly consulting her colleagues as they ran to the station. 'The hooded man on the opposite platform just strolled away. Neither has been apprehended yet and the man hasn't technically done anything illegal. But keep your eyes peeled.'

An ambulance was parked on the pavement by the station, which was cordoned off by the police. Nina told Mercy to wait outside, flashed her badge and stepped underneath the tape.

The night was freezing. Mercy had on her leather jacket and black scarf and she hugged herself near an old Roman wall by the entrance. The wind whipped at her hair. It was nearing the hour when the station would be shut anyway but there were still plenty of inconvenienced people milling around its mouth. Mercy cast an eye across the wide road to where the Tower of London stood, ancient and illuminated. Regret swallowed her.

Why had she let Bill slip away like that? It was easily the most reckless thing she'd ever done, which was saying something. Had she really thought that he'd just shoot Kistler and then be apprehended without further incident? What if someone innocent had been caught in the crossfire? Or, on a subconscious level, had she really just wanted Bill to escape. Once she'd solved her dad's murder, and gotten his killer to admit it, had she just wanted to be his friend again?

Her throat began to choke with sorrow. He was the man who'd killed her dad. But, even now, she couldn't help but feel he was the better of them and that her investigation had doomed him. Already she was beginning to wish that she'd minded her own business and spared him this terrible end.

But, as quick as it came, her mind rebelled against such self-loathing. *Fuck that.* After all, it wasn't her who'd set out on a murder spree instead of just reporting Victor to the police. Bill had forged his own destiny and now the only people left to channel her anger toward were his killers. Her eyes scanned the faces of passers-by for them.

Then she spotted the motorbike. Out on the busy road that separated the tube station from the Tower of London. The black bike had two riders, wearing matching helmets. A smallish woman was driving while a man held onto her waist. She saw the man's helmet turn subtly toward her as they sped past.

In that chilling moment she knew that it was the people who'd stolen her phone up Lewisham Hill. It was even the same bike.

'That's them!' she cried as they turned right onto Tower Bridge. 'They're getting away!'

She screamed even louder as they crossed the river. But the police were focusing on the scene below and, by the time she got anyone to listen to her, the motorbike was long gone.

# EPILOGUE

*Later that year*

Slow and mournful string music plays over the intro. An ominous piano theme builds underneath. Almost immediately, her father's familiar rasp is heard.

*'Christopher mate. Chrissy. It's your dad. This still your number?'*

The sound quality is scratchy, which works for the noirish tone. Every episode begins this way; with Mercy getting misgendered in the most dismal call she ever received.

*'Listen, son, it's a filthy night and I'm drunk...'*

The recording is edited and cuts out a lot of his heavy breathing, grunting and swear words.

*'I know I've not been the best dad.'*

Another voice interrupts. This one is a soft, clear Liverpudlian accent contrasting with her dad's rough cockney.

'In the early hours of a storm-battered winter's morning,' the voice tells the listener, 'private investigator Ray Tyler made the final call of his life.'

*'It was that afternoon in my office, when you was still my little boy,'* Ray continues as the opening music becomes creepier. *'You heard me talking, right? Doing that deal...'* an elongated pause is artificially added to stress the significance, *'... with the Long Needle!'*

'Ray is speaking to his only child,' the presenter cuts in, 'perhaps conscious that an unseen killer was pursuing him in the rain.'

*'I know you were listening.'*

'Hours later, on December 20th 2019, his body was found floating in the Thames. His death was pronounced an accident. And that's how it would have stayed, were it not for the tenacity of a most unlikely sleuth!'

The word "unlikely" irritates Mercy because what, as if she didn't already know, was so fucking unlikely about her?

'I'm Matt Wren. For over twenty years I've been chief crime reporter for the Crier on both a national and local level. During that time, I came to know Ray and his partner Bill Mance – now infamous as the Whetstone spree killer. Back then I could never have guessed at the dark secrets these men harboured...'

This annoyed her too. Considering that Wren had originally hired them to hack the phones of innocent people, his claim that he'd no clue they were dodgy was questionable.

'... and the terrible violence that lay in their wake.' The ambient music becomes even more sinister as a third voice is edited in.

'When I was little, I looked up to Dad and Bill' – Mercy always winces when she hears this bit, and not just because she doesn't like her own voice – 'but the more I uncovered...' Her voice fades out and Wren finishes the sentence.

'... the more Mercy Tyler learnt that the men she idolised were the opposite of heroes!' As the doomy theme reaches its climax, Wren's voice rises. 'This story has already become the stuff of crime legend. It revolves around the Neale brothers – Britain's most notorious gangsters – the Whetstone massacre and a mysterious assassin still at large. Join me as I try to untangle the thread of the Long Needle. Welcome...' – big crescendo – '*... to the Needle Drop!*'

A needle scratches on vinyl. Then the music changes to something rockier. An electric guitar playing something that, at first, sounds like 'London Calling' but not enough that the podcast would have to pay for it.

'A Town Crier Production,' a calmer voice informs us as the music fades out.

'On this, the ninth episode of the Needle Drop, we continue our series of exclusive interviews with Mercy as she guides us through the sordid web of sin she uncovered at her family business. Mercy, welcome back to the podcast.'

'Happy to be here.'

As soon as the news had broken that Bill had been killed after confessing to multiple murders, every news outlet in the country had wanted exclusive rights to Mercy's story. Having interviewed her on the previous day, Wren was by far the fastest and most insistent of these tabloid suitors, but Mercy had told him to get stuffed. She was too traumatised to sell the dreadful details.

At least not as quickly as that.

Hours after her confrontation at Limehouse, but before Bill's fatal showdown at Tower Hill, a narrowboat called The Long Needle had been set alight up the Lee Navigation canal. Nobody was inside as it drifted upriver aflame but, when finally extinguished, little evidence remained of whoever had been occupying it. According to the Canal & River Trust, it had been registered to Julian and Meredith Kistler. Little trace of these people existed outside of this documentation but the Trust provided police with a photo ID of this Julian person. As she'd expected, it was the same man who'd been presenting himself as Jamal on Valentine's night.

'That evening in Brixton I told this guy everything I then knew about the contract killer my dad spoke to,' Mercy had eventually explained to Wren's listeners on a previous episode.

'How did that come up?' Wren had asked.

'It was a date,' she'd answered, 'I always end up over-sharing. And somehow, perhaps through the police,' she theorised, 'he must've heard about my claims that I'd even spied on 'the Long Needle' when a teenager. I'd even been extremely vocal about it before I'd returned from Spain and had tried to interest the media with my story. I can only assume that, on learning this, he wanted to see if I recognised him. I guess the plan would've been to kill me if I posed a threat. But he soon realised that I had everything wrong and must've assumed it was safe to let me live. After establishing that, he made an excuse to leave.'

'What was his excuse?'

'He pretended he'd only just realised I was transgender,' she answered, 'and ran off in faux-disgust.'

Eventually, as a global pandemic changed the world, it became apparent that the agency wouldn't survive without a serious cash injection. And so, disregarding her principles, Mercy accepted that she needed to sell her story to the highest bidder, which turned out to be the Crier. The deal she struck with the media organisation that owned it included exclusive access to the recording of her father's final words, the Neale tapes she'd recorded from Spot's nightclub, and, most importantly, Bill's confession. Mercy was also contractually obliged to take part in this wretched podcast with Wren. It was a demeaning trade, but it helped keep the lights on during her first difficult year as an investigator.

'Today is listener's questions,' Wren announces. 'And, as you can imagine, there are plenty of them!'

Rather than see her as the quirky 'detective with a difference' that Wren was always billing her as, the podcast audience generally seemed to distrust Mercy. She'd received a lot of online abuse ever since the show had become "lockdown's No 1 True Crime podcast," much of it transphobic. There were trolls bombarding the M&T twitter account with offensive hashtags and at times it had seemed like a coordinated attack.

'Lots of people are asking about Nick Neale,' Wren begins. 'Mercy, your actions helped acquit him of the Whetstone massacre. Has he contacted you to express gratitude?'

'Nope.'

'What about any of the other salubrious characters you captured on tape in the nightclub? Have they been in touch?'

She thought again about the vile anonymous messages she'd been receiving online.

'Not to my knowledge.'

'It may interest you to know that we reached out to Nick and asked if he'd like to take part in this podcast. He refused.'

'OK.'

'Apparently, he's working on a rival podcast that will present his side of the story. Will you listen to that when it drops?'

'Probably not.'

'Okay, well back to twitter. @StuartPoole1974 doesn't so

much have a question as a comment. He takes issue with your assertion that Sarah Neale's death wasn't suicide.'

'He can think what he likes.'

'Do you think the police will ever catch these Kistler people?' Wren asked.

'Not especially. The police are looking for a hooded woman who struck Bill in the back with a fire extinguisher and was then seen legging it from the station. And they're looking for the Kistlers who destroyed their floating home and disappeared. But, outside of my statements, they've no reason to link the two. Sarah's death still looks like suicide and Bill confessed on tape to every murder they actually care about. So no, I don't think they're poised to catch our couple now.'

'What about you, Mercy? Are you going to continue trying to sniff out this man you overheard in your dad's study all those years ago?'

'I've a business to run.'

'But aren't you worried they'll sniff *you* out?' Wren asked. 'They might want you silenced.'

'You can't live life in fear,' replied Mercy, who was actually considering buying a gun.

'Perhaps you'll get a creepy phone call,' Wren suggested, 'like at the end of *The Silence of the Lambs.* "Hello, Mercy. I'm having an old friend for dinner." Something like that.'

'Maybe.'

'Do come back and tell us if that happens.'

In April Mercy had moved back home to quarantine with her furloughed mum. It had become apparent that she couldn't keep paying rent on her Lewisham flat with agency money, especially considering the steady losses that they'd been making ever since Ray had died. And now, with Bill also deceased, Nina gone, two remaining employees to keep paying and an international virus shutting society down, it looked unlikely that M&T Investigations would survive the year. She wondered if she even wanted it to.

Facemasks lay discarded on the Southwark pavements, a form of litter that hadn't existed when she'd started working there. It was late November and Mercy returned to the building with the peacock feathers painted on the corner wall. She removed her own mask, unlocked the front door, climbed the musty stairwell and entered the office that had been empty since lockdown. She pulled up the window blinds and looked down to the street below. A grey Nissan was drawing up outside and driving it was the young woman with whom she had an appointment. Mercy drew back from the window, crossed over to where the kettle was, flicked it on and peered into the tin containing mouldy biscuits. She was throwing them into the pedal bin as her visitor buzzed the door.

'Lisa,' she beamed with enthusiasm when they met. 'How lovely to see you again. You never change.'

'Mercedes,' her late partner's stepdaughter said, stepping into the main office. '*You've* changed.'

They didn't shake hands or hug but instead attempted an awkward elbow rub in a parody of social distancing measures. The last time Mercy had seen her was when then were both in their teens and before Bill had divorced her mother. She was Lisa Sweeney now, no longer Lisa Mance. Mercy wondered if Lisa remembered the gender-swapping games they'd once played as children. This was the first time the two had met since her transition.

Lisa had been bequeathed Bill's flat, his car, some money, as well as his half of the agency. But it was only now that the two inheritors had been able to meet face-to-face to discuss how the future might work. Lisa was a nurse and a mother and looked deeply tired. Today she had a rare day off from her long hours at St Guy's hospital. She wore glasses and an apricot cardigan over a white top. The year was turning cold again, but the radiators had stopped working. Mercy had turned some portable heaters on to warm the place, but they took a while to have any effect. Once she'd made them both a cup of camomile tea, Mercy invited Lisa to join her in what was once Bill's office.

They exchanged small talk. Mercy asked about Lisa's children, what her partner did for a living, and whether now was a good time to sell Bill's flat. In fact, they were keen to talk about anything aside from the two men from whom they'd inherited the business.

'No offence,' Lisa said, broaching a thorny subject, 'but I can't see this agency lasting with just you at the helm. Is it true that you only started here in February?'

'I'm new to the game,' Mercy admitted after swallowing some tea. 'But if you check those figures,' she indicated the papers she'd rested in front of Lisa, 'you'll see we're managing to stay afloat in these challenging times. Which reminds me.' She adopted the same warm but professional manner Bill had used when sat in that chair. 'Maybe we could pay you your share in the form of a wage. I know you don't work here but there are advantages to pretending that you do.'

'I'd prefer it,' Lisa said, 'if things were run straighter from here on.'

'It's hardly a big deception,' Mercy smiled and pointed at the statements with a pen that still had a hidden voice recorder in it, 'but our accountant advises me it's cleaner from a tax perspective.'

'Is that the same accountant who handled Victor's

money?' Lisa asked. 'When we were kids we knew who funded this agency, it was a thing that was talked about openly. You and I used to laugh about it. M&T was a front. Our parents were dining off prostitution money, robbery money, drug money. Murder money. That makes me sick to think about now, but it also raises the question of how this agency is expected to survive now the Neale tap has been turned off.'

Mercy leaned back into Bill's chair.

'That's an outdated view of our income,' she responded. 'We're more solvent than you're suggesting, even without the blood money. For instance, our social media profile has raised considerably during my time and that's resulted in increased revenue.'

'I've heard the podcast,' Lisa replied with a sniff.

'You're right though,' Mercy ignored the disapproval, 'it won't be easy going forward. The future will be tough here.'

'The future will be tough everywhere,' Lisa told her as she placed her now empty cup onto the desk. 'And I feel like you've changed your tune. In our email exchanges this summer you agreed that, once lockdown was over, we should be selling this business for whatever its worth. Seriously Mercy, what changed?'

Later, as Mercy stood by the window and watched Lisa get into Bill's old car, she wondered what *had* changed? Everything Lisa had just said was true. And yet she still felt compelled to make a success of this if she could, to be a private investigator. Was this a deluded ambition? It wasn't the first time people had tried to dissuade her from following a path that she knew to be right for her.

Lisa drove away, but still Mercy remained by the window. She asked herself, was keeping this agency alive simply an exercise in maintaining the legacy of two men who didn't deserve one? Would it be better if she packed it in, moved from London, and pursued another career, a different life, one that might welcome her more?

Behind her a phone rang. It was the same line on which the hitman had called. Was this him calling back, as Wren predicted he would? Or might it be a new client with a case, one that would prove a profitable distraction.

Whatever, she should answer it. So, she stepped away from the window and drew further into the office, trying not to mind the cold.

## THANKS FOR READING

I hope you enjoyed *Ask for Mercy.* If so, I'd be very grateful if you could leave a review on Amazon or anywhere else you fancy. I'd love to hear your thoughts.

Also, if you'd like to read more from Mercy's world, I've written a prequel novella called ***Find the Needle*** which is available for free and at the touch of a button. The story is set in 2004 and shows how Mercy's father Ray first tracked down the man she later comes to call The Long Needle.

To download the free story, and receive regular updates about my upcoming books, simply sign up to my newsletter. My website is James-benmore.com

And feel free to follow me on social media.

# ABOUT ME

As well as writing *Ask for Mercy,* I'm the author of a trilogy of novels about Jack Dawkins, otherwise known as the Artful Dodger from Charles Dickens' classic novel *Oliver Twist. Dodger* was published by Quercus in 2013 and was soon followed by *Dodger of the Dials* and *Dodger of the Revolution*.

The Dodger novels will soon be revised, republished and rebranded by Top Sawyer Books under the new series title *The Dodger Papers.*

My next book, a thriller called *Hauser and the Vultures,* will be out soon from Top Sawyer Books. Plus, a sequel to *Ask for Mercy* is in the works.

For regular information, visit my website Jamesbenmore.com and sign up to my mailing list.

# ACKNOWLEDGMENTS

*Ask for Mercy* was a labour of love, both in terms of the writing and in getting it published. As proud as I am of the book itself, I'm equally proud that I managed to get it into your hands eventually.

And I couldn't have done it without the help of some amazing people.

To help me create in Mercy a character who'd ring true, I reached out to a number of transgender readers who advised me on how best to fashion an authentic trans character. It's not for me to say if I succeeded but, in particular, I want to thank Ugla Stefanía Kristjönudóttir Jónsdóttir, otherwise known as Owl Fisher. Ugla read every page and gave invaluable advice, their thoughts and comments having a particular impact on the sections relating to Mercy's childhood.

Also, the writer and feminist campaigner Jane Fae was generous with her time and advice at an earlier stage of the writing process.

My first draft was almost 900 pages long, a ridiculous length for anything that isn't an ancient religious text. Thankfully, professional editor Dan Holloway was available to help me wrangle it down to a more acceptable size. And Georgina Asfaw's forensic eye for detail made her the perfect copy editor and proof reader. If you're in the market for an editor yourself, I would heartily recommend either Dan or Georgina.

Special thanks to Christian Regnaudot who's been my most enthusiastic reader ever since my first schoolboy scribblings. He read this manuscript in its pre-edited form and gave plenty of encouraging suggestions. Another supportive friend was Luke Deckard whose understanding of the private eye genre cannot be beaten. Other valued readers include Anna James, Alice Furse, Grace Flahive, Stevie Williams, Paul Sweeten, Tes Asfaw, Bridget Arsenault, Zoe Morgan Chiswick and Ciorsdan Glass.

On the publishing front, I'm indebted to Mark Dawson and James Blatch for their Self Publishing Launchpad course. I doubt I would've had the wherewithal for such an undertaking without those modules. The Alliance of Independent Authors (ALLi) also proved useful during complicated moments. And crime novelist Amer Anwar talked me through his own history with self-publishing over a friendly pint.

Thank you to Stuart Bache of Books Covered for creating such a cool, dynamic cover. Love it.

But my biggest thank you must surely go to my large and loving family, and especially to my brother Harry who provided incredible support during the publication phase.

*Ask for Mercy* is dedicated to everyone in my family; past, present and future.

Top Sawyer Ltd

Printed in Great Britain
by Amazon

30958431R00303